# ARISE AND SHINE

# ARISE AND SHINE

## DEATH OF THE PARTY
## BOOK 1

### Kleggt

Podium

Podium

# ARISE AND SHINE

## CHAPTER ONE

# Live, Laugh, Languish

*H*mm, *was it damage avoidance or damage mitigation that was more effective?* The pencil tapped on the paper Character Sheet three times before spinning around. The eraser scoured the hapless number from the designated box.

"Are you going to wait on the customers or not?" A figure in her peripheral wiped her hands on a grubby apron before putting them on her hips.

Sally looked up to see the short, portly figure of the diner owner, Doris, standing midway in the doorway to the kitchen. She seemed unable to decide whether not burning the food or chastising the one waitress in the diner was the most important thing at present. Her hazel eyes were still soft despite the scowl.

"They're fine, Miss Doris, barely even moving a muscle." Sally waved her free hand toward the general horde of Sunday morning breakfasters.

Most were contentedly murmuring about their week or chewing through the cooked flesh and eggs the cook had drowned in grease. None of them looked particularly needful of her attention.

Doris shook her head, her gray curls bobbing about as she resigned to heading back to the fryer. "Just pay attention, okay?"

Sally scratched at her blonde hair and glared around the room again, seeing if anyone dared require more coffee or needed to pay their bill. None met her challenge. Sunday morning was perhaps the dullest time in the diner—anyone up this early had no right demanding such prompt service.

Resigning to double-check that there was still enough coffee to dispense, she turned around and narrowed her blue eyes at the glass pot atop the heated plate. The dark liquid inside was at an adequate level. *Oh*—Doris had mentioned she changed the coffee brand this morning due to a stock shortage. Sally turned the adjacent dark container around on the desk to read the name and wrinkled up her nose. *RatJuice?* No complaints from the customers yet . . . but that was terrible marketing.

She returned to her sheet and slowly filled the empty box . . . with the *same number* she had just erased. She exhaled and fiddled with one of the ribbons in her hair as the box was purged of numerals once again. It had taken all week to get to this point, but the character was *almost* close to being complete. It was by no means min-maxed, but everything about it had been curated to be authentic and effective.

The small sketch of her character, "Krunk," stared back at her in silent judgment at her indecisiveness. Krunk had it all. Strength, charisma, and a cool hat. Probably even a suitor or five if Sally really wanted to drive home the fact that the character was just escapism from her own insecurities.

"Oh, what system are you playing?" A nervous voice roused her from a focused stare at the paper.

She looked up to see a man, probably only a little older than she was, eyeing up her character sheet. He had messy brown hair and green eyes, and his shirt had Goreblaster written across it. It looked like one of those terribly over-the-top, obscure band shirts with barely legible text. The usual Sunday crowd was nearer the grave—other than the occasional weekend office worker, so his sudden appearance was a surprise.

"Technically," she said as she twirled the pencil awkwardly before dropping it on the floor, "I am not playing . . . yet."

"Ah, you don't have a group?" He raised his eyebrows.

The question wasn't meant to be judgmental, she knew, but Sally still recoiled mentally from her own slant on it.

"I haven't been into *Hobgoblincide* for long," she lied, mentally hiding away and drawing a curtain around the stack of books and unused characters languishing in long-forgotten piles at her house.

"That's fair." The guy rubbed the back of his neck. "I'm, uh, Theo. You should come by the Card Dungeon sometime—there are a few groups you might be interested in joining." He slid money across the counter with a smile.

"Sally." She nodded in return before remembering she had a name badge on. "Do you have a group?"

"I do." He smiled, heading toward the exit. "But it's only for the *worthy*." A brief, awkward wink was the last she saw of him as he left out into the world.

Sally pursed her lips and frowned as she watched the door close behind him, rattling on its hinges. Was that a challenge, flirting, or just being condescending? In theory, whichever was the correct answer, it still made her want to try to get into the party.

Did Doris serve him earlier? She looked down at the money presented—the perfect amount for the basic breakfast and all-you-can-drink *RatJuice* special. Sally frowned and shuffled it off into the till—surely she would have remembered serving him earlier?

Her nerves struck up, overriding her brief confidence. She didn't know anyone else going to the shop; what if she embarrassed herself? After building her ideal character for so long, what if she made a mistake or ruined it somehow? Now sitting lonely atop the counter, the character sheet seemed like a bad idea waiting to happen—an invitation to disappointment.

"Sally?"

She started and turned to the gruff projector of her name. It was just Reginald after some more coffee. She sighed and picked up the heated pot.

Reginald was a regular, to the point where the diner was like a second home to him—or maybe even his first. Every day he would spend as much time as possible there, drinking coffee and slowly reading the newspaper. Always in a brown tweed suit and matching hat. Same chair. Same table. He was as much part of the furniture as the strange mammal statue Doris had placed at the end of the counter over a decade ago—not that Sally had been here that long, *thankfully*. She had no intention of working here until she died.

"Sorry, Reg, I was miles away," she said as she poured his fresh coffee. "Anything good in the papers?"

"Never is." He shrugged glumly. "Always sounds like the world is ending." His tiny eyes peered out from craters of wrinkles, and his gray-flecked beard cradled a slight smile.

"Well, even if it does, you've still got this place." That didn't sound like a great comfort out loud, but Reginald seemed to perk up and nod in agreement.

"*Order's up, Sally!*" A shout came from the kitchen.

The metal slats that covered the window to the kitchen opened up, and two plates of hot, greasy food were placed on the shelf. The sweating face of Doris peered through. "Table three!"

"Roger that, Miss Doris." Sally clunked the coffee pot back onto the heated plate and grabbed the two plates.

The kitchen window shut behind her with a *clunk*, and she sighed. It wasn't that she didn't enjoy her job. She had just been here way too long. What had started as a summer holiday job to get her more social—or at least, that's what her parents had said—had turned into a few years of waiting tables. *Waiting* to wait on tables. School had passed, and it became a full-time thing. The work was simple, and Doris paid well enough . . . but she *had* been languishing.

She smiled to the customers—a couple in their late middle age—a skill long practiced and automatic. To an outsider, Sally was all the confidence and friendly sass that you'd expect from such a quaint, out-of-the-way diner. But inside, interacting with people was an awkward and alien concept. One that often never passed the required pleasantries of this familiar setting. If only she could kill off that part of her brain.

Sally returned to her side of the counter, *the safe side*, and squatted down to pick up the pencil. The momentary hiding spot, away from the dozen-odd customers and the persistent glare of the morning sun, was a relief. A small wall of aged wood and commercial function. The shade was almost enough to let her sales face melt away—but then the diner door swung open with a small jingle. She stood, ready to greet the new customer—but it was not a graying mortal intent on devouring a cooked breakfast.

The familiar unkempt face of the other diner worker strolled in. His shirt was untucked and his almost-black hair a messy thatch. With the amount of thin ice he skated on, he could go professional once he inevitably got fired.

"What's with the tie, Charlie?" Sally pointed at the wonky, partially loose black tie around his neck. "Got an interview?"

"Not quite." He beamed beneath tired eyes. "They say to dress for the job you want."

Sally raised an eyebrow as he slowly walked toward the kitchen. "What job *do* you want, Chuck?"

He shrugged in response. "No idea, but it'll come quicker with this on, right?"

"You're an hour late for shift. The only thing it'll make quicker is giving Doris easy access to throttling you."

He waved her off, entering the kitchen—the muffled raised voice of Doris vibrating through the wall as she chastised his tardiness, *again*.

Sally shook her head and smiled. Charlie had only been there six months and had been a thorn in Doris's side nearly every day—it was a wonder why she kept him around, but the old owner had a soft spot for them both. In truth, she saw the boy as a little brother too. As a single child herself, it was nice to—

*Crash.*

She turned to see the sluggish glances of the diner patrons move over to Reginald.

"So sorry, dear—I knocked the coffee off when moving my paper."

It was hard to be annoyed at the earnest apology as the old man's tiny, sad eyes looked up at her. Plus, it was just a cup—it's not like anyone died. Sally grabbed the dustpan and brush and went back around to clean up.

"Not to worry, Reg. Let me sweep this, and I'll grab you another one."

"Thank you, you are too kind."

She smiled as she brushed the last of the shards together and scooped them up. Finally standing, a weird vertigo sensation made her wobble. Putting a hand on the nearby table, a frown weighed heavily on weak muscles.

"Oh, must have gotten up . . . too . . . fast." The words came out slurred, and as she tried to move her hand, a weird numb sensation filled every limb. Something smelled strange too, but her foggy brain couldn't place it.

Maybe she just needed some rest?

Sally closed her eyes and let the darkness take her.

## CHAPTER TWO

# Dead Language

> *System error . . . incorrect parse // retry? Retry aborted. Running safety diagnostics . . . Maintaining System stability . . .*

**S**ally blinked.

The barest amount of moisture rubbed over her dry eyeballs as she struggled to focus. A strange cold, weighty feeling ran through her body, receding gradually as the feeling returned to her extremities.

It was daytime. A rough haze of amber filtered in through the windows—she must be indoors? Shadows intertwined with the wave of light now reaching her brain. A few more blinks and whatever blur that remained washed away, now leaving her lethargy to slowly process where she found herself.

Tables and chairs next to a long counter with stacks of cups and cutlery behind. All of it a polished light wood, the slight discoloration of spilled . . . food and drink. The waning light reflecting across the glossy surfaces sought to illuminate a word in her currently very blank mental dictionary. *Diner.*

This was a *diner.* The sole thought sat in her lethargic brain like a hotdog in a bowl of porridge. Familiar, but wrong. But why was it wrong? Why was it familiar? The questions pained her bowl, cracking it. Threatening to leak the tasty porridge across the floor. Dark shapes shuffled into view, breaking her from the terrible food analogy.

She was not alone. As her ears joined the fray, the groaning and shuffling of the *others* surrounding her solidified that fact. Shambling figures of pale, decaying skin and glowing red eyes slunk around her—seemingly paying her no heed. Sally tried to move her head, the muscles in her neck painfully reluctant to do the task.

Sally looked down at her hands.

At this point, she would have expected her heart rate to start pounding in her chest, to fill her hearing with the drums of fear. Instead, she stared down at the pale gray skin that now ran from her fingertips all the way up to the shoulders of her sleeveless top.

*"Wowzers."* Her voice came out dry and cracked. She looked down at her feet and wondered why she had been sleeping standing up. Or was it even sleep?

"You shouldn't be able to talk." A harsh, rasping voice echoed around the diner from behind her.

Startled, Sally spun around on resistant legs, almost toppling over one of the undead occupants of the building. With sore eyes, she saw the one responsible for the statement hovering about six feet off the floor. A disembodied skull, enveloped in an eldritch purple energy.

"Who are you?" Sally croaked once more, yapping her mouth to try and get some moisture into her desert-like talking box.

"I am an Observer," the skull responded, seemingly frowning despite being unable to do such a thing, "and zombies aren't supposed to talk."

*Zombie.* There it was.

"Hey, *skullhead*, I have a lot of questions." Sally glared around the room for some kind of liquid, eventually locating a half-full glass of something dark. "But let's start with . . . what are you observing, and why?"

"Technically, I have already broken the rules by talking to you." The skull hovered a little lower and looked over toward the window by a barricaded door. "Observers aren't meant to talk either."

Sally followed the gaze as she gulped down the stale mouthfuls of liquid from the glass. "Something out the front?"

"What? No? Stop observing *me*—that's not your job."

"I don't think I have a job, not anymore." The memories of her past life were itchy, and she scratched at her tangled blonde hair as she walked over to the window. Did she even have a past job?

*"Stop, stop, stop!"*

Sally pressed her nose up against the window, flaring her nostrils out. A woodland took up the majority of the horizon, with a handful of other buildings that sat lifeless over to the left of her view. The pathway from the diner led alongside patches of grass, which perhaps at one point held verdant greens and collections of vibrant flowers—but now was just dry and desiccated.

Perhaps the most interesting thing of all, however, was a trio of figures standing about thirty feet down the road.

Her brow furrowed further, trying to take in all this newness. "Who are they? And why do they have numbers over their heads?"

Sally crouched down farther so just her eyes peered above the windowsill. A thin layer of dust and grime encrusted the edge of the glass, slightly obscuring the group with a mottled filter of brown and gray.

"You . . . can see the numbers?" The voice from the Observer sounded more confused than aggressive this time.

"Mhmm." Sally narrowed her eyes as she focused on the strangers. "There's a little symbol too."

There was a brief pause as the skull floated down slowly beside her. "Tell me what you see."

"There are three people there. Two of them have a plain circle with the number one. Then the other guy has a number three, and his symbol is . . . holy looking?"

"Two Novices and a Cleric. The numbers are their class levels."

"Huh. *Adventurers?*" More familiar but blurry words slid behind the spotlight of her understanding.

The Observer said nothing, turning away from the eyes of Sally to look around the diner. She followed suit.

The maybe dozen fellow zombies wandered aimlessly around the room, unaware of the situation. Now that she focused, she could see numbers above the heads of the other undead. Zero point five.

"Seven hells," she whispered. "Are we a beginner quest? The Cleric is hoping to power-level his friends by killing us?" Her sluggish mind started to race, gathering speed as if having clambered over the apex of a hill to find nothing but rapids beyond.

"This is highly unusual. Zombies aren't supposed to be able to talk or see power levels. That would only be possible if you were . . . " The skull tilted slightly as if trying to get a better read on the woman.

"What's my level and class?" Sally looked around, trying to find a number above her head, but only the faded wooden panels of the ceiling returned her scouring glare.

"Odd, I can't access it. You should just be an unnamed zombie, 0.5." The Observer hovered up higher in the room, almost perching atop the candle chandelier. "No class."

"I have a name; it's Sally," she snapped, somewhat unsure of how she remembered that name or if the statement was even true. "And I *can* be classy." She pouted, taking the comment out of context on purpose.

The zombie girl folded her arms across her chest and tapped her foot on the stained floorboards. It was only a matter of time before the adventurers would burst through the door and kill all the dead inside. For what? Experience and loot? Is that how this sort of thing worked?

"Hey, you!" She accosted the nearest zombie, once an older gentleman in his sixties with a long graying moustache and tweed suit with a matching hat. "Do you understand me? Stand over there if you do."

The aged deceased stopped in his current aimless tracks and turned to regard the woman now demanding things of him. With a brief hesitation, his glowing red eyes turned to the side, and he began shuffling over to the area indicated.

"Yesss!" Sally hissed but tried not to celebrate too loudly in case the figures outside heard her. Now she could make a plan!

"This is highly, highly irregular," the Observer buzzed to himself from up on high.

The Cleric sighed and pinched the bridge of his nose. "For the last time, this is really simple. You hit the zombies, I will heal you if you are hurt, and once they are on low health, I can *[Holy Nova]* to finish them off."

"That'll level us up, yeah?" The male Novice, a gruff redhead, stood waving his sword around in the air like a sparkler. "I want to choose my class already."

"It's kind of scary—what if we get surrounded?" The second Novice was a timid blonde-haired girl, holding her sword as if it were a particularly smelly piece of garbage.

"It's a simple building; we just have to go out the door if there is any issue." The Cleric drummed his fingers on the end of his mace. This was the third group of Novices he had agreed to boost for gold and so far, the most problematic by half.

"What about if we don't level, or want to level *higher?*" The male Novice planted his sword into the grass and frowned hard at the darkened diner ahead of them.

"We can do another building, but that will be more coin." The Cleric shrugged. "For now, worry about the task at hand. Enter together and focus on one zombie at a time, support each other, and most importantly, *don't panic.*"

Sally waited behind the counter, her back against the wooden shelves as she sat on the cold floor. Most everything was cold, but perhaps that was just her current undead condition. It stood to reason that if her heart wasn't beating then the warm, tasty blood also wasn't circulating through her body. *Tasty blood?*

"I want to advise you not to do this," the Observer called from the ceiling, "but I'm not really meant to interfere either way."

"Well, at least keep your voice down, Mr. Spooky-skull," Sally hissed, distracted from any further self-reflection.

"I am Observer unit HM-3.3."

"Oh. I'll call you *Humphrey,* then." Her smile was sinister in the shadowed recess of the back side of the diner.

The skull hovered down beside her behind the counter. "I'm not sure we should fraternize, but that is a suitable name."

Sally furrowed her brow at the empty sockets of the Observer. "So you're here to watch the adventurers kill us? Then what?"

"It is my job to report the balance of the world. Seeing who comes out on top."

"Report to whom? Stop telling me you're not supposed to talk to me, but then still do it." As much as she wanted answers, she thought that if you were going to draw lines in the sand, you should stick to them.

"Survive this encounter, and I might tell you." Humphrey somehow grinned as he floated back away, seemingly unable to shut his skeletal trap.

*Pretty annoying for a floating head*, Sally thought. Just what had she woken up into? Her life before this was a blur. Did she work at the diner? Were adventurers and levels a thing from the world where she had been a living person?

Just as this thought crossed her mind, she stopped as if frozen. A sound filtered in from outside, gradually increasing in volume—footsteps getting closer. The "good guys" were making their move.

"Okay, get ready, everyone!" she whispered as loud as she felt safe to, the boots of the eager adventurers nearing the door by the second.

There was a pause as a deathly silence cast its shadow across the diner. No breath was taken, and no groans uttered, the anticipation growing into a lump in Sally's stomach.

With a loud crack, the door burst open, shattering the quiet as three figures stood silhouetted in the fragmented opening.

"Huh, where are the zombies?" the red-haired Novice bemoaned as he took his first steps.

Hastily.

*Unprepared.*

## CHAPTER THREE

# Command and Conquer

The red-haired Novice took four short steps into the diner; weapon outstretched in accusation at the building that was apparently devoid of promised undead. It was at his fifth step that he snagged on something, and in his haste he tumbled to the floor face first, sword clattering across the wood away from him. As he rolled over to see what had been affixed to his boot, the female Novice spoiled the reveal.

"The zombie was *under the table!*" The gasp became a starter light that flickered along the fuse of their despair as around a dozen zombies crawled from, or flipped over, the furniture they had been hiding beneath. One of them got stuck and lumbered forth like a hideous tortoise.

As the red-haired Novice tried to kick away the shoe-grabber who was now fruitlessly gnawing on his thick leather boot, a second zombie lunged from the table beside where he fell. The flash of red eyes was his only brief acknowledgement before the undead man bit into living flesh, the searing pain only heightened by the shock of the assault.

"Ack! Help!" he called out, trying to shove away both attackers.

"Help him!" The Cleric growled at the panicked Novice still standing. He calmed himself and began channeling a spell. "*[Healing W—*"

*Thunk.*

The holy spellcaster winced away from the pain, the spell faltering as his attention was broken. Sally ducked back behind the counter and grabbed another glass mug, a wide grin spread across her face. The ambush from the zombies wasn't all that complicated, but their options had been limited. As she peered slowly over the countertop, it looked like it had had the desired effect.

With the Cleric interrupted, the two Novices had five zombies bearing down on them—just about too much to handle. The wails of the fallen one increased as help was no longer on the way. Sally shuddered. The pained pleas of her would-be killer were music to her ears. It was concerning, or at least, part of her believed so.

She watched as the female Novice cut down one of the zombies before her sword lodged in the torso of the second one. As she struggled to remove it, the old gentleman zombie grabbed at her arm, waylaying the adventurer and allowing a couple more undead to pile into the attack.

"Oh, God!" The Cleric looked panicked now as the female Novice screamed—overrun by the superior numbers. He went to prepare a spell but faltered, weighing up the effort.

Sally jumped up onto the counter and stood proud. "Nice try, magic-boy!" She cackled over the sounds of screams and feasting undead. "Go find your easy experience somewhere else!"

The Cleric glared with confused eyes at the zombie woman gloating over him from across the room. He opened his mouth as if to reply, but part of the horde split off after him, and with one brief look at the two fallen, he turned and made haste out of the diner. With the zombies reaching the threshold, she waved them back.

"Ah, let him go." Sally shrugged and sat down at the edge of the counter. "Is he really a class level of three if he can be beaten by one mug? I don't mean *me*."

The zombies paused at the doorway, a slightly forlorn look of wanting passed over them before they turned back to what remained of the Novices. The Observer floated down from his vantage point to hover beside the strange woman.

"That was an interesting outcome."

"Meh." Sally cocked an eyebrow at the skull. "They would have planned to stick together. We just needed to break them up a little and overwhelm, interrupt their carry."

"Simple, maybe. But not something a zombie would have thought up or been able to enact."

Sally swung her feet back and forth as she sat. She didn't *feel* like a zombie. There was undoubtedly a degree of undeath to her, but despite how tasty and red the Novices looked, there was no desire to consume them. Her friends seemed to be all about that, though.

"Oh!" She watched as a [Level Up] arose in gold lettering above seven of the zombies, and their Power Level changed to One. "Some of the gang leveled up!"

"So did you. Look at your wrist." The tone of Humphrey's voice had the barest hint of excitement to it. If Sally didn't know any better, she would think he had started to develop a vested interest in her advancement.

Upon her wrist was a golden star. It hadn't been there before, and it had a weird shimmer to it, like a hologram. With one gray finger, she pressed it, prompting golden text to appear in the air before her.

Error

"Oh, neat?" She pressed it again, and a strange buzzing filled her ears before it suddenly popped, and text appeared in her vision.

Level Up
Skill Gained: Command Dead
Party Option Unlocked
Title Gained: *the Unliving*

"Pfft, *the Unliving*? That's a pretty dull name. Shouldn't the zombies get the cool stuff, as they did all the work?" She crossed her arms and glared at the Observer.

"How strange . . ." Humphrey zipped around behind her to take in the text, which he could apparently also see. "You are a named Monster now . . . but the Party option is only for Player characters."

"Did I not just command the dead? Why am I only now getting the skill? Seems cheap."

Humphrey sighed and gradually started to bob in a circular motion around her. "I don't really know; you shouldn't have been able to in the first place. Consider this your proper crowning."

"Are there many skills?"

"I'm not a New Players Guide, Sally the Unliving. I wouldn't burden your mind with things you do not need to know at this stage."

Sally pouted and slid off the counter to the floor, dusting off her grubby red skirt. "You think Sally and her friends will be dead soon, so you don't care to answer."

"I can neither confirm nor deny my feelings on the matter."

Sally paced around the room, avoiding the new, fresher stains on the floor. This was a lot to take in. First, she was dead, and people wanted to kill her. But secondly, she could also get stronger and protect those around her by killing those people.

"Didn't even get to pick my class," she huffed. "Looks like I can have four friends, though. I'll pick . . . "

She pointed out three of the Level One zombies, then, with a sigh, turned to the older gent with the tweed suit. "Sorry, old friend, you have the job of looking after these weaklings." Sally jabbed a finger into the soft shoulder of the zombie, who gave a vague acknowledgment of his task in return.

Another Level One zombie would fill out the party . . . but she paused as she observed one of the shamblers. He was a little shorter than the rest, with a thatch of messy dirty-black hair and an outfit messy even for a walking corpse. There was something about him that was familiar, but she couldn't quite place it. "You're in, 0.5. I'm going to call you . . . Chuck."

Party 5/5

"Alright, my group, go stand over that side. Don't get killed for a little bit, and I'll give the rest of you names too." She pointed to the right side of the door-way, and an elderly couple and a businessman-looking zombie joined Chuck.

"You are picking this up rather fast," Humphrey noted while hovering around the diner. "If you hold down the STAR, you can bring up the Party information."

"Yeah, no thanks to you, Humps." She stood with her hands on her hips before relenting and pressing the odd STAR on her wrist. Immediately a window was brought up in the side of her vision.

Chuck (0.5) - 100% HP
Zombie (1.0) - 100% HP
Zombie (1.0) - 100% HP
Zombie (1.0) - 100% HP

"I can check out all my friends. How convenient. Health and power, just like a . . . like a . . . ?" Sally paused, unable to draw the comparison, before shrugging it away. "Are you going to tell me who you're doing this peepin' for now?"

"*I suppose.* I've already broken the terms of my service, so what's a little extra exposition while I'm at it?" The skull came to settle down at eye level.

"Should I sit down for this or—"

"I observe for the Architect. While their name might imply they are the cre-ator of everything, it is more accurate to say they are the underlying force behind the abilities and statistical—"

"They're the god of *numbers go up*? Got it. So they have you check up on things to make sure the math isn't going all loopy?"

"Again, your choice of words is . . . bemusing, yet not far from the truth. I was sent here to ensure there was nothing untoward happening with this experi-ence boosting. And then you turned up."

Sally sucked in a large lungful of air before slowly exhaling. "So I was a nor-mal zombie, and then suddenly I became super smart and capable. Despite being an Observer, you didn't see that happen?"

Humphrey hovered in the air in silence for a few seconds, the facial expres-sion of the skull unmoving. "*Yes,* well. Perhaps whoever burdened you with such enlightenment leaned a bit too hard on the sass button."

"Either give the information or scoot." She waved him away and headed toward the open doorway to peer out. In fairness to the floating skull, she was being especially . . . open with her thoughts. It was as if a chunk of her brain that usually weighed her down was missing. Which was quite likely, all things considered. Though she stalled, trying to remember where she drew the comparison from.

The sun had gotten tired of any adventure thus far and had begun settling in behind the forest. The last grasp of amber beams slowly rescinded to be replaced by tendrils of cool shade. That would be much nicer weather to travel under—Sally had no intention of staying put and being a target again.

It was a slim chance that the small group of weaklings would be the only tribulation in her unlife. In fact, just being a zombie would be a magnet for those who felt the need to defeat evil. Not that Sally felt particularly evil . . . even if the corpses of the Novices smelled delicious right now.

Sally turned back around to the increasingly gloomy diner. "Whatever part of me is meant to tingle when there is danger—it's doing so. No doubt Mr. Cleric will return for revenge or send some higher-level group our way."

"Now that some of you are higher level, you'll be worth more experience." Humphrey seemed to agree. "Even if you're not that much more dangerous. Zombies don't really unlock many skills as they level, just some statistical increases."

"Boneface." Sally shook her head with a tut. "They'll be crawling out of the woodwork once they hear about the talking zombie girl. I'll be on the bounty board by morning. Figuratively, or literally, depending on how this world works, I suppose."

"So, what are you going to do about it?"

A wide, sharp-toothed grin spread across her face as she turned back to the outdoors, grasping the cracked door frame.

"Why don't you *watch and see?*"

## CHAPTER FOUR

# Stale Air

Sally took her first steps into the outside world. This part of reality had less familiarity to it. Sure, there were trees and patches of grass—the things she knew *existed* on a base level. But, historically, this area was new information to her already cloudy head.

A cool evening breeze ruffled her red skirt and blonde hair as she narrowed her eyes at her surroundings. The diner looked to be the first building that the road led to, and then as the overgrown cobbled street carried on to the left, a small group of buildings in a U shape made up what could be considered a small town. *A townlette,* she mused.

Two shops, a bunch of residential buildings, and—at the farthest point—a larger building that must be some kind of town hall. Everything was made of the same light wood as the diner, perhaps locally sourced. The darkness in the depths of their windows and open doorways in the dying sunlight confirmed her first impression that the whole micro-village was either abandoned or similarly filled with rotten shamblers.

"Hey, Humphrey?" She waited for the Observer to follow her outside as the four members of her group slowly caught up the short distance. "Is it just zombies here, or is there anyone special?"

"I couldn't tell you even if I knew; I am only here to observe. Remember?"

She narrowed her eyes in response. "Have you *observed* anything more than zombies here? Y'know, when you haven't been constantly blabbering at me."

"Nice try. I suppose I can return my report now and receive any admonishment for breaking protocol. If I disappear into a mist, then it was nice knowing you."

The skull paused in the air as if frozen in time, and the eldritch energy surrounding it became a glowing white flame that flickered upward, enveloping the Observer.

Sally shrugged and looked back at the gloomy buildings. There were still questions left unanswered, so hopefully the skull wouldn't go away so soon, but she would need a plan either way. The hall would be the best bet for a defensive structure. *Possibly.* She mostly liked it because it looked the most castle-like. Being a named Monster and all, a decent place of residence seemed like the next step up.

Staying in the small area would probably not go well in the long term. They would need to keep moving so that adventurers wouldn't come by and wipe them out. *Soon.* There were already too many questions weighing on her mind; the thought of traveling in this unknown world would put her off-balance.

*Stabilize*, she told herself, *then think calmly and logically.* Sally turned and watched some of the zombies meander out of the diner. Her four chosen shamblers stood in a loose formation behind her, idly waiting for direction. For an awkward moment, she half expected them to talk or give some kind of signal. They did not. While Humphrey was still in a state of . . . communication with the Architect, she prodded at the STAR on her wrist. Interestingly, she found that it could rotate. Micro menus popped up depending on which point of the STAR jutted out toward the back of her hand. There were very few options. However, some things must be hidden until unlocked or needed. With a brief amount of fiddling and muttered curses, the skill description for [Command Dead] popped up in front of her on a big semi-transparent window.

---

[Command Dead]
Range 30 ft - Passive
Creatures with the <Undead> tag will be more likely to follow commands within this range and have a bonus to completing the command successfully. Only works on <Undead> at or below the user's level.

---

That was more helpful than the floating skull, but not by much. She wondered why the language was so imprecise. "More likely" and "bonus" didn't exactly provide a granular experience of whatever this existence was. Maybe there was a skill for seeing the numbers; that would be it. She was the same level as the zombies for now, at least, but did that mean a specific class level or total level? There must be some difference. The STAR spun again, and she brought up a Party member and their details screen.

---

"Chuck" - Level 0.5 Zombie
Health: 100%
Skills: None

Other than the Monster Level, this one was similarly ambiguous. Being in a Party didn't seem to give much benefit, so far, other than being a little nosey. With a quick flick-through, none of the other zombies had anything special going on aside from the change in level. Humphrey buzzed and shook in the air before the white glow encompassing him returned to the simmering purple of before. He took a moment to attune back to his current surroundings.

"Well," he said, eventually adjusting himself in the air to address Sally, "there's good news and bad news."

"Good first." *Always go good first*; that way, you cannot listen to the bad after and pretend it didn't exist.

"I have been forgiven of any error I have made in talking to you—"

"Including doing so now?"

"Yes, but the bad news is—"

"*That* was the only good news?"

"Now." He sighed, looking like he regretted ever starting the conversation. "The bad news is now I have been assigned as your personal Observer."

"Creepy." Sally crossed her arms. That meant the Architect had some interest in her and was keeping tabs. It reminded her of the first week at the diner when Doris had watched her every move. Sally rolled her tongue in her mouth—those were memories of her previous life? *Doris* . . . The name conjured up a rough round shape, but it lacked detail.

"It appears you are special." The Observer woke her from trying to piece together that puzzle. "I'm here to watch and make sure you don't do any…damage."

"Like *Hit Point* damage, or irreparably knocking some intangible screws loose in the structure of the System kinda damage?"

"*Yes*." The skull hovered slightly higher in the air to avoid her scowl. "The latter, mostly."

She sighed and bit her lip. This was turning into more of a pain than she first thought. The "classless Monster" stomped back over to the diner doorway and yelled at the remaining dead inside. "Alright! Everybody out. If they want me to break the System, then I'll need y'alls help."

"That's not what I . . . " Humphrey sighed and decided it wasn't worth the effort to continue his objections as they fell on deaf ears.

Sally stood and beamed as the half dozen or so remaining undead filtered past her out of the diner. Even the elderly gentlezom in the tweed suit followed despite his sad, but still glowing red, eyes.

"Sorry, bud. All hands on deck until I leave this little nook of forgotten civilization." She gave him a pat on the shoulder as he passed. You never knew when an extra pair of hands would come in useful when it came down to it.

"*Hillan*. That is what this place is called." Humphrey shuffled down closer to her as a small *ping* on her wrist STAR lit up.

"Location information? Neat, but I'm not going to stand here and read it." Sally shook her head and narrowed a glare at the skull. "So, *now* you're my Beginner's Guide?"

"I have been granted allowance to furnish you with some information. So long as it doesn't go against my scheduled duties or affect the System in any way."

"Sure." She rolled her eyes as she remained unconvinced. "And we know how much you like sticking to protocol."

Before the Observer could object, Sally turned and pointed toward the supposed town hall of Hillan. "Onward!"

With sluggish ambition, the horde of zombies began shuffling in that direction, the haunting groans and scraping of feet against dirt signaling the inevitability of their arrival. Or it would if there was anyone else around to hear it. Currently, it was enough that she could hear it.

"A little quieter, people, please." She rubbed her head as her thoughts bounced around like a bee in a balloon. In response, the moaning volume dialed down a couple of notches. *[Command Dead]* proving it was worth its weight in gold already.

"What are your plans now?" Humphrey questioned as they joined the throng in walking to the building. "Not only now, but also long term—let's say next day, week, and month. Assuming that you aren't dead by then. Re-dead."

Sally was silent for a few moments. The mass of bodies around them subsided, as they had soon breached the front of the group due to their less-shambling pace. Her Party members were also at the forefront just behind them, although their pace was barely any quicker than the rest. Just as the floating skull was about to figuratively prod her again, she spoke up. "As I am, I will be hunted by adventurers and the like. That means I will need to get stronger and get a stronger Party to support me." She looked up to the darkening sky as distant stars twinkled back at her. "For now, just survival is enough. Until I know what this world is, how it works."

"Very wise." The Observer hovered higher up and turned to watch the group of zombies following the woman, allowing them to pass him as he stopped. Something akin to a smile curved at the edges on his skeletal face. "I will be watching your career with great interest."

## CHAPTER FIVE

# Dead Space

Sally slammed the large town hall doors closed behind her and slumped against them with a sigh. The short jaunt across the small village had picked up a few extra stragglers, and now her horde had grown to nearly three dozen, if you included the zombies already waiting for her arrival in the building. Which she did.

"Quite spacious in here, is it not?" Humphrey hovered idly in the air nearby.

It was modestly spacious. The main portion of this town hall building was indeed that—a large hall that could probably seat all the residents of Hillan, should it be required. Currently, the mass of tables and chairs had been stacked at the side walls, leaving the main hall space clear. She was thankful for this due to the number of bodies meandering around. Although the under-the-table trick worked once, she doubted it would a second time. Plus, all the zombies would be bumping into everything at this point.

"*[Command Dead]* didn't have a target limit, right?" It was mostly a rhetorical question to herself; she could still remember all the information on the useless tooltip.

"What are your plans?"

"Quit asking me that, Humps." She scowled up at the looming skull. "You are literally the worst *Observer*."

"I'm not usually this talkative." He moved up and down in the approximation of a shrug. "You are just different from all—"

"All the other girls?"

"All other Monsters."

"Yeah. Monsters don't get this STAR thing either, right?" She held up her wrist to show the silver star that seemed to float a few millimeters from her skin.

"Only Players do." The Observer nodded and swung down closer to Sally's face.

"Then . . . what *is* a Player?" She scowled at his empty eye sockets, searching for an answer that made sense.

"I'm . . . sorry, Sally the Unliving. I am unable to answer that."

"You don't know, or you are not allowed?" She sighed and slunk to the floor, burying her head into her knees. Either way, she wasn't getting an answer, and the depth of what she didn't know sank in, smothering her.

"Nobody really knows much about the world when they come here; you are not alone in that regard."

"So *people* come here? Then they get assigned as a Player usually, but not usually a sentient Monster?" She raised her eyebrows as the skull tried to back away.

" . . . "

"The Architect is going be so annoyed with you." She smiled, climbing back to her feet. "Welp, best get our defenses sorted, and we'll see which of us gets vaporized first!"

There were two other doors exiting the wooden hall—a small one to the right and a marginally larger one at the back. The side room seemed like as good a place to start as any. With a creak, the door swung open to the darkness inside. "You'd think I'd have better night vision as a zombie."

"There's only so much light your ocular . . . bits can pick up." Humphrey floated into the room over her head, his purple energy giving just enough dim light to see.

"Too busy yapping during anatomy class? This looks like a storeroom." Sally stepped farther into the cluttered room, squinting at the dark shapes illuminated by the Observer's glow.

A few stacked wooden chairs, a couple of cabinets and cupboards, and a broken mop and metal bucket. Sally picked up the wood-only part of the snapped mop and waved it in the air. She wrinkled her nose and turned to the skull. "What, no 'Makeshift Club' or Inventory stats?"

Humphrey just stared blankly back at her.

"I'm just . . . I don't have any useful skills to attack with, right? I feel pretty weak and reliant on my friends out there." She jabbed the splintered end of the mop toward the hall.

"Players usually start as a Novice and have a *[Novice Strike]* skill. It's like a normal attack but has—"

"Yeah, yeah, either gimme it or let's move on. If I'm some kind of necromancer, I should have . . . like a bolt attack or some way of dealing ranged damage."

"Necromancer isn't a class that you can—" Humphrey began before the zombie woman turned and began opening the cupboards.

Nothing. Well, not *nothing*. But just the random odds and ends used for cleaning or repairing the hall. There was a box of candles, some tools, a couple of spare chair legs, and a handful of things that had degraded away to dust and mulch. She grabbed the tools and chair legs and brought them back out to the hall, putting them in a pile.

"Candles would be nice, but it would draw too much attention. Let's check the back." She pushed through the crowd of swaying corpses, muttering unnecessary apologies until the space at the back was reached. The door here appeared to be locked—on account of the rusty-looking padlock on it. Sally turned and whistled out to her Party, who emerged from the horde over to her.

"Reckon you could break down a door?" She smiled and flexed her skinny arms to further the point.

As one, the Party lumbered over to the door. Chuck arrived first and slammed his meager body weight against the wooden entryway. The business zombie stood over him and pushed against the door, as the elderly couple assisted by giving their body mass to the effort.

"Is there like some kind of roll that happens? Invisible dice or stats comparison? My skill says it makes things more likely to succeed."

"If there were, it would not be something *you* would be privy to." Humphrey moved closer to the straining zombies.

"But *some* people can see it? Can you? You can, can't you? *You can.*"

"Y-yes. Well, sometimes." He spun back around to face her. "There are different levels of Observer, which determines how much of the System they can see."

"Otherwise, you wouldn't have been able to see if there was anything weird going on with the experience gained at the diner?"

With a loud groan that reverberated around the tall ceiling of the hall, the wooden door eventually relented, the old hinges cracking and splitting from the wood. The Party collapsed inside the room, landing atop each other and squishing Chuck.

"Oh, look, a learning opportunity." Humphrey slightly grinned. "Check your Party status screen."

Sally tapped the STAR button and read the image that burst forth.

---

Chuck - 92% HP

---

"Poor Chuck took a little damage, the red part?"

"Correct!"

"Fascinating. How do I make it not red?" She folded her arms as the screen vanished again.

"Beats me."

"Is that a request?" Sally growled as she stepped through the doorway, over her Party trying to untangle themselves.

The space beyond became illuminated by the skull as he came in behind her.

It was a long, single room that seemed to serve a dual purpose of both kitchen and office. The closest side had desks and drawers, and a wide window looking out to the gloom of night outside. The far side had a stove and counters for preparing food. As her eyes adjusted to the shapes coming into focus, she realized there was something in one of the chairs.

*A skeleton.*

She bounded over to it across the dusty floor and leaned over to look into the empty eye sockets. It sat, head rolled back slightly and slumped in the chair as its arms dangled to the floor.

"Anyone in there?" she cooed before stepping back and frowning. "How do all the bones stay together in this position?"

"It's probably that—"

"Oh, there's a note in front of them." She blew the dust away and picked up a sheet of paper before turning it over and then around. "Why can't I read it?"

"It's probably that—"

"Never mind, it's not words—it's a drawing! A pretty terrible one, though. I mean, I've heard the term 'starving artist' before, but this is . . ." She paused and put her hands on her hips.

". . . Everything okay?"

"They should change the skill name to [Command *Un*dead] if I can't make the bone-person do things." Sally shrugged and looked over the scrawled map again. She turned ninety degrees to the left. Tilted her head to the side. Moved the paper close to her face with a squint. "They hid a weapon in the stove." She eventually rolled her eyes. "That does not look like a stove, though, but using deduction and context clues, I was able to—actually, let's just get it."

"Be my guest."

"I'm already *Mr. Bones*'s guest," she said, curtsied before the skeleton, and placed the paper back where she found it.

Her footsteps echoed against the wood slightly as she approached the kitchen end, where she knelt in front of the stove. The small metal door popped open with a squeak of hinges in need of a good oil and revealed a dark pit of ash. Or what she hoped was just ash. She dug around with her hands before a smile lit up her face.

Sally turned around and plopped a rectangular box on the table. Despite the bedding it had just come from, it was in almost pristine condition. Iron bracing ran along the sides and filled out the corners—not particularly ornate, but enough to make the box seem well-defined—a respected box among lessers. Plus, the white question mark painted on the front was interesting. A small pair of weapons crossed were imprinted below it. At a squint, they looked to be an axe and a sword.

Humphrey sidled along beside her. "A *[Melee Weapon Chance Box]*, how peculiar."

"Aw, I wanted a ranged weapon." Sally pouted but drummed her fingers on the surface. "Tell me how it works then, guide-skull."

"You bind to it with your STAR, and then it opens, and you receive a random weapon. White box can have anything from the lower tier of rarities—a medium tier would be the rarest drop from it."

"*Neat*," she whispered. "Let's save the tier explanations until after I somehow roll something higher than possible, yeah?"

"I'm not sure that—*yes*, alright, then." Humphrey resigned, his lack of eyelids narrowing over his lack of eyes.

Sally held her wrist over the box, eyes aglow as the STAR shone a bright white. She edged closer as the light spun around the box bracing, the question mark pulsing with a similar white glow. With a hiss of invisible steam, the lid popped open, and something rose up from within.

## CHAPTER SIX

# Internal Organ-ized

**S**ally gasped as the weapon rose from out of the box.

"*A dagger?*"

The dull-silvery blade hung in the air and rotated as if it was waiting for her to claim it.

Sally stared at it and moved closer. "Not a dagger that can raise my kills as zombies? Or enchanted to do double damage on Tuesday evenings?"

She grabbed it out of the air, and whatever magic held the display together dissipated—the box now just an inert tray of wood on the table. With a few test swings, the dagger cut through the air easily enough.

"No stat box for this either? What's the point of the random chance without tangible stats to compare?" She growled as she cut more of the air.

"Odd, there should be something. Maybe you need to activate it, like how you had to level up to unlock skills." Humphrey floated farther back to be well out of the way of the errantly swung blade.

"Makes sense, actually; I'm betting Monster equipment doesn't have stats, correct? So I need to convince the System that I'm a Player?" Sally put the dagger carefully into a small leather sheath that had appeared on her belt at some point.

Humphrey was silent for a few seconds before answering. "Most Players aren't usually this self-aware."

"I spent a lot of busy-brain time with Systems in my previous life . . . " She scratched her head. "*I think.*"

The Observer said nothing further, so Sally shrugged and returned to the main hall. Her Party had managed to untangle themselves and stood awaiting their next task. With a glum smile, she gave Chuck a pat on the shoulder. It was hard to see how hurt he was visually—being a zombie left you with icky-looking patches that would count as injuries on a living person already. Finding a way to heal her pals would be a needed step on her journey.

"Right!" she commanded loudly to all the zombies present. The shifting of dozens of pairs of red eyes to focus on her was briefly unnerving, but she continued. "I expect that miserable Cleric would have gone and whined to some tougher friends about our little dining experience." She nodded to the several diners who still had Novice-gore caked across their fronts. "And they'll probably come back for revenge."

She took a deep breath into useless lungs. Speaking in front of crowds wasn't something she was used to, but it felt exciting now. "It's time to put together our next plan for when they do." A big smile crossed her face at the multitude of groans that passed for a response.

Sally felt *powerful.*


"Killing zombies is pretty beneath us," a raspy voice of a figure clad in dark leather bemoaned as their footsteps rang out against the stone road.

"As I said before"—the Cleric clenched his jaw—"there's *something else* there. Some undead Monster with some manner of intelligence."

"A ghoul, maybe? There wouldn't be anything high level like a vampire out here," the third person in the group muttered to themselves, wiping a sweaty hand on their robes.

The Cleric exhaled through his nose. The fact that he had to bribe the Ranger and Wizard to come out so quickly was mortifying. Having lost the gold from the Novices earlier, it had now turned into a costly day. If he could at least kill that zombie woman who had mocked him, it would bring him some peace.

"You didn't want a tank, neither?" the Ranger pestered, going over points they already had discussed before leaving the nearby village of Yarch.

"They're zombies. We can easily keep out of range between the three of us, especially if they're still in the diner."

The Ranger shrugged in response and looked out into the forest while idly tapping his fingers on his slung longbow.


Sally peered from a dusty window halfway up the wooden wall of the town hall, atop a stack of chairs. She had heard footsteps, and now that the bobbing globe of lantern light had started to sway up the end of the road, she knew trouble loomed.

"Everyone shush," she hissed down at the horde of zombies shuffling into battle positions. "They're here!"

Three figures emerged from behind the scenery, enclosing to a generous thirty feet away from the diner. She narrowed her eyes to barely pick out the details above their heads. Ranger . . . Wizard . . . and the Cleric from earlier. All Level Three. That wasn't terrible, she considered; just by numbers alone, the zombies had more power to them . . . depending on how levels scaled.

She watched, eyes growing wide, as a small ball of light formed in the distant hand of the Wizard. Then, in a short second, the ball flew out and into the open doorway of the diner. An explosion of amber and yellow flashed, blowing out the windows of the building and illuminating the whole mini village. Just as soon as the attack had occurred, the magic flames flickered away—surprisingly, not setting the entire structure alight.

"*[Fire Blast]*," Humphrey whispered from way too close. "Slightly different than *[Fireball]*, the latter of which would have set the building on fire."

She frowned and watched the small group approach the diner. The Cleric led the way and stopped at the open doorway before he turned to the other two in animated conversation.

"*Idiot*," the raised voice of the Cleric echoed around the town, "*what do you mean only once per day?*"

"Low-level casters." The Observer rolled his empty sockets.

The Ranger walked slightly closer into town along the overgrown, patchy pathway. The cloaked figure knelt and ran their hand through the dirt. He then stood and gestured toward the town hall, the other two cooling off from whatever argument they were having.

"*Wet biscuits!* Alright, they're onto us. Deep breaths now." She breathed in and out slowly, despite not having the mortal need to. If there was one thing she was thankful for, it was that the lower floor did not have any windows at the front—most of the natural lighting came in through the windows higher up or from skylights in the roof. *It probably looks quite pretty in here during springtime,* she mused, before shaking the distracting thought from her head. It meant the only natural way in would be the door.

The Ranger drew his bow and notched an arrow, his footsteps approaching the hall until they stopped about forty feet away. The Cleric and Wizard joined him, and they began a murmured conversation.

"This is bad," Sally whispered to the skull, hiding away from the window briefly. "Three ranged classes against my slow pals?"

"*Yes,*" Humphrey confirmed helpfully.

Sally peered back out of the corner of the window. The Ranger had now nocked an arrow that had a very unfriendly blue glow pulsing around it.

*Hells!* There was no way the horde could cross that distance without being cut down. She was now glad she hadn't stationed her Party in one of the side buildings—although they would briefly distract the enemy, it would just have weakened the main group of zombies.

She waited for the inevitable impact of whatever skill the Ranger was casting with his arrow . . . but nothing came. Another peek revealed the trio had started arguing again—murmured, but their body language suggested they were only keeping it down so as not to disturb any zombies.

This gave her a brief moment to think. *Perhaps* her plan might work; it just needed risk, patience, and sacrifice. *Probably a miracle too.*

"Psst! Everyone to the walls, slowly. You five go meet our unwelcome guests."

The zombies that had been patiently waiting at the back of the hall began to filter to the left and right flanks, hugging against the wall as quietly as they were able. Which, to their credit, wasn't too loud, considering. The handful of unlucky shamblers moved to the doorway below her and, after a brief amount of effort, pushed it wide open.

A streak of blue flashed across the space between the two groups as the arrow had been let loose. As it struck the first zombie stumbling through the opening, lightning arced from the impact. Tendrils of white-blue light flickered between the other nearby *z*'s, and they shuddered and fell to the floor. The smell of burnt flesh and singed clothing filled the hall.

Sally held her breath by instinct, saddened at the loss of her undead thralls but not wanting to give her position away. A buzzing filled her head, and she winced before a new UI popped up in her vision.

"What's this?" she hissed with narrowed eyes as the buzzing pain slowly vanished.

"Combat UI when engaging a new foe—most turn it off unless it's a special battle." Humphrey sidled up against the wall, not wanting to catch an arrow either, despite being unable to be seen by the opponents.

"Yes, yes, turn it off." The UI vanished, and she peeked through the window. She could just barely hear the conversation between the trio of Level Threes.

"Can you see any others?" the annoying Cleric asked.

"Not from here. You really pulled us out here for a handful of zombies?" The Ranger seemed both disappointed and frustrated.

"Any others would have come out too." The Wizard was quieter but seemed to agree with the Ranger.

Sally licked her lips. The next part was a long shot but might work if the adventurers were slightly divided. With a sigh, she readied herself.

"Oh, help, please! These zombies have me trapped!" She tried to sound as much like a maiden needing rescue as possible.

Humphrey raised himself to see through the window. "Don't worry; they can't see me. They appear to be arguing again."

She strained her ears to try and pick their voices back up, but they had lowered them as they deliberated. They must not have bought it. Plan B would need to be conjured into her brain sooner than intended—

The Observer turned back down to her. "Oh, looks like two of them are walking this way. The Cleric is just throwing up his hands in resignation."

Sally turned to her Party, who sat on the makeshift scaffolding made of chairs and tables she had built into an archway over the door. With nervous confidence, she gave them the thumbs up and withdrew her dagger.

## CHAPTER SEVEN

# Hairline Fracture

Clerics, they are all the same." The Ranger spat on the floor as he walked toward the dark opening of the town hall, bow raised, and arrow notched.

"More interested in purging zombies than saving a life in distress," the Wizard murmured in agreement. After all, zombies couldn't talk—the voice they heard had to be someone who needed help. There was nothing quite as satisfying as a side quest you just happened to run into by chance.

Especially one that didn't involve running over half the continent to deliver some cake ingredients. At least the cake had been good, though.

The Cleric continued to seethe through clenched teeth. *How dare they?* To come all this way and still be so stupid and clueless. He had half a mind not to support them . . . but then, if they did kill the zombie woman, he wouldn't get any of the rewards. With a deep sigh, he begrudgingly followed behind them at a safe distance, idly flicking through his Combat UI. The fact that it was blank was curious but not abnormal.

He shrugged and drew his spell book and mace.

*This better level me up again.* Sally shook her head. Though . . . getting out of the situation with her unlife would be a fair middle ground. She itched from sitting so long, perched precariously by the window—perhaps some combat would relieve her of that problem. Yet again, she faced a situation where she just had to wait and listen as footsteps drew closer.

Her hand gripped tightly to the handle of the dagger was oddly clammy. She had never struck anyone—in this life and whatever was before—that she could remember. It was kill or be killed, and she was quite partial to being on this side of the grave. Did Monsters or Players respawn? That would be a question for the skull when they had—

The Wizard and Ranger had reached the threshold of the doorway, pausing for a second as their eyes adjusted to the dark interior.

"Blue blazes, there's a lot of them. You think the lady trapped is in the back room?" The Wizard raised his hand, and a green glow started building.

The Ranger shrugged, raising his bow. "No idea. Let's clear these out and che—"

He didn't get to finish the sentence as the rickety bridge over their heads collapsed—helped in part by Sally kicking out one of the supporting legs. They both looked up as tables, chairs, and the four Party zombies dropped down on them.

The Ranger managed to dodge backward, tripping onto his backside but avoiding the majority of the debris and falling rotters. Not so lucky was the Wizard, as the furniture pinned him to the floor, causing his spell to fizzle out. A sheen of blue light flickered over the panicked arcane user, some manner of shield preventing the initial bite attempts from the Party.

"You have lightning resist, right?" the Ranger yelled as he tried to scramble to his feet and ready his bow.

The Cleric dropped his mace and helped the Ranger up. "*[Healing Word].*" A spell began to form in his other hand, ready to heal the Wizard after the zombies had been cleared.

Sally leapt from the tower of tables, a good fifteen or so feet in the air. Everything seemed to go in slow motion as she fell toward the Wizard, trying to free himself from the zombie's grasp. She had just enough time to savor the fear in his eyes as he noticed her descent.

As if knowing her intentions, the Party moved to the side, which allowed her a clear route to her target.

She landed, pain flaring up her legs as wooden furniture buckled and split beneath her landing. With the full force of her fall, she jammed the knife downward into the unprepared Wizard's throat, gouging the basic weapon to the side with little resistance.

Blood sprayed out, covering her waitress uniform and face as the Wizard fell dead, shocked eyes lolling back toward the remaining adventurers.

"Miss me already?" she hissed out at the Cleric, licking the blood from the blade as her eyes glowed bright red. The added psychological damage was always worth being a little extra.

Both men paled, mouths agape, before the Cleric regained his composure—a brief flare of anger overrode his fear.

"That's her!" he sputtered as he stepped backward. "She can control these dead—kill her!"

As if to prove his declaration correct, the zombies that had been waiting in the wings started to clamber over the debris and pour out of the town hall, red hunger in their eyes.

The Ranger leveled a quick arrow at Sally, and she flinched, expecting the piercing pain—but Chuck flung himself in the way, the arrow taken in his eye socket. His body flopped over onto the ground, and the light of his eyes faded.

The horde surged past her, giving her cover as she seethed, teeth bared as she tried to process the death of her Party member.

"Impressive." Humphrey hovered down to her. "They are back to having the advantage of range now if you plan on just standing here."

[Holy Nova]. A bright dome of radiant white light pulsed from the Cleric, burning up the nearest zombies. The Ranger let loose a couple of arrows, downing several more undead.

Sally flipped her dagger around and sprinted off the pile of wood and Wizard, sidestepping as she ran so that a zombie was always between her and the ranged pair. The horde was gaining ground but losing the war of attrition.

The Cleric wiped the sweat from his brow with his long brown robes and scowled. "Keep an eye on her; she is approaching."

"I can see that, god-boy; I'm just trying not to get overwhelmed," the Ranger spat back, landing another arrow in the forehead of a nearby undead.

"Yes . . . quite." The Cleric wrinkled his nose and scanned the crowd with panicked eyes. With a swift motion, he brought his mace around in a wide arc, striking the Ranger in the back of the head. "Sorry." The robed man shook his head as he turned and fled from the betrayal.

The Ranger stumbled forward, staggering on unsure footing as his hand reached up to his cloaked head. He spat on the floor as his vision spun and went to turn toward the traitorous adventurer—but before he could focus, a body slammed into him, knocking the air from his lungs as he fell against the stone floor. The musk of decay filled his senses before the pain of sharp teeth ripped into his throat.

Sally stood and wiped the gore from her mouth, allowing the slower zombies to finish the job. She hadn't wanted to eat them before, but the taste of the Wizard's blood was . . . *pretty neat* actually. Not in a full three-course meal kinda way, more like cotton candy that melted on your tongue and was a fun treat.

She stepped forward away from the throng of dead eating the Ranger to watch the Cleric's cowardly escape.

"You are an affront to God!" he yelled out from a safe distance. "I will be telling the Guild about you—your days are numbered, fiend!" He escaped down the road and behind the tree line, his fist outstretched and shaking the whole way.

"That was unexpected. Though, a hypocritical Cleric? Not saying *duh* . . .

but . . ." Sally sighed and pocketed her dagger. She wasn't sure if she still had adrenaline rushes, but whatever buzz had made her stab and eat people was wearing off, and she felt tired.

"He probably would have been fine if they attacked together," the Observer noted as he flew lazily through the air. "I've never witnessed such reckless self-preservation from an adventurer before."

Sally licked her teeth clean. Why were they all so sharp? "Hey, Humps, who is the 'Guild'?"

"He probably meant the Adventurers Guild. They facilitate quests, officiate the laws governing adventurers, and all the boring stuff." The skull turned to look back at the reduced horde in front of the town hall.

"Ah, so they'd be the ones putting a bounty on me or setting some kinda . . . standard of Party that would need to come zap me?" She rubbed her legs now, sporting some minor cuts from the furniture, but surprisingly she hadn't bled much. Perhaps *not* surprisingly.

"*Yes.*"

She tapped the STAR to bring up the Party information. She hadn't realized it, but she had lost the elderly man during her rush. However . . .

"Huh." Sally walked over to the debris pile by the door and squatted down by her fallen Party member. "You seeing this, Humphrey?"

The Observer paused as if going over the same overlay in his own vision. "I do. Peculiar."

Chuck lay across a split table, mouth agape and arrow stuck through one eye into his brain. His body was limp, and his eyes were devoid of any light. The UI showed a full red bar, yet he hadn't been removed from the Party like the old man had been.

"Aw, buddy." She patted his shoulder. "Why aren't you properly dead?"

Level Up

Her STAR shone a bright golden color as several text pop-ups appeared over the heads of half of the zombie horde.

"Aw, nice!" Sally flexed her noodle arms in celebration. "Why are my pals only Level 1.5 now instead of two?"

"Some Monsters scale differently, so they have part levels. Minor stat increases make it a smoother leveling process for, uh, Players."

It looked like leveling up had replenished part of the Party's missing Health Points. Except for Chuck, who—

The zombie in question stood up and staggered into position, the arrow still in his eye socket.

Sally frowned at the UI—he had returned to full health, but . . .

"Chuck, you've gone down in level to 0.3. What are you playing at?" She tilted her head, but the short zombie did nothing to respond.

"Hmm." The Observer similarly tilted himself. "I suppose you'll go up in power at least."

"Of course." She beamed, pressing the golden STAR. "Oh!"

Surprise and wonder filled her red eyes as three skills popped up. *Pick One*, the hovering text said in bold letters.

"I didn't know I'd get to pick!"

"Generally, that is the method. First four levels, you have a choice of three skills, and the fifth level has a keystone ability for your class. After the fifth level, you can either advance your class, multi-class into something different, or just keep at it—within certain limits."

"Mine didn't work like that," she huffed. "I still don't even have a listed class."

Sally paused her complaining and narrowed her eyes, weighing up the options before making her choice.

---

**Pick One**

**[Drain Life]** Ranged, 40 ft - Replenishes some of your HP by damaging the target

**[Grasping Hands]** Area Effect, 10 ft radius - Any creature entering this space is slowed

**[Mighty Aura]** Passive Aura - Party members have increased Strength and Constitution

---

## CHAPTER EIGHT

# Handful of Bones

Skill Gained: Mighty Aura
Stats Increased

The skull seemed perplexed with her choice. "Interesting, that skill is not built into any class that has access to those other two options."

"That's why I chose it, Humps. Sure, the ranged attack would be handy, or even the area slow . . . but, uh—I forgot where I was going with this."

"You want to support your Party?" The Observer nodded at her.

"Sum of the parts, and all that. I don't want to be like the annoying Cleric and think so little of my Party members. They may only be zombies for now, but we could be a lot stronger in the future because of my choices now."

"You're really in this for the long term?"

Sally looked almost insulted at the question. "What choice do I have? I didn't ask to be a Monster—and after tonight, we can agree that the term is loosely granted, huh?"

"It's not my position to place judgement. For what it's worth, you are interesting to observe."

"Aw, don't go all soft on me, Humps. I don't trust your 'number-daddy,' but you are cool enough." She smiled and turned to the horde of zombies, crossing her arms in thought.

For a brief moment, the purple energy surrounding the Observer turned the briefest pink-peach before returning to the eldritch purple.

"I can't travel with twenty-odd zombies," she huffed. "Not only are they slow, but they will attract unwanted attention. I alone already will—but a group of flesh-eating undead will be too much of a hindrance. As cute and adorable as they all are." She pouted and turned back to the floating skull.

"What are your plans now?"

"To find more powerful friends. Then, I don't know, destroy the establishment—maybe God?" Sally shrugged.

"That's . . . I'm not even going to address that. That would be a lot of adventuring parties to be the pooper of."

"Well, whatever I used to be, I may not have been the life of the party . . . but here, I can be the *death of the party.*"

"That would make a good tagline, maybe even title."

"I doubt it—oh. Chuck, come here." She beckoned the Party member over before she plucked the arrow from his socket with a wet sucking noise. "Such a goof. I suppose I need to replace a Party member with . . . that one."

Zombie has joined the Party

"You did promise you'd name them if they leveled up again," Humphrey reminded her, bobbing around her in an arc.

"Ack, fine. Funny what you choose to know and tell me. Chuck, Grams, Suits, and . . . McDoots." Her head rocked back and forth. "Is that too demeaning? I suppose this is just my nickname for them, rather than actually forcing them to live under my given cringe identities?"

"*Yes.*"

"Thanks, Humphrey, always a good chat. So, tell me, do I get quests or do I have to wander blindly throughout the world in search of danger and tasty meat suits? *People.*"

"There should be a quest menu under your—"

"Oh! More importantly, can I loot these dudes?" She jerked a thumb back toward the dead adventurers.

Humphrey made a shrugging gesture in the air, shifting up and down. "Monsters can't loot, usually."

Sally approached the Ranger, waving off the zombies who were finishing their snack. Strangely, it did not repulse her to see the state of what remained of the man. It did make it a hassle to try and dig around for valuables, though. "Is there not a way this is gamified?" She waved her hand at the chewed-up mess.

"*Yes.*"

"Humphrey, I swear . . ."

"Use the STAR if you can." The skull floated slightly farther away to avoid her ire.

"When did we even start capitalizing that," she muttered. "I don't even want to know if it's an acronym." Sally pointed the odd device at the corpse and jabbed at it.

Nothing happened.

She prodded it repeatedly again, impatience building a scowl across her face. Then, a buzzing started in her head once more. A screen popped up, filled with nonsense numbers in a disjointed pattern—pressure built up inside her skull as the word "ERROR" burnt into her mind. The throbbing almost deafened her before a *pop* cleared her head.

> Inventory Unlocked
> Parse//Read Error . . . Scan Unl

"Oh, cool, I get headaches and broken abilities. Whoever made *this* is the true monster." Sally rolled her eyes and jabbed her finger on the STAR once more. This time a small window popped up.

> 10 Gold
> Longbow - Common
> Arrows - 18
> Small Medicine Pack

Sally took the med pack and gold. As much as she had wanted a ranged weapon, the longbow looked like something she had neither the skill nor the muscles to use. Not that she could check her own stats yet. With a sigh, she wandered over to the Wizard, his face still agape in shock after she had sliced a gash in his exposed neck.

> 15 Gold
> Zap Wand (3 Uses)
> Spell Components (4)
> Lucky Rabbit's Foot

"Hold up!" She whistled. "This a magic trinket, Humpster? The wand sounds useful too." Sally hit *Loot All*.

The STAR was spun to find the Inventory tab, which soon opened up to a large UI screen. Reaching the trinket, it was pulled out of the part-digital screen and appeared in her hand. She clipped it to her belt.

> Lucky Rabbit's Foot: +1 Luck

"Hah, wasn't so lucky for the rabbit, right?" She beamed around the clearing looking for the Observer. "Nor for the Wizard, I guess."

She sat down on one of the least broken chairs littering the doorway and looked out into the village of Hillan. Well into the middle of the night now, the area was only lit by the two moons in the sky. It was almost serene, like watching ducklings paddling around a pond. Except it was bloodthirsty walking undead. *Oh!* An undead duck might be a nice pet.

As she placed her head in her hands, the Observer made his appearance known by clipping the doorframe as he hovered beside her.

"Everything okay, Sally the Unliving?"

"Pfft, who knows." She closed her eyes. "I'm pretty sure I used to work in that diner as a normal person. Now I've just eaten part of a man trying to kill me because I've woken up as a zombie—one that defies the laws of this world."

"True, but you—"

"I'm also followed around by a floating skull that is watching me to see exactly how I break the rules and only gives me information at random."

The Observer said nothing but looked at the sky with the zombie woman.

"I'm sorry, Humphrey. Just venting, and I know none of this is your fault." She sighed and gave a sad smile to the skull. "Do I even need to sleep? I can't tell if I am tired or just . . . dead."

"It's okay, Sally. I hope one day to be released from the constraints placed upon me. And, *yes*. Even Monsters need to rest sometimes."

"You think we will be safe here for the rest of the night?" She looked around at the empty houses. It was a remote location for sure, the gnarled wear of the wooden structures, the dust-laden surfaces—all a testament to this.

"*Yes*." Humphrey caught her glare. "I will awaken you should anyone approach, and you have these zombies still, as a safety blanket."

"Thanks, Humps." Her frown turned upside down. "We'll spread the *z*'s out, put some lit candles where I am not sleeping—to draw attention away."

"Smart." He nodded. "I have no arms, so I will just bob about and provide mood lighting."

Sally grinned and hopped to her feet. "Just what I've always wanted from a third party constantly spying on me!"

They had chosen one of the empty residential houses as their base for resting. Despite being dusty and relatively plain, the bedroom was surprisingly comfortable. A single bed with a worn but unsullied mattress, a bedside table with a few desiccated flowers, and a set of drawers. Above the bed hung an amateur painting of the village.

For the undead woman caked in gore, it was quaint and peaceful. Under the soft purple lighting of the Observer, who watched out of the single window, she soon fell asleep. Her Party rested just outside the room on the second floor, spread among the landing at the top of the rickety staircase and the grime-encrusted bathroom. A few select shambling corpses were placed downstairs, with the rest split between the other nearby buildings.

The sleep went by fast, dreamless, and uninterrupted. Sally awoke to the bright morning sunlight cascading through the window, illuminating the bed and the rest of the room, save for the shadow of the floating skull.

"You've been there all night?" She yawned and swung her legs over the side of the bed, throwing back the covers.

"As I said I would. I do not need rest. Just a mandated two-week holiday, annually."

She brought up the Party UI and saw that everyone had been fully healed overnight, including herself. "I thought I felt better," she murmured and wiped her eyes. "Is there a way I can clean my uniform? I mean"—Sally waved her STAR around—"like with magic instead of *effort?*"

"*Yes.* In the right location." Humphrey moved across the room, close to the door. "I'll let you know when the opportunity arises."

"Thanks." She rolled her eyes, trying to decide if that was helpful or not.

"So what's the plan for—"

The STAR lit up in a brighter silver. Sally shrugged and poked at it.

Login Bonus: Day 1 - Receive Gift?

## CHAPTER NINE

# Ground Earth

New Player Starter Pack Received
10 Gold
Basic Weapon Chance Box (1)
Basic Armor Chance Box (1)
3-Day Exp Boost (+10%)
ERROR

They sure do like to labor me with all these *Errors* to clutter up my Inventory."
Sally rolled her eyes. "Shouldn't I have received this stuff yesterday?"

"Technically, no. Or . . . " Humphrey looked the woman up and down. "You are still not exactly a Player. The System is trying to fix the 'broken pathways,' and it must have activated after your sleep."

Sally blew air out her nose. This was becoming a headache. Getting all the Player things in disjointed, delayed, or buggy fashion would put her at a disadvantage. She quickly flipped through the STAR to see how her Party members were doing—all okay—before switching the Inventory and bringing out the two Chance Boxes from the 2D hologram into the real world. Or however "real" it actually was.

"Can I tap both at the same time?" She held her wrist above the first one and raised eyebrows at the skull.

"Sure, why not."

The STAR lit up the first, and then the second with a white light that spanned around the box bracings. The white question marks atop the boxes pulsed with a similar glow. She leaned in closer, the light illuminating her face as the anticipation built.

With a puff of wispy steam, both boxes popped open one after the other, items inside rising into the air. Both of them Common quality.

"Pfft, another dagger!" Sally wailed, her hands thrown in the air in frustration. "And the second box is . . . shoes?"

"*Yes.*"

She plucked the gray *[Common Basic Boots]* from the air and put them on. They happened to be the correct size, only now they weren't boots anymore—they looked like her sneakers. She wasn't too sure how she felt about being in her waitress uniform for the rest of her unlife, but at least the shoes were comfortable.

"Usually, there's a toggle," Humphrey interjected, lowering down to inspect the footwear. "To either show the item or your cosmetics equipped. Doesn't work that way for Monsters, however."

"Seems like Monsters get the short end of the stick here, huh?" Sally pocketed the second dagger, and the two boxes remained inert and empty on the bed. "If I get a dagger out of my next box, I will write the Architect a very strongly worded letter."

"Their response time is . . . Oh, you were joking. *Ha-ha.*"

Sally frowned at the skull and looked over to the window. Would the sunlight cause them a problem? It was quite likely that slow-walking some decaying bodies down wherever the road led to would at the very least be a stinky affair. Whether that translated into actual health damage or status effects was another thing entirely—and not one she cared to get a half answer out of the Observer. Looks like her options were limited.

"We're going to go through the woods." Sally clapped her hands together and looked around the room to see if she had all her possessions. Everything being held in the intangible UI would take some getting used to.

"Certainly. In which direction?" Humphrey followed her searching gaze around the furniture with his own.

"That one." She pointed at the wall before turning roughly eighty degrees, having forgotten her exact place in the town. "Away from here and avoiding the most danger that we can. Maybe gobble up some low-level adventurers?"

There was no response from the floating skull as he watched her head toward the door.

"Oh." She spun back around. "Do people respawn?"

"Players? No. Monsters? Sometimes no. It depends."

"You?"

Humphrey paused, trying to work out if that was a veiled threat. "The souls of the deceased go somewhere, but I am not privy to that information."

Sally tilted her head. So there was something after this life—or unlife. The Wizard and Ranger she killed last night were now at peace, but was that in some kind of heaven or were they reincarnated as Monsters—or even back into another version of this reality? That would be a bridge to cross when she got to it—hopefully, not by testing out her own mortality.

With a shrug, she went back to the door of the bedroom. The Party had gathered and assembled in the downstairs kitchen, which was pretty bare and had no brains stored away in the pantry. Every surface was covered in dust, the specks of which danced in the illuminating beam from the window as they disturbed it with their shuffling about.

"How long has this place been abandoned?" Sally rubbed her finger along the counter. The sink had a layer of grime around the plughole where a small plant had started to grow.

"If I told you, I'd have to kill you. Oh—you are dead already. *Ha-ha.*"

The zombie rolled her eyes. "Was that laugh genuine? It sounded like your sarcastic one from before."

"I have never had to laugh before. Is it with a different inflexion, like *hA-hA*?"

"N-no. Let's put a pin in that." She grimaced at the weird noise coming from the skull. "And how about my answer?"

"Three weeks or so."

"Huh?" Sally leaned her elbows on the counter and rested her chin in her hands as she tried to gaze through the dirtied window. A furrowed brow bore down on her red eyes. "That doesn't make any sense."

Everything looked like it hadn't received a lick of care for years. The other *z*'s were clearly the past residents or visitors—surely? That made her think, though . . . How long had she been here before the "awakening"? She narrowed her eyes as she watched the skull bob in the air.

"You have a lot of brains for a zombie—*ha-ha*. I can see you postulating; care to make a guess?"

She bit her lip and stood up straight, sighing. "If you tell me one thing, I think I can guess. How long have *you* existed?"

"Three weeks or so."

Sally closed her eyes. It didn't really make anything better and just made the groans and shuffling of her Party more pronounced. Not that it was *horrible*—it had quickly become background noise, but for a mind already cloudy with the facts, it put pressure on the conclusions trying to form.

"So, the System was created less than a month ago, but the environment has the appearance of being an established setting?"

"Wouldn't be much fun if everyone were newborns on a barren flatland."

The flicker of a different color pulsed through the Observer, too quick for the zombie to notice which—only that there had been a change.

"So why am I a zombie and not a Player?" She crossed her arms and glared at the skull.

"That's what I am trying to find out. Remember the whole 'Observer' thing?"

"*Clearly not.*" Sally threw up her arms in resignation. "So I am the only sentient being that gets to be stuck in a Monster body instead of becoming a Player?"

"Now . . . this is where it gets muddy." The skull tilted side to side as if trying to arrange the thoughts in his head. "There are sentient Monsters, of course, and some have skills or other abilities to a degree. But they are more grounded in the setting . . . They don't have—"

"They don't have the System blaring large screens in their faces? They aren't *gamified?*"

"As always, a curious way of phrasing things, Sally the Unliving." The immovable facial features of the Observer almost seemed to be grinning.

Sally leaned her back against the counter. Her Party stood against the opposite wall where some decrepit shelving nudged them into awkward standing positions. Not that they were a paragon of perfect posture anyway. Chuck especially seemed to be having an awkward time existing as he gazed up at the cobwebbed ceiling with a pained look on his face.

"You know, Humps." She eventually sighed and tilted her head at the skull. "We can't be best buds while you're still spying for the Overlord."

"I . . . uh . . ." the Observer stuttered. Before his sentence could completely form, he was interrupted by a piercing buzz coming from the zombie.

"Ahh, frickin' STAR!" She growled, waving her arm in the air in hopes she could push away whatever droning had filled her head. A pop filled her ears, and the ceaseless noise vanished.

She peered down at the cursed shape with a scowl. It was glowing golden again, but not as bright as when she had leveled up. With a sigh, she pressed the top of the STAR and watched as the menu spun around.

---

Quests Now Available

---

"Usually, you'd get those almost straight away. You certainly are a late bloomer."

Sally clenched her teeth and glared at the skull. "You want to tell me what the deal with quests is before I crack you open and see if there's anything worth eating in that bonehead of yours?"

Humphrey slowly rose up toward the ceiling. "Certainly, *ha-ha.* When not receiving a quest directly, the System will offer you a choice of three options to complete. There are usually Combat, Social, and Exploration quest options so that all manner of adventurer may find a rewarding fit for how they spend their time in—"

"Alright, alright. You don't have to sell me on it. Hopefully, one of them will be in the direction of the woods—and Social sounds like a wash given the company I keep." She jerked her thumb toward the bored-looking walking corpses.

She popped her finger onto the STAR to bring up the three quest options. "Huh, interesting. I guess I will pick . . . "

Transport a Crate of Cloth to Merchant {Paulo Wrathon} in {Yarch}

Successfully Tame a Pet

Investigate {Tomb of the Lost King} in the Cemetery

## CHAPTER TEN

# Copse and Robbers

The animal taming quest?" Humphrey questioned, raising eyebrows he didn't have.

"Don't judge." She pouted. "The tomb isn't going anywhere, and the woods are nearby."

Sally put her hands on her hips in defiance. She might as well get some experience and reward, as it's so close by—and she could even nab herself a cute critter as a pet! Or emergency snack, if we are being honest. Her Inventory pinged a notification.

> Creature Taming Lure (1)

"Neat. Is it a 100 percent chance that it works? They only gave me one. Plus, what does it work on? What if I change my mind?"

"*Yes.*" Humphrey paused just enough time for the frustration to show on Sally's face before continuing. "*Ha-ha.* Why don't you read the item description?"

"I'm mostly just tired already from the vague technobabble I've been presented with so far. But, okay."

She pressed through the menus to bring the item up. Her red eyes briefly scanned over the fuzzy text before she closed it.

"Alright, so that answered some of what I asked. You know what? Let's just go do it. This kitchen is getting stuffy, and I am getting hungry."

"You're the boss," the skull agreed diplomatically.

Stepping out into the daylight was an uncomfortable shock. Being directly under the sun made her skin itch like she was wearing a winter coat. It turned out that being unable to sweat was one of the downsides of being undead. Cold in the shade, sweltering in the sunlight.

"Alright, stick to the shade, troopers. No sense arriving at our destination half-cooked." She shuffled over to the meager shade offered by the house.

Overall, Hillan was quite beautiful in the light of day—idyllic, even. If it weren't for the faux-decay of abandonment, this would be a quaint retreat from whatever passed as a city in this world. Maybe everywhere was like this. Sally shrugged to herself; there was just too much world to explore that there was no point thinking about it all at once.

"Humphrey?" she asked, shuffling along the wall to keep to the shadows. "Tell me more about stuff."

"That's . . . a really vague—"

"Like, levels and classes."

"Alright." Humphrey swung out in front of the conga line of walking corpses, trying to shift along to the end of the street where the road left the town. "Players start as Novices, and once a Novice reaches Level Five, then they can choose a class. Their level is then reset, and they start anew in their designated class. Every five levels you can—"

"Upgrade to a further class within your class type?"

"*Yes*. But your level doesn't reset at this point, so for example, the Wizard you so easily murdered yesterday was Level Three—he would have been a Level Five Novice before choosing the Wizard class. If he had lived to see Level Five, he may have chosen an advanced class—say, Fire Wizard, but still have been Level Five."

"Then at Level Ten Fire Wizard, he could advance again?" Sally raised an eyebrow and paused as they reached the corner of the last building on the row. Just the vast expanse of the stone road lay before them now, but the beckoning shade of the woods lay a good thirty feet away.

"*Yes*. You really are smarter than you look." The skull rotated around to avoid the narrowed glare of the zombie woman.

"How many advanced classes are there, or what's the max level?" She took a deep breath and ordered the Party across the road—taking off at a stiff jog herself as they shuffled slowly behind.

"Base classes have differing amounts of advanced classes. I'm not actually sure of the exact amount, but the maximum level is fifty."

The Observer watched in silence as the zombies made it slowly across the road, hovering high above them, not bothered by the sun. As Sally collapsed against the first shaded tree, he bobbed down beside her.

"So there's between one and ten advanced classes for a base?" She panted and clawed at her face, willing the excess heat to escape her dead flesh.

"Potentially, but the most common is around five, I'd say."

The Party clamored into the shade beside them, looking equally disgruntled by the overly warm sunlight. Traveling only at night would be a problem and totally inconvenient if they were going to be searching out adventuring Parties to . . . eat. Was that what she wanted to do to them? Things were a little hazy right now.

Sally spread out on the grass, lying down on her front to try and allow the grass to cool her. "Anyone Level Fifty yet? It's been three weeks or so, right?" Her voice came out muffled from being buried in the greenery.

"Outside my authority, I'm afraid. Just statistically speaking, though, no. I would be surprised if there were any Parties over . . . Level Twenty, maybe." Humphrey tilted as if trying to parse the mathematics inside his skull.

"Is it most common to adventure in a Party, then?" Sally rolled onto her back to look up at the canopy and watched it shuffle gently in the breeze.

"*Yes*. Almost required, really. Perhaps the closest to mandated without being the law as possible." The Observer turned away from the conversation, his purple glow flickering in color again.

For a few short, silent moments, Sally felt peaceful looking up at the branches and leaves above, with the occasional glimpse of a clear blue sky as the covering leaves shifted. It was cooler here, and the haze inside her head faded. She closed her eyes and briefly felt like this was all a dream.

"This is the west Hillan Woods." The skull broke the silence, accompanied by the buzzed notification of her STAR giving her location information.

"*Not reading it.*" She closed her eyes. "Getting knee-deep in a lore excerpt just sounds like the quickest way to getting ganked."

"It has a list of the animals native to this area of the woods, though, for your quest." Humphrey hovered over her and looked down, blocking her view.

"Just tell me the coolest one." She sat up and waved the skull away. "We both know that I'm going to go for the weirdest thing possible."

"Well, it depends how you define 'coolest', but there are frogs, owls, spiders, dire badgunks—"

"Wait, what's that last one?"

"It's a mix between a badger and skunk, with the personality of a raccoon." If the Observer was capable of slow-blinking, he would have done so.

"I feel as though you are making that up." Sally folded her arms and scowled at the floating skull.

"I assure you I am not. Your bestiary doesn't seem to be activated yet, huh? Perhaps encountering one will knock the System straight."

Sally exhaled and stood up, wiping down her skirt—for all the good that did. Creases were the least of her worries when it was covered in blood, dirt, and remnants of the adventurers that had tried to cross her. Which was mostly still blood, in fairness. She wondered how far the Cleric had gotten in his machinations to come back after her and whether he had a proper Party. Probably not, given the way he treated the Ranger.

"Do I get experience from killing wildlife or other Monsters?" She turned to watch the Party, who seemed to have gotten distracted by a bird and were all staring off into the same tree.

"Monsters *can* level up through the killing of other Monsters or neutral creatures, but it is usually at a very reduced rate. Killing Players gains a lot more experience, by comparison." Humphrey looked up to see if he could see the bird too.

"So clearing out Hillan would have gotten me little more than a sore arm and pang of guilt."

"*Yes.*"

"Party, group up! Alright, we are heading into the woods proper now." She beamed as her troupe of corpses turned and acknowledged her. "Don't go running off after the first tasty snack you see. We will have to be clever and quiet if I am going to trap this . . . badgunk thing."

If *[Command Dead]* got through to them, they made no show of it. As much as Sally adored her undead friends, without them having the necessary brains to at least acknowledge her requests, it would make this whole ordeal tougher than it needed to be. Plus, they couldn't gain many skills, according to the Observer.

"The dire badgunk is especially smelly when warding off larger predators, but otherwise wily and thieving in its bullying behavior toward smaller animals."

Humphrey waited for her response before slowly arcing around next to the Party to observe her. The zombie woman looked glum.

"Pets take up a space in your party too," he added, unable to read the situation.

"*Aww*, so unfair," she whined. "They should call them thieves of joy. Am I right, gang?"

The Party did not respond.

"Well, usually the quest is for Novices before they fully unlock the Party function—other than a few classes, pets are more of a hindrance once you start to—"

"Hush, Humps." Sally shook her head. "You are already making this harder than it needs to be. I have to let one of my babies go so soon?"

"*Yes?*" The Observer rose slightly higher to look down at the collected group of shamblers. Babies would be one of the last words he would use to describe them.

Sally pouted and sighed. No sense bellyaching over it, or was that just her hunger for mortal flesh? Her Party had managed to ward off a small group of Level Three adventurers—with some luck and a horde of zombies to assist. What would happen if they came across a full five-person Party, a group that wouldn't get caught out by slow corpse-walkers?

"Well, let's get moving. We aren't getting any stronger listening to me yap.

You're rubbing off on me, Humphrey." With a brief smile, she shook her head at the skull and began striding off into the woods, slowly followed by four zombies.

The Observer looked back to Hillan briefly, narrowing his eyes at the smallest moving object in the distance, before turning and floating off back toward the odd zombie woman.

## CHAPTER ELEVEN

# Stench of Death

If there was one thing that you could say about trees, it was that they were pretty consistent. Indeed, each had their own individual knots, branches at different angles, or different slants to their growth—but after a few dozen of them, they all looked like big brown rods that just got in the way.

Sally growled as she stumbled over another scarcely visible tree root hiding in the grass. The *[Common Basic Boots]* she had received from the Chance Box obviously were not enchanted to protect against making a fool of oneself. She only fared slightly better than the rest of the Party, who moved slower but were just as clumsy.

"Where badgunk?" she grunted at the floating skull.

"Beats me. No, that still wasn't an invitation." Humphrey floated out of reach, just in case. "From what I can tell, we have managed to scare off any living critter way before you've even gotten a sniff of them. Partially because they get a sniff of you."

Sally stopped and watched the zombies shuffle noisily through the short shrubbery and grasses of the woods. She had tuned it out, but on reflection, they weren't exactly a subtle group even without the stench of decay about them. She pinched the bridge of her nose. All this walking about in the daytime was making her cranky. Perhaps wandering around aimlessly hoping you would just stumble into a clue was a terrible idea. The Party paused around her, and she allowed the silence of the place to sink into her once more.

Birds chirped in the distance. The canopy leaves shook gently in the breeze, a low rustling that rose and fell as the ripples of air ran through into the distance.

There was the faint glimmer of . . . running water? A stream or small brook that bubbled along, somewhat nearby. Speckles of sunlight danced through the shifting gaps of the overhead cover, with the occasional block of illuminated earth to traverse where a gap in the trees allowed it through unabated. Beautiful, perhaps. Were Sally not a living corpse, this would be relaxing. But it wasn't; it was a mess of things getting in the way of her intended quest. It was a maze of potential hiding places for things that wanted to hunt her down and kill her. She clenched her sharp teeth, wondering if the frustrations she felt were a side effect of the heat—or her need to eat once more. She had been able to resist at first, with the Novices, but once she had tasted the blood of the Wizard . . .

"What do badgunks like to steal?" Sally relented and directed a question at the idle Observer to distract herself from the bad mood.

"Mostly food, but they are known to covet adventurer items—they have the *[Pickpocket]* skill."

Sally grunted and withdrew the spare dagger, walked over to a tree stump and placed the weapon upon it. She then took out the Taming Lure—a strange object that looked like a fishing rod but with a red bobble on the end instead of a line. "Alright, everyone . . . *play dead.*"

The Party stood for a second, taking a brief moment to process the command. Slowly, one by one, each zombie collapsed to the floor and lay there unmoving. Sally did the same, slumping against a tree a few feet away from the stump in a sitting position, head lolled to the side with her tongue out.

"Allow me to perform recon," the skull offered to the corpse. "I am sure this is not against protocol, but I will float up and observe for approaching creatures. And then notify you appropriately." Humphrey hung in the air, waiting for a response. But the dead body remained unmoving. "Wow, you are too good at that." He relented and floated up into the air.

Sally couldn't resist the smallest of smirks curling up at the side of her mouth—before she quickly reset to her blank expression. With the Taming Lure hidden in her hand under a short bush, she realized that she should probably have looked more into how the blasted thing worked. Did she have to remove a Party member first? Was it just point-and-click? Did she have to weaken the target first? She blamed Humphrey for the lack of information.

Time passed. For the lack of care she had for the idyllic beauty of nature previously, now that she had cooled down and the stress had passed, it *was* pretty relaxing. The sun had scooted its way across the sky, and, thankfully, the positions the Party chose to lay in remained shaded for the most part. Bugs and flies had gathered to see what the hubbub was about with the group of newly dead— but seemingly had no luck in accelerating the natural process.

She tried not to think about the fact that she was also a living corpse. At least she had some of the facets of one—for the most part, other than quickly overheating, she just felt like an average but very stiff and achy human. The brain fog was a little concerning, but in comparison to her Party, she couldn't really complain.

Instead, Sally took this downtime to try and make sense of the jigsaw puzzle pieces in a big pile in her brain. Why was she here? What was before this? The diner was familiar, and her uniform hinted that she perhaps worked there—and knew Chuck in some fashion. She could imagine doing daily chores. Serving customers, pouring coffee, and cleaning up after closing. Were these actual memories or just false ones she was placing?

She cursed the System, whatever it was. This constructed reality was unfair. Not only because she had a glitched existence between Monster and Player, but being dragged from her previous life and being set upon by who knows what—

The STAR blinked red, illuminating the shaded patch of grass in a crimson glow.

"Oh, that's not good." Humphrey sunk down from his lookout point.

"What?" She tried not to move or make much sound, but her eyes darted toward the skull.

"Red means bad. *Usually.*"

Her eyes narrowed. The STAR stopped blinking but remained a dull red as it awaited her to check the notification. It didn't look like a badgunk was coming, but should she blow their cover, just in case one could be on the way?

The Observer bobbed in the air expectantly.

Sally sighed and reached over to press the notification, sitting back up straight. "If I miss out on completing my quest because of this, I'm using the Taming Lure on you."

"*I don't think that would work.*"

A screen flashed up as the STAR was pressed, large letters looming over the zombie woman.

Bounty Taken Out: 250 Gold

She tilted her head back against the tree and exhaled at length.

Humphrey moved to try and meet her gaze. "Do . . . do you want me to explain?"

Sally put her hands over her face. "No, I want off this wild ride, Mr. Bones."

"It's a pretty low bounty, considering." The Observer ignored her muffled wails. "They underestimate you."

She let her arms flop back to the floor and tilted her head at the skull. "Flattery will get you nowhere, Humps. Give me the facts."

"The nearest town will have a Bounty Board with a general description of you. It will update once you get closer to a big enough town. Adventuring Parties can accept the task, but it's a formality and doesn't confer them any further benefit other than knowing you left the area."

"How do I get rid of the bounty?" Sally waved a hand in the air as if to shift away the target on her head.

The skull said nothing, blankly staring back at her.

"Humphrey . . . how do I get rid of it?" She stood to her feet now; fists clenched at her side. Red eyes glared at the Observer.

"Once there has been a bounty issued . . ." The skull began to float away slowly. "There are only two ways in which it can be rescinded: if the original placer of said bounty removes it . . . or, well . . ."

"If the bounty is completed?" Sally growled back at him. The Cleric must have placed it, and he didn't seem like the type to have a change of heart on such matters.

"*Yes.*"

"You forgot a third way." She punched her fist into an open hand. "We need to *beat up* the Bounty Board."

"Ill-advised." Humphrey visually recoiled from the suggestion. "The Adventurers Guild that it is tied to is basically the foundation of the System. You would have to be—"

"I'd rather be crazy than dead!" Sally winced after raising her voice, the brief echo rolling down through the woods and spooking away a couple of birds—no badgunk for this already-dead whiner.

"I'm . . . sorry to upset you." The Observer looked down at the floor slightly.

"It's not you." Sally sighed and looked at her Party still lying prone. "I've just been feeling the System is unfair, and I've been getting the short end of the stick."

Humphrey said nothing once again, content to wait for the zombie to fill the silence.

"Perhaps I shouldn't complain so soon, though. Just because I have a glitched existence and a bounty on my head doesn't mean it's all bad, right?" She slumped as if hoping to be told otherwise.

"Normally, killing a few Level Threes would net you slightly more bounty. Either the Cleric cheaped out on you, or the Guild wasn't convinced of your proficiency."

Sally stretched out her jaw muscles. So quickly had her whining been glazed over. Was this intentional due to the Observer's directive, or was he just being a jerk-head? *Yes,* she thought, in a tone mocking the floating skull.

"Sally?"

"Mmm? Oh, so the System has the final say?"

"*Yes.*" Humphrey nodded, unaware of the internal scream inside the woman's head.

"So if I dismantle the System, then—"

"Shh!"

"Don't shush me; you know that—"

"*No*, I mean—listen!"

Sally paused, her red-hot rant cooling off in the chamber as she focused her hearing. There—rustling in the bushes. An odd tempo of movement, but it was definitely getting closer. As silently as she could, she sat down on the floor, nary a couple of feet from the prized dagger sitting inert on the tree stump. A dead-blank expression crossed her features while her eyes subtly stared over at the bushes where the sound was coming from. Her grip tightened on the Taming Lure as her arm tensed, ready for it to shoot forth like a magic wand. She could see the movement now, bushes and leaves shaking as the creature approached.

And then, with one bounding movement, the small beast leapt across the gap toward the bait.

With one swift motion, Sally rose from position and leveled the Taming Lure, activating it with her intent. Her mouth hung open as the end of the lure started flashing between a red and green glow.

That *did not* look like a badgunk.

## CHAPTER TWELVE

# Spattering

It did, however, look like a very *cute* gunk.

The round, almost spherical blob of blue jelly-like substance looked up at her with a shocked expression. Tiny black eyes that floated to the surface welled with misted fear and betrayal—the coveted dagger just but a small leap away from its grasp.

"That's a Blue Slime," Humphrey answered sagely. "You can tell by the way that it is."

"You didn't mention these." Sally stood in awe at the semi-transparent creature as the lure started to pulse green more frequently than red.

"You did interrupt me."

"So what do I do—" Her question was interrupted as the Taming Lure burst with green light and small sparkly stars, a wave of relief washing over the Slime as it became friendly.

---

Blue Slime successfully tamed
No room in Party
[Make Space] [Release]

---

"No, no, I don't want to release you. Oh dear, our friendship was so short-lived." She turned with a glum expression to her zombie friends, who were still doing a top-tier job of being inert corpses.

She brought up the Party menu and cycled over to McDoots. She sighed as she brought up the options and selected *[Kick]*.

The zombie, formerly known as McDoots, clambered to its feet awkwardly. As if a spell had been broken, it slowly observed the group around it and then started lumbering off back in the direction of the diner. Sally briefly considered keeping it around with *[Command Dead]*, but that sounded like more effort than the zombie may be worth.

Blue Slime has joined the Party

"Maw, so sad to see him leave. But let's see what Bubbles can do."
She flipped through to the Party information screen for the new pet.

Bubbles (Player Pet) - Blue Slime
Skills: [Absorb Water] [Nibble]

"Bubbles?" Humphrey questioned rhetorically. "They will act in a similar manner to your . . . zombie companions, as they are a Monster you control."

Sally knelt and prodded the Slime. It wobbled around and cooed at her, much to her delight. "I've only had Bubbles for two minutes, but I will kill anyone that hurts them. What is the maximum level for Monsters?"

"It is also fifty. Usually, a Monster won't get too much higher over their starting level—due to their slower experience progression, but also the reward for killing them increases, and they end up hunted by adventurers."

"So for a Monster to even level up sets them aside from their kin pretty quickly?"

"There is a gradual scale. One level over, the Monster is Experienced. Two levels, and they are an Elite. Three is Champion, and four is Mini-Boss."

"Five levels is Boss, then?" Sally popped the Slime on her lap, sitting on the tree stump, and slickly stroked the gooey surface.

"In theory. In three or so weeks, however, it would not be possible for a Monster to attain such a level." The Observer reconsidered this statement with a head shake. "Unless they destroyed a town of the highest-level Players, maybe."

"Best add that to my checklist, then," she muttered back. "Though—I get levels like a Player rather than a Monster, right?"

"*Shrug.*"

"You . . . can't just say that."

"It appears that you have the experience curve of a Player, but your skill selection is unlike any of the classes." Humphrey bobbed around and looked back out into the woods.

Sally waved her hand through the menus, trying not to let Bubbles slip to the floor. The Slime wasn't exactly making her dried-gore-encrusted uniform any better, but also not really any worse either. She frowned. "I can't see an experience bar anywhere, though?"

"No?" The Observer floated back down and stared blankly closer to her face. "You're just slightly off."

"Aw, nice! I just need to find a hapless Novice or two in these here woods, and then *chompin' time!*" She shooed the Slime off her lap and wiped her hands on the sides of her dress as she stood. "Or hope to not run into evil adventurers after my bounty."

"*Yes.*"

Sally glared at the skull. "If you had a neck, I'd wring it. Welp, no point standing around here all—"

"Ahem." Humphrey nodded his head toward the STAR as best as he was able to.

It was glowing a dim golden color, eager to be pressed again.

"Oh, quest complete, right?"

Quest Complete
Error Experience
5 Gold
Basic Armor Chance Box (1)

"Did my experience go up at all?" Sally folded her arms. This error business was really getting on her nerves. "Five gold is meager too, but at least it wasn't another dagger box."

"Experience did go up—you're just slightly off."

"You said that *last time!*" She waved her hands in the air in frustration.

With a sigh, she withdrew the Chance Box from her Inventory and opened it up. The small fanfare of the item reveal was starting to grate on her nerves. In part because getting basic Common items was underwhelming.

The hiss of the opening box drew the attention of the whole Party as the object emerged.

Common Basic Boots

"Rah!" Sally immediately grabbed them and chucked them into the bushes some twenty feet away.

Humphrey made the wise choice not to remark on the outburst.

"Let's just go do the stupid tomb quest then." She shook her head with a sigh. "It's in . . . a direction, right? Why do I not have a map?"

"Well—"

"Monsters don't have maps, right? Just more evidence the System is broken. Or maybe I am broken? People don't go into Monster bodies, right? Only Players? Am I the only hybrid, Humphrey?"

"Sally. You are asking so many questions that my '*Yes*' will have no meaning."

She bared her sharp teeth at the skull. "I'm just pretty hungry actually; where can we take Bubbles and get some fresh Novice meat?"

"*Shrug.*"

The woods felt a lot calmer now that it was heading into the latter part of the afternoon. Shade had spread wider, and they had fewer periods spent avoiding the direct sun. Sally kept her eyes peeled for Parties of Novices, but unfortunately for her grumbling stomach, they hadn't caught sight of a thing.

It was acceptable, if not a shame, that any wildlife was easily scared off by their approach. They would be worth little experience, even if their internal meaty bits would satiate her hunger. But surely any adventurer worth their salt wouldn't be similarly scared off? Not that she wanted particularly salty ones, but by now, she wasn't too fussy.

"We aren't wandering into a high-level area or something, Humps?" she wondered to the skull.

"No, not for a while. I would warn you if that were the case." The Observer had spent this leg of the journey a few feet above the woman, keeping an eye out for any potential danger.

"Aw, how protective," she teased before looking back at her Party.

"Your existence is unique—my interest is only academic," Humphrey murmured to himself, rising higher in the air.

She grinned and allowed him to go unheard to save his embarrassment. She hadn't known many skulls in her life—none that weren't hiding away in a face, at least—but despite his annoying tendencies, Humphrey was at least the closest thing to a friend she had in this world—ten points for the floating Observer.

Bubbles had received bonus points in her mind for being slightly faster than the zombies. The Slime did make a *boip* sound every time they hopped, which was becoming ever more grating every ten minutes or so. She shuddered, remembering the weird noise it had made when Chuck tripped over it at some point when the Slime had been distracted eating some woodland garbage.

It was safe to say that Sally was tired of walking through the woods. At first, sure, it was enjoyable. A brief holiday through nature with warm sun, slight breeze, and all the shades of green you could shake a lure at. But now, she missed walls. The structures and stability of something carved out via intent. She idly wondered if the Novice Players had a quaint little starter town nearby, a sense of community and a place to grow new friendships or forge strong Parties.

And she wondered if she could *eat them all*.

Doubt welled up in her stomach, pushing the hunger to the side for a brief moment. Could she even kill anyone? Without tricks up her sleeves, a group of Level Three Novices could easily roll the zombies—and she was no melee expert.

These ill seeds of sinking confidence had a familiar but distant taste to them. She closed her eyes and took three deep breaths, in through the mouth, out through the nose.

"Everything okay, Sally?"

She opened her eyes to the skull floating in front of her, at arm's reach. They had stopped in a narrow pathway between trees and bushes, almost a natural alleyway between groupings of plant life. The zombies stood idle and surprisingly quiet. Bubbles hopped beside her and gazed up with those tiny, innocent eyes.

A smile spread across her face as she turned from the blob creature to the skull, opening her mouth to confirm—but stopped.

Sally turned to the left as a rustling of leaves came from the side. Before she could draw her dagger, a figure jumped forth. A humanoid shadowed from the sun, a darkened shape of light-brown leather and dark iron. Their weapon—a shortsword—was already in mid-swing.

A flash of pink light followed the blade as it swung down in a huge arc, catching the sun in a radiant blaze.

Bubbles *popped*. The impact of the attack sent globules of slimy jelly splashing against her legs and the grass around them.

> Party member Bubbles has died

Red hot anger burned through her eyes, before they met those of the assailant. Sally froze in place and gasped.

## CHAPTER THIRTEEN

# Taste of Blood

T*HEO?"*

The slime-murderer paused and stumbled backward as he brushed the messy brown hair from his face.

"W-what the . . . *Sally?*" His green eyes darted wildly between the zombie woman before him and the three other undead who glared at him eagerly.

"Stand down, for now," she hissed back at her Party before addressing the man again. "You killed my pet, you jerk." Sally crossed her arms and kicked a lump of the former slime away.

"I . . . Why are you a zombie? And you can talk?" His words stumbled out of his mouth as he struggled to process the situation.

"More importantly. . . " Humphrey hovered down and made himself visible to Theo. "How are you a Level Seven Novice?"

Sally frowned and checked above the man—the Observer was, of course, correct: a number seven and the icon for a Novice hovered over Theo.

"Let's have a seat," she said and sighed. "And we will go over everything, okay?" She sheathed her dagger and gestured to a log lining the passageway.

Theo nodded and put his sword away nervously.

The rest of the Party went and followed a butterfly around as the pair sat down, the Observer hovering in front of them. Sally was surprised to find she was not nervous sitting next to the man dressed in basic leather armor, but why should she be? Theo, however, looked like he was sweating every last drop from his body—threatening to shrivel up.

"I'll start." Sally smiled diplomatically, "It's quite the coincidence seeing you again, Theo. I see you have become a Player in this world."

"Yeah . . . everyone kind of did. I woke up near the diner, but it looked overrun by the undead, so I went into the forest to do some . . . starter quests."

"I was in the diner. So were my friends here. I didn't get to be a Player." She frowned and looked down at her feet, covered in slime.

"Oh, you're an actual *Monster*, then?"

"Do I look like a Monster, Theo?"

He licked his lips to wet them. "I mean, *yeah*. For a zombie, very sassy maybe, but you are also traveling with a Party of Monsters too . . . I didn't know they could do that." He frowned and glanced nervously at the three corpses glaring up at a branch where the bug had landed.

"Monsters can't," the Observer interjected. "Sally is an interesting case where the System has put her between Player and Monster."

She nodded. "I don't have *all* the Player stuff. It's . . . glitchy." Turning her head back at him, she pulled a confused face. "So how are you Level Seven? Humps said Novice goes up to Five?"

"Humps?"

"That's me." The skull nodded. "Humphrey, Observer for the Architect."

"Ah." Theo gulped. "That is more concerning than the group of zombies. Well, after I hit Level Five, I just got rid of the pop-up and continued killing— I've been farming Blue Slimes around here, so I'm sorry about your pet."

"It was super rude." Sally scowled. "But the blue blob *was* getting super annoying."

"The little *boips* constantly, right?" Theo smiled at her. "I was farming their cards—I just need two more."

"Cards?" Sally questioned, giving Humphrey the side-eye.

The skull sighed. "Monsters have a rare drop of a collectable card that grants benefits to the wielder. You can have five active at a time, and there is usually a bonus for five-of-the-same or specific sets."

"I don't have that!" Sally wailed and slumped back. How many other parts of the System were unavailable to her?

"Even so, the System shouldn't let you go past Level Five as a Novice. I suppose Blue Slime is the least masochistic way to do that, though." The skull tilted as if considering the possibilities.

"What does the card do?" Sally sat back up, still deflated.

"I'll show you." Theo tapped his STAR.

Blue Slime Card - Uncommon
Novices Gain +10% Experience

He shrugged as the picture faded away. "It'll be the most efficient set for leveling higher as a Novice. I think a full five of them give a bonus to attack damage or something too!"

"But . . . why be a Novice? Don't you only get one attack skill?" Sally's red eyes searched Theo's face for an answer before it sunk in. "Oh, you complete ass—you get reborn into a world like this, and you're going for a meme build?"

"I managed to get in contact with some of my old friends, but they're going all tryhard with it. Full part of complementing classes, all tactics and min-maxing. I'm all about the joy of the experience, making it memorable, you know?"

"So you don't have a Party?" Sally stared at the Novice's neck and wondered if he had looked that tasty in the previous life.

"No, I'm not a fan of how they seem to be a forced necessity to be able to progress."

Her eyes lit up. "That's great. Do you want to join mine?"

"I'm not sure I'd . . . fit in." Theo glanced past her once more to check up on the zombies. "I'm not a Monster."

"That's okay." Sally shrugged. "I won't hold that against ya. I'll even help you with your goal of . . . what, being the first Level Fifty Novice?"

"Correct." He beamed, returning his gaze to her. "But what is *your* goal?"

"Don't tell the Observer here," she said as she winked at the skull, "but I'm planning on taking down the System and giving the Architect a stern talking to."

Theo whistled and rubbed his chin. "That sounds like a worthy task. Killing some Slimes one day, killing God the next—right?"

"I will advise against such action." Humphrey attempted to scowl at the pair.

The Novice rubbed the back of his neck. "I feel like I will be a hindrance more than anything, though. As you said, I only have one attack skill. The equipment I will have available is also restricted. As will my options for—"

"Yeah, yeah, Sally doesn't care. *As you said*, it's about the memorable experience, right? We are using the *Party* to kill the *Party*."

Theo smiled and nodded. "You know, you certainly seem much more confident in this world. None of my friends seemed to remember our past lives."

Sally leaned forward, the shadow of her hair obscuring her eyes. "I have one question for you, Mister Novice."

"Uh—yes?" Theo leaned backward in response; brow furrowed in brief panic.

"Do you want a piece of this bounty?" She pointed upward at the icon she knew that he would be able to see.

He swallowed. "Nope. No offense intended, but that amount of gold isn't worth the risk of fighting you and your friends over there."

Sally slumped back and exhaled. "Sucks. I really could do with killing and eating you. I'm *so* close to leveling up."

"I'm sorry to disappoint?"

"You joining or not, then?" If she couldn't eat him yet, the least he could do was stay around to act as an emergency meal for when they were on the road.

"I will have to decline . . . for now." He held his hands up in apology before continuing. "I need to get the rest of these cards, and it might take a little time. I've been at it for two weeks and only have three."

"But after then?" Sally pouted.

"After then, sure. Just send me a message if you leave the area—or I can message you when I'm done?" He wiggled his STAR toward her blank expression.

"Message?"

"Oh, wowzers." He shrugged. "You didn't even get the proper Novice tutorial stuff, huh? Let me try this anyway." Theo held his wrist out and gestured for the zombie woman to do the same.

Sally held her STAR over his, and there was another droning whine in her head. She held her hands to her eyes as the pain threatened to make her eyes burst from their sockets—before a *pop*! Relief washed over her as a new menu rotated around her wrist.

"I'm okay," she assured the Novice, seeing his worried expression. "The System does not give its gifts freely. Now, how do?"

"Like this." Theo smiled.

Theo: Hi, Sally
Sally: oh, neat

Humphrey bobbed above them, taking an inert interest in the development. "You can only send messages to people you have scanned with. Or with Party members if you ever needed to talk privately."

"Really?"

Sally: Hi, Chuck!
Chuck: aaaaaaaaaaaaaaa

"So, where are you heading next?" Theo rubbed at the stitching on his leather bracers.

Sally closed the chat window and tilted her head. "Do you know where the tomb is around here?"

"Sure, pretty much straight south from where we are now. Can't miss it as after the woods is the Bloom Plains, and there's a big Cemetery right there."

She idly rubbed some of the dried flakes of blood from her dress as she tried to imagine it. Why did she want to go there? "Dead friends *are* nice." She shrugged. "But thank you for being understanding, Theo."

The Novice reddened slightly and tried to wave her off. "Please, it's nice to talk to someone who isn't gargling the Adventurers Guild's . . . poleax. Speaking of, did you need any equipment? Novices can only trade Common gear I'm afr—"

"I have *shoes.*"

Theo blew air out of his nose. "Here, then, I can trade you a full set I have spare. Blue Slimes drop those Chance Boxes pretty regularly. Shame I mostly seem to get—"

"Daggers?"

"Yes! *Right?*"

Sally gestured to the Observer, arms flailing to emphasize their point.

Basic Common Cap
Basic Common Armor
Basic Common Bracers
Basic Common Leggings
Basic Common Gloves

"What kind of weapon do you want? Again, just the basic stuff." Theo brought his Inventory back up and cycled to the Weapons tab.

"Um. Do you have anything ranged? A crossbow or magic staff?" Sally had no idea if those were actually things in this world.

"Depends on if your DEX is high enough, but I have—"

"I can't see my stats."

Humphrey idly wandered off to try and curtail the walking dead trying to climb into part of a tree.

Theo scrunched his nose. "Wow, really handicapping our Party, aren't we? I'm assuming you'll replace the zombies with other misfits along the way?"

"I don't suppose any of your friends were a Cleric?" She avoided his question, not wanting to think, or dare even hope, that he might be correct in his assumption.

"No." He shook his head. "They decided to split healing between Paladin and Druid, I think. Here, just take these."

Common Shortsword
Common Crossbow
Common Staff
Common Buckler
Common Mace

"Thanks, Theo." She grinned, excited to try out some of the new loot he had given her.

"No problem, but perhaps now you can do something for me, Sally?"

He leaned forward. His warm, meaty face to the side of her cold, dead one. In her ears, the sound of blood pumping through his veins almost drowned out his soft voice. The hairs on the back of her neck rose, tingling with anticipation.

Her eyes widened as he whispered his request, and a long, sharp-toothed grin spread across her face.

## CHAPTER FOURTEEN

# Dirty Deeds

Theo was pretty nice, wasn't he?" Sally almost skipped through the undergrowth as the light of the day began fading into dusk.

"Mmm," the floating skull replied.

"Don't be jealous, Humps." She paused and waited for the shambling corpses of her Party to catch up.

"It is just worrying, that's all." The Observer had been mostly quiet since parting ways with the Novice. "First *you*. Now *him*."

"I can have more than one friend." She shook her finger at the skull that glowed purple among the shaded woods. "Just because he is a snack—figuratively and *maybe* literally—it doesn't mean anything."

"What? No, I mean the glitches. You shouldn't be able to discard the class selection once you are a Level Five Novice."

"Are you going to report it to the big boss?" She crossed her arms and began to look around to see if this would be an okay place to stop.

". . . No, not right now, at least." Humphrey shook side to side.

It seemed to be a decision that was conflicting. Sally had started to get a good read on the skull, despite his lack of ability to show any change of emotion. If the Architect didn't like Theo, they might force him to change class. Or something even worse.

She shook her head at these thoughts. Theo had given her a task, and she had agreed to fulfill it. It was the least she could do for all the equipment passed to her—even if it was basic. Sally shivered, remembering the words whispered in her ear. How *surprising* they were. How *excited* they made her. She wiped the drool from her mouth. *It was their secret*, she reminded herself.

"This is a slight detour from our trip to the tomb," Humphrey announced, mostly to try and bring her out of her stupor.

A shrug was the only response offered back to him. Was it unfair to keep the Observer in the dark about the quest given? It probably wouldn't matter either way, but a promise was a promise. If there was one thing Sally was, it was a woman of her word. Probably starting after she said she would kill whoever hurt Bubbles. As much as the level up would have been nice, another ally might save her in the future. In a handsome, if really lackluster Novice-y, way.

It was only another two minutes into their trek before she held her hand up, and they all stopped as one. Humphrey hovered down beside her, almost at head level. They both remained silent as they moved over to a bush and crouched down. The Party of zombies did similarly to whatever cover they could find in the area. Within the darkened gray shadows of dusk, their sinister red eyes glowed.

Movement could be heard ahead of them—the tell-tale signs of footsteps through leaves and grass. The murmured tones of low voices carried through to the clearing where they lay in wait.

"It's getting late though, Jake." A whiny male voice was the first to be picked up.

A female voice responded to him, her tone already fed up. "Stop whining. We've already killed so many today; the drop is almost guaranteed."

"That's not how—"

"Both of you quit it. Gabs and Raleigh have already gone home. Let's just pop a couple more and then head back to camp. Tomorrow is another day." A third voice, another male—this one slightly gruffer.

"*Fine,*" the first voice relented.

Sally licked her sharp teeth and slowly withdrew the crossbow, ensuring her dagger was ready to hand if needed.

"Oh, I see," the skull whispered before heading up to the apex of the clearing.

With a deep sigh, Sally lowered her eyes. "*Bloip!*"

"Wait." The female voice came from maybe two dozen feet away now. "Did you hear one?"

"A *sick* one, maybe?" the whiny voice responded.

Sally narrowed her stare at the grass by her feet. "*Bloip!*"

"Came from over there," the gruff voice signaled, pointing in, hopefully, the direction of the party.

With bated breath, she waited as the footsteps came slowly closer. Much quieter than expected—if not for her focus on trying to track them, she doubted she would have picked them up over the breeze rustling the leaves surrounding them. And then she had visuals.

Three Novices stepped into the clearing, each similarly dressed to how Theo had been. They had been slightly off on tracking her voice, so they entered past the bushes nearby, and their meandering put themselves almost totally in the middle of her Party.

A crooked smile flexed across her face as she slowly leveled the crossbow at the small group stalking ahead.

"What's that?" The gruffly voiced and mace-wielding man at the front peered out, getting a glance of Grams. "Zombies? What are they doing—"

A quick *twang* snapped across the clearing as the bolt struck the Novice in the side of the neck. With a panic he dropped to his knees, clutching at the blood flowing from the wound.

The zombies leapt forth with a groan, gaining some ground on the startled opponents before they resolved their combat nerves. Level Three, all of them.

Sally dropped the crossbow and snaked forth, keeping low and allowing the rest of the Party to be the distraction. The smart thing to do would be to take out the female Novice while her back was turned, *but* . . .

She dove atop the wounded Novice, tearing the bolt from its nestled place and biting into the warmth of his neck. This was bliss—almost immediately, the hunger pangs that had built throughout the day were sated. All it took was a little chomp. But there was nothing stopping her from completely feasting on—

Party member Grams has died

At the last second, she rolled to the side, a sword blade cutting down her right arm. *Pain.* She stood and gripped it with her left hand, red eyes blazing out into the darkness.

The female Novice had struck her after felling Grams. In the background, Chuck and Suits had taken a bit of damage—her UI flickered up to show Party status—but they had finally overwhelmed the man and dragged him to the floor.

"What in the *hells* are you?" The sword of the Novice was shaking, panic written across her face.

"I'm Sally," she replied, drawing her second dagger into her off hand, "and you're farming in my friend's spot."

"W-wha—"

Sally burst forward, getting in close to the Novice as she raised her sword back. She collided with her opponent before the *[Novice Strike]* skill could be used. Her sharp teeth gnashed into the leather armor as her arms wrapped around the Novice trying to wrench her off.

A wild kick to Sally's shin caught her off-guard, and she flinched backward, letting go of the woman briefly. Thoughts of fleeing washed over the pale and clammy face of the Novice, her resolve broken. Before she had a chance to react, Sally lunged forth recklessly again. The panic in the woman's eyes turned to shock as a dagger found a place just under the leather armor, into her stomach.

The Novice collapsed from the sudden pain, dropping her half-raised sword as the zombie bit down on her neck.

Crimson waves of odd euphoria passed through the limbs of Sally. Each bite into the exposed flesh of her victim became more feral, and a growing desire welled up from her gut. *Consume*, it said. *Gorge on the weak.* She hesitated at first, her past humanity balking at the scene playing out, before she eventually gave in.

Sally feasted.

After a few minutes, Humphrey floated back down from his perch.

"Before you say anything . . ." Sally pouted as she rolled away from the corpse. "I don't feel proud of myself. *No*, that's a lie. That was pretty rad—other than losing Grams."

"*Yes.*"

"But also . . ." She waved her wrist in the air. "I got that level up!"

"Just barely. Level Three Novices are scraping the barrel a little." The skull took a moment to visually absorb the corpses across the woodland floor.

"If they want me to be a *Monster*, I will be." She shrugged, lying back into the cool grass. "Wow, why do I feel drunk?"

"Maybe you ate too much."

"Well, perhaps if they didn't want me to eat them, they shouldn't have made Players so tasty." Sally yawned. Okay, perhaps she had overeaten.

She pressed the chat menu on the STAR, shrugging off the level up for just a few minutes—just to build the suspense up a little.

Sally: hEY Theooo
Theo: Hi, Sally, all good?
Sally: Our little secret has been taken care of xoxox
Theo: Amazing . . . and scary—thank you!
Sally: find ur dman Cards so we can kill God alrdy

She closed the chat without waiting for a response. This feeling in her stomach was not great—or rather, it had been too great. She had supped from the fountain of vitality and was now too healthy to live. If she was about to pass from this System, her one regret was that she didn't eat more people.

As darkness fell across the world, Sally closed her eyes and joined it.


"Sally. *Sally?*"

The zombie rolled over and spat out a mouthful of grass she had apparently been chewing in her sleep. *Had she slept?*

"Mrff," she growled and sat upright, head lolling on her shoulders as her body tried to function. It was light out again—but only barely.

"Good thing nobody came looking for your bounty while you were unable to be roused. It *has* increased, by the way."

Sally squinted up at the skull, the glimmers of early morning sunlight falling through the shifting canopy into her red eyes like a hail of broken glass. Why had she even fallen asleep? One glance at her even redder white shirt brought the memories back.

"Only by fifteen gold," Humphrey continued, giving her a stern glare from empty sockets, "Novice lives aren't worth too much, apparently."

"Ouch. The System doesn't pull any punches, huh?" She stood and brushed the dew from her rather dirty-looking dress. As she looked over at her first meal, she nodded her head. "What's the point of all this class business if I can pop a guy in the neck with a bolt and kill him?"

"The starting levels are very . . . *realistic*? Though, take my word with a pinch of salt, as I only have the System as a base measure. After a few level ups, you start getting more resilient to basic damage."

"Brutal." Sally shook her head and turned to her two remaining zombies. They were sitting patiently on the grass, having both feasted and rested themselves too. It was a shame that she couldn't make new undead or find a way to bring some back from the diner or even reanimate the ones that died again.

She turned to the floating skull, who seemed to be waiting patiently for something.

"Monsters are usually created by the System, right? They don't have *people* in them?"

The Observer was silent for a few moments. "*Yes.*"

"Are there NPCs that aren't people too—sentients that aren't from the previous world?"

"Maybe I should be observing the Ultra-Novice instead; he asks less questions. *Ha-ha.*" He waited for the awkward pause to pass—which it didn't. "*Yes,*" the skull eventually sighed.

"Okay, neat. I was worried." She crossed her arms. "You know, whether it was morally okay to ingest innocents? But if they are just constructs of the System, then I don't feel so bad."

Humphrey hovered in silence.

"Oh, I never chose my level-up skill!" Her wrist rose with the gleaming golden STAR attached. "There's a message from Theo too."

Theo: You must be good luck. Found the fourth card this morning!

"Wow, my messages from last night were pretty cringe. Do I get drunk off eating people? Best leave him on read for a bit." She flipped through the menu to receive her leveling rewards.

**Pick One**
**[Upheaval]** Area 20 ft Radius - Turns Target Area into Rough Terrain and does Minor Earth Damage
**[Hex: Slow]** Curse - One Target becomes Slowed and Lethargic
**[./Puppy]** Passive//Error - #Mar A to Parse-Sector Override . . . Compiling, Compiling . . . Retry Parse?

## CHAPTER FIFTEEN

# End of the Line

*[Hex: Slow]*

**W**hat, you're not going for *[./Puppy]*?" Humphrey asked, the slightest of smiles peaking at the edge of his jaw.

"Like I need any more errors in my life." Sally shook her head. "It was clearly bait."

If her friends were going to be slow coaches, then the Hex may level the field somewhat. Even if she switched them out for towering stacks of hamburger meat, like Theo, being able to slow down an enemy would be an advantage. *[Upheaval]* sounded alright but didn't really appeal to her.

"Level Three now," she told herself. "Any more surprises from the System? Anything I can now unlock?"

She let the silence of the woods around her answer the somewhat rhetorical question. It was another pleasant day, by all accounts, as the sun gradually rose. The light breeze rustled through the part of her hair that wasn't matted with dried blood. She yawned, despite the good rest. Another day traveling and avoiding the sun wasn't the worst thing—but no doubt it wouldn't be that easy. Sally flicked open her chat.

Sally: Already have more skills than you, hamburger

She closed the chat. "Alright, let's get going to the tomb . . . " She peered out at the dense woods, turning almost a half-circle in trying to determine which direction to stroll.

"It's this way." The skull rolled his lack of eyes, before heading off in a direction she wasn't looking.

"C'mon, boys." She waved at Suits and Chuck. The pair shambled along after her.

"There's a small body of water nearby," the skull offered as he floated along, "so you *could* get cleaned up."

"Giving me lots of help now, Humps. You sure the big guy will like that?" She smiled at the Observer, with a quick flash of a wink.

"Making sure you are presentable does not go against my directive," he responded, not looking back down at her.

"Are you going to join my Party now that I have openings? *Very* lucrative position."

"I . . . am unable to—even if I so wished it. Observers are not capable of joining Parties." This time he did look back at her, a hint of emotion on his skull-face. Was it sadness? Disgust?

Sally hopped over a fallen log and stopped for a moment to watch her two zombies clamber over awkwardly. "Are stats a choice too, like . . . where to assign them?"

"*Yes.*"

"Hmm, does that mean mine are still unassigned? Or, because I am a Monster, they are automatically allocated? Wait, don't answer if that's just going to be a yes."

The Observer glanced between the woman and the two zombies picking themselves off the grass floor.

"Can you see stats? What did Theo have?" She leaned toward the skull with eyebrows raised, her hands pressed together in exaggerated interest.

"All Strength."

Sally giggled—that sounded just like the dolt. She could picture him now, building for full damage with *[Novice Strike]* and trying to kill things in one hit, before they could turn around and paste him. She licked her lips thinking about him in paste form.

"I can tell your distribution but not the exact numbers. They are oddly as cloudy to me as they are to you."

She frowned up at the floating skull, drawn from her daydreams of Theo sandwich spread. If she wasn't currently able to select her stats, did it matter that much how they were distributed? "Pass. Let me know when I have some agency."

They slid down a short, muddy embankment and her disguised boots splashed in a shallow stream. It flowed weakly, perpendicular to their direction of travel.

Chuck landed face first into the water, having tripped on the way down the decline of terrain. Suits stumbled through awkwardly but maintained footing.

"Could you *be* any more accident-prone, Chuck?" She brought up the Party information screen with a shake of her head. "You took more damage from that than you did fighting the Novices last night."

With a flick of her hand, the menus of the STAR spun around, pending notifications ignored as the holographic text disappeared. Sally began to walk downstream, watching the flickers of sunlight roll along the slight current of the water.

"What were we going to the tomb for again?" Humphrey flew up beside her. The question seemed more leveled at digging into her thought process rather than an admission of absent-mindedness.

"The quest said just to 'investigate,' which I guess for a Player means go stab some undead. For me, that means go find some friends." She kicked a loose rock into the stream.

"Seems like more a hub for danger," the skull responded flatly.

"Is that a veiled warning? I had considered that we wouldn't be the only ones questing there." Sally pushed her blonde hair from her face and smiled up at the Observer. "More chance for us to eat some newbies, right? I need those level ups. *[Mighty Aura]* is nice, but something with regeneration or speed would fit better—especially now, with *[Hex: Slow]*."

"I just don't want to go back to my normal job so soon, *ha-ha*."

The trek along the small ebbing stream was perhaps the most serene leg of their journey yet. Grass became richer shades of green, the breeze seemed to lull, and with fewer undead causing a ruckus in their wake, the creatures of the woods were heard—even if not seen. Within a dozen minutes, the small group arrived at an open area where a small pond had developed at the end of the water flow.

A pool of reflective and surprisingly clear water glimmered under the gaze of the morning sunshine. Small flowers and other greenery sprung up from around its edges—almost looking like mini-woods of their own, with blooms of white and yellow among deep verdant grasses. A butterfly of mottled reds and black fluttered from a grouping of flowers and out into the woods beyond.

Sally whistled at the view as she knelt by the edge of the water and looked at her reflection.

"Huh. I do look quite the state, and my complexion has seen better days." She touched the surface of the pool, sending the barest of ripples out.

"For a corpse . . . I've certainly seen worse. There will be an option on your STAR to clean yourself up."

She wasn't too sure whether to take the first part of that as a compliment or not and gave the skull a narrowed side-eye, but relented and checked out her wrist UI.

[Clean/Wash?]

After a quick tap, she watched a progress bar fill over the course of five seconds. With little fanfare once it was completed, her clothes were as good as new. She peered back into the pool and the previous smears of dark, dried blood were gone from her face and hair.

"Not sure how I feel about that." Sally held her arms out to check their cleanliness. "It seems a bit arbitrary."

"*Ha-ha.* I suppose it does seem out of place considering you have had to do most things manually." Humphrey floated out over the pool and looked down at his own reflection.

"Pfft." She took her boots off, the visual of her sneakers also vanishing, and sat with her feet barely in the water. "Feels odd . . . Not as relaxing as expected, but still a relief for my weary soles. Let me check my notifications."

---

Theo: Level 8 (:

---

"Show off." She smiled, closing the chat. It had been nice seeing Theo. Despite their brief meeting in the before-time, he was something of an anchor to reassure her that she wasn't going mad. Asking her to get rid of the Novices farming in his area was surprisingly callous . . . It excited her. Her toes tapped in the shallows of the pond. She hadn't been this bloodthirsty in her previous life, *right?* It had been all too easy to become the role of a Monster—or perhaps that was by design. Surely if she had been reborn as a Player, she would have just as eagerly been slaying Monsters—so it shouldn't be *that* different. Eating people still felt a little weird, though.

Chuck also reminded her of her past. A familiar figure that she couldn't quite place yet. Even that didn't make much sense, though. Where was his soul? If he had become a Player, then why was he a zombie here? But if he hadn't become a Player, then where was his soul? Surely not still in the zombie; Humphrey had said Monsters were System-created. Herself being the exception, of course. Still, it did make her worry about the clumsy zombie.

She turned her gaze back to the Observer who was still looking at himself in the pool. "Humphrey, am I evil?"

The skull turned to regard the zombie, his purple energy illuminating a circle of the pool beneath him. "Morality is relative."

"Weak answer." She shook her head. "Does the System regard me as evil?"

The Observer floated across the pool close to her as ripples expanded and slowly faded from his movement. "As a Monster, your goal is to be a hindrance and obstacle to Players, which you have been doing. As a Player, your goal is to grow in power and defeat obstacles. I'd say you are doing well in the eyes of the System."

"Doing *well,* but not doing *good.*" She sighed and ran her finger through the soft dirt at the water's edge.

"That is a conundrum you will have to reconcile yourself; I am not here to judge." Humphrey turned away slowly and tilted to the side.

Sally paused and frowned in the direction he was looking, holding a breath of air. The gentle breeze roamed through the leaves of the trees around them, the slight sound of birds chirping from behind, and a few lazy insects buzzed around the edge of the water.

Even the two zombies took the unspoken hint to remain silent briefly.

Panic gripped her as she heard the unmistakable noise of footfalls up ahead.

## CHAPTER SIXTEEN

# Loss Prevention

There's nothing in these woods that are really that dangerous." The Fighter shrugged, brushing her long black hair away.

"*Nothing that dangerous*," the short Ranger spat as he kicked through a vine tangled around his boot. "Not during the day, at least."

The group's Cleric, a petite woman with large blue eyes, tutted and shook her head, causing the hood of her light gray robes to fall back and reveal flowing blonde hair. "Don't go getting all conspiratorial, Bren. The Hillan Woods and surrounding areas have always been safe for night camping."

The Ranger pulled a face. "You heard the two Novices wailing back in town, though—no contact with the rest of the group. Something killed them *real* quick."

"Serves them right for being Novices still." A red-headed Rogue pushed past to the front of the group, shrugging unapologetically. "Even *we* are still pretty behind the curve."

"Better slow than dead," the Cleric chastised, pulling her hood back up.

The fifth member of the Party said nothing. Their plate armor glinted in the sunlight as they stopped in place, full helmet turning to the side.

The Ranger caught their gaze and walked over in that direction. "Oh, there's a small pool over here—good eyes."

"Gods forbid we have a Ranger that chose any kind of tracking abilities." The Fighter rolled her eyes and stepped into the clearing.

The Cleric hustled them out of the woods with a sigh. "Go get cleaned up; it won't be too long before we get to the Cemetery."

"Ah, you won't be complaining when we get into a fight." The Ranger shrugged back at the Fighter, ignoring the nagging. He took out his waterskin to be refilled and narrowed his eyes at the pool. The water looked clean enough to drink. "Weird." The Rogue knelt on the other side of the calm water. "There's a pair of *[Common Basic Boots]* just sitting here."

Sally cursed through clenched teeth as she peered out from the dense bushes that only barely hid her location. She could at least be thankful the two zombies were well-practiced in playing dead, but her eyes blazed red with anger.

A full Party of Level Threes, except for the Knight at the back—they were Level Four.

Attacking them now would be folly. Even on a skill-to-skill basis, it would be their sixteen versus her three. The element of surprise wouldn't get them far either, and she doubted that the zombies could chew through metal armor. Instead, she settled for gnashing her teeth and trying to pick up what they were talking about.

Humphrey had remained over the pool, his ability to cloak himself from those he did not wish to see him a handy ability for recon. She would have to poke him for clarification—if they didn't find her.

The mud was cold through her outfit as she lay prone among the shrubbery. Despite wearing the armor Theo provided, it still felt like her linen shirt was the only thing between her bare flesh and the earth beneath her. Typical that she would need to get cleaned up again so soon.

Her fingers dug into the soil as she seethed. What was this feeling that burned within her? Fear? No, it was closer to anger. Disdain. Her tongue ran across her sharp teeth. Maybe some envy or jealousy as well, she might admit. Time seemed to stretch on as she watched the figures mill around, murmuring about her boots, the Cemetery, and other meaningless banter. *Sally hated banter.*

Eventually, they began to leave. The Knight seemed to be pensive, thoughtful even, and lingered briefly in the clearing before joining the rest of their Party. Their voices got slowly farther away until they became inaudible. The Observer came down to the impromptu hiding position.

"Coast is clear." He nodded.

Sally let out a long, stale breath, before pushing herself out of the mud. Indeed, her white shirt now had a few streaks of brown down the front. "At least I'm not dead. *Deader*," she grumbled to herself. The softer soil did feel kind of nice on her bare feet, however, and she took a second to squash it between her toes.

"Seems they are heading to the Cemetery too," Humphrey offered as he looked back to the direction traveled.

"Figures. I would have thought someplace like that would have been cleared out by now." She hopped out of her hiding place and tried to avoid getting caught in the rougher bushes as she went back into the clearing.

"Perhaps I was too vague about respawns." The skull rotated slowly. "I just didn't want to give you false hope about your own mortality."

"System-created Monsters can respawn, but anything with a soul can't?" She stuck her toes back into the water to wash the mud off.

"There are also some Monsters with the Unique tag that do not respawn."

"Gotcha—ah, *dammit.*" Sally narrowed her eyes around the edge of the pool. "They ran off with my boots."

"It was the Rogue, *ha-ha.*"

She shook her head as she brought up the menu to clean off her clothes. As it progressed, she tapped the STAR to bring up chat.

Sally: Tomb might be trouble. If I die, I just want you to know . . .
Sally: I wish I killed and ate you x

If the walking steak dinner had actually chosen a class, then he would at least be able to contribute better to the Party—but even then they were sorely outpowered. It was also not very likely she could find more Players compassionate to her cause . . . and willing to murder other Players in the way. Her STAR *boiped.*

Theo: Stay safe
Theo: Just think, a Level Fifty Novice would be a meal all the sweeter ;P

*Bloody tease*, she thought with a smile, closing the UI. There was no use complaining about it; there would be no further pals to be found in the reflection of the pool. The Cemetery may have enemies, but it would also have undead to control—a possibility to gain an upper hand.

"I think you were about five feet away from your bounty being visible," the skull idly announced as he hovered over the calm water once more.

"Arrgh, why tell me that?" She scowled and searched her Inventory to see if her sneakers were in there. Thankfully, they were.

"Your luck knows no bounds, *ha-ha.*" The Observer laughed awkwardly as he turned to watch the two zombies stumble out of the undergrowth.

With her sneakers back on, Sally brushed down her newly cleaned clothing. She didn't feel too lucky, the *[Lucky Rabbit's Foot]* notwithstanding. There was the option of staying back near Hillan, perhaps just farming out some more Novices . . . but even that had danger. Word had already gotten out about her. If more Novices started disappearing in the area, then it would only draw more higher-level Parties out.

She gazed out to the woodlands surrounding them. The way to the Cemetery—the direction the enemy Party went—was at a slight decline. With a glance, she looked over at the Observer, who was staring in the same direction.

"Penny for your thoughts, Humps?"

"Did you see their Party name?" He slowly turned to meet her look.

"Parties can have names?"

"*Yes*. Their name was *The Skullsplitters*. Very gauche." The Observer shuddered in the air.

"You're not a real skull, though?" Sally crossed her arms and tilted her head slightly. "Like, you're just a construct made in the image of one?"

Humphrey did not respond but turned back to gaze in the direction of the Cemetery.

The zombie villainess tapped her foot on the ground. Parties having names would make it easier to discuss specific ones without getting confused. *The Skullsplitters* were the first full Party she had come across, and they were pretty intimidating too, all things considered. No doubt on their way to go split skulls down near the tomb. Beating up her undead friends would be their last mistake.

"We'll give them a slight head start, and then follow them in. Avoid them if possible, but hope to find more allies down at the Cemetery if we need to engage." She nodded both at the Observer and her two companions, who had joined them at the cusp of the clearing.

"As good a plan as any." Humphrey smiled with his teeth.

"Glad to have you on board." Sally rolled her eyes and then perked up. "Oh! I never redeemed my daily prize thing, eh?"

"*Yes.*"

She spun around the STAR in search of the right menu. Despite there being few options, it took her three go-arounds before finding where it was hidden.

---

Login Bonus: Day 2 - Receive Gift?

---

"Yes please, System."

---

20 Gold
ERROR
P:
ERROR

---

"*Really?* How do I send a complaint, Humphrey?" She scowled at the fading text before turning toward the skull. Her finger wagged in accusation.

"I will forward this to my manager."

Sally bared her teeth at the Observer, narrowing her red eyes. She flipped through her Inventory—nothing new had been added. The Errors must really be—

"Oh, what's this?"

Humphrey moved closer to see the hovering screen showing her stored items.

"Looks like whatever 'P' was supposed to be. That isn't usually something given to Players through the reward program . . ."

She withdrew it, her eyes sparkling with wonder.

Monster Summon (M)

Sally whistled. "The Error taketh and the Error giveth, huh? I should use this now, right? Right now? *Right?*"

"You can, but if it is something untoward, then it will set you at a disadvantage."

Untoward? Like something really noisy, perhaps. Or something on fire; that would be pretty bad for their current situation. She stared at the item in her hand: a small ball of swirling yellow energy made of glass. The summoning item was smooth and almost felt warm in her dead hand. Waiting *would* be the sensible thing to do. There could be no telling where such an item could come in clutch at a last-ditch moment.

However, only a fool would rely on chance when things were dire.

She threw the glass ball to the floor, shattering it. Sparks of yellow lightning arced around a light blue mist that spewed forth from the broken summoning item.

A dark figure loomed out from the cloud.

## CHAPTER SEVENTEEN

# Gathering Moss

What is *that*?" Sally stood with mouth agape, looking up into the bright yellow eyes of the creature that had been summoned.

> Woodland Lurker has joined the Party

"Nice," Humphrey interjected, "you're starting to get more of the HUD pop-ups that Players get."

"That's a terrible name, though; let me call you . . ." She squinted at the Monster and put her finger to her lips.

The Lurker was easily seven feet tall, although almost a foot of that height was its humped back. Almost built like a gorilla, the Lurker's two long arms looked comical against its shorter legs. Moss and leaf-like fur covered its whole body as if it were a walking bush—a part of the woods come alive. It blew warm air from its nostrils as it leaned down closer to the zombie to give her a sniff.

"Friendly, huh? Let's call you . . . Big Dave!" She swept through the STAR while absentmindedly patting the creature on the head.

> Big Dave - Level Three Woodland Lurker - 100% HP
> Skills: [Thrash] [Lurk]

"Neat. Look, Humps, a Level Three Monster with some skills. It doesn't quite make things equal, but it's a start." Sally walked around the Monster to give it an inspection. "Dave's arms are wider than I am!"

"Indeed, quite the formidable force—"

"Why can't I name the Party?" She peeked back around from the back of the Monster, and her finger jabbed at the STAR beneath her scowl.

"It requires a full Party of at least First Class Players." Humphrey swiveled around the side to look at the woman better.

"That figures." She sighed as her arms flopped to her side. "More anti-Monster rules from the oh-so-great System. With a capital *S*, apparently."

Big Dave grunted and shrugged their wide shoulders.

"Exactly. Dave gets it." Sally nodded her head sideways at the lumbering beast.

"We should have enough of a distance between us and the 'splitters now . . ." The Observer avoided the potential conflict by turning to zoom over to the edge of the clearing.

"Gotta decide who your loyalties lie with *eventually*, Humps." She shook her head as she gestured for the rest of the Party to follow on into the woods.

"I don't . . . My directives are very . . . I'm here to *observe*, Sally."

"Yeah, yeah." She waved the stuttering skull off as the Party passed. "It's not me you're trying to convince."

Humphrey hovered in place as the footsteps of even the slow zombies started to fade off into the distant trees before he shook himself and followed along.

The slight decline of the ground in this part of the woods made traversing slightly easier. Only slightly, as, for the most part, it just made it so the zombies stumbled into roots and tangling bushes at a marginally greater speed. Sally was tempted to hop atop the back of Big Dave—who had no issue with the jaunt through the woods—but that probably would have come off as rude.

Humphrey had been mostly quiet for the better part of the journey so far. *There had been truth to my words*, Sally thought, even if it was a bit harsh on the skull. You would have thought that the Architect would have made their System maintenance bots more . . . emotionless? She wondered if there was a higher-tier Observer watching over Humphrey to see what he was getting up to.

"Ah, hells." She snapped her fingers and shot a frown at the canopy above. "I forgot to loot those three Novices last night."

"*Yes.*"

"You would have told me if there was anything worth grabbing though, right, Humps?" She gave the skull a sheepish grin, trying to patch up the distance she had wedged between them.

"They didn't have anything you would have been able to use to kill God."

The reply came calm and measured, but there was the slightest hint of tongue-in-cheek tone to it—enough to make Sally smile—despite his lack of both tongue and cheeks.

"They tasted alright though. Sorry if I push you too hard. I know you have a job to do." She looked to the floor as the skull floated down alongside her.

"Tell me, *Sally the Unliving*, are you happy?"

"Happy?" The question caught her off guard. She rubbed the back of her neck before running her fingers through her blonde hair. "I suppose I have accepted the lot I have been given and am doing my best to live in a manner that makes me happy."

The Observer turned to her for a few seconds before looking back at the direction they were traveling. "I see."

"Are *you* happy?"

"Conflicted. *Ha-ha*. Previously, completing my tasks as designated was enough to content me. For three or so weeks I have been satiated by my role in the System."

"But now?" Her red eyes looked up at him with one raised eyebrow.

"I have been observing some interesting things." His eldritch purple color briefly flickered red to pink, and then back to purple.

Sally smiled and hopped over a fallen log. She stopped to watch Big Dave pick up each zombie and place them on the other side before clambering over. Even with the heat of the day starting to feel a little uncomfortable, it was a brief moment of bliss. The Woodland Lurker snorted as she gave them a pat on the arm.

"How close am I to leveling up, Humps?"

"Still quite far—you did only just level up." The Observer shook his head.

"True. I haven't even used my new skill yet—my other two are passives, so it will be fun to do something more than *run up and bite people*." The STAR menus popped up so that the skill could be read again.

"A proper Party fight will be a lot different from the easy pickings you've had so far." Humphrey floated backward as he moved in front of her. "Not to put a damper on your achievements so far—"

"I've killed *seven* people."

"But the skills and abilities of five people working together, and the fact that they won't fold after a single surprise attack . . . It will be a learning experience for you."

She pouted at the Observer partially obscuring her view. "Do you think heading to the tomb is a mistake?"

"I think everything since you opened your eyes in the diner has been a mistake. *Ha-ha*—just a joke." The skull tried to walk back the comment on seeing her expression sour. "Truly, I believe you are capable."

"You need to choose a lane, Humphrey. I'm the one that is supposed to be an emotional mess given that I am recently now a person that eats people. In some weird world. Where I also want to eat the only living person I recognize from my previous life. I wonder how the pork chop is doing. How long between messages before I should assume he has been killed by the Slimes? Or worse, what if there is another half-Monster out there like me killing Novices? Maybe I should—"

"Sally."

"Huh?" She looked up from her hands where she had been staring.

"Everything is okay."

She walked quietly, looking at the purple skull as he rotated beside her once more. Her sneakers crunched against fallen leaves and errant sticks. A frown crossed her brow as she looked down, wondering why the sudden amount of noise. Even the lighting was dimmer now despite no increase in canopy cover.

The group paused, and she took in her surroundings for the first time in minutes. It was as if they had suddenly changed season into autumn. The previously green trees were now a mix of oranges and browns, and the ground was now littered with dried and desiccated leaves. An overcast sky filled in the gaps between the shedding branches with a muted gray.

Humphrey nodded toward her. "We are getting close."

Sally: Almost at the Tomb

There was no immediate response. After ten seconds she closed the chat with a shrug. If the fool had gotten himself killed and she wasn't around to eat him, then she would be super annoyed. Her fingers drummed on her arm as she sighed.

"Is there resurrection magic in this . . . System?" The question felt awkward, like it had the taste of the world from before. A language forgotten but familiar.

"*Yes.*"

"More information, bonehead." She shook a fist at the Observer. "Please."

"It's a skill only some Third Class jobs get, so not anytime soon. There are items too—but very rare."

"I bet there are special limitations or conditions on its use too, huh?"

"*Yes.*"

"*Architect dammit*, Humphrey." Sally shook her head. The Observer couldn't be any more annoying if he tried. If resurrection was a difficult thing, then maybe she wouldn't waste it on her meal ticket. However, she didn't have any better candidates yet. It was unlikely it would work on her . . .

Big Dave grunted and hunkered down, causing the rest of them to stop. Humphrey rose up higher—a sure sign that something was afoot. Sally pressed up against the Lurker and peered at the tree cover. Chuck and Suits just lingered in the background quietly.

Far ahead, maybe eighty to a hundred feet through the darkened and dead trees, there were dark shapes moving.

Sally gulped. Did they catch up to the *Skullsplitters* without realizing? If the enemy Party had taken a rest, then that was certainly possible. Had they noticed—oh, the shapes were getting closer. She slipped out her crossbow and loaded a bolt, eyes trying to dart to the surroundings for an opportune place to hide or escape.

The Lurker narrowed their eyes as their fur rose in anticipation.

Sally cursed her inability to have a rising heartbeat—or to sweat. It made the brief panic uncomfortable and awkward as she leveled the crossbow and squinted with one eye down the sight.

Sixty feet away, a group of shapes moved closer. Was it five? It was hard to tell between all the twisted, dead trees.

Fifty feet, details started to form on the silhouetted figures. Metal armor glinted in the dull overcast light.

Forty feet, her finger clasped around the trigger. She held a lifeless breath.

Thirty feet . . .

## CHAPTER EIGHTEEN

# Teeth of Stone

Sally gasped as her finger fell from the trigger.

*Skeletons?*

Four shambling figures of nothing but bone and metal armor came clanking into view. Rusted swords hung from limp arms, dragging through the loose dead leaves cluttering the woodland floor. A baleful green glow emanated from their otherwise empty eye sockets as they regarded the zombie woman with blank emotion.

"Aw, they're sad and lost!" Sally jumped and punched the air, stowing the crossbow back into her Inventory.

"You can tell?" Humphrey hovered down.

"*You can't?*" She walked up to the first one to enter through the brush toward them and gave it a pat on its metal helm. "The nasty *Skullsplitter* Party probably came through here and killed their friends. Isn't that right?"

The skeleton nodded stiffly.

"*See!*"

Skeletal Warrior has joined the Party

"Only Level One, but that's okay. We don't judge in my Party." Sally beamed as she spun up the STAR.

Skeletal Warrior - Level One - 100% HP
Skills: [Slash]

The skeleton walked over to join the rest of the group, while the three others milled around at the edge of the tree line. There may not be any room left in the Party, but she could still use *[Command Dead]* to do something with them. It would probably make more sense to dump Chuck and get another Skeletal Warrior . . . but she had a soft spot for the zombie. As long as that didn't get her dead. *Deader.*

"Not going to replace the—"

"I've already had that discussion internally." She waved the skull away. "He stays for now."

"We are but a few minutes away from the Cemetery if the skeletons are out this far. Are you ready, Sally the Unliving?"

"Ready to get a new title," she murmured to herself, before straightening her back. "Let's get this dumb quest done and not get murdered by Players."

Now that she was more focused on the surroundings, there was something comforting about it. Was it just how dead everything looked? The cooler air from the heat of the sun being obscured? It felt more home than the diner had, despite the Hillan building having that odd familiarity to it.

Sally stopped and knelt, brow furrowed. *Bones.* She brushed leaves out of the way to reveal a whole skeleton—albeit one that seemed to have exploded apart. Dave grunted off to the right, and as she followed their gaze there was a second— and maybe a third—pile of bones about two dozen feet away.

"Looks like we found the rest of the warriors." She shook her head. If only she could raise them back. "Oh, neat, I can loot their skulls."

Skull (1)

"I just need to find some purple paint now, eh, Humphrey?" Her nose wrinkled up as she stuck her tongue out at the Observer.

The floating skull did not respond but instead flew up into the air near the lower branches of a dead tree. He cast his eyeless gaze across the Party and the surrounding area, finally staring off toward the supposed direction of the Cemetery.

Sally followed where he was looking and tried to piece together his thoughts. It can't have been too long ago the *Skullsplitters* had come and . . . split these skulls. Well, technically the skulls were in pretty good condition, and her Inventory now sported three of them. They would definitely come in handy at some point and not just be cluttering up her space forever. *Definitely.*

"Everyone on good behavior." She spun around to her cohort, index finger outstretched. "We are getting close to a dangerous zone, so be quiet and alert."

The Lurker murmured and lowered their head, while the zombies and skeletons mostly just twitched in a way that indicated they at least heard her. Chuck especially seemed enthused about the orders given and almost tripped on his own feet as he moved closer.

"A rallying cry for the ages." Humphrey hovered down closer. "Apologies, that was sarcasm. *Ha-ha.* Just a little nervous."

Sally smiled and looked out from the edge of the woods. There was a darkness that obscured the details beyond a certain part. As though there was a thin fog—a miasma that clouded the area and prevented seeing farther than a hundred feet or so. Perhaps a potential benefit to their attempt at closing in to the tomb with subtlety. The last thing they would want is to be spotted from half a mile away, or even half a kilometer away.

Nevertheless, they persisted onward.

Gravestones. Jutting forth from the landscape like rows of gray teeth in an ogres maw. *Just the lower jaw though.* Sally looked briefly to the sky to make sure there were none above. The gloomy clouds overhead seemed devoid of grave markers and teeth alike. Now free from the obstruction of the woods, they had emerged into what was possibly a Cemetery overcompensating for something.

As they had reached the edge of the tree line, the dead foliage had become more sparse. There was still the errant tree or two, even a desiccated garden in odd places, spread among the graveyard. Everything was covered in a layer of doom— steeped in it. The grass was dry and brown, the earth gray and cracked, and the stonework of the markers and scant buildings was weather worn and crumbling.

"It's beautiful," Sally gasped, eyes wide. The same dark fog obscured how long this Cemetery stretched on for, but even within its bounds, it would have to house hundreds of the buried. There were a number of mausoleums and supposed tombs dotted around the many gravestones—but perhaps more pressing were the scattered remains of more Skeleton Warriors.

"So much for the cavalry option," the Observer mused as the zombie woman knelt to retrieve the skulls from the fallen.

The Lurker whined and hunkered down; their yellow eyes darted around.

"Aw, Big Dave, I know there isn't much tree cover here." Sally stood back up and cradled the moss-covered fur head of the beast. "We will stick to what obstacles we can as we check which tomb we are meant to be investigating—and then we are out of here as soon as possible."

The creature seemed to be somewhat comforted by this plan and rose back up to their full height. Chuck was caught on the ruined metal fencing that they had been able to stroll through unhindered.

"Wow, looks like we have a natural *[Find Traps]* user." The floating skull rolled his empty sockets.

"He can't help it." Sally scowled at the Observer as she strode back over to pull the zombie from the metal pole his shirt was caught on.

With a brief rip, the dirty white shirt tore, and Chuck stumbled forward, tripped, and landed face-first in the dry dirt with a deep thud that belied his short frame. He lay there and didn't move for a few seconds, as if stunned or moderately embarrassed.

Sally sighed. "Up you get, poppet." She brushed some of the dirt from his front as he wobbled to his feet, for whatever good that would do. Her red eyes searched his face, trying to get a hold of the familiarity she held for the clumsy fool. His previously damaged eye had recovered back to normal—some magic of the System, she assumed—but the gaze he returned was vacant and devoid of any of the personality that was slipping from her memory.

She frowned and gave his shoulder a squeeze, before turning around to face the more pressing situation. Her concerns over the zombie would have to wait till they were in a safer position. The STAR on her wrist *boiped* as she received a chat notification.

> Theo: Got the last card ;P
> Theo: Will make my way to the Cemetery
> Sally: Be quick—running out of space in the Party

"The quest didn't specify which tomb it was, right?" She closed the menu system and narrowed her eyes at the nearest building.

"I'm afraid not. Exploration quest is exploration-y." Humphrey floated around in an arc, trying to shake the constant stare of Big Dave.

"Bit of a rough second quest."

"Much like your skill choices." The Observer rose higher up. "You are not following traditional advancement. There are three buildings nearby that are explorable."

With a nod, they started to head toward the closest one. The building was a roughly square structure made of thick stone slabs. Dark vines engulfed the back corner and the black metal bars of the gate covering the entrance were rusted and worn. A pitched recess led somewhere underground from behind the barred doorway.

"It's locked." Sally pointed at the almost comically large padlock on the side of the gate.

"*Is it?*"

She frowned at the Observer, just catching the tail end of a flicker of red in his otherwise purple glow. With a huff, she turned back to the lock—which was now unlocked.

"It was obstructing my duties . . . " The skull looked away, off into the distance.

"Best have the same outlook when I have a blade to my throat." Sally grinned and shook her head.

The gate squealed gently as she opened it. She bit her lip and resisted the urge to squeak it back and forth. Putting a signal out to any adventurer in the area that they were here would be one of the sillier things to attempt. Maybe later.

Humphrey came down beside her to offer his glow as lighting. A short staircase of less than a dozen stone steps covered in muddy leaves led down into a short passageway. The walls were cool to her touch. Relaxing even. Her fingers brushed across small indents in the brickwork—and a brief panic about traps quickly became a realization. Under narrowed eyes and the scant light from the floating skull, she was able to pick out carvings of names and dates. Those that were buried here?

Big Dave and the others stood at the entrance on guard. Not only would the large beast not be able to comfortably fit down into this small tomb, but Sally had no doubts that Chuck would fall down the stairs and break himself.

The short passageway led to another small set of three steps as the room opened up to a chamber. Humphrey's light barely illuminated the featureless wall on the opposite side. In the middle of this room, a raised stone plinth stood—atop it was a wooden box . . .

No—this was a *treasure chest*.

"Odd place to keep treasure," Sally mused, her voice dampened but still echoing in the underground chamber. "It is probably a . . . disguised Monster?" She could feel a name sitting in the back of her muddled mind, something from the before-times, but it couldn't reach her tongue.

"Suspend your disbelief a little; perhaps the owner wanted to take their possessions with them to the afterlife." Humphrey looked particularly menacing in the otherwise pitch-black room, his eldritch purple glow illuminating the recesses of his empty sockets.

"Pfft." She brought out her dagger and jabbed it into the wood, tense and expecting something to burst out. The sharp sound briefly reverberated up throughout the stone.

No Monster surged forth.

"Best open it then." She shrugged.

With the weapon stored, she grasped the lid and lifted, eyes widening as a familiar hiss of clear mist was expelled by the chest.

She looked within to see her bounty earned.

## CHAPTER NINETEEN

# Grave Intentions

50 Gold
Common Basic Boots
Scroll: Savage Strike (1)

I am completely whelmed. At least I got some boots back?" Sally shrugged, bringing up her Inventory to switch them on. "I may as well check out this scroll while I'm here. One use, I take it?"

Savage Strike: Your next Melee Attack deals 100% more damage

"*Yes.*"

"*Skullsplitters* had a Rogue. Why didn't they come to get the chest?" She crossed her arms and began walking toward the exit.

"Probably the terrible rewards; they must be here for another, more specific reason." The skull followed her out.

"Sorry, gang, nothing too fun down there." She gave the Lurker a pat on the arm after emerging from the tomb.

The next one wasn't very far away. They passed by rows of gravestones, some ruined or crumbling. Sally noted that they were all worn enough that no names could be made out. That seemed convenient. Whatever passed as a pathway through the Cemetery hardly differed from the dried earth that the graves sprung up from. Once again, Sally wished she had the ability to raise the dead—*just think* of the army she could raise against the System.

"So, Humps," she began as they closed in on the next tomb, "is the Guild like a centralized organization, or . . . ?"

"There's an official hall in the nearest town. Usually, the bigger hubs in each area have a hall that is run independently but is still part of the overall organization."

"I really need a map. What's the closest hub?"

"Poppybrook. It's the main town for Novices and early-level First Classes." The Observer easily reeled off the information and then paused, remembering what the woman would be using it for.

"How are they defended? Is it like—"

"*Nope*." Humphrey stopped in midair and shook. "Quit trying to involve me in your plans of rebellion. I am sure I can be easily *unmade*."

"I feel we keep going in circles with this, bud. I bet you the guardians of the Guild hub are a powerful Party or something . . ."

" . . . "

"*Ahh*, you're too easy to read!" She placed her hand on the cold stone of the next tomb and stuck her tongue out. "Maybe the System is too predictable . . . aside from little ol' me, of course."

This second one was not locked, and the gate shuddered as it struggled to swing on rusted hinges. As Sally stepped down into the depths it became clear that it was built exactly the same as the previous one—except on coming to the steps of the chamber there was no chest waiting for her. Instead, two pairs of baleful green eyes glared back at her.

"New friends, come with me," her voice echoed briefly.

She smiled as she returned to the surface once more. The gloomy sky may look like it was threatening rain, but she dared it to even try. Alongside her full Party, there were now five Skeleton Warriors that appeared to be able to take brief commands easily enough. It almost made her regret letting loose all of the dead in Hillan. However, there would have been no chance she could have hidden from the *Skullsplitters* with them in tow, and even with their full force, it wouldn't have pushed that battle in their favor.

If she was going to head into civilization soon, would it be an advantage to have a weak horde alongside her? That question would have to marinate. They would have their uses against the weak and System-created, even if they were immediately mashed by the higher-level Parties. The whole thing was a hastily put-together plan if she was honest with herself.

Dismantle the Adventurers Guild's hubs to reduce the efficiency of the Parties and give the Monsters a reprieve. Amass her own strong Party and stomp her way through the System until they get a meeting with the Architect themselves—and hopefully get some answers on how the souls of Players got here. And why. And how dare they?

"This one looks much bigger."

The Observer took her out of the distracted thoughts as the group trod through dirt and dead vegetative slurry. It was a bigger tomb—even on the outside it was nearly twice as wide as the prior two, and decorative pillars rose up at each corner to display worn gargoyles. Or cherubs? The amount of wear and decay made it hard to pick out the details beyond just looking a little creepy.

Sally glanced around first. No sign of anything. No living dead, and no living . . . uh, living. The gloom still sat obscuring the far distance making it difficult to judge how far into the Cemetery they were—and as she looked backward, the woods too were now out of view. She put the likelihood of it going on infinitely about fifty-fifty.

"The doorway is wider on this one," she thought out loud. "I think we should *all* go inside—something is giving me the creeps." Turning back to her group she frowned. "Except for Suits—you stay up the top of the stairway here and be our canary."

"Very tactical." The floating skull nodded as the male zombie groaned in resigned acknowledgment.

"No smarm from you, if you please." Sally shook her head and opened the wide gate. This one did not creak or squeal, which seemed like a bit of a rip-off. Totally didn't get the memo about the area theme. With one step inside, she waited for the Observer to catch up and provide some light.

"You know, most Novices start with torches."

Sally just clenched her teeth in response. If Humphrey was trying to dissuade her from destroying the System that she felt gave her a bad deal, then reminding her about these things wasn't helping his cause. It probably came across as a little selfish to want to destroy the world around her just because she had a rough start. There was something that was underlying though—a knowledge that this wasn't right. She could remember the time before, and Theo must have some knowledge too if he recognized her. Whether the rest of the Players had the same mentality was something she would need to find out.

At least, when they weren't trying to kill her.

The start of the tomb began similarly to the smaller ones; a passageway began at the bottom of a dozen stairs, and engravings lined the cold brickwork. Sally waited for a second for the group to filter in behind her. Dave helped Chuck up when the zombie inevitably fell down the stairs.

"Chuck! You're going to run out of health before you need it, and I'm not wasting this med pack on you." She crossed her arms and waited for the clacking of bones to shuffle down the stairs as the handful of Skeleton Warriors joined them in the near darkness, leaving Suits up near the opening.

"Looks like it goes farther in." The Observer bobbed too close to the top of her head, setting her hair abuzz.

Where usually a couple of steps would lead to a small plain chamber, instead this room was slightly bigger, with a domed ceiling. Across from them, the wall had some kind of mural carved into the stone—the exact details were too hard to pick out in the wide shadows cast by Humphrey's purple glow. Two doorways sat on either side of the mural, closed and made of dark wood with latticed black iron bracing. On the walls on the left and right of them as they stepped into the recessed chamber were two armored statues of stone, cobwebbed and glimmering in the low purple light.

"Come with me." Sally spoke to the statue on the right. It did not heed her call. "Eh, was worth a try."

"Hmm," Humphrey murmured from above.

"What is it?"

"*Oh*, nothing."

She narrowed her eyes at the skull. "Are you observing things and not sharing? Telling me there is something to notice but then denying it is gaslighting, you know."

The Observer sighed and moved over closer to the mural. As it illuminated, further details were revealed. It seemed to be of some kind of armored warrior—with a crown? No, it was just an ornate helmet. The stonework wasn't super detailed; perhaps the area surrounding it had been painted to show the background of the overall design at some point but had since faded with time.

"Oh." Sally squatted down and looked at the boots of the carved man. There was a faint red line that ran up the sides of the boots—it almost glowed in the darkness but was too thin to have been seen from a distance. She ran a dead finger along it. There was an odd tingle to it.

"A Party using torches probably wouldn't have seen that," Humphrey noted, unsure of whether he was being complimentary or not.

"Yes, but what is it?" *What would be tingly and part of a mural?* Sally stood and put her hands on her hips, head tilted in thought. The easy answer would be . . . magic. But what good did that answer do her?

The Observer was silent now, which usually meant that he didn't want to interfere with whatever decision she made. Sally pressed her STAR and brought up her Inventory. This was probably a waste, but fumbling around in the dark with a bunch of dead bodies wasn't her idea of . . . Oh, no, that didn't sound that bad actually. The tombs had been quite relaxing. Cold, quiet, and comforting in a claustrophobic way.

She pointed the *[Zap Wand]* at the wall. "Uh, do I have to call out skills when I use them?"

"No . . . no? Why would you do that? There's no benefit in—"

"Zap!" Sally yelled, and an arc of blue-white lightning flickered from the tip of the wooden stick to the boots of the mural, briefly lighting the room and causing the undead to shirk away.

Humphrey tutted.

"*Observe that.*" She smirked and looked back at the wall. A cobweb of red lines now coursed up from the boots, making their way up through the legs and torso of the carved knight. Two prongs of red eventually reached to the part of the helmet where the eyes would be, and small orbs of glowing light briefly lit up before fading.

A shifting of stone caused Sally to level the wand at the left statue as she watched it swivel around out of the way, the grinding sound stopping to reveal a hidden passageway.

She walked toward it and peered inside. A corridor that immediately went to the right and then a staircase that spiraled down out of view. Sally hummed to herself as she gestured for the horde behind her to follow. Humphrey lit the way, the purple light illuminating further thick dust in this secret area.

The spiral staircase only made a couple of twists before reaching the next level of the tomb—thankfully not far enough where Chuck could cause himself further damage when he eventually stumbled into the back of Big Dave. The Lurker had to squat down as they moved, looking rather uncomfortable in the enclosed space. A doorway blocked their passage—a heavy wooden door with an insignia of the same helmet that the mural wore.

Sally pushed it open and stumbled into the room. "There's a little step right there," she pointed out and righted herself as the rest of her group filtered in.

This chamber was twice as wide as the one above, along with the step that ran around the outside of the perimeter of the room; the walls were also decorated with carvings and paintings of battles from a different era. In the middle of the chamber on the smooth stone floor was a low table also made of stone—but the table was a darker, almost unnatural color.

Sitting on a throne made of equally odd, black stone at the other side of the room was an armored figure. Or rather just the armor—the helmet sat on the knee of the reddish-black-plated body, the head completely missing and empty.

Sally gasped and moved toward it, half expecting the Observer to start yapping on about the lore of the place.

Then a UI message popped up from her wrist.

Party member Suits has died

## CHAPTER TWENTY

# The Arisen

Sally shot a panicked look toward the door. *"Close it!"*

Skeleton Warrior has joined the Party

A whirl of curses spun around inside her head. This was a very bad position—perhaps she had been too overconfident, too lackadaisical with her abilities. She shot a glance toward Humphrey, who had hovered into the middle of the room near the ceiling, ready to observe.

"This is where Theo shows up just in the nick of time, right?" She clenched her jaw as the skull did not respond. Even if the super-Novice did manage to get here in time, there was nothing he would be able to do against a full Party.

"Told ya we should have checked all the tombs on the way in."

A brash voice carried faintly down the stairs toward them—it sounded like the Fighter of the *Skullsplitters*. A softer response was given but was too muffled for Sally to make out.

She hissed at the Lurker. "Hold the door. Make sure they can't get through." With a deep breath of stale air, she withdrew the crossbow from her Inventory. She had to keep a clear head. The doorway was perhaps the only advantage they had—with the staircase being only a few feet away, it would create a bottleneck.

Big Dave braced themself against the door, heavy brow furrowed in determination. She ordered the two Party skeletons to stand either side of the door, but a few feet back. The assortment of random warriors she told to gather near the middle of the room around the table. Without being able to control or support them as well, they'd do better to draw focus away from herself in one corner—the right side of the door wall—and Chuck in the other, opposite her.

It would be nice if she could give the walking meatloaf a weapon or maybe just wrap him in a pillow. He was already half dead—but he might be of some use if he didn't die too quickly.

"Someone's opened up a passageway here." A voice came from above, closer now.

She again glanced up at the Observer. He was focused on the door, his expression cold and hard to read. Her teeth ground together, as she was unable to sweat. Footsteps could now be heard on the staircase—easily a handful, though it didn't take much to guess this was all of the *Skullsplitter* Party.

"Let me check for traps first," the Rogue complained from the staircase.

"There's hardly any room to move; I'm sure it will be fine." The Fighter again, closest to the door.

The Lurker flinched as the door attempted to budge, steadying themself with grim determination.

"Huh, it's stuck." The Fighter pushed again, jostling Dave but unable to shift them.

Sally began slightly regretting being so cynical about the Architect; maybe they were a great person, and this was all a big misunderstanding? The pit in her stomach told her this wasn't the case. But perhaps she could be free of this weird world, whatever death here truly entailed.

"Looks more like something is blocking it," the Ranger now called from the spiral stairs. "If someone opened the passage they might be here still."

"Hello?" The Fighter banged her fist on the door. "Anyone in there?"

There was no chance pretending to be a Player would work this time. One whiff of the door opening and it'd be clear they were a bunch of Monsters. The loose huddle of Skeletal Warriors looked anxious, eager to get into battle even if outmatched. She glared at them and willed them to stay put with *[Command Dead]*. At least, she hoped she could do that with just a powerful side-eye.

"No response." The shrug from the Fighter could be heard through the door, in part due to her armor shuffling about.

"Allow me."

This voice was new—deep, gravelly, and calm. The clanking of heavy metal boots on the cold stone floor nailed shut any second guesses about this being the armored Knight. Murmured complaints of people squeezing out of the way of their approach were then punctuated by silence.

Sally stared at the Lurker, eyes trying to bore through the creature so that she could see what was about to happen, what their plan was so that she could try and counter it. A splintering sound and a flash of pain across Big Dave's face was the introduction to the answer she sought.

The Lurker stumbled forward from the door and attempted to clutch at their back. Behind them the longsword of the Knight had pierced through the door; crimson blood ran along the silver blade. As Dave turned back around with anger flaring in their eyes, the door was kicked open.

A torch was flung into the room, casting bright amber light throughout the chamber, shadows hauntingly dancing against the wall as the empty skulls of the warriors were lit from underneath.

"Why is there a Woodlands—oh, *undead*!" the Fighter called from behind the Knight.

"Nice and easy," the Rogue called and rolled into the room beneath the grasp of the Lurker as Dave rushed forward to clog the doorway once more. The red-haired thief brought up a hand crossbow and knife leveled at the nearest skeleton before a frown spread across their face as their arms didn't move as quickly as they expected.

*[Hex: Slow]*

Sally shot her crossbow at the slowed Rogue, striking the figure in the side, piercing their ribcage. A pained expression flared in their face along with a sudden panic as the Skeleton Warriors they thought easy to dispatch now closed in on them.

"Han needs help," the Ranger growled, an arrow barely skimming past the Lurker and striking a skeleton in the shoulder, causing it to stumble backward.

"I can't see them; you're in the way!" The panicked voice of the Cleric came from the stairwell, the bottleneck working as hoped.

Sally shook as she loaded another bolt into the crossbow, trying to shrink farther into the corner. A second bolt might put the Rogue closer to death, but if the skeletons could finish them off, then she should save—

A bright flash of blue light filled the chamber for a split second, and then Dave roared in pain. The Lurker's right arm was hewn from their body, radiant blue light still dancing across the edges of the wound as blood began to spray to the floor—the hum of the Knight's sword almost like static in the air. An arrow from behind followed up, striking Big Dave directly in the face for a critical hit.

Party member Big Dave has died
Skeletal Warrior has joined the Party

She flicked through the STAR and licked her teeth. It was a distraction, but giving a skeleton a boost from *[Mighty Aura]* might make a difference. The Rogue had grabbed hold of one of the Skeleton Warrior's arms to prevent it from landing a blow, but a second one carved a slice in their flank; pain and sweat covered their face. They looked dizzy, woozy . . . *ripe*.

The Knight stepped into the room and the two warriors on guard stepped forward to engage. In their heavy plate, the rusty sword of the first just bounced off, and the second was parried, a counterattack easily splitting the skull from the neck.

Party member Skeletal Warrior has died

Sally froze at the sight of, surely, her imminent doom. The torchlight flickered off the bright armor, giving them an almost demonic visage. The crossbow would do nothing against them; neither would the swords or teeth they had. As the Knight turned to smite the second warrior, the Cleric ran into the room, hands glowing with a bright yellow light.

The bolt left the crossbow. Sally watched as the light from the healing spell faded, and the eyes of the Cleric widen in slow motion. One of the eyes anyway, as the other had a bolt through it. The healer started to collapse, and the Knight turned to catch her. The plated figure then looked up and saw Sally.

"Bren, Healing Potion—NOW!" the Knight boomed, passing the dying form of the petite blonde over to the Ranger entering the room.

A second roar came from the stairs as the Fighter rushed in using a skill—and the warriors surrounding the Rogue turned to immediately face the new threat, almost entirely forgetting the near-death Rogue.

Sally backed against the wall, trying to think of a way to escape the enclosing Knight as their blade started to glow blue. Ideas were short.

"What in the blazes is that—" the Ranger began, fumbling for a Healing Potion to give to the held Cleric. "I can see the bounty, but—*oh, Gods!*"

The Knight turned back to his Party, as did all eyes in the room briefly, as a figure in flames grabbed hold of the Ranger from behind and bit into his neck. Blood spurted from the wound as his own clothing started to set alight; the Ranger dropped the Cleric to grasp at his wound as the aflame zombie also fell over and laid still.

The Fighter growled as her weapon cleaved another skeleton into fragments. Having finished off the last of the warriors, she rushed over to help put out the fire on the Ranger and heal the injured pair.

"I don't know who you are," the Knight growled as he turned back to face the shrinking Sally, "but you will pay with your life for this." He leveled his blade back at the zombie woman as she slumped into the corner. He was now just a couple of steps away from striking her down.

Her hand gripped the handle of her dagger and trembled as her mouth ran dry. *Was this it?* A single tear rolled down her cheek, knowing that she would never get to gobble up Theo.

As she felt the shadow loom over her, the static energy of the magic crackling through the Knight's blade made her skin prickle. The sword drew back, and her muscles tensed, prepared to try and run. Try to escape.

A red flash of light burst through the chamber, briefly blinding everyone.

The smell of burnt dust was accompanied by the sound of creaking metal and plate grinding against smooth stone.

"*Ha-ha,*" a booming laugh echoed deeply around the chamber. "*Ha-ha-ha-ha-ha!*"

## CHAPTER TWENTY-ONE

# Ascension

As the blow from the Knight stayed, Sally risked glancing at the sound of the familiar—if now a lot creepier—laugh.

In front of the throne, the ancient armor now stood. Dark silver and burgundy decorated the ornate plate, and a constant burst of red flame emanated from the back of the helm. In his plated hands, the Death Knight held a greatsword that glowed with the same red energy as the helmet.

The face of the helmet twisted into a devilish grin. "*Ha-ha*," it reiterated. "I think you'll find the woman does not die *today*."

Humphrey has joined the Party

"These three are barely holding on." The panicked Fighter's eyes darted between the new figure and the Knight. "We need to get out of here."

The Knight hissed and looked down at Sally, disgusted by her. After a brief moment, he relented and turned toward his Party—ready to help them escape.

"*Ha-ha!* Not so fast, Mr. Virtuous . . . *[Compelled Duel]*." Humphrey lowered his gaze as he leveled a finger at the retreating Knight.

The Knight stood frozen in place, halfway to stepping toward the fallen Cleric, as the Fighter had the Ranger over her shoulder, the Rogue supported by her arms. "What are you doing?" she whispered angrily.

"Uh oh, looks like you failed your save—*ha-ha!*" The Death Knight flexed his head side to side and raised the greatsword. "I've always wanted to do this."

Sally sat speechless in the corner, eyes darting between the frozen Knight and the apparent Death Knight–Observer—if he was even still that. Slowly, so as not to draw attention to herself, she brought up his details on the UI.

Humphrey - Level Ten Death Knight, Undead Humanoid
Skills Unknown

The Ranger threw up across both the floor and the Fighter.

"*Uh!* Seriously? C'mon, we need to—" The Fighter yelped and stooped to one knee, dropping the Ranger and sending the Rogue stumbling toward the spiral stairs.

The Knight turned like a statue toward Humphrey and readied his own sword. "Who are you? What are you doing here?" The words came through clenched teeth.

"Well." Sally smiled, rising back to her feet at the gesture of the Death Knight. "We aren't huge fans of the System, or the Architect—or even the adventurers that come around and kill everyone."

"That's right," Humphrey growled. "So we are going to destroy everything—bit by bit. *Ha-ha!*"

"But . . . you're *Monsters?*" The Knight held his sword in a ready position and tensed up.

"That seems to be a matter of . . . perspective." Humphrey grinned widely and launched himself toward the opponent, his greatsword flickering through the air with a hiss.

Sally tore her eyes away from the clash and ran over to the doorway. The stairwell was empty save for the Ranger lying sprawled across the floor. She ground her teeth together and weighed up chasing down the escapees—they were heavily injured, but that was a sure way to get herself overwhelmed by accident. The Ranger looked . . . unwell to say the least, and rather unappetizing, unfortunately. She hadn't gotten to eat from any of them.

The sound of sharp blade against metal came from behind her, and she turned to witness the duel. Humphrey was remarkably quick with the large blade and seemingly enjoying every second of the battle. As proficient and well-armored as the Knight was, it was clear the level difference was against him. Every blocked blow put him on the back foot; already his strength was waning. His reactions slowed as lethargy set in.

Still, the adventurer was giving it his all, causing the Death Knight to block and dodge around to avoid the flashing blade, neither of them seemingly able to land any decisive blows.

A clang reverberated throughout the chamber as the Knight's armor was split and dented. The greatsword burned with intensity as if it hungered for the carnage. Humphrey had pushed the foe back to the far wall.

"Nothing personal." The Death Knight grinned, arms wide in feigned apology.

The Knight roared and darted forward unexpectedly, his longsword blazing a bright blue glow. Static buzzed through the air as the tip struck the burgundy breastplate undefended and Humphrey opened his mouth in shock.

"*Ha-ha!*" His expression turned to an evil scowl as the blue blade just slid off his armor, the attack having no effect. "You had no chance from the beginning."

The Knight stepped back, now pressed against the wall. He almost dropped the sword as he fumbled around his belt for something.

Humphrey raised his free hand, palm outstretched toward the panicked man. *[Drain Life]*

A foul mist of green-purple swirling energy pulsed out of the Knight in a stream that made its way into the outstretched plated hand of the Death Knight. The adventurer shuddered, arms limp and no longer searching around his possessions as his sword clattered to the floor.

"This makes *me* the winner." Humphrey grinned, somehow affixing his large sword to his back.

Sally ran over to the collapsing Knight and threw the helmet off. His eyes were rolled back in his head, and he looked dried out, but food was food. She bit through his throat and savored the sweet taste of his remaining life force.

"You coulda done that sooner." She scowled at the Death Knight as she wiped the gore from her mouth along her arm. "Saved the rest of the Party?"

Humphrey folded his arms and looked away. "It was no easy decision to become this. I have severed my connection with the Architect, abandoned my duties to the System, and gone against the very nature of my creation."

"Aw, just because you couldn't bear to see me die?" she teased and walked over to the smoldering body of Chuck.

She hadn't received the notification of his death . . . Bringing up the UI she could see that he was on zero Health Points again. She knelt and brushed some of the ashes from what remained of his lower trousers. "It's not shorts season, you goof."

Chuck rolled over, half his face blistered and sloughed off from the burn damage, and slowly started to get to his feet despite his apparent lack of being dead.

"Huh." Sally shook her head before her STAR *bloiped.*

Level Up

Humphrey sat on the edge of the obsidian table, oddly interested in having the ability to do so now.

"Chuck—you leveled up too, but you're down to Level 0.15. How does that even work? If you get even clumsier from this, I swear I will leave you behind." With a sigh, she tapped her own level-up notification.

Nothing happened.

She jabbed at it again, and again—but the message just stayed put. Maybe she just had to give it a minute. Perhaps the System had performance anxiety.

"Strange, the Ranger seems to have turned." Humphrey idly drummed his fingers on the table. "I'm not sure it's supposed to work like that."

She turned to look at the figure lying by the door, who now had started to shuffle to his feet. His complexion was certainly more on the green side—and he didn't have glowing eyes before. "Perhaps Chuck is the alpha zombie?"

They turned to watch said zombie staring up into the corner of the room away from everyone else.

"Doubtful, *ha-ha.*"

"So you're just a Level Ten Death Knight now? No fancy background knowledge?" She walked back over to the Knight, being careful to move the flickering torch further away from Chuck.

"*Yes.* I no longer observe. To put it in a metaphorical sense, while I do not have library access, I have still retained the pages previously read."

Sally mulled this over as she crouched down by her last meal. Having a powerful Monster in her Party was certainly a big boost—she shot a sad glance over to the body of Big Dave—but a System-linked untouchable knowledge bank had advantages too. It was done now, at least. No sense in aching about it.

She smiled at him as she started to loot the Knight. "At least now we can be proper friends, right?"

"I can assure you that had no weight in my decision." The Death Knight looked away at the wall.

---

240 Gold
Healing Potion
Dried Meat (5)
Sturdy Necklace
Sturdy Ring
Secret Note

---

"I'm leaving his armor there because there's no way I'm wearing plate." She stuck her tongue out in disgust. It looked like the Knight liked to stack Damage Reduction, which made sense. For all the good it did him. She put the accessories on and felt slightly more resistant to pain . . . maybe? She brought up the Secret Note.

---

Secret Note: Within Walls, Lands Afar, Broken Ground, Crimson Mar

---

"Some kind of poem," she murmured. A problem for another day. Time to try and level up again.

The menu buzzed, but her repeated presses did nothing.

"Humphrey! I am broken; it won't let me level up." She held out her wrist and pouted toward the Death Knight.

"Hmm." He stood and came over, kneeling slightly to be level with the held-out STAR. "There is something I may be able to try if you're willing?"

"Please." She nodded and then tilted her head as he drew the greatsword. "Unless it involves cutting off my arm."

"*Ha-ha.*" Humphrey grinned and placed the sword to the stone floor and knelt before her. "*Sally the Unliving*, I hereby pledge to be your champion, to protect your life and obey your commands. I will travel with you in every venture until my death."

"That's very sweet—and slightly creepy, Humps, but—"

The level up text fuzzed and vanished, before being replaced by a notification popup.

---

New Bodyguard: Humphrey, Death Knight - Level Three
Level Four Boss Monster Ability Unlocked
**Choose your Affinity**
[**Melee Affinity**] Increased: Health, Melee Damage, Defense
[**Ranged Affinity**] Increased: Speed, Ranged Damage, Critical Chance
[**Spellcaster Affinity**] Increased: Mana, Spell Damage, Spell Critical Chance

---

## CHAPTER TWENTY-TWO

# Gloomy Skies

Tough choice, Humps." Sally scratched her chin as she looked over the three options. "My crossbow has been working out pretty well—and with you up front, I shouldn't need to melee and put myself in too much danger. No offense."

"None taken, my liege." The Death Knight performed an awkward half-bow.

"*No*—don't do any of that. I'll . . . cast you out of service or something." She waved her hand at him in frustration. "It's bad enough that your level reduced. I guess a bodyguard has to be a level below their boss?"

"*Ha-ha*, astute as always." Humphrey folded his plated arms across his breastplate. "But you haven't considered spellcasting?"

She shrugged. "I only have *[Hex: Slow]* at the moment, and with my random progression there's no guarantee I will get any cool spells soon." Sally closed her eyes and rubbed her forehead. There was the taste of a memory avoiding her attempts at retrieval. Mentally she chased it around, eventually getting a handful of it—enough to guide her decision.

Melee Affinity Selected

She frowned at the Death Knight who had his head tilted in interest. "Just because you are a tank, it doesn't mean I don't need to think about my own survivability. There's no use being ranged or magic if I get easily squished." She sighed and relaxed her brow. "I won't always be able to rely on you to keep me safe."

"Preposterous! It is my sworn duty to—"

Sally hushed him with a wave of her arm to all the broken skeletons and the corpse of the Lurker. "Plus," she added with a wry grin, "how could I *trust* you when you gave up your previous duty?"

"W-what? That's—that's not fair," Humphrey spluttered.

"Just kidding. I appreciate it, skull-knight. We're proper buds now." She smiled and dusted off her hands on her dress. "Oh, that reminds me. Where are we heading next?"

"You haven't handed in your quest yet." The red flames lapped gently at the back of his helmet. Now that combat had ended, they had simmered down to a gentle wave of crimson energy.

"Oh yeah, this STAR thing takes some getting used to. Especially when it doesn't work properly half the time."

Quest Complete
50 Gold
Uncommon Weapon Chance Box

"Oof, always with the random stuff." The menus spun around atop her wrist. "Dang it, just accepted a quest without seeing the options. *'Clear the Goblin Cave'*—it's near a place called Yarch. What kind of name is that?" She raised an eyebrow at the Death Knight.

"Wasn't me that named places, *ha-ha*. Yarch is a small village close to Hillan. It's on the way to Poppybrook."

"And Poppybrook is where we go to eat the Guild, right? You can tell me more about it now that you are my minion." Sally beamed, and her eyes twinkling in the flickering light of the torch still on the floor of the chamber.

"There are three parts to this that make it an ill-advised plan." Humphrey cleared his throat. "But I will tell you as long as you never call me a minion again." He waited for her nod of agreement before he continued. "Firstly, Adventurers Guild hubs are the central points for Parties to gather to do official boring business—so it is likely there will be several groups in the immediate vicinity."

"Uh-huh, got it. An all-I-can-eat buffet."

"Secondly," the Death Knight continued, "the building itself hosts the most powerful Party in the region. They get to influence region policy and get a few boons in return as long as they act as stewards to the Guild."

Sally nodded.

"And lastly, this Guild Party will be protecting the Guild Core—an artifact that helps bind elements of the System together. These often have defensive layers of their own—traps, spells, and even Monsters."

"Like a dungeon?" She tilted her head. Kill the weaklings, eat the strongest defenders, and survive the dungeon to pierce the heart.

"*Yes.*" A brief lick of flame curved out from the back of his helmet.

Sally tapped a finger on her hip thrice before bringing up the STAR.

Sally: Almost died. Can't believe you stood me up
Sally: New plan—meet near Yarch

"Alright, no point waiting for the tasty snail to respond. Let's get out of here. It is starting to feel stuffy."

Zombie has joined the Party

Humphrey nodded and watched the Ranger fall in line to the will of his new boss, who was currently busy collecting the skulls of the fallen warriors.

They were one Party member short, but if Theo ever managed to catch up, then that'd be fine. Basic Zombies were starting to lag behind in level though—especially Chuck. Sally narrowed her eyes at the walking corpse, who was now just leaning face-first against the wall. It probably just felt cool on his burnt skin, she decided, feeling bad for the unlucky zombie again.

"Shame you cannot loot the Ranger now, as he has become a Monster." The Death Knight grinned.

"But if I killed him now, would he drop his Player gear?"

"Hmm, *inconclusive.*" Humphrey shrugged and made his way toward the stairs.

Sally grabbed the torch. After waving it about to try and douse the flame, she was amused to find she could just jam it in her Inventory while it was lit. There were probably a few ramifications to that kind of thing, but she didn't let it cloud her mind. With the chamber drowned in pitch darkness once more, she hopped toward the stairs where the red flame of the Death Knight briefly illuminated the doorway.

"Whoa!" She tripped over the small step and scuffed her knee on the floor. "Ah, I'm injured!"

"I'm not carrying you up the stairs." Humphrey grinned from the first couple of stairs. "I'm not the gallant type of knight, *ha-ha.*"

"Yes, so I have observed." She stood and brushed herself down again. "So did you lose all your cool abilities becoming Level Three?"

"*Yes.* I now only have *[Adrenaline]*, *[Minor Resistance]*, and *[Grave Strike].*"

"Aw, the duel one looked really useful." She pouted and made a mental note to check the details of his skills later.

"I hope to regain it as we grow."

As they reached the top of the stairs and into the upper chamber of the tomb, a trail of scuffed blood led along the dusty floor toward the exit. Sally knelt and ran her finger through it. She stared at her outstretched digit with a furrowed brow.

"I don't know why I did that." She looked up at the Death Knight. "It was obvious what it was." She licked her finger.

Humphrey stared down at her with empty sockets, unflinching as she wiped and licked her finger across the trail a second time. "Perhaps you need some fresh air."

"Uh-huh," she agreed, only briefly considering just running her tongue along the floor before she stood and started to lead the Party back outside. She winced as the dull light of the overcast sky flooded her eyes.

The air was . . . Well, it wasn't stale and stuffy. Sally was breathing, as it felt like it was a natural reflex rather than a mortal necessity. So although she didn't feel the full benefit of the clear air, it was a welcome change. A few steps out from the tomb, she stopped and waited for the others to catch up.

"How long does it take for these low-level Monsters to respawn?"

The Death Knight looked around at the still-empty Cemetery. "Too long to be worth waiting around for, if that was your intention."

"Dang." She frowned at the gloom preventing her from seeing farther. "Hey, wait, did I ever respawn? Before . . . all this?" She waved her STAR in the air in front of him.

Humphrey regarded her with a blank expression, the flames at the back of his helmet the only movement for a long handful of seconds. "I do not know. I was not in the diner that long."

She narrowed her eyes. Perhaps the answer didn't really matter. Even if she had been killed a few times and just respawned back in the diner, now that she had her soul . . . it was more real? Her tongue ran across her sharp teeth. There was something definitely strange about the whole process that was currently beyond her understanding. *Another* problem for *another* day.

"Which way to"—she paused as Chuck tripped out of the tomb and landed flat on his face—"Yarch, then?"

The Death Knight put his plated hands on his hips and turned, eye sockets narrowed at the gloomy, shapeless horizon. Eventually, he pointed his finger past them, almost back the way they had come.

"Killing goblins doesn't sound like my kind of thing; perhaps there will be some way to subvert the quest when we get there?" She sighed and began walking as Humphrey fell into step beside her.

"Not everything has to be a subversion just because you are different. I'm sure you could just ask them to join you, and then we can all have a jolly time sacking Yarch together."

"So you agree, then?" She beamed and nudged his arm. "Oh, while we walk, let's see what trash I get from the Chance Box?"

"As you wish. Just don't stab me if it's another dagger, *ha-ha*."

"No promises." She winked, drawing the box from her Inventory and running her STAR across it.

A green light flickered around the edges as the question mark adorning the top pulsed.

With a hiss, a blue mist poured from within the box, and a shape rose from within it.

Small sparkles of light fell from the object, reflecting in Sally's widening eyes.

## CHAPTER TWENTY-THREE

# Foreshadowing

t *is* a dagger."

Rare Dagger of Luck

Sally exhaled and withdrew the new blade from her Inventory. It had a slight blue sheen to it and a nice leather grip. She would perhaps admit that it was a much nicer dagger than her common ones, even if she still couldn't bring up the item details properly.

"Luck is self-explanatory, at least." Humphrey shrugged, standing slightly farther away from her. "If you keep it equipped on your belt, you'll gain the stat boost even when not wielding it directly."

"Thanks." She held back a sarcastic response. Luck wasn't a terrible statistic to improve, at least in theory. Depending on how the System calculated things, it would either be super effective but random or too low a chance to really come into play. If only she could see her own stats too.

They walked in silence for a few minutes, passing by the tombs they had previously entered and plundered. This time instead of heading up through to the woods, they found a path that led at a slight angle away.

"Sticking to the road might be more dangerous," Humphrey warned, "but will lead us almost straight to Yarch."

"I'm okay for a little danger." She grinned and wiggled her eyebrows. "I should be Level Five next, right, and get some kind of keystone ability?"

"Perhaps." Humphrey looked thoughtful. "For a Player class that is true—for you, we will have to wait and see."

Sally pouted. If her next level-up was another boring passive skill, she would be quite annoyed. Buffing her Party was all well and good—but as a boss Monster, she should be able to hold her own in a fight. Especially if there was a Player version of *[Compelled Duel]* or some kind of taunt like that Fighter had used.

As they left the Cemetery onto the road, the fog of gloom faded around them, and they were able to see the normal distance once more. The rough stones of the road were slightly overgrown with grass in places but stretched on into the woods for quite a distance. The farther they traveled from the site of graves and tombs, the brighter and clearer the skies were.

"I don't feel so lethargic in the sun now." Sally winced as she looked upwards, but the light didn't seem to burn as much as previously.

"One of the benefits of being a boss." Humphrey grinned. "You get minor resistances to certain conditions and maladies."

The armor of the Death Knight was even more eerie in the direct light. A mix of dark burgundy and blood-red metal, with dark silver edges and details. His once plain expression surrounded by purple glow was now a menacing grin that burned with intensity. It was a good look for him.

"How does it feel? Being a Monster now, I mean."

He regarded her with a tilted head and then looked up to the sky. "I had always wanted legs."

"*. . . And?*"

"They are very tiring to utilize constantly, *ha-ha.*" He grinned, and his helmet flame grew slightly more intense. "I feel like more of a real person now rather than a tool, if that answers your question, *Sally the Unliving.*"

"It does." She smiled back. "And you said I'd be getting more titles?"

"*Yes.*"

Sally opened her mouth to respond when instead a notification popped up on the STAR. "Oh, this must be Theo."

Marius: Where are you, corpse?

She wrinkled her nose at the little picture beside the text. "It's the deranged Cleric. How'd he manage to message me?"

The Death Knight paused, and they stopped on the road as he leaned down to stare at the message. "That is odd; I'm not sure of the workings of—"

Sally: Sorry, I'm not into you like that

Humphrey sighed. "It's probably best not to antagonize him."

"That was like the least bad thing I could think of—I didn't say anything about his mother . . . yet. Wait, do we even have parents here?" Parents, now that was a weird lump in her pea-soup brain.

*Bloip.*

"Hmm." The Death Knight stood back up straight and put a hand to his chin. "I am aware of parents existing as a concept." *Bloip.* "But not whether yours are here, or the exact—" *Bloip.*

"Oh my gosh, *this guy*. Where's the block option?" Sally scowled at the messages popping through.

> Marius: Reveal your whereabouts!
> Marius: I already have a group after you
> Marius: And I wouldn't date a loathsome creature like yourself
> Marius Brent Blocked

"His signaling was all over the place there. Also—Players have real names? How quaint."

Humphrey tilted his head as they began walking again but didn't press the issue.

"Walking the road might be a sure way to run into the Party he mentioned, but that's on the assumption that they'd have a clue where to look; this is a big area and—"

"As a boss Monster, you are now easier to find." The Death Knight raised a finger. "Where a bounty will say what Region you are in, being a boss Monster, the location can be narrowed to a smaller area. Like, *the Cemetery*."

"People can just grab that information from the town at will?" She was shocked at how brazen and unfair that was. That definitely seemed like a breach of her privacy.

"*No.* Only through a magical item—a *[Kill Contract Scroll]*. When used, it gives the location of a random boss or Elite Monster."

"Are you also an Elite Monster, Humps?" She raised her eyebrows.

"*Yes, ha-ha!*" His mouth opened wide as a burst of flame exited the back of his helm to emphasize his outburst.

"*Great,* that means we are twice as likely to be found, then."

"Oh. *Yes,* you are right." He rubbed the back of his armored neck apologetically.

Sally sighed. Turning towns into rubble and breaking the System was hard enough if they had the element of surprise, but now if random groups would be hunting them down as well—well, that just didn't seem fair. *The unfairness was the point*, she reminded herself, as she received another notification.

> Theo: On my way

"Not even an apology or promise that he has been seasoning himself," she huffed, closing the menu. "We need to teach that man some manners."

"It will be useful to have a Player in the Party." Humphrey scratched his chin. "One that can access all the normal Player things, I mean."

Sally chose to ignore this slight and carried on down the road that followed a gradual curve through the woods. Trees adorned the raised grassy embankments on either side, shade cast intermittently over their path. It was another calm that surely must be hiding some form of impending anguish.

"There must be interesting locales just off the path, right?" She narrowed her eyes into the woods to either side.

"Yes. Various locations for quests, Monster dens, and resource-gathering nodes."

"There's crafting?" Sally looked glumly at her lack of menus.

"To a degree. It is mostly useful for Player Housing and making gold to pay the—"

"What can I craft with . . . a dozen skulls?" She poked at her Inventory window, squinting at the collection of skeletal parts.

The Death Knight shrugged.

"Is it worth us looking for any side quests, then, out in these woods? You have map information still, right?" The text from her STAR flickered away.

"Probably not." Humphrey looked out into the dense trees to the side. "You are unlikely to get any decent reward or experience from anything in this area."

"That's sad. I was hoping we could—" Sally stopped mid-sentence.

She whirled around to face behind them, her rare dagger drawn from its sheath. The Death Knight drew his greatsword and stood back-to-back with her as the two zombies started walking a slow circle around the pair.

"What is it?" Humphrey asked, eye sockets narrowed.

"I thought I heard something . . . or could sense something . . . I'm not sure."

The path on either side remained clear—the woods were too dense, and it would be easy to hide away behind one of the countless trees. For a moment, the only sounds were the rustling of leaves in the light breeze, the shambling footsteps of the Party zombies, and the low hum of Humphrey's flickering helmet flame.

Sally relaxed and slowly put her weapon away. She continued to scour the way behind them with her red eyes, trying to spot any slight hint of movement or something amiss. With a shrug, she relented and turned back around. The Death Knight looked her way as he put away his sword but did not seem to see anything that she couldn't.

"Weird, perhaps my brain is just playing tricks on me. I only got to eat one adventurer." She patted her stomach and pouted at Humphrey. "I wonder which way the rest of them went—the tasty blood trail just petered off outside of the tomb."

"Let's hope they found a different way to Yarch so you can finish them off—*ha-ha!*" A gleam of red light sparked in the eyes of the Death Knight.

"I'm salivating already." She beamed, literally drooling as they continued down the path ahead.

A few minutes later, as the undead group became dots on the horizon, the faintest sound of exhaling was followed by darkened shapes slipping from between the cover of the trees.

## CHAPTER TWENTY-FOUR

# Wound Up

I'm getting pretty tired of walking," Sally whined. "When do we get horses?"

"When you've earned one." The Death Knight sighed. "Walking is so much worse than floating."

If she didn't know any better, Sally would have assumed they were stuck in some kind of loop. It had been perhaps a couple of hours of following this road, and the scenery hadn't changed by much. If not for the sun waning toward the late afternoon there would have been almost no indication that any progress had been made on their journey. On reflection, the walk from Hillan down to the Cemetery had taken a little while. If Yarch was farther away, it made sense—it was just so *boring*.

"I know we said no side quests, but we have to break up this monotony. Also, find someone to eat. *Something*."

Humphrey scratched his chin in contemplation. Then he looked around the woods on either side as if he could gain any sort of clue as to whether something was nearby.

"No." He shrugged. "It will not be long before we are at the goblin caves. You should save your energy for that."

Sally looked up at the Death Knight with a scowl. In that weird armor, he stood almost a full head taller than her, and certainly had a more appropriate figure for fighting. "Alright, then, Humps, my manager *slash* assistant, tell me how you even got to take over that suit thing—how does that work?"

"In lore terms, this was the ancient warrior Ark'han the Lost. He fell in the Bleak War where it is said he fought on for an hour even after being decapitated."

"That's . . . I guess they can just make up anything, huh?"

Humphrey grinned widely. "Pretty handy, as I was the missing piece of the puzzle—I just had to reroute some of my energy into merging with the potential Monster. A simple task for someone as powerful as—"

"So Ark'han would have been some kind of quest boss for higher levels? Since you were Level Ten before."

"*Yes.*" The Death Knight flexed his fingers and looked up to the sky as they walked. "I'm not sure why that is something I could do as an Observer—but we have both seen how fallible the System can be."

Sally nodded. That all seemed to make some manner of sense. As much as anything in this world did, at least. Although she had secretly hoped he would join her cause, it was still a surprise how much he had willingly sacrificed to help her. Having someone she could trust was a relief. She puckered her lips and frowned.

"Do you think we can trust Theo?"

Despite his lack of face flesh, Humphrey managed to look taken aback. "You have doubts?"

"It's not that. He just seemed to be on board with the plan almost immediately. He is certainly an odd cookie—"

"And a *Player.*"

"And a Player, yes. I just hope he can join the Party in proper terms rather than . . . " She looked back toward the two zombies shambling along behind them as she drew a finger across her throat.

"As a Novice he will pose no threat to us, no matter how high his level gets. Perhaps still more useful than Chuck, though." Humphrey cocked an eye toward the barely living corpse.

"Hey! Leave him outta this. He is unusual, just as you and I are. He just hasn't had the opportunity to . . . flourish yet."

The Death Knight grinned and looked back toward the road ahead. "You're just interested in what will happen if he gets to Level Zero."

"No!" She threw her arms in the air. "But what will happen, do you know?"

"*Ye*-no, I do not."

Sally opened her mouth to respond but then paused. Her brow lowered, and her eyes darted toward the woods on their right. "Noise," she hissed unnecessarily as the rumbling sound grew quickly in volume.

The cracking of trees and crushed bushes reverberated around the space around them as they drew their weapons in anticipation. Soon a large silhouette bounded forth, shattering the tree at the edge of the embankment and sending the shorn parts over their heads like nothing.

A ten-foot-tall humanoid snarled down at them, his singular eye glowing blue. In his hand, he held a giant club, almost as wide as one of the trees crushed in his path, the tip of which had sharp, bladed barbs embedded into a wooden head. Weird sigils and markings were painted on his bare skin, a leather loincloth adorned with bones the only item of clothing worn.

"Oh, hi." Sally beamed nervously. "Would you like to join my—"

The club slammed down in the place she had been standing, the zombie barely able to dodge out of the way in time as shards of broken stone road peppered her. She rolled and stumbled back to her feet, clutching at her arm as the pain took hold—one of the barbs had just caught her.

Humphrey leapt forward, a pulse of red energy flowing over his armor as he activated *[Adrenaline]*, causing his movements to speed up. As he parried the follow-up swing of the cyclops, he stumbled backward from the force.

"I miss being Level Ten already," he growled, empty eye sockets blazing with fury.

Sally pointed her Dagger of Luck at the cyclops and cast *[Hex: Slow]*. Almost immediately, the large Monster seemed to become lethargic—allowing the Death Knight to circle around past the next swing. She commanded the two zombies to stay back on the road.

With a deep breath, she ran in closer, dagger at the ready. Humphrey had circled around the Monster, causing it to rotate and face almost back into the woods. With a flash of red light, the greatsword carved a crimson line across the stomach of the lumbering cyclops.

As the beast roared in anger, Sally slipped up behind him and jammed her blade into the back of the Monster's knee. Her mouth salivated as the warm blood ran out from the piercing wound, his thick skin not enough to resist the attack.

And then, pain and pressure—a weird sense of weightlessness before she crashed down on the hard ground and rolled. Her brain caught up as she wheezed and tried to stand. One of her arms no longer worked. Distracted by the damage she had inflicted, she hadn't seen the backhand of the club's handle swing. She spat blood on the floor. *Wasn't it interesting that she could do that while still undead?*

"Sally!" Humphrey yelled out, breaking her from her stupor.

She had just enough time to flatten to the ground as the club whizzed past in a slow arc inches above her. The injured right arm flared up in agony. Her dagger . . . It must still be in the cyclops, or on the floor somewhere? She rolled onto her back and brought up her STAR, pressing it with her nose as her right hand hung limp.

The Death Knight slashed at the Monster, causing another large gash in the left arm and then the left flank of the cyclops. Droplets of red spattered out across the worn gray stonework of the road. The greatsword pulsed with dark arcane energy and his helmet's flames increased in intensity as he clashed against the large club. Splinters of wood dropped to the grass as the long blade cut into the wooden weapon.

Humphrey strained against the strength of the overbearing cyclops, having to relent against the show of power as a meaty left fist came in to strike at him unguarded. The blow rattled out as his metal armor shook, and he was knocked backward.

Sally swore under her breath. Trying to fiddle with the UI without the use of her hand was stressful and frustrating—who would design such a hindrance in their System? Finally, she retrieved the item she was after, just as a shadow loomed over her.

She looked up to see the large eye of the cyclops blazing down at her, his mouth agape and grinning with fist-sized teeth arranged awkwardly, like they had been too indecisive when growing in. As the club raised into the air, she struggled to level the crossbow in her off hand—thankful that she had stored it away loaded—the weapon shaking as she moved it to a more vertical position.

The thick arm of the cyclops tensed as he brought the club down, and Sally clenched the trigger of the crossbow.

With eyes closed she waited for the inevitable end. It did not come as quickly as expected.

*"Could . . . you please . . . move!"*

She opened her eyes to see the Death Knight standing by the cyclops, holding the large Monster up so that he didn't fall atop her. A crossbow bolt sat lodged dead center in the single eye. Sally rolled across the road, wincing every time her injured arm struck the path, before, finally, Humphrey could sidestep and allow the weighty giant to collapse to the floor, dead.

"Thanks, Humps. You're my knight in flaming armor again." She stood on her feet, wobbly, and gave him a weak smile.

"That's . . . not a normal place for a cyclops to be." He wiped his sword on the Monster. *"Level Five Elite."*

"So, that's meant to be a challenge for a full group of Level Fives? I feel like we took it on pretty well considering, then?"

"Hmm. There is something more to it than that—but I think we will cross that bridge when we get to it." He stowed away his greatsword on his back as his flames gently died down.

"The only thing I feel like crossing is this Med Kit off my Inventory list." Sally again struggled to navigate the STAR without the use of her right arm.

"Once you are done with that, come loot."

She murmured under her breath as she brought out the supposed healing kit. A small progress bar appeared over it. At least she didn't have to do any actual field medicine. She sighed. Once complete, a warm rush of green energy filled her before quickly dissipating. Her arm felt . . . better—still stiff, but at least movable.

With a stumble over to the corpse, she leaned against the large flank of the cyclops. Was damage meant to feel this painful? A headache began to throb. The prospect of more walking threatened to turn it into a handful of mental nails for sure.

She tapped against the dead body, again wishing she had some kind of zombification spell, and her eyes fell over the loot that had dropped.

"Humphrey! *What in the—*"

## CHAPTER TWENTY-FIVE

# Dead End

The glow of purple reflected off the Death Knight's armor, casting deep shadows within his empty eye sockets. "There we go; that is the unexpected amount of luck I had anticipated, *ha-ha!*"

Sally plucked the item from the air with a furrowed brow. A rectangle not much larger than her hand and flat except for some slightly raised details on one side. The artwork on the card stared back at her with its single eye. Her grip tightened as a buzzing filled her head—a familiar pressure that eventually released with a *pop*.

Card Feature Unlocked

"Alright, alright. What does this . . . cyclops card even do?"

Cyclops Card - Rare
For every 4 Strength you gain 1 Constitution
Card Equipped: 1/5 Slots

"Wowzers, that seems . . . excessive? How high do stats go?"

"*Yes.* The soft cap is one hundred. Given that you seem to have something odd going on with your stats already, this is perhaps problematic." Humphrey brought his hand up to his chin in contemplation.

Sally shrugged. Without seeing her stats, there wasn't much she could do about it. Even if there *was* a problem, it sounded more like something that would work to her benefit. You could never have too much Strength or Constitution, right? It would only make her more able to survive in this strange world.

"More to the point," she said as she retrieved her dagger from the cyclops's leg, "is what was this meanie doing out here at his level? Also, why did he not join my Party?" She shook her head.

"They are usually mountain creatures; it is unusual for a Monster to wander so far from their spawning habitat."

"Unless they are like me." She beamed and sheathed her blade.

"I don't think anybody is like you." The Death Knight shrugged. "Perhaps the System is just fraying at the seams more than we first thought."

That stood to reason—if anything, they had almost encountered more unusual activity and errors than normal things: Chuck with his lowering level and not being able to die, Theo with avoiding choosing a class and being super tasty looking, Humphrey disobeying his directive to help her out, and now Monsters in odd places.

She took a look through the rest of the belongings of the felled foe. Surprisingly, despite his lack of pockets, the cyclops had managed to hold onto a great deal of coins and miscellaneous boring stuff.

134 Gold
Skull (3)
Healing Potion

"I'll leave everything else. No point in getting my Inventory filled up with gross junk. Can't stand clutter. Are you listening, Humps? *I can't stand it!*"

"Yes. I did hear you—I am just ruminating."

"*Can't stand it,*" she whispered to herself, shaking her head. Skulls were *different* though. Skulls were neat and stacked into one square, and one day she could make a throne with them, or one of those archways for a garden—maybe even a weapon. Like a skull-trebuchet!

Her arm was at least back to almost normal. There was a weird darker green discoloration to most of it, which she assumed would be bruising if her blood still worked that way. She wasn't sure if the System knew how living corpses were supposed to react. The Healing Potion—a small glass filled with a bright red liquid—was stowed on her belt. As much as she could use it to get back to top form, you never knew when it could come in handy.

"We'd best head off," Humphrey eventually concluded, apparently having dropped whatever thought process he was lost in. "I'd rather we get to the caves before dark."

"There're no Monsters that are dangerous that come out at night though, right?"

"*Yes.* No *Monsters.*"

Humphrey had been correct in that they shouldn't dally around for too much longer, for, as their destination drew closer, the waning amber of the setting sun soon flooded the sky, bringing with it long shadows from the looming trees.

"How have we been walking nearly all day and gotten no farther," Sally complained, her body slack and hunched over as her legs ached.

"There's a science to it." The Death Knight tapped on the side of his helmet. "Roads are usually free of most danger; the wilderness has all the bad stuff. As this is the newbie area, it is quite . . . bland."

"Aside from our big ol' friend back there." She jerked a lazy thumb backward. "Plus, the feeling like I am being watched."

"No doubt we are."

Sally straightened back up and raised an eyebrow at him. "You think so?"

"Yes. Not by Monsters. That isn't too likely. But Players, Observers, and maybe others? We are an interesting Party."

"If the Architect wanted to, could they just . . . *[Smite]* us out of existence?" She fiddled with part of her hair.

"That's a strong . . . *maybe.*"

They walked on in silence for a while. Chuck and the dead Ranger—Sally decided to call him Frank—stumbled on behind them at a slight distance. The former had somehow managed to regenerate the flesh and clothing that had been burned away in the tomb fight. His health was still deep red on the UI, but otherwise, he looked as he had the previous day.

The road was mostly shadowed now as the sun had sunk closer to the horizon, with beams of orange occasionally making their way through the gaps in the trees. It was cooler now, and the light breeze that had flourished throughout the day had increased its efforts a little. Eventually, some rolling hills could be seen through the dense woodland, a few peaks rising up in the distance.

"We are just about there." Humphrey pointed with an outstretched digit. "The dirt pathway here will lead to the goblin caves."

She squinted her eyes. There was indeed a dirt pathway coming up. "Do we need to worry about the goblins? They aren't like . . . Level Eight and more sharp edges than necessary?"

"I'm not sure how many edges are necessary—"

"One, maybe two—*max.*"

"But they are low level. Their danger mostly comes from greater numbers, but between the four of us we have almost a whole brain, I reckon . . ."

"So just funnel them into a choke point. Fair enough." She nodded and started to think of potential scenarios as they left the road to follow the dirt path.

Perhaps "dirt path" was a little generous. There was a slightly worn path in the ground that wound and meandered around the slightly sparser trees. It was a breadcrumb trail to guide those with little navigational skills—or no map, as the case may be.

"So you go in first, alright?" Sally had decided that was the best plan in almost any scenario that didn't involve eating Theo. Humphrey *was* the designated minion.

"As you wish." He turned and nodded deeply to her, almost bowing—an unnecessary formality to make her uncomfortable.

"Chuck and Frank are best used behind me to protect against flanking or anything sneaking up on us. I will support you in taking out weakened ones if you get overwhelmed." She rubbed her chin and tilted her head.

"Sounds like a reasonable plan, *ha-ha*."

"You aren't convinced?" The laugh didn't have the usual ridiculous pomp to it.

"Being away from my connection to the System has left me feeling a little lost without access to the knowledge I am used to accessing on a whim. I would not say that I am scared, but the unknown has brought fear into me even when it is unwarranted."

Sally frowned at the Death Knight. "These are valid thoughts, Hump. You did a brave thing, and I'm here to support you through it." It was unlike the skullhead to be anything but annoying, and he hadn't shown any amount of trepidation when fighting the cyclops—or maybe she was too focused to notice.

"Thank you, *Sally the Unliving*. I hope to fill the hole of not-knowing with other, more joyful things." The flames at the back of his helmet lit slightly brighter.

"I hope to fill my tum with some gobbo meat." She grinned, giving him a light punch on the arm. "At least, if they are edible and don't taste like regret."

It was then that the cave came into view. Less than a handful of trees ahead, a dark toothless maw spanned across dark gray stone—a hill of rock rising above the tree line. The entrance was perhaps just over a dozen feet in width and height, a rough circle almost. Just outside the cave, a bucket, two stools, and what remained of a campfire lay strewn across the scuffed clearing.

Sally approached cautiously as Humphrey drew his greatsword. The chairs looked like they were for guards to sit at, maybe? She knelt by the campfire, licked her finger and touched the wood within. *Still warm.* "Still warm," she repeated with a hushed tone as the Death Knight could not read her mind.

"Lots of boot marks through the muck and dust too," Humphrey added. "Not goblin-sized either."

Sally sighed and gazed off into the darkness of the cave. It would be just her luck to arrive just after some Party had already come through and cleared it out. What did that mean for her quest though? Did she just have to wait for them all to respawn? Could she just wander in and receive the [Quest Completion] even though she did none of the work?

Actually, that second one sounded quite preferable. "Let's check it out." She signaled to the Death Knight with a nod. "See what actually happened?"

"I will lead the way—perhaps you can make use of that torch now rather than relying on my radiant personality, *ha-ha!*"

That was more like the Humphrey she knew. She winced and stumbled back a couple of steps as she withdrew her torch, forgetting that it would come out fully lit. She took one last look back to the woods and road behind them, shooing Chuck out of her line of vision, but nothing untoward caught her eye. With a shrug, she followed the Death Knight into the cave.

If the entrance had been any indication, the inside of the caves confirmed the fact that something was amiss. Or, at least, the dead goblin bodies did. *Imagine raising a zombie goblin army.* She sulked internally once more—one day, raising the dead would be a power in her grasp. She demanded it. There were at least half a dozen in just this starting area of their once home.

Silently, they gingerly walked over slain goblins, broken furniture, and shards of split rock. They stopped in a wide chamber to observe the destruction. In a way it was haunting—the flickering light of the torch casting dancing shadows from the lifeless bodies of the short Monsters. In another way, it was plain annoying that they missed out on all this experience and loot.

Humphrey put away his sword and shrugged before folding his arms. "Sucks for us, I suppose."

Sally groaned and rubbed her face with her free hand.

She was about to complain some more when her voice caught in her throat—a sound from the other side of the chamber stopped her dead in her tracks.

The Party slowly turned their heads as a barrel at the side of the room slowly started to tip over with an ominous *creak*.

## CHAPTER TWENTY-SIX

# Small Blessings

The barrel clattered to the rocky floor and its contents launched out toward them. Sally pulled her dagger out but paused in surprise at the dark shape that rolled across the floor, as it stopped just before them.

"Hello!" A small, green face beamed up at them, eyes slightly askew from her dizzying arrival.

Sally scrunched up her nose at the small goblin girl lying upside down. Her dagger wavered in her hand before she relented with a sigh. "Who are you?"

The goblin girl righted herself and dusted off her plain brown dress. Both the dress and the beige undershirt she wore were stained and grubby—perhaps from what was inside the barrel. Once again she beamed up at the Party before speaking. "My name is Bella. What's yours?"

"I'm Sally, and this is my friend Humphrey." She knelt as she jerked a thumb back toward the Death Knight, who was looking more perplexed than the zombie. "The other two are Chuck and Frank, but they don't talk much."

"Momma said I talk too much." Bella looked shyly at the floor. "Or, at least, she used to."

Sally sucked in some air and glanced around the room. "Are . . . any one of these your momma?" A finger jabbed in the air toward some of the dead goblins.

"Oh no, Momma just moved away." The bright smile returned to the young goblin's face. "Bad adventurers came here and killed everyone, but not me!"

"Is that because you hid, little one?" Humphrey stood a little closer but still loomed over the little girl.

"No Mister, I hid because I was scared of the dark." She gave a quick glare to part of the chamber not currently lit by the torch. "I didn't die because I *can't* die."

The Death Night raised his lack of eyebrows toward Sally.

"Well." The zombie tilted her head. "What do you mean by that?"

"I'm Bella the Invincible! You can try it out if you like. I trust you."

Sally brought her dagger and placed it to the neck of the goblin girl, who did not flinch.

"*Whoa, whoa!*" Humphrey interrupted, waving his hands and kneeling with them. "Why would you go straight for the throat? Just try and cut the back of her hand if you must."

Sally opened and closed her mouth a couple of times waiting for words to come out—but none did. With a shrug, she removed the blade from Bella's neck and put it against the back of the offered hand. "If I get overcome by bloodlust and start eating you, I apologize."

"Okay!" Bella beamed and stared wide-eyed at the blade against her skin.

Sally paused, gradually seeing the girl as less of a loot pinata and more of an adorable pinata. She drew the blade of her dagger across the goblin's hand. At first, nothing happened—and then a long crimson rivulet formed across the wound.

"*Owwy!* Why'd you do that?"

"Oh, I'm sorry—I thought—"

"Hah! Just kidding." Bella stuck her tongue out and waved her hand in the zombie's face. The blood began to disappear, and the evidence of the act vanished within a few brief seconds.

"*Ha-ha!* How curious!" Humphrey narrowed his empty sockets and regarded the small girl with curiosity.

"What do you think?" Sally turned to him, eyebrow raised. "Really over-the-top regeneration?

"Most likely."

Bella yawned and rubbed her red eyes, pushing her dusty black hair away from her face. "So what are you doing here? You don't look like adventurers."

"We are here to . . . uh." Sally scrunched her face up thinking of a different reason than wholesale slaughter. "We are looking for strong Monsters to join our Party." Her almost-grimace of a smile was probably not as convincing as she had hoped.

"A Party does sound fun . . . but maybe you could help me instead? Do you know the way to where Momma lives?" Her eyes widened, the torchlight dancing alongside her excitement.

"I don't know where anything is . . . Humphrey?"

The Death Knight shrugged. Somehow, his face had softened. "This is the only goblin cave I know of. Do you know where your mother went, little one?"

Bella twiddled with a loose strap of her dress and kicked some dust slowly from the cave floor. "No, not really? She said there is a place with special water nearby? Some of the clan were sick, as they are not as invincible as me!"

Sally sat on the floor and crossed her tired legs—a yawn escaping from her mouth as well. With a gentle toss, she threw the torch to the floor so that she could rest her chin on both palms as the little goblin sat down opposite.

"Special water? There's a Rejuvenation Fountain not too far from here—that would be my best guess." Humphrey sat down too, his metal armor scraping against the rock floor as it shifted into a comfortable position.

"Sure?" Bella nodded, seemingly able to inflect the majority of her sentences into questions.

"But sleep here first, right?" Sally frowned at the Death Knight. "Or should we be traveling more at night, given our dispositions? I think we burnt ourselves out too much walking in the day."

"*Yes.* To the sleeping at least. Respawn won't be for a while, so we're as safe as it can get."

"Amazing. So, Bella, if you join with us for a bit, we can help you out and protect you." Sally grinned at the goblin.

"Okay!"

---

Bella has joined the Party

---

Sally sent Chuck and Frank back closer to the entrance by a bit—the least they could do was be an early warning system for anything approaching. If the goblins respawned around them in the cave, then that would be an interesting morning alarm, but she trusted that Humphrey had a reasonable guess on when that might actually occur.

Having an invincible Party member sounded good on paper, but a child with no ability or weapon proficiency wouldn't be of much use. She doubted that they could roll the girl into battle to absorb blows . . . unless they strapped her to a shield. No. That was a crazy thought from a tired brain. A self-healing shield was a poor use of such power.

They briefly arranged some of the unbroken furniture with the largest shards of those that did not survive the carnage into a makeshift barricade. It split them from the two zombies near the front, but the more time they had to react to danger, the better. A handful of bedrolls and furs not matted with blood were fashioned into beds for the three of them—more comfortable than the bare, rocky floor.

"Sally?" Bella rolled over and furrowed her brow.

"Ya-huh?" She was staring at the ceiling. The flickering of the torch was keeping her awake, but they had kept it out for the goblin girl.

"You are a weird-looking goblin."

"Mmm? Oh—my green skin? I'm actually a zombie." She turned her head to the girl to see her reaction.

"Oh? Okay!" Bella beamed and closed her eyes. The rattling sound of the Death Knight snoring did not seem to bother her.

Sally looked back at the ceiling as a new message popped up in the air next to her.

Quest Updated - Goblin Cave: Find Momma

She gave the retreating text a half-smile. While this had certainly been a less physically taxing adventure than planned . . . it was still odd. Stale air slowly exhaled from her lungs as her eyes closed. Everything seemed to be a series of odd events—but could it really be anything else? If she was a normal Monster or a normal Player, then her life would probably be more normal. Instead, not only was she a mess, but also a mess magnet.

She drifted off to sleep with thoughts of her previous life playing on her mind, trying to smudge the memories so the different shards could join and be more cohesive.

A finger prodded her awake. She growled and had to hold herself back from gnashing at the imposing digit. As her red eyes blinked back open, the goblin girl was squatting down next to her with a wide smile across her face.

"Wakey-wakey! You sleep like you're dead? *Heeee!*" She squealed and ran off, happy enough to be an annoyance.

Sally groaned and sat up. Soft sunlight filtered in from the cavern entrance, barely making it far enough to properly light their chamber but giving enough ambience so the torch was not needed. She gingerly flung it into her Inventory fully lit again, being careful not to burn herself.

Humphrey was leaning against the wall, arms folded. "Careful running about in here," he scolded Bella gently before turning to the zombie. "Oh, morning, Sally. I hope you rested well."

"A full sleep that has restored all our Health Points—hard to imagine that ever being bad. But I hope you did too." She smiled and dusted herself down.

"It was exemplary! *Ha-ha!*" He beamed back at her and then his expression dropped. "First time I have ever slept. It was frightening—how do you reconcile the gap in consciousness?"

"I guess . . . we don't? It's a nice break from existing, at least on a functional level. Did you dream?"

"I did!" Bella hopped over beside them. "I did! I dreamt of adventurers coming to kill me, but they couldn't no matter what they tried!"

Sally pursed her lips. Perhaps better to just move on from that. The girl seemed happy enough. Her eyes caught the empty sockets of the Death Knight, and it seemed he had the same thought.

"I did not." He shrugged, turning his gaze away and back toward the cave entrance. Chuck was in view and staring up at the rocky ceiling with great intensity. "We should move soon. We need to get to the Rejuvenation Fountain and start to make plans for Yarch."

She nodded and brought up her STAR—there was a notification in the chat.

Theo: Almost died to a bunch of orcs. Didn't think they came out this way
Theo: Camping for the night to recover—will meet near Yarch, give coords if you can

"Tall stack of BBQ goodness almost died," she repeated for the Death Knight, "said there were orcs. He is totally going to be a liability for us, huh?"

"Probably, *ha-ha*." Humphrey grinned before rubbing his chin. "*Orcs* though? Interesting."

"What's this?" Bella pointed to the menu hovering over the STAR. "There's a weird bit here that doesn't match?"

Sally frowned and brought her wrist closer to her red eyes. It was like a part of the menu had wrapped around and gotten lost behind whatever UI box it had been assigned to—only the barest of blurred white text lingered at the edge of the holographic display.

"I never saw that before, Bella—good eyes!" She beamed down at the little girl who seemed overjoyed by the praise. Sally tried to jab at the near-hidden text.

On the third attempt, she struck the mystery, and a buzzing static filled her head, causing her to clench her hands against her temples—a vertigo sensation lolling her forward.

Humphrey reached out to steady her as something in her skull popped, and then the tension was relieved as a notification popped up in front of her blurred, watery eyes.

CHAPTER TWENTY-SEVEN

# Un-Found-ed

Map Unlocked

*Finally*," Sally hissed as she wiped the water from her eyes. At least her tear ducts seemed to work? She was sure that would be useful for some dramatic moments in the future. Like when she finally got to eat Theo, and he tasted gorgeous.

"You okay?" Bella tugged on the side of her skirt, withdrawing her from the brief daydream.

She looked down at the small goblin, the girl's red eyes wide and worried. Did all Monsters have exceptionally cute children? It made the prospect of Players blazing through and murdering everything that little bit more sinister and cold. Not that she would have done any different—though, if faced with the "humanity" of Monsters like Bella, perhaps her blade would have faltered.

"Yeah, I am. I have . . . stolen some of the power that adventurers have, to use to help Monsters." She smiled and gave the goblin a pat on the head. "It just takes a while to activate and is uncomfortable."

Bella cooed, wonder filling her eyes. "So you're a *hero!*"

Humphrey scoffed, and Sally clucked her tongue at him, crossing her arms. "I'm what's known as a boss Monster." The goblin practically vibrated with joy at this revelation.

"Do you have a fancy title?"

"I'm *Sally the Unliving!*" She unfolded her arms to strike a somewhat heroic pose.

"That's . . . okay!" The smile on Bella's face faded a little, but she still seemed enthusiastic.

Humphrey coughed and gestured toward the outdoors with a nod. "Should Sally the Unliving lead the way?"

"I have a neat little navigation . . . arrow thing." She pointed to a cone hovering over her head that they couldn't see. The transparent-white shape jostled and turned depending on which way she was facing. "After we sort this fountain problem and get Bella somewhere safe, we will sit down and go over the map and the functions."

The Death Knight nodded and pushed himself away from the wall. He began to move some of the furniture out of the way so that they could pass. The two zombies standing guard looked just as bored and absent-minded as they always did.

Sally stretched out her arms. Sleep on the hard floor hadn't been softened that much by the furs found. Perhaps she had been spoiled by the bed in Hillan; it wasn't too common for Monsters to have a nice bed to sleep in. Her Inventory opened up, and she took one of the Common Daggers out.

"Here." She passed it to the little goblin. "Just in case."

Bella bit her lip and immediately tucked the blade into the leather belt around her dress. "Momma said not to play with knives."

"Well, this one isn't for playing." Sally raised an eyebrow at the girl. "You may be invincible, but this is a tool for defense."

"Okay!" Bella nodded enthusiastically.

Humphrey grunted, more to let them know he was done shifting chunks of wood than that the process was exerting. He had seemed eager to get moving, which was not entirely odd but still raised a slight suspicion in the mind of the boss zombie.

With just a brief glance back around the chamber, they began to head out, Chuck and Frank joining along as they passed. Chuck was now back at full health but still had his reduced level. At least the other zombie was relatively regular—if you discounted the fact that he was once a Player that Chuck had turned.

Rather than let herself get caught up in another conundrum of how this whole existence functioned, she instead bathed in the warm light of the morning as she stepped out of the cave. The evening gusts of the day before had all but left, and the trees stood patiently, allowing the sound of birdsong to be the prime melody of the woodlands.

"It looks like it is . . . that way." She pointed farther away from the road, almost behind the hills where the cave had been carved into. "It looks like we will have to circle around."

"There will probably be an easy route close by—the System doesn't think much of Player intelligence." Humphrey grinned, flames dancing behind his head.

"What's a Player?" Bella squealed up from beneath them.

"They're, uh, basically the adventurers that come to kill you." Sally scratched the side of her head and narrowed her eyes at the goblin. "Say, Bella, if you're invincible, you must have survived more than one attack, right?"

"Oh, yes! Everyone dies but they come back after a couple of days—but they don't remember?"

"But you do." The statement weighed heavily on the zombie as she tried to imagine the poor goblin having to witness her clan cut down around her every few days. Was it any relief that they came back? She shuddered.

The Death Knight caught the look on her face and tilted his head as they rounded the rough hill. "Do not forget that these Monsters are System-created. They live and die with little consequence as the System determines."

"Like yourself?"

Humphrey opened his skeletal mouth but promptly closed it.

Sally didn't think that the System should make that sort of determination. Sure, the Monsters may not have souls—or the freedom to choose a life outside of their designated role—but that didn't mean that they shouldn't be allowed control. The talking skull had managed to escape his constraints, and she hoped that he could see where she was going with this.

Bella skipped along ahead of them by a few feet. The little goblin seemed perfectly capable of avoiding her fate. Maybe due to an error in the System? With a flick of her STAR, she brought up her Party Member's screen.

Bella - Unique Goblin

"Huh, says she is Unique," she murmured to the Death Knight flanking her.

"Momma always said that too!" The girl with apparently exceptional hearing giggled.

"Odd." The flames from the back of his helmet flickered in contemplation.

As they clambered over a group of small boulders, they hopped down onto a path. Again, only a slightly more apt name than the worn passageway to the cave, but this one at least seemed to conveniently pass along a clear route into this part of the large hill. A baby mountain, even.

She shrugged and helped the goblin jump down from the rocks. As obvious as it was, the route would take them to their destination, which was the minimum you could expect from a path. As Chuck fell from the rock onto his front, taking some damage, she opened up chat.

Sally: Going to Rejuv Fountain south of Yarch

Sally bit her lip and frowned as she went to close the UI.

Sally: Bring seasonings x

She hissed a curse at herself and went to catch up with the others.

Slowly, as their walk ascended up the hill, they rose above the level of the tree cover. A carpet of gentle waving greens covered almost as far as the eye could see, the morning sun illuminating everything and making the gaps in cover all the more obvious. A rough circle where a town sprung from the green—like a tree stump of darkened wood and red tile. Smaller clearings left pockmarks in the green fabric of the region, a sliver of different shade signifying the road they had traveled not too far off.

Sally narrowed her eyes—trying to see any Monster or Players in the nearby area. She wasn't sure whether to feel relieved or concerned. Something still didn't sit right in her head, an awkward lump that refused to let her sit at ease.

"If you are wondering why it is so quiet," Humphrey said and joined her gaze, "in the three or so weeks, most Players have moved on from this area." He briefly shifted his focus to the goblin squatting down, observing a bug intently. "*Most*, but not all. After the first week, when a lot of Players died in the second area, people started to slow down a bit—no use in rushing."

"So the ones still remaining here are either incompetent or extra cautious."

"Both equally dangerous in their own ways, *ha-ha*." The Death Knight gave her a pat on the back, his plated hands not jostling her slim frame as much as she had expected.

With a few more twists and turns, they eventually made it to some kind of plateau. The rock was a worn gray, almost smoothed intentionally—perhaps just buffeted over time from the elements . . . though that would have to have been artificially so. In the middle of this rough thirty-foot circle sat a fountain made of white marble. Smooth folds had been carved into the main body of the object, with an ornate swan-like creature rising from the middle.

A soft trickle of water ran from the beak of the bird statue as it looked to be caught mid-escape from the fountain proper. Just at a cursory glance, it would make more sense for there to be a spout rather than a trickle. Sally held her hand out to stop her troop as she narrowed her eyes.

On her own, she gently trod toward it. It was beautiful in design and showed no signs of wear from the elements. The interior of the fountain became visible as she neared it—a low pool of clear water. Totally devoid of any sort of algae or moss or little bugs that you would perhaps expect from running water left to nature. The bottom of the fountain was clearly visible, a plain circle of white marble slightly lower than the ground she stood upon.

Circling around the white marble, she couldn't help but lose her gaze on the horizon. Now even higher than the trees, she could see out to where the woodlands finally ended and new regions of different shade and texture teased their existence. She licked her sharp teeth as the unhindered breeze rolled through them. She looked down at the far side of the fountain and saw a satchel flattened against the ridged wall. With a gesture for the group to come over, she knelt and retrieved it.

Setting it on the edge of the fountain, another breeze rolled through, rustling her hair. Something felt odd though, different to the first gust.

Her skin prickled, and words caught in her throat as she turned around.

The sharp pain of a dagger plunged into her back.

## CHAPTER TWENTY-EIGHT

# Blood and Water

Sally coughed out blood as she spun around, the shape of a man appearing behind her, emerging from thin air with a shimmer. The damage from that one attack was huge, with pain like nothing she had experienced so far, and her STAR buzzed with low HP warnings.

Her last-minute reflex to turn was the only thing that had prevented the blade from burying straight into the back of her neck. The sweat and scowl of the assailant, half of his face obscured by a black bandanna that matched his dark leathers and cloak, gave credence to his intended plan.

She dodged a follow-up attack and hit him with *[Hex: Slow]*—drawing her own dagger in the process. Even with the slowing curse he was remarkably fast. His eyes burned with an unnatural green glow that wafted around his hands.

> Party member Frank has died

She stumbled backward out of the reach of the Rogue and glanced over at the group. Three more figures in similar garb were among the Party. Humphrey roared out as twin blades screeched along his armor. His *[Adrenaline]* activated as he reached for his sword, red flame bursting from the back of his skull.

Chuck had taken a blade to the chest and was wrestling with a Rogue with flowing blond hair for control over the stuck dagger. A battle he was likely to lose in short order. Sally cursed and switched her *[Hex: Slow]* over to this opponent and spun to face her own attacker. She had not seen Bella but didn't fear much for the invincible goblin.

The green-eyed Rogue stepped toward her, a second dagger in his off hand, blades of silver flickering in the sunlight as they carved through the air toward her. She was stepping back toward the edge of the summit, closer and closer with every attack dodged. She grabbed an item from her belt and chose the right moment.

She leapt at the man as the momentum of his attacks was at a lull. The sharp points still pierced her skin as she collided with the surprised man, putting him slightly off-balance. Her own dagger found purchase in his upper arm—not an efficient place to damage, but the pain caused the Rogue to drop one of his weapons, loosening the pain in her torso. Sally popped the cork from the Healing Potion and downed it as she leaned into the still-held blade.

The empty glass bottle dropped to the floor, and she grabbed the offending arm holding the dagger in her gut. As the Rogue tried to withdraw, her hungry maw opened wide. She felt strong. She felt powerful. She watched the Rogue try and recoil away, but fear painted his eyes, and panic overcame him.

*Blood and warmth.* Her sharp teeth ripped out part of his neck.

Crimson stained the soft gray of the hilltop as the gurgling bandit slunk to the floor. One hand tried to stem the flow of blood from his neck, the other fumbling for healing of his own.

"Steve is in trouble," a gruff voice called from the fray behind.

It was dull to her, as if half the woods away. All that she could feel was a weird beating inside her . . . a heartbeat? Not her own, surely—perhaps that of the fallen. *Steve is in more than trouble.* She scoffed and brought her sharp blade down, straight through his leather armor into his heart. The pounding in her head stopped.

The scrape of hardened metal against stone drew her attention to the rest of the battle. She turned in time to see the greatsword of Humphrey radiate dark energy and slice a leg off one of the Rogues in a brutal upswing. A second Rogue had taken a nasty wound across the chest, black leather armor split and darkened by blood, and had taken some steps backward in fervent thoughts of escape. Chuck had overpowered the last of the Rogues, assisted by the *[Hex: Slow]* and was happily making a feast of his bounty.

*[Hex: Slow]* hit the nervous Rogue as they turned to run—stumbling in confusion as lethargy suddenly hit them. The second thing to suddenly hit them was a crossbow bolt, and they flopped heavily into the rocky floor.

The Death Knight stood over the maimed attacker, his sword resting across his shoulder as his eyes blazed bright red, jettisoning angry flame into the summit's breeze. He had been injured but did not bleed—instead, he just looked more furious at the injustice.

"*Wait*," Sally hissed, wiping the blood from her mouth. "They could be useful."

She stumbled over to the figure who was almost sweating as heavily as they were bleeding. Sally felt a weird elation mixed with discomfort. Not nauseated, but the kind of jittery excitement you feel from the depths of your stomach. She knelt, stabilizing herself with hands on her knees, as she observed the Rogue.

This must have been the gruff-voiced one, although they looked anything but gruff right now. Their light blue eyes were a contrast to the rough five o'clock shadow and heavy brow that now rose high in panic. It was obvious they were in pain, and Sally was no sadist, but she needed some answers.

"Why'd you do this?" She shook, more from unease than anger.

"C-came here to kill ya," his earnest reply came, his gruff voice now uncertain, afraid.

"Dumb." She shook her head. "Only four of you and you didn't even focus on me. Whiffed your one shot and now look what happened."

The Rogue's eyes darted over to Chuck chewing at the guts of the blond-haired Rogue and then back to Sally. "N-not four of us." A wry, panicked smile curled up the side of his face as rivulets of sweat coursed down his round face.

"Not . . . " Sally frowned as her eyes scoured the area. "They were hidden and kidnapped the goblin?"

A coughed laugh erupted from the injured Rogue, seemingly finding some bittersweet ending to his plan. "We'll take her and do what we do to all M-Monsters . . . "

"One last question." Sally stood and dusted off the gray rock dust from her dress. "It was the annoying Cleric that sent you, right?"

He said nothing, but there was the faintest hint of recognition that gave it away. The Rogue licked his lips and jabbered soundlessly, perhaps about to try and negotiate or throw more hurtful comments.

"Humps." She gestured to the Death Knight. She was at her limit for compassion for those who decried Monsters but were one themselves.

The greatsword burned with the dark energy of *[Grave Strike]* and carved through the air in a clean arc. The head of the Rogue sailed off into the tree line below.

Sally held her head in her hands for a moment, trying to exhale the vertigo and the unease from her system. She couldn't wait to eat that miserable Cleric. Theo was a delicacy, but whatever the Cleric was called, she just wanted to gnaw and gnash and mulch that scrawny frame until nothing but bone and gristle remained.

"You alright?"

The heavy hand of the Death Knight rested on her shoulder. It was oddly comforting. She bit back the sobs welling in her throat and raised her head from her hands. She smiled up at the demonic skull of her friend, but her eyes gave away what emotion lay inside.

"Being a Monster is not easy," he said softly. "Players can kill us with abandon as they see us as below them—not real. When it comes to morality, the ethics of taking a life . . . We are not different to them, and they to us."

"Nobody hunts Players down just for trying to exist, though." Her lip wobbled as she tried to throw out an exaggerated pout to mask her feelings.

"Nobody yet." He grinned, his lack of eyebrows raising.

"You big jerk." Sally gave him a light punch to the chest and a smile. "I can be an ethical villain still, can't I?"

The Death Knight shrugged and stood away from the zombie, then turned his head to the path. "Should we try and find the little one?"

Sally looked around at the carnage atop the summit. Chuck was contently sitting atop the remains of his meal. Gore caked down his front. Three further Rogues lay in pools of blood, the red marring the plain gray of the smooth rocky hill. Spatters of crimson—some of them her own—dotted the plain white marble of the fountain.

"You think I have time to loot?" She bit her lip.

The Death Knight shrugged once more. "You are the villain here, *ha-ha*."

She cursed under her breath and jogged uneasily over to each of the bodies in turn, scolding Chuck for being lazy and letting Frank die in the process. The blond-haired Rogue surely would have died from embarrassment from losing to such a low-level zombie. Had they not already died from being killed.

348 Gold
Uncommon Leather Hood
Uncommon Leather Chest
Uncommon Leather Gloves
Uncommon Leather Boots
Rare Leather Leggings
Poison Supplies (5)
Speed Earring (2)
Healing Potion (2)

"I'd say that was worth the trauma." She brushed down her new armor set—which still appeared as her waitress outfit. "Not as light as the basic gear, but it should offer me more protection, right? And these Speed Earrings are pretty cute—I'd wear them even if they weren't useful." They dangled from her ears, golden kite shapes with some kind of shiny gemstone that swirled between a verdant green and mustard yellow.

"*Yes.*"

Sally felt a little bad that Humphrey couldn't enjoy the looting experience—perhaps there would be some other way to improve him? With one last glance, they began heading away from the fountain, her satchel stuck in her Inventory for the time being. Whatever the fountain was actually used for, she no longer cared.

About twenty feet down the winding path she stopped and knelt. Humphrey stopped behind her, and Chuck stumbled straight into the back of the Death Knight.

There was a little blood on the path. She ran her finger through it and licked the crimson off. "This blood is *blood*." She twisted her head around to confirm to the pair, who were giving each other evil glares after having collided.

She stood and moved ahead—another drip of blood. Her feet increased their speed, her new boots comfortable, as the splashes of blood became more frequent.

They rounded a corner, almost running now, and stopped.

In a large smear of crimson, the prone figure of the small goblin lay, tiny hands clutched to her stomach holding bloodied shapes of reds and pinks.

## CHAPTER TWENTY-NINE

# One Life to Live

Bella!" Sally called out and raced down the path.

The prone figure rolled over and sat up. Blood matted her black hair and soaked through her clothing. Despite the macabre sight, a wide smile beamed out from behind the gore.

"Are you . . . okay?" Sally stopped and knelt beside the girl.

"Adventurers are full of these warm squishy bits!" She held up a handful of what looked to be intestines.

Humphrey caught up and glanced over the area. The trail of blood led off to the side, over the outcropping. He peered over before returning to the pair with a nod.

Chuck sped past them, tripping and sliding almost a dozen feet down the path before striking a rock wall.

Sally winced and then picked up a rather bloody dagger from beneath where the goblin had been lying. "So the bad person tried to make off with you, and you gave them a . . . little stabbing until they dropped you?"

"Only for *defense*." The goblin nodded.

"Neat." The zombie boss sat down on the floor and crossed her legs. "A full Party of Rogues, huh?"

"It has advantages." The Death Knight leaned against the rock wall to watch over them. "Lots of very high-damage attacks and evasion. No tank or healer though—you could see how easily they came undone without any support."

Sally nodded. It could have gone much differently though. It was perhaps only by luck that she had noticed the breeze being blocked by the invisible figure beside her—it set her on edge enough to avoid what was possibly a certain death blow. Once the element of surprise had worn off, she quickly overpowered them with her strength. They had made the mistake of attacking the zombies and focusing on Humphrey first. Either they had anticipated the assassination would have been easier to pull off or underestimated who was the true threat.

"You got rid of the mean adventurers? They won't come back?" Bella's red eyes looked up into Sally's own.

"Players don't come back." She nodded, giving the girl a pat on the head.

"*Good.*"

Sally smiled sadly. It *was* good, but being the final end to someone was a weight. To kill a Monster was bad enough when they may respawn in the future and be real again—regardless of if their memories were retained—but for a Player it was final. It's what made potentially eating Theo all the sweeter.

"Let's have a look at this satchel, huh?" She brought up her Inventory and drew out the small brown sack. It was made out of some kind of rough hessian fabric, a leather strap running from one stitched side to the other. Sally flipped open the small flap and peered inside. From within, a sheet of paper and an odd rock were retrieved.

The writing on the page did not make sense to her—and not because this one was actually a drawing. She thought what were possibly words seemed to be disjointed and incomplete, leaving the page looking like a gathering of cut grass. The stone was smooth and almost flat, with a series of lines carved onto one side.

"Oh! I know this one!" Bella beamed and reached for both objects as they were easily relinquished. "Momma used to play this with me all the time!"

Sally watched as the goblin lay down on the floor with the paper in front of her, humming a tune as she placed the rock onto the paper. Her feet gently kicked at the air as her brow furrowed, her hand twisting the rock and changing its place between the mess of lines.

"It says"—Bella hopped to her feet—"there is some kind of village hidden nearby, and there is a password."

Sally raised an eyebrow at the Death Knight.

"I . . . know of no other villages in this area." He shrugged, scraping his armor against the stone wall.

"It's a *secret*," the goblin whispered. "That's why there is a password?"

"That's where your momma is?" The zombie stood up and stretched out her back. Although she had healed the damage from the attack, there was an uncomfortable ache where the blade had struck.

The little girl nodded enthusiastically. "The note says the entrance is at the fountain; you have to speak the word to enter, and it takes you there!"

"Convenient. Hey, Chuck! We are going back up." She waved at the slumped heap of zombie still mashed against the wall farther down the path. Reluctantly he heeded her call and shambled his mangled body into a walking position.

"I hope we eventually put him out of his misery." Humphrey shook his head. "Perhaps he will just respawn back at the diner and live a simple life of getting killed by low levels until none remain."

"Nah." Sally shook her head. "You'd be crazy to assume there would only be one . . . wave of Players. Is that what it was?"

"Everyone did come at once, pretty much. Perhaps you are correct. Certainly, as Players die off there might be a need to replenish them—why not also to backfill some of the earlier zones?"

Sally nodded but just looked over to the sea of green. Three or so weeks wasn't really enough time to establish a new normal. What would this place look like in a couple of months or a year or two? It wasn't likely that the Architect would just let the Players run dry and leave the world inhabited by aimless, System-created Monsters. What even was the purpose of all this? She exhaled through her nose to push the thoughts away.

"I've noticed all the Players so far have been human." She tried to distract herself from the big questions.

"Yes. Any human you see is a Player; there are no System-created humans and no other choice when Players . . . enter the world."

"So who runs all the towns?"

"It's usually other humanoids with different ancestries—dwarven, elven, gnomish, and the like."

Sally scratched her head, undecided on whether that was cool or made no sense. It was certainly an odd choice, either way. At the very least, it would make it easier to spot potential enemies or those that were less of a threat.

They reached the summit once more and strode over to the fountain, not paying much heed to the corpses or crimson marring the area. Bella hopped onto the marble wall with a little struggle before turning back to face the group.

The goblin cleared her throat and then glared at them. "You have to be touching it." She waited as they each stepped up and did so, Chuck just slumping against the side. "Alright, and the password is <XXXXXX>."

Sally's ears dulled with a whining pain as the word struggled to parse. Unlike the System trying to fix itself, there was no pop of released pressure—just a lingering ring that reverberated throughout her skull. What followed was intense vertigo as a blue light fully encompassed her vision.

There was the brief feeling of falling—and then just as quickly, it ended.

She opened her eyes to a polished black floor. As she pushed herself up, she could see slim lines of turquoise running along every foot or so in two cardinal directions. A grid. Some source of light shone her way as Humphrey groaned and righted himself.

"Momma!" Bella hopped to her feet and ran off to a group of shadowed figures.

As Sally's eyes adjusted, she could see the handful of figures were also goblins—albeit older ones. As one with long choppy hair cradled Bella, a second goblin in dusty leather armor came closer.

He was pale, his normally green skin instead almost fully white, and his eyes were dense pools of obsidian that barely reflected the red of Humphrey's flame.

"You are safe here, outsiders." His voice was uncanny—a smooth and comforting tone where you would perhaps expect something scratchy or vile.

"Where . . . are we?" Sally rubbed her face. The almost limitless expanse of darkness surrounding them was nerve-wracking.

"You are in a place where the System cannot reach, I have carved this space from under its watchful gaze. We are all outsiders here."

Sally blinked a few times. The goblins in the background all looked . . . alive? Not constrained to their designated paths—free.

"You are all glitched, Unique forms shunted by the error of the System?" The Death Knight echoed her conclusion; his voice steeped in curiosity.

The goblin shook his head but smiled. "We prefer not to use those terms as they have negative connotations. Despite the fact we only have one life to live now, we see our new existence as a blessing."

"Same here." Sally smiled, pointing a thumb back at herself. "But with your new free will, why hide away? Are you just scared to die?"

"We seek to exist without the threat of adventurers, who are an ever-present threat. What would you have us do? We are but a handful of goblins only recently formed."

Sally sucked in a lungful of empty air and raised an eyebrow at Humphrey. "Well . . . how would you like a village? If you want a place in this world, you have to take it, live in it, and defend it just like anyone else."

"This . . . *is* our village." The white goblin gestured to the featureless expanse.

"No. This is a den of selfishness, thinking you can hide and covet your precious lives lest you lose them and what you think makes you different." She wagged a finger toward him. "You follow me into battle, and you prove how much value your life has by how willing you are to die for it."

The goblin spluttered, black eyes darting around the nothingness as if an answer lurked hidden away. "L-let me confer with the others." He scowled and made his exit with a short bow.

"A surprisingly rousing speech." Humphrey titled his head toward her to murmur his approval. "Although you are unlikely to win over hearts by calling them selfish for wanting to exist."

"Pretty sure I just stole that from somewhere." She shrugged. "I'm still new at this boss stuff. But imagine not only taking the village but setting it up as a home base for Monsters like us."

"I have my concerns, but I am willing to see how it plays out, *ha-ha*."

After a brief muttering of conversation, the pale goblin returned, a tired look on his face.

"We have agreed that we will assist you to take the village, whatever that may entail. Bella seems to think very highly of you." He cast a nervous glance over at Chuck, who stood completely still, dazed by the dark expanse. "Your words may be sour, but there is a sliver of truth to them."

"In that case, we should head back out of here and meet up with Theo!"

Bella has left the Party

Sally pouted, but her dead heart warmed slightly to see the little gobbo so happy to be back with her mother. A bright blue light flashed into view again, pain flaring at the back of her sockets, before a cool breeze made her realize they were now back outside the fountain.

She slumped against the marble wall of it as notifications popped up on her STAR.

Quest Complete
Daily Reward Available

"Huh, I always forget about that one."

## CHAPTER THIRTY

# Second Meat

Quest Complete: Find Momma
Experience Gained
50 Gold
Weapon Enhancement Kit
Armor Enhancement Kit
Daily Reward Received
Medium Medical Kit (3)
Stat Booster (1 Day) (1)

**S**ally pursed her lips and checked out the information on two of the items.

Weapon Enhancement Kit
Improves a Weapon by +1, Max level +7, One Use
Stat Booster (1 Day), Increases all Stats by 10% for 24 Hours

As much as it tempted her to use them, she instead stowed them away in her Inventory. You never knew when you might need them for later—a better weapon might be around the corner. Perhaps not at this hilltop summit where there was nothing but a failing fountain and a handful of error goblins worriedly listening to Bella explain how all these corpses came to be.

"You killed these adventurers?" The pale-white goblin had returned to them as her Party sat against the marbled circle of the supposed Rejuvenation Fountain. His brow was furrowed over his black-orb eyes, but he no longer looked nervous.

"Yeah, we've killed, what . . . at least ten Players by now?" She raised her eyebrow at the Death Knight beside her.

"Fourteen, I believe."

The pale goblin whistled. "My name is Henkk, by the way. Two *k*'s."

"Sally, Humphrey, and Chuck." She pointed between each of them. "One *k*."

As Henkk went to speak, they all paused and turned as a figure emerged from the pathway onto the summit: a man with messy brown hair and basic armor, who looked rather taken aback by the congregation currently before him.

"Ah, if it isn't Mr. Fifteen." Sally beamed and got to her feet. "Don't worry; he is with us . . . *for now.*"

"Um, hi." The Novice waved awkwardly. "I'm Theo."

"Theo is just as intent on breaking the System. This is Henkk; he has started gathering Monsters who have been afflicted by similar errors as we have."

Bella strode over with dagger in hand. "Is this not an adventurer?" She scowled at the man and weaseled over to hide behind Sally's legs.

"Technically, yes." Theo rubbed the back of his neck. "I don't really like it much here and have no interest in the arbitrary System this so-called Architect has burdened us with—expecting us to dance to his tune and join Parties in the—"

"So cute when he wants to destroy reality," Sally interrupted, trying not to drool. "Henkk and these . . . four other goblins have become Unique through their glitched existence, and so if they die . . ."

"They die for good, like Players." The Novice nodded. He turned toward the white goblin and knelt, head bowed low. "It would be an honor to fight alongside you for the cause and put my life on the line fighting for a better future for us all."

Sally short-circuited for a brief moment.

"Aren't you really weak, though?" Henkk frowned at the prostrating man. "I mean, us goblins aren't much for fighting, but you don't look like much either."

Theo maintained his bowed position, perhaps to hide his embarrassment. "What I lack in skill . . . I make up for in dedication and . . . perseverance?"

"I've heard worse, *ha-ha*." Humphrey walked up beside them. "You have the full Blue Slime Card Set now, then, yes? Then you are slightly more than useless."

"I've done better than that." Theo smiled, raising his head as a glimmer of light spun from his eyes.

"*Oh?*" The Death Knight tilted his head, interest filling his empty eye sockets.

Theo held out his hand; two rings adorned his fingers. The first was a ruby red gem with a hatching of silver carved into it that sat on a silver band. The second was a purple stone that seemed to absorb the light instead of reflecting it, and its band was dark black.

"Surely it doesn't work like that—*oh*, but the Card bonus too." Red flame danced from the back of Humphrey's helmet as he shrugged and shook his head with a smile.

"What does what now?" Sally wanted in on the details.

"Blue Slime Card full set reduces the cost of using *[Novice Strike]*. The Ring of Expert hit causes all melee hits to land but do severely reduced damage. The Youngling band allows you a follow-up strike if your melee strike does below a certain threshold in base damage." Humphrey beamed devilishly.

"So it's a death of a thousand cuts type thing?" She sucked in air at the incredulity of it. Here she was struggling against assassins and giants, and the forever-noob had devised an even more meme way to ruin his build.

"It's base weapon damage too, so using a wooden shortsword I only do one point of damage, but it's then boosted by my Strength and Novice bonuses when it actually hurts them." Theo stood back up and brushed the dust from his knee. "It's just a shame I don't have any points for other useful stats."

"Oh, here." Sally fiddled with her ears. "Take these earrings—they'll increase your Speed."

"That's great! Thank you so much, Sally." He took them and pinned them to his ears, the pretty jewelry vanishing once they were properly equipped.

"No problem. I am sure I will get them back eventually." She winked and tried not to stare at his chewable ears.

"So." Henkk cleared his throat. "About this village?"

Sally nodded, and as a group they sat down in one of the least corpse-y areas of the summit. After Henkk and Bella, they were introduced to the other three goblins.

First was Oleb, an oddly portly goblin who could consume rock and wood with no effort and no ill side effects. Second was Frena, Bella's mother. She could see long distances like a hawk. Then last was Jaxk, a thin, twitchy fellow who was apparently immune to fire. It wasn't exactly a ragtag group of elite mercenaries—but everyone had a place, no matter if their part was big or small.

Theo has joined the Party
Henkk has joined the Party

Sally beamed across at the Novice as he accepted the invite. Theo managed to keep his cool despite how often she was creepy around him. Either he had accepted that she was a threat—or no threat—or he really needed to put more points into Intelligence. It wasn't even an attraction thing, just familiarity mixed with forbidden fruit. She was hard-coded to want to eat fresh humans. She blinked as she realized she had been staring.

"What plan do you currently have?" The honey voice of the pale goblin seemed authoritative despite his diminutive figure. His apparent glitch was being able to create a portal to some kind of netherworld—a "hidden" place within the System.

"Well"—Sally wiped her mouth and looked over at the Death Knight—"I was thinking go in at night, kill everyone. Uh. Then the village is ours?"

Humphrey groaned and rolled his lack of eyes. "It is good fortune that you have me on our side. May I explain how the village structure works?"

The zombie nodded. "Assuming it is different than the Guild towns, yes."

"It is similar. There are a group of System-created village leaders—"

"I bet there's five," Sally murmured out the side of her mouth.

"One of them being a village Champion who is the final defender. Once all five are dead, the village will stop being populated."

"That seems like a strange way to design the System." Theo frowned and leaned back on his palms.

"*Yes, ha-ha.* I believe there was part of the System that was trialed but not fully implemented yet. Some offshoot of the Grand Tournament where guilds could have control over—"

"There's a *tournament?*" Sally's eyes lit up, and she didn't fail to notice that Theo had a similar reaction.

Humphrey sighed and rubbed the temples of his helmet. "Let's try not to die among the weeds before you go plotting future arcs, please."

Sally pouted but gave a raised eyebrow and knowing gaze to Theo, who returned it in kind.

"So," the Death Knight continued, "your original plan of entering the town at night and murdering everything is what we are going to do. But we need a focused approach."

"Hit the location of one or two of the known Leaders before they can gather or call reinforcements." Theo stroked his chin.

The goblins remained quiet for the most part, seemingly feeling outclassed or simply content enough to follow along with whatever plan was concocted. Henkk seemed to be absorbing the most information, perhaps because he felt responsible for those of his clan that had become Unique.

The white goblin spoke up. "And what of any adventurers?"

"We'll need to kill them too. Probably as a matter of urgency." Theo shrugged.

Sally felt her face flush—or was that just the anticipation? Maybe worry? Hopefully, not just excitement that Theo wanted to murder Players. What was it about killing Players that felt so good? She squirmed in her villain era.

"Agreed." Humphrey nodded. "Although it is most likely to be Novices and lower-level classes, if any, we must keep our wits about us and deal with the greatest threat."

"Hopefully that Cleric is there so I can pop his head off," Sally said a little louder than intended. Seeing the confused or concerned looks from some of the group, she clarified. "He attacked me before but ran off, and he also sent this all-Rogue group to assassinate me."

"How'd that work out for them?" Jaxk peeped up from the back.

" . . . Not *great?*" She frowned.

"We've got maps now," Humphrey interjected. "Let's go through a proper plan—it is near midday—that gives us time to decide on a strategy and get there by nightfall."

"Sure, sure." Sally waved her hand. "But now let me name the Party."

They sat in silence and watched her spin the STAR menus around, selecting the wrong options a couple of times as her brow furrowed further.

Eventually, her face lit up as the deed was done.

Party Renamed: The Outsiders

## CHAPTER THIRTY-ONE

# Sun Fall

I t was dark.

The cool breeze of the evening rustled through the shadows of woodland as tiny specks of amber light hung in the near distance. Illuminated by the slight red glow of the Death Knight, Sally huddled down behind a grouping of bushes.

"You remember the plan?" The voice of Humphrey was calm and level but still got her feeling a little anxious.

"Of course, we've gone through it several times since we left the fountain. Four groups for four of the Leaders—attack at the same time. The last chap is hiding away in the garrison so better to join up to kill him last."

"*Yes, yes*—I know it too; you don't have to tell me, *ha-ha.*"

She narrowed her eyes at the Death Knight. She supposed it made sense that she had been burdened with him. Theo would have been too much of a distraction, all alone here in the dark woods . . . It would have been the second worst decision, probably slightly after making Chuck one of the team leaders. To be fair to the clumsy zombie, he had the easier task.

Her STAR spun around, and she opened Party chat.

Sally: Team Dead in position
Theo: In position
Chuck: aaaaaaaaaaaaaaaaaaaaaaaaaa
Henkk: We're as ready as we'll ever be

"They didn't use their team names." She pouted at the Death Knight, who shrugged in response.

Together they crept from their hiding place and approached the village edge. There wasn't a lot of activity that could be seen in the sparse areas of lantern-lit glow. An occasional guard meandered through the cobbled roads, but it was by no means well-defended. From the map, the town formed a rough star shape with five roads converging to a central mass; buildings sprung up in the gaps like moss around a tree.

Their targeted Leader was perhaps the second most dangerous—which wasn't saying much. An elven blacksmith residing in their quarters in the forge. Even the System-created slept. There must have been no coincidences allowed when making this village, as each lower road "prong" had one of the Leader's residences, with the fifth one in the garrison at the apex of the village. It made the upcoming fight somewhat linear and structured . . . if everything went to plan.

They reached the back of the forge and crouched down behind a set of cut logs around twenty feet from the stone building. She ran her tongue along her sharp teeth. Trying to get the timing right on the first blow would be difficult, as once the alarm was raised, things would start to get dicey. Humphrey had no idea if the village was big enough to have a Champion. A bridge to cross when they got to it.

Henkk: We have the signal

Sally gulped. Frena had been put up as watch, being able to see the whole village from atop one of the trees. Her signal meant that the rotating guards were at their farthest points from the Leaders' positions. This was the point of no return.

Sally: All Teams Go

Theo sighed and closed his STAR. He had already drawn his wooden shortsword, but his hand rested on a sheathed dagger. Sometimes a meme was not enough. His footfalls were near silent as the grass of the woods turned to soft dirt—and then he was there, standing atop a stone doorstep. The backdoor of the inn. With a deep breath, he pushed the door open. Thankfully, it was not locked. Double thankfully, it didn't make an awful creak as it slowly swung on its hinges. Darkness loomed directly inside, but he stepped within to close the door gently behind. It wouldn't do to get caught by the guard patrol if they circled back.

With controlled breathing, he stepped from what must be a storeroom into a dimly lit corridor. A stairway led upwards directly to his left. A wide doorway in front of him opened into a tavern area, with two low lanterns illuminating the dark wooden tables and edges of chairs. Two figures sat hunched over empty steins, a dull snore radiating through the empty space.

As he licked his dry lips, he made the first step to head to the next floor.

Halfway up the staircase a floorboard creaked.

Theo winced. Droplets of sweat started to run down his back. He had neither the stats nor the inclination for a stealth mission. How Sally had convinced him that it would be a smooth and uncomplicated task, he did not know. The fact that he talked himself up in agreement—that he could do fine solo—was on him, though.

Here he was, in a Party, just like he said he wouldn't be. He had told himself it was different, but the bread and butter of it was the same. Perhaps he wanted a Party after all. He had just needed to find the right one. Just the right amount of crazy and different.

As he reached the top of the staircase onto the landing, another wooden board complained of his presence.

He had passed four doorways down this wide corridor—the goal being the single one at the end leading to the innkeeper. The decor, he had tried not to be distracted by. A plain rug of faded design, drab paintings of forest landscapes, a small table with a miserable-looking potted plant. All bathed in dim shadow.

A door started to creak open from behind, and he slowly turned to meet the wide-eyed surprise of a sleepy Novice.

Henkk gave Frena the thumbs up to know that the plan had been put into action. He clenched his jaw and tapped nervously on a side pouch. He didn't think the goblin woman would have been too pleased that they were using her daughter as an assassin, but surprisingly she had been okay—even eager—about it.

He held his hand out, and Bella took it, nerves at the edges of her bright smile and wide, red eyes. "Remember," he said softly, his honeyed voice barely making it to her ears, "say the word and you will come back out."

She nodded and took a deep breath, her knuckles almost whiter than Henkk himself as they held her dagger.

The pale goblin frowned and closed his eyes, pointing an outstretched finger at the wall of the hospital.

Bella vanished from the light breeze of the open outdoors and briefly felt as if she were floating through mud. Her breath was squeezed from her lungs as the sensation weighed in on her.

And then it ceased. Wooden floorboards were beneath her hands and knees. She blinked slowly and fought the urge to gasp air inwards. Slowly, carefully, she allowed her lungs to reinflate through her nose as her heartbeat pounded in her head.

Snoring filled her ears. Close by. She allowed her gaze to scan past the immediate flooring to her surroundings. A small room lined with shelving. Cupboards and the smell of something . . . sharp? Like the medicine Pa used to make.

Beside her, a bed. She turned slowly to face the wide wooden frame. Atop the bed, sheets were bundled over a figure facing away from her. The blue linens rose and fell with every snore. Gingerly, she got to her feet.

One step. Two steps.

Each light footfall brought her closer to the figure—a sleeping elf with long blonde hair and a sharp goatee. Bella frowned. This wasn't an adventurer or currently a huge threat to her well-being. It was a person sleeping. Would they try to kill her if the roles were reversed? *Probably.*

Her held dagger glinted in the dim lantern light. It was for the good of the clan. She would do it.

Third step.

The figure shuffled restlessly and turned over, facing the goblin girl as she froze in place.

Bleary blue eyes flickered open.


Chuck groaned.

Jaxk raised an eyebrow at Oleb, who shrugged. "Must be the signal?"

Chuck started stumbling toward the back of the library as the slim goblin lit the torch.

Oleb licked his teeth and took a bite of the stone wall, a mouthful coming free just as easily as if it had been made of cake. A second bite widened the hole, and he salivated at the odd meal.

Jaxk yawned and sniffed the air. *That was an odd smell.* He turned and saw that the zombie had been caught alight by the idly held torch. The goblin's stomach immediately stuck in his throat in panic.

He tried to waft the flames off the zombie as Oleb sped up his chewing, but if anything, it had just increased how much the zombie burned.

The hole was just about big enough for the goblins to fit through, but the zombie would have to squeeze.

The flame-immune goblin pushed Chuck toward the hole, flames licking against his own skin to no effect.

"*Hells!*" Oleb whispered, removing himself from the situation and wiping his mouth. The torch had been discarded in panic and had now lit up some drier brush in the surrounding area. He waddled up to it and started to try and stamp it out—a job much better suited to the other goblin.

Jaxk fell through into the library as Chuck finally popped through, the zombie immediately stumbling into a bookshelf. With a brief groan, the shelves collapsed backward, sending the aflame corpse sprawling across dusty tomes, which burst into flame with comedic effect.

"*Hey, what's that noise?*" A deep voice boomed from above, freezing Jaxk in place.

* * *

Sally frowned at the distant figures. Most were shades and shadows among the places the village's lanterns did not reach. Team Firehazard looked a little brighter than she would have expected, but it was hard to judge from this angle. With a shrug, she made her way to the side of the stone forge.

She cursed the building—it was perhaps one of the harder ones to breach in the village and much more suited to the rock-eating goblin. The blacksmith inside was rumored to be a competent enough fighter. In comparison to the other Leaders, anyway. The forge had no back entrance or side doors and no windows to breach on the lower floor. There was just an opening where the forge itself sat, among an anvil and other darkened shapes used in smithing that Sally cared not for.

They stepped inside, paying caution to the village center that they could clearly see, and quickly skirted back into the enclosed side of the building. Two identical doorways blocked their way. One to the back storage room and one that led to the quarters of the blacksmith above. Neither had markings or a way to identify which was which.

With a shrug to the Death Knight, she held a stale lungful of air and reached for the first door.

Sally pulled on the handle. It didn't budge.

She pursed her lips and frowned. Was it locked? Maybe she should just try the other door then—but her gut had said this one. She gave it a slightly harder tug, and yet still it did not relent.

Humphrey tapped his foot impatiently.

With clenched teeth, she gestured for him to try the other door. *This one was hers*, after all. She stared at the handle and tried to see if there was some manner of visible lock that could be picked or broken. Not that she could pick locks . . .

The Death Knight grasped the handle of the second door firmly and braced to pull it before they both froze in place.

"Eh, what's all this, then?" A voice resounded behind them, rising in both fear and anger as a rattling noise rose from the speaker's belt.

They both spun around as the small object reached the lips of the patrolling guard.

A shrill warning blasted throughout the sleeping village.

## CHAPTER THIRTY-TWO

# Blood Moon

**W**hat are you doing?" The Novice rubbed their eyes. "Don't you know how late it is?"

The rising wave of panic flooding through Theo abated briefly. Of course, he just looked like a normal Novice, just a little out of place. His wooden sword was of little threat, surely.

"Couldn't sleep. It's a damned blood moon tonight." He relaxed his posture and gave a shrug at the young man giving him the once-over.

"Is it, huh? Perhaps that's why I was having a bad dream . . ." He turned as if about to retreat back into his room before looking back at Theo. "How are you at such a high level?" There was curiosity there alongside the suspicion.

"It's a secret class that you can unlock—but totally not worth it." He waved his hands in the air in an attempt to wash the conversation away. "You don't get any additional skills or benefits."

The interloping Novice frowned and shook their head. "Whatever man, just be quiet."

Theo grinned apologetically as the door started to close, almost in slow motion. It got to the last few inches—

And then a shrill scream of a whistle erupted from outdoors.

Not only did the door swing back open, but the sound of footsteps and muffled voices echoed dully from the other rooms.

He turned as the main door at the end of the hallway burst open. A large woman with a hefty mace stood in the doorway, backlit by her room's lantern.

"You are not right." She scowled, heavy brow weighing down her pale face. "Enemy in the inn!" Her voice echoed through the whole building.

The other rooms opened, and a handful of Novices stepped out, clutching at their basic weapons with both fear and anger in their eyes.

Theo dodged the first swing of a Novice. It was an amateur attempt. Even with his oddly distributed stats, his hard-learned experience fighting the wilderness around the world gave him a slight advantage. Though, against seven enemies in this tight space . . . He was used to being able to kite trouble around.

Even in this dire circumstance, he was reluctant to attack.

Despite trying to disassociate these last few weeks, he found himself unable to stomach how very real this had become. Staying solo and fighting Blue Slimes made life simple—he needn't have to worry about much. Just kill, collect, and camp out at night. Did it matter that the last thing he remembered was leaving the diner? This was the new normal now. He could live it and keep his mind free of any deeper considerations.

Then Sally showed up.

He pushed a Novice away as they drew closer and blocked the swing of a mace from another with his wooden sword. Sally had been like a key, sliding straight into the mental lock he had put in the past, allowing the weight of his situation to sink back into his gut. Now he had followed the zombified version of the girl he had a brief conversation with into attacking Yarch. A village with very real Players living in it.

Theo exhaled. The rate of his breathing had increased as his footwork scuffed around on the worn rug—trying to get the low levels caught up in each other trying to attack him. The spark of trying to escape back down the stairs had flared up, but where would that leave him? Back in a hostile town with a group following him—and ruining Sally's plan.

A shortsword cut into his free arm, a sliver of pain that worsened as he bent his arm in recoiled shock. He ducked the follow-up from a second opponent and shoulder-barged the first to the floor. This was Player vs Player—and PvP was heavily penalized by the System. The punishment would be—

The innkeeper struck his shoulder with her mace. A dull pain numbed his whole right arm. His grip loosened as he fought against the debilitating blow. He hopped backward into the wooden wall, almost falling through into one of the open doorways—that was it! He rolled across the room as the mace struck the wall, wood splintering to the floor. A lantern lit the empty bedroom, and he stood poised at the doorway.

A choke point would have to do. With a staggered sigh of resignation, his wooden sword bathed in a pinkish light as he readied his *[Novice Strike]*.

Bella yelped, and the Healer yelled back in shock too.

By reflex she dove at him, dagger sinking into soft mattress as he rolled to the side and fell on the floor. The little goblin jumped atop the bed and readied a pounce.

Immediately, a blast of radiant energy struck her in the face, knocking her back. It . . . hurt a tiny bit, but then it was fine. She rolled to the side, getting tangled in the linens as a blade struck into the bed.

A shrill scream of a whistle filled the air, shaking the small windows of the room.

It was enough of a brief distraction that she could wiggle her way backward from the trap of the bed, dropping to the floor. She was no match in a one-on-one fight. Escaping would not be good—they were relying on her.

"Come out, you devil-rat! What are you doing here?" The man's voice was shrill and stern, causing her to recoil against the wooden frame.

How dare he call her such names though? It was mean and unnecessary; shouldn't elves be nice? As the Healer stepped around the bottom of the bed, she leapt forth and stabbed the man in the foot.

He hissed in pain and lashed down with a shortsword, catching her in the back of the head. Crimson droplets spattered across the clean floor as the man healed himself with a spell.

"Better tell the guard," he growled, turning away from the prone body.

The Healer fumbled for the latch on their door. Sweat ran down their brow—what a rude awakening that had been. To think a goblin could somehow make it into the village—into his very bedroom, even! He gripped the handle and went to turn it.

Bella launched herself silently from the floor and wrapped her arms around the taller man's leg. The Healer jumped in shock, having thought the girl dead. As he went to strike down at her with his sword, she glared up at him and opened her mouth.

"Cabbages," she growled.

Then, with a brief suffocating weight placed upon them, she vanished from the bedroom.


*"The library is on fire!"* the voice called from above.

Jaxk thought about running, but as he turned to the hole, Oleb was there with the torch. "Finish the job," the portly goblin hissed, "and be quick; there's a bunch of—"

A shrill scream of a whistle reverberated around the whole of Yarch.

He swore, grabbed the torch, and began moving from shelf to shelf catching the books alight. As the flames danced in his eyes he watched in frustrated amusement as the zombie managed to clamber and fall into a second bookshelf already, spreading small fires to the opposite side of the library near the wide doors.

The librarian emerged from the staircase to the right, wielding a long staff of polished wood and wearing either red robes or some really comfortable sleepwear. "Goblins?" he bellowed.

Jaxk flinched as the elf readied a spell and pointed it toward the small Monster. *[Greater Firebolt]*!

Jaxk just blinked as the burning energy of the spell shot across the room and struck him. He would be the first goblin to put his hand up and admit to not being the sharpest tool in the pit . . . but why the librarian would use a fire spell in the currently aflame library was beyond him.

The librarian looked equally as blank as the spout of fire just petered out ineffectively against the goblin.

Scratching his chin, Jaxk turned to see Oleb chewing around the base of the wall, heading toward one of the structural supports. With a shrug, he drew a dagger and leapt atop one of the burning bookshelves. The dancing embers played in his eyes, and the librarian buckled from the intimidation.

Chuck drew the old man's gaze away from the hellish goblin as he clambered over a table to get closer.

With shaking hands, the librarian began preparing a new spell.


Sally leapt forward, taking the guard by surprise and ramming her dagger in the underside of his jaw, her strength carving a large wound through his throat and spraying blood down her arm.

"Interesting," she hummed as he slumped to the floor. "I have no urge to eat the System-created."

"Bloody marvelous." Humphrey rolled his empty sockets. "How about worrying about the town being alert now?"

She wiped the blood onto her red skirt. "I'm sure it'll be fine. All the teams will have done their jobs, and we'll just mop up—"

The second door of the forge swung open, and a large burly figure stomped out. Eschewing the norms of elfdom, the blacksmith was heavily built and well-muscled, wearing just shorts and boots. A thick beard to match a tight cropping of black hair. The pointy ears looked more like afterthoughts to his design. In one hand he held a thick hammer with a short handle, and in the other, an axe with a blue-tinged blade.

"Undead?" he roared, almost excited at the prospect of a fight. "My specialty." The hint of blue in the axe flared up into a flame.

"Uh, gentlemen first?" Sally sidestepped slightly behind the Death Knight.

"Gladly!" Humphrey grinned, the flames of his helmet flaring out as dark energy pulsed around his greatsword.

Sally turned toward the town square, where the doors of the garrison opened, and a large armored figure strolled out, accompanied by a score of more guards.

"*Oh, for fu*—" As if things couldn't get any better.

Sally tried to recoil against the inside of the forge while peering out at the gathering town guard. The clash of melee behind her was making that difficult though, with the Death Knight and blacksmith whirling and flailing about behind her. She winced as the noise of metal on metal drew the eyes of the town captain and his guard.

There had been a yell over in one of the other buildings, and the library had started to smolder from any opening that allowed it. She could almost hear the crackle of wood splitting and burning if it weren't for the periodic clangs of the fight.

She turned back to them with a scowl. Humphrey had taken some damage, but the heavily muscled elf was sweating heavily, with two long gashes across his chest.

"Seal the deal, Humps," she hissed. "We have company imminent."

"*Yes*. I'm just going to—"

A clang rang out—the blue glow from the blacksmith's weapons pulsed as they struck the Death Knight.

Humphrey dropped to one knee, and his sword arm slowly lowered.

## CHAPTER THIRTY-THREE

# Endless Night

*[Novice Strike]*

The wooden sword struck the innkeeper's arm, and a brief flash of confusion animated in her face at how the seemingly useless weapon hurt so much. Theo flicked the blunt blade into another strike, the trail of pink energy a continuation of his first skill. He could certainly feel the difference from the Speed Earrings Sally had given him. His layers of bonuses and item interactions caused the second blow to twist into a third—the weapon almost moved of its own accord, willing him to make further attacks.

It had disorientated the innkeeper. The blows had come quicker than expected and for much higher damage than a Novice with a wooden sword should be able to deal out. As she tried to retreat backward, Theo shifted toward her, his flurry of blows unrelenting. The eighth . . . or maybe the tenth blow cracked the woman in the neck, and she dropped to the floor.

The crackling pink energy fizzled out as the sword returned to its normal state. Theo wiped the sweat from his brow and tried to catch his breath. He eyed the gathered Novices, who had also paused, unsure of what to do next as they saw the important figure fall.

"We don't have to do this." Theo gripped his sword tighter, holding out his open hand in a gesture to diffuse the situation. His arm still stung from his earlier wound, and he wasn't keen on adding to that.

He watched as the collective eyes of the group rose above his head.

*Bloip!* His STAR shone red with a bounty notification.

"Shit."

Bella dropped to the grass, the cool breeze rustling through her hair. Rolling to the side, she bumped into Henkk. The pale goblin looked shocked, to say the least.

She turned, fumbling for a weapon, expecting to see the surprised Healer lying in the grass after the weird teleportation.

Her mouth opened, and she frowned.

Lying on the grass on the outside of the building was an elven leg, barely covered by a scrap of nightshirt that waved in the breeze.

"Send me back in." She pulled on the cloak of Henkk. He shook his head clear and rested a hand on her.

Another wave hit her—pressure and nausea flooded her body as she then popped back into the building.

The Healer was lying up against the door in a pool of crimson. Their missing leg was now healed over but still missing. A pale sweat and tired eyes on their face. Upon seeing the goblin appear back into existence, he was startled and raised a shaking hand to begin casting a spell.

Bella ran and leapt onto the man before he could mumble the last of the incantation, landing on top of his body. She muffled the spell as her arms wrapped around the head of the Healer. He struggled against her as a wide grin spread across her face.

"Cabbages," she hissed for the final time.

Jaxk jumped down from the bookshelf and snaked around the tables and chairs to approach the librarian. As dumb and stubborn as the zombie was, they were at least a distraction.

He rounded a corner and winced as a sharp crackle of blue energy shot through the air and struck the burning corpse. A melon-sized hole cratered through Chuck, yet he still stumbled forward.

The librarian cursed and began to head back up the stairs, beginning to prepare another *[Zap]*. Jaxk stopped and watched the zombie trip up the first step, face-planting on the wooden stairs, but avoid the spell, which arced over his head into the wall behind. The stairs became alight with fire.

"Doing my work for me," Jaxk murmured to himself, shaking his head. The librarian cursed once more and tried to move along the walkway to the upper rooms.

With a large groan, the supports bent beneath his weight—Oleb appeared to give a brief thumbs up before continuing to weaken the building by eating it. Within seconds the whole thing shook, sending the librarian toppling to the wooden railing, bursting through, and tumbling back to the ground floor.

Jaxk watched the figure fall, landing atop a table which shattered dramatically. He sighed and walked over to the groaning body, quickly sticking his thin knife into the throat of the prone Leader.

"You should get out soon," Oleb called, with mouth half-full of stone. "Even if the fire doesn't kill ya, this place'll collapse soon."

Jaxk wiped his blade and sheathed it. Time to join the rest of the Party in the center of the village.

The blacksmith growled out in pain as the crossbow bolt struck his forearm, waylaying his attack on the stunned Death Knight. His eyes blazed as he turned to Sally, pulling the bolt out with his teeth.

"Not sure that is advised," she growled, dropping the ranged weapon and bringing out her dagger. "You can bleed out quicker doing that."

Her opponent hesitated, wanting to finish off the Death Knight but not wanting to lower his guard for the zombie to attack. He was bleeding and heavily damaged—perhaps his only option would be to wait out healing . . . if the Healer ever showed up.

The sound of metal boots marching across stone was enough pressure for Sally to want to act. Even if the large elf was frozen by indecision, Humphrey wasn't recovering, and she was running out of time. She tensed and then sprung forward.

*[Hex: Slow]*

The arc of anti-undead enchantments on the blacksmith's weapons slowed just enough for her to avoid the blows. Sparks rang from the floor as the axe blade carved the air just beside her. Sally kept trying to flank the sweating elf, hoping to draw his attention away from Humphrey. She tried to bring up her Party UI as she leapt back from another dual-weapon attack.

Error: Restricted

*Typical.* Was this the System choosing an opportune time to glitch up, or was there something the captain could do?

The blacksmith's hammer grazed her arm, and the tingle of the magic energy repulsed her. It felt dangerous. Despite being slowed, the elf levied an almost constant barrage of blows—and with the extra reach he had over Sally's dagger she found it hard to approach. With a feint, she threw the dagger.

At this range, it cut the blacksmith but fell to the floor—it hadn't the momentum to do much more. In the brief flinch of the elf, she slid in and launched a heavy punch straight into his gut.

It barely moved him.

"Hah! Got you now!" The wide grin of the bearded elf shone out through his shadowed face as he readied his weapons at the zombie.

A flash of red carved his head clean from his neck as the sinister glow of Humphrey's *[Grave Strike]* arced through the air.

"You mean '*Ha-ha*'!" He grinned, the flames from his helmet flickering but weak.

"Here." She threw a Healing Potion at the Death Knight, who caught and ingested it immediately. "We need to get to the town square now and hope that everyone else was successful."

"*Yes.*" Humphrey nodded and fell into step with the boss Monster.

As Sally stepped into the open air, a weight sunk in her stomach at the sight of the group marching toward them. The imposing figure of the captain, in polished silver armor, holding a halberd, strode out in front of perhaps fifteen other Yarch guards. If it was any consolation to her panicked nerves, there didn't seem to be any Players among them.

The pair stopped at the midway point of the southern end of the village. The library to their east was alight now, flames licking up the sides as part of the roof collapsed. Two small figures, silhouetted against the fire, came out to join them—Jaxk and Oleb. Chuck was nowhere to be seen.

From an alleyway, Bella and Henkk came to join them. The girl's dress was smeared with blood, but she otherwise looked in good spirits. The white goblin, however, appeared to have had his fill of the adventure but was here and holding a dagger tightly.

From behind them, the tavern door slammed open, and Theo stumbled out, immediately throwing up across the cobbled flagstones. He was covered in blood, his armor was worn and scuffed, and his pallor was off-putting—even for Sally. He wiped his mouth with his sleeve and with a shallow smile stumbled over to the group.

"You all look like garbage." Sally beamed. "But I am glad you're all okay."

"Mfff." Theo shrugged, convulsing as he tried to keep more of his dinner from escaping. "So, who set off the guards?"

Sally raised her hands up and shrugged. "Who knows." She held his gaze silently as his eyes narrowed.

"I hate to spoil a reunion." Humphrey cleared his throat. "But someone is waiting for our attention."

She turned to see the captain and his retinue standing around thirty feet away. They had stopped but stood at the ready, awaiting order to charge.

"Foul undead and assorted Monsters," the captain called out, his voice deep, carrying throughout the village, ". . .and murderous Player."

Theo waved sheepishly.

"You have assailed this fine, pleasant village. You have slain four of its Leaders. Sent the rest of the populace into hiding within their homes. *There is only one punishment for this,* and as I stand here before you today—"

Sally nudged Theo. "Isn't it weird how they always monologue?"

He nodded, keeping his eyes on the captain. "If the endgame is death, then why not just go straight to the fighting?"

"—on behalf of the Crown, he who sits atop the marbled throne of—"

"Yeah, right? We should be kill-on-sight."

"—and with the power granted to me, I hereby—"

"Hey!" Sally interrupted the captain. "Can we skip this cutscene?" She wrinkled her nose at her Party and lowered her voice. "We don't have much healing, right?"

Party UI - Error: Restricted

Theo shook his head slowly as the armored elf stood literally shaking with rage at the group. "I used the Healing Potion you gave me. I have two *[Small Medical Kits]*, but those take a little time."

"They are unlikely to wait for us to recover, *ha-ha*."

Sally scowled. An all-out battle was not the best use of their skills, not against superior numbers. She tried to read the levels of the guards and captain, but her eyes just burned. Something was not right, adding to the unease that she had—

Chuck stumbled out from the crackling ruins of the library. No longer aflame, he was burnt beyond recognition—almost skeletal—blackened, dark flesh clung to a small percentage of him. He brought a sickening meaty smell to the already smoky night air.

She turned back to the gathered group ahead of them, the captain leveling the pointed end of his halberd right at her.

"*Guards—attack!*"

## CHAPTER THIRTY-FOUR

# Gathered Before Dawn

Humphrey stepped in front of the boss Monster as she loaded her crossbow. His sword blazed with the fell energy of *[Grave Strike]*, illuminating their position in a dim crimson glow. Theo prepared his *[Novice Strike]*, the stress on his face visible even through the sweat and grime. The goblins looked panicked for the most part—aside from Bella—and Chuck just stayed lying on the floor.

Sally peered out from the side of the armored Death Knight and shot a bolt off into the quickly approaching crowd. The captain had seemed content enough to let the mass of generic guards flood ahead of him—one of which was struck by her ranged attack. Just the upper chest. Not a killing blow. She quickly wound the crossbow back.

She could almost smell them now. Boots thundering across the stone, their angered expressions yelling and grimacing as they prepared for the clash. If Sally had a clearer mind, she might question the amount of sentience these System-created had—how deep did their feelings, their sense of self go? The second bolt flew out and struck a different guard in the thigh.

This first guard stumbled straight into a wide upswing from the Death Knight, his large blade cleaving a deep gash through their torso. Blood flicked through the air, dappling the throng as the first guard fell, defeated.

And then the battle was truly upon them.

Sally drew her rare dagger and went to move to engage the front line of the guard—but Theo stepped in the way. The Novice swung forward with his wooden sword, a blaze of pinkish energy arcing through the air. He struck a guard and immediately twisted into a follow-up attack—blocked—but a third twisted its way into the bracer of his opponent, disarming the guard. He moved as if in a dance led by the unconventional weapon.

Humphrey burst into red energy as he activated *[Adrenaline]*, his greatsword having no issue in carving through whatever passed as armor. Sally fell in behind the Death Knight, lashing out at a wounded guard that stumbled past, her dagger finding the exposed neck. Soon they started carving a bloody path through the regiment. She found no joy in it. The System-created were not interesting to her, nothing but obstacles in the way. Humphrey had taken some damage, but most attacks were not strong enough to pierce his full-body plate.

The goblins were being just as opportunistic as she was. They helped finish off some of Theo's opponents and were being avoidant, drawing out lone fighters and then piling on. Oleb had chewed small lines in the path, tripping and causing uneven footing for the guards approaching. Then, when they had an advantage, all four would pile on with a flurry of merciless dagger strikes.

*[Rallying Cry]*

A wave of blue light flashed through the crowd, briefly illuminating the village square. Humphrey's greatsword struck out at an opponent but was blocked; his attack was rebuffed as the remaining guards retained a light blue color to them.

Likewise, Theo met with more resistance. He had managed to fell two guards and damage a handful more all with the same use of his skill—but his next strike against the buffed guard fell short, and he was knocked back. He stumbled, lethargy taking its toll as sweat dripped from his face, and he took a blade to the side of his stomach.

"Theo!" Sally growled, casting *[Hex: Slow]* on the guard attempting an overhead swing to follow up at the reeling Novice.

It gave Theo enough time to just bring his sword up for a block, bracing with both hands. Bella slid into the scene from between his legs and stabbed the guard in the lower leg.

*[Novice Strike]*

The face of the Novice was nothing like what Sally had seen before: a tired, focused scowl set on his face, his eyes cold and teeth clenched and grimacing. He stood stooped slightly as blood ran down his side. Though his hand shook, there was still the determination to keep on fighting.

She turned from him before he could start his next skill—a guard swung at her, a shortsword aimed at her arm. The metal rang against her dagger as she managed to divert the path of it away, her arm numb from the vibration. Sally grabbed the guard with her off hand and headbutted them, stabbing them in the shoulder and then neck as they recoiled from the blow.

Humphrey barreled into her, and she tumbled to the floor into a painful roll. As she righted herself to scowl at the Death Knight, she saw him with the halberd blade partway through his left shoulder and the large captain holding onto the blunt end of the weapon. She quickly switched *[Hex: Slow]* onto the armored figure while she had the chance.

Things had been going . . . okay for the group. She risked another quick glance around. Theo looked terrible but again was flickering around a pair of guards—taking a few cuts himself but layering up damage even on the Rallied opponents. Jaxk had taken a nasty-looking cut to the head and was being helped by Henkk. She watched as a guard jabbed their sword toward Oleb and the goblin ate the incoming pointy end. Frena then rushed the confused opponent, having now joined the group with a sharpened spear.

She turned back to the captain clashing with the Death Knight. Humphrey's left arm sagged, hanging limply as he stepped backward while parrying the assault from the last Leader of Yarch. Sally brought out the *[Scroll: Savage Strike]* and activated it as she stalked toward them. The paper burnt and disintegrated from her grip as a red glow started to swirl around her held dagger. She dodged and spun away from an interloping guard, not wanting to waste the double damage on such a lowly foe. Theo flickered in to strike at the attacker, a blur of pain and pink light.

Sally cursed as she ran forward, hopping over the bodies of the fallen. If only she had better skills. Despite things still being in their favor—all it would take would be losing a goblin or, dare she think it, Humphrey, and the tide could easily turn against them. Even as she closed the short distance, she could see the fire from the back of the Death Knight's helmet had dimmed.

She timed her arrival for just after the captain had swung at Humphrey, the clang of blades clashing also signaling her arrival. Dagger outstretched, she barreled into the large armored form of the Leader, ramming the blade into the side of their stomach. A guard clocked her on the head immediately after, and she dropped to the floor. Her vision started to fade.

At first, a numb sensation flooded her. Then, the cold cobblestone of the village square sank through her prone body. The sound of muffled fighting grew clearer, and she blinked. A familiar pressure filled her head—but instead of a *pop*, there was just a slow, steady release. She felt calm, almost like she had just napped. Even with the surrounding chaos. The fighting, the heat from the fire, the wet feeling at the back of her head.

She shook—or rather, someone was shaking her.

"Sally." The voice of Theo came from above her. "*Get up.*"

She did. Not because of the concern or the urgency of the request. Not because she felt like she could gorge on his tasty flesh. Not even because he was fast becoming a trusted friend.

She rose from the floor because she was angry. His hand was warm against hers as he helped her up to unstable footing. Her eyes turned to him, blazing bright red, but she saw past him to one of the few remaining guards leveling a blow toward the unaware Novice.

As the blow came down, the burnt figure of Chuck lumbered into the way— his skull splitting in twain from the blow, spraying what remained of his brain matter across them.

Party member Chuck has died

Something burst inside Sally. She pushed Theo to the side and grabbed the guard by the throat, crushing their windpipe even as the body of her former Party member was still falling to the floor. Where was her dagger? It probably didn't matter. She twisted the mace from the now dying guard. Humphrey was still on the back foot and lagging even further; the captain was still slowed and now injured from her attack, but two guards had positioned themselves in between them, all as the melee had progressed.

She stepped forward with confidence, despite feeling light-headed. The first guard swung, but she was quicker, the mace striking the opponent's wrist, shattering the bone and sending their weapon clattering to the floor. Sally lurched forward and bit into the arm that came up to support the broken one. The blood was . . . different. Plain. Average. A world of difference compared to the joy of consuming a Player. Yet still, it felt sustaining in some way.

Restricted

The STAR hummed as Theo flashed beside her.

"Get the captain," he growled, sounding groggy and pained.

She nodded and slipped past as he engaged the other guard, arriving at the duel just as the Death Knight was struck and knocked to the floor.

"Hey! I'm your opponent now!" Her voice rang throughout the village.

The captain paused over the prone body of Humphrey and turned to the approaching zombie. "*Oh*, you're approaching me?"

Sally spat blood as her eyes flared bright crimson.

"I can't eat the shit out of you unless I get closer."

## CHAPTER THIRTY-FIVE

# Endure the Dark

The captain turned to her and held his halberd in position to guard, wincing slightly at the dagger still wedged into his side.

Even with the *[Hex: Slow]* upon him, the captain was fast. Sally knocked the first strike wide with the mace, the shock shaking down her arm, but didn't have much chance to retaliate before the armored Leader was in the midst of a follow-up.

She ducked beneath it—a dangerous maneuver that risked her losing her head, but she spun out from it and struck the wedged dagger with the head of the mace, further digging it into the Leader. Off-balance, she lunged into the captain as he recoiled from the pain. Despite her Strength, in his plate armor he was immovable and didn't budge as she slammed into him. Sally dropped the mace and grabbed a hold of her dagger, twisting it before withdrawing it from the wound. The captain pushed her back with a kick.

As she stumbled back a couple of feet, she grinned and licked the blood from the blade. Still plain, but it felt energizing. A dagger was a terrible weapon in regard to reach, but the extra Luck might help. *Maybe.*

The captain was breathing heavily now. For all the gamification of stats and Health Points, getting stabbed in the gut still hurt pretty bad. It was only a matter of her Strength mixed with the double damage of *[Savage Strike]* from the scroll that had allowed her to even pierce the plate, she assumed. Behind her, the clamor of battle had subsided.

The soft footsteps of a group of goblins joined her, as did the panting Theo. Even Humphrey managed to scrape himself up off the floor and level his blade at the now very outnumbered captain. No guards remained standing, and save for their labored breathing and mutters of pain, a silence filled the village square full of the dead and weary.

"Just who are you?" The captain clenched his weapon tighter, his voice still remaining firm despite his predicament.

"I'm Sally, and I am the death of the System." She darted forward as her Party joined her.

Against the coordinated effort of the Party, the captain had no chance. His attempt to attack first was blocked by the Death Knight as the goblins all scooted in from below to stab and harry his movement. Theo knocked his off hand away with his wooden sword, leaving the Leader wide open for Sally.

She barreled into him and bit out his undefended neck—somewhat cliché but fast becoming her signature finisher. The gurgling as the elf collapsed was sweet music to her ears. She spat the tasteless blood onto the dying captain.

"Well done, *Sally the Unliving.*" Humphrey sat back down on the floor to hold his limp shoulder. "You have defeated the five Leaders."

She groaned and dropped to her knees, the lethargy sinking into her battered body. Likewise, the goblins and Theo took an arrangement of sitting and prone positions on the floor. Only Bella looked particularly cheerful, despite being soaked in blood.

Sally closed her eyes. They felt warm. "So . . . what now?"

"You'd need to appoint new Leaders, I suppose. This is . . . unprecedented." Humphrey shrugged with his good shoulder.

She licked her lips and opened her eyes again. The lantern light surrounding them felt brighter. Maybe she was just tired. "You alright, Theo?" The Novice was balled up, hiding his face away.

A couple of moments of silence passed before his response came. "Can't feel my arm or legs. Feeling pretty conflicted about the whole evening."

That was understandable. He was a Player after all, and he had not only murdered a handful of other Players—real people—but openly waged war on the System by clearing out a village.

"Do I have to do some kind of ceremony speech, or . . .?"

"Be a lot cooler if you did." Humphrey looked at her blankly.

"Fine." She huffed and stood up on shaky legs before clearing her throat. "As Sally the Unliving, boss Monster and destroyer of the village of Yarch, I hereby appoint the following new Leaders."

All eyes turned to her now, the goblins all bloodied and worn, Theo looking as close to death as she felt; even the Death Knight was enamored by her next words.

"Bella, a small goblin with strength of heart and innate healing, you are the new Healer for Yarch."

The girl beamed and nodded eagerly.

"Jaxk. Immune to fire, you shall stoke the furnaces of the forge as the new blacksmith. Frena, with your vision to watch over others, you will make a great innkeeper. Oleb . . . uh, you're the librarian because of your insatiable appetite for . . . knowledge?"

Oleb shrugged.

"Lastly . . ." Sally smiled. "Henkk, the leader who wanted to protect and keep safe the glitched and Unique, I can think of no better captain to guard our first outpost."

The white goblin bowed with a brief nod.

Henkk has left the Party

A blue light shimmered around their feet; a light circle of energy persisted beneath each goblin where they stood or sat.

"Oh, I can [Heal] people now!" Bella jumped into the air with excitement.

"Do it, then." Sally's eyes widened. "*Please.*"

"Sure, that'll be five gold, Miss." The goblin girl beamed up at the zombie with her hand outstretched.

"F-fine." Sally frowned but handed over the money. She watched as the goblin put her hands together and a green glow flowed between them like a tether. She began to feel pretty good . . . She brought up her UI to see her Health bar rise to the top. "Wow, that's super nice. Shame we can't take you along with us now."

Humphrey coughed from the side.

"Okay, okay." Sally rolled her eyes. "How much to heal everyone here?"

"Uh!" Bella wrinkled her nose as she counted each of the presently injured. "Ummm . . . thirty gold?"

"Don't all rush to pitch in." Sally shook her head and withdrew her gold. Not that she had been paying attention to how much she had accumulated, but she was certain she had enough.

The small goblin went around in turn and healed them in a similar manner. She crouched down by the charred and crumpled form of Chuck and prodded at the zombie. "Not much I can do for him, Sally." She turned back to the boss and gave an exaggerated pout.

Sally sighed. "It was inevitable. He was the last of the diner zombies and had only made it this far by glitched miracle." She was still pretty sad about it, though. As goofy as Chuck had been, he had also been pretty effective at turning the tide of their fights.

"So, what are you going to name your first village?" Humphrey stood up and stretched his sore arm out.

"Henkk is the captain now, so it's his choice."

"Oh!" The white goblin narrowed his pitch-black eyes and glanced around the dimly lit village. "How about . . . *Sanctuary*?"

"It's cliché." Sally shrugged. "But sure. The first foothold of the *Outsiders*—the glitched and the anti-System-ites."

"The new Leaders will need to bind to their buildings overnight." Humphrey folded his plated arms. "I will assist in clearing some of the bodies to the outskirts."

"Thanks, Humps." Sally watched the goblins scarper off to their various new homes, and she jerked her thumb over to a bench with a nod to Theo.

They sat down on the smooth wooden surface, the glow of a lantern above them slightly rocking in the light breeze of the night. The Novice leaned back and closed his eyes, facing toward the clear sky.

Sally bunched her hands together and tried not to stare at his exposed throat. "You doing okay, Theo?"

"Maybe." His single-word reply not doing much to encourage that fact.

"It's the emotional toll, right? Something the healing doesn't fix."

They sat in silence for half a minute before the Novice sighed and turned his head toward her. "I must have made a good impression on you at the diner, huh?"

"Perhaps. It's different here." She smiled sadly. "In this world, you're only as attractive to me as a fully loaded burrito would be."

He blinked slowly in response before looking back toward the night sky. "Burritos *are* pretty damn awesome."

"Right?" She kicked the side of his leg. "You're an anchor for me, a reminder that this isn't my real life. It's taking a lot of self-restraint not to turn you into my next meal."

"Well, I do appreciate it." He smiled and sighed. "I was trying to avoid thinking about that by keeping to myself while in the System. When you showed up . . . I had to face the reality of the situation—"

"Or lack of reality."

"Yeah, and I think although the path you intend to travel is going to be futile . . . it's the right thing to do. I don't want to be part of this game . . . or alternate world . . . or whatever we have been forced into."

"Even if it kills you?" Sally raised her eyebrows.

"Even if it kills me."

"Even if I eat you?" Her eyebrows raised further.

"Even if . . . Well, let's have a rain check on that?" He smiled and sat back up straight. "I've got a bounty on my head now. I may be worth more than a quick bite to eat."

Sally resisted telling him she wouldn't make it quick. "Big outlaw now, are ya?"

"Probably kill-on-sight for most Parties now. The System doesn't take too kindly to Player-killers." He shrugged and idly ran his finger down his wooden shortsword.

Restrictions Lifted

She looked down at her STAR, which now buzzed with information—most notably a golden light shone from it, duplicating the glow that also radiated from Theo's.

"Looks like that little stunt leveled us all up." He grinned, going through his menus.

Sally *boiped* away the Party notification to show that Humphrey and Theo had leveled up and pressed onto her own.

Level Up

Level Five Boss Monster Keystone Unlocked

Undeath Affinity

Party Aura – Increased Constitution and Resistances

**Pick One**

[**Summon Zombies**] Summoning (3/Day) 2–5 Zombies are summoned under your control

[**Dark Healing**] Party Healing Spell 60 Mana, 2m Cooldown - Undead within your control restore 20% HP

[**Call of the Grave**] Single Target Curse - Target takes increased damage from all sources

## CHAPTER THIRTY-SIX

# Fresh Light

Despite her excitement at now being able to *[Summon Zombies]*, Sally managed to drift off to sleep in the tavern with relative ease. Theo hadn't been too pleased with seeing the bloody handiwork he had made outside of the bedrooms—but having two locked doors between him and the jaws of the zombie woman had eased his mood.

She awoke to a knock at her door, the pillow she was chewing falling out of her mouth as her bleary eyes adjusted to the daylight. "Uurf?"

"It's Theo. You should come see this."

She rolled from the bed and tried to stretch out. There wasn't as much ache through her limbs as she had expected—a good night of rest seemed like powerful enough healing magic even without the help of the Healer goblin. Stumbling lazily over to the door, she opened it to see the Novice standing there. He looked as refreshed as she felt.

"Let's get some breakfast? If you can eat normal food?" He shrugged and nodded his head toward the stairs.

Sally nodded back and gave the room a quick once over before leaving. It was partially odd that she slept in her armor and that all her possessions were kept in some intangible space, but it also seemed perfectly natural. It was something easier to just not think about.

Even as they reached the top of the stairs, the light streaming in from the windows at the top of the stairwell, there was something immediately odd—*noises*. Specifically, the murmur of voices. Sally hopped down the stairs, turning at the bottom to see the table-laden tavern to the left.

It was bustling.

Nearly two dozen goblins sat at the tables. Drinking, eating, and generally having a good time.

"I spoke to Humphrey earlier. Apparently, as the five Leaders are goblins, the System has populated the village with goblins," Theo said from behind.

"Neeeeat," Sally hissed, turning and pushing past the Novice to exit the kitchen door.

The village itself took a few seconds for her to process. Not only were there now scores of goblins going about their daily System-assigned lives, but the structures had also changed. The buildings were now of a darker gray stone, with accents of red. Wooden spikes adorned the edges of the roofs, and fiery braziers had replaced the lantern posts. The garrison at the top of the village now sported two banners of crimson, each with a painted skull upon them.

"Pretty impressive, huh?" Theo nudged her with his elbow. "The first Monster-controlled Player-town. All because of you."

Sally nudged him back. "I had some help, you tasty sack of sappiness. I have an itchy feeling though. Where's Humphrey at?"

"He said to bring you to the forge."

She groaned and rolled her eyes. "If this is some kind of crafting or refining tutorial, I will be super justified in eating you."

"That's not—oh, we just skipped breakfast there, huh? You go on ahead. Let me pick you up some . . . meat, I suppose?"

"I guess—I haven't even eaten a brain yet. I'm not sure if that's a thing here in this world." She shrugged and waved him off as she set off toward where the Death Knight should be.

Eating a brain just sounded inconvenient—Players kept them locked away in their stupid skulls, which were a pain to get into even with her current Strength. Oh, she didn't even try to loot all those dead guards and Leaders. She cursed herself. Hopefully, the bodies would still be in the pile wherever Humphrey dragged them out to.

A pair of smiling goblins greeted her as she passed. Everyone seemed so happy and accepting of her. A village full of Monsters happened to be anything but that—they were no different than the elves that lived here previously. Just a little smaller and greener. Something seemed odd though.

Stopping, she tilted her head to observe the goblins moving around. They all seemed normal enough . . . Oh—that was it. There were no children. While she was no expert on the subject, there were definitely none that were as small or spritely as Bella was. With a shrug, she made a mental note of this oddity and carried on her way.

She arrived at the forge to find Jaxk hammering away at something. The fire-immune goblin had already grown in size and bulked up, his slender frame now muscled and bare to the elements. He placed down his smithing instruments as he saw her approach and leveled a wide grin at the zombie.

"Eh, good morning, Sally. Looking for Lord Humphrey?"

"*Lord?* Yeah, Theo said he'd be over here. You seem to have settled in here pretty well."

"It was certainly a surprise this morning." The goblin scratched at his soot-covered head. "But I feel like I have some kinda purpose now, a place to live and people to protect. Even if the gobs walking around aren't Unique, they're still my people."

Sally smiled and looked back out at the village. It was certainly something worth protecting. Even if nothing was real, it was something they had earned. Something taken back from the unfair System. Roping them into her crusade had been a little heavy-handed, perhaps, but they had stepped up more than she had expected.

The backroom door swung open, and the plated figure of Humphrey strode out. He looked slightly different, and the curiosity must have been evident in Sally's eyes as the Death Knight grinned and stood tall and proud.

"I had Jaxk give me a little upgrade, *ha-ha!*" His armor looked sturdier, maybe thicker in places, and better defined. "Getting your arm nearly hewn off is not fun."

"I can imagine." Sally nodded. "So—increased defense?"

"*Yes.* Increase in my armor class and mundane resistances." The Death Knight paused and crossed his arms. "You never asked what I received from leveling up."

Sally rolled her red eyes. "Out with it, then, Lord Humps."

He opened and closed his mouth before surrendering the information. "*[Will of the Dark Lord]*." He opened his arms wide to exaggerate the reveal.

"Uh-huh. What's it do?"

The Death Knight deflated slightly. "It's an Area of Effect Stun if you must put it in base terms. Long cooldown. Save check against Willpower."

"Well, that's much cooler than what Theo got at least. Which was nothing." She grinned and leaned against one of the non-heated counters. "Though the item interaction he has going on seems to be working well."

"It is inefficient, but, professionally, I am very interested in how far he can push it." Humphrey rubbed his chin with his plated hand. "He needs more Speed and Base Weapon Damage."

"So, Strength items? We really need more loot."

"That's why I asked you over here." The Death Knight grinned, his flaming helmet flickering. "We need to get stronger and probably quite quickly."

Sally clucked her tongue. "It's the village, right? Either Players or the System is going to come fight it?"

"*Yes.* Astute as always. In two days, a regiment from Poppybrook will arrive to reclaim the town. Between now and then, Players may attempt the same."

"Thankfully, it should mostly be low levels around here?"

"*Yes.*" Humphrey tilted his head, his eye sockets narrowing. "But stronger Parties may travel over for the challenge."

"*Arse.*" Sally rubbed the bridge of her nose. "But you have ideas, right?"

"Always, *ha-ha!* Now that we have a base of operations this makes things a lot easier for our progression. It depends whether you want more loot, more experience . . . or more allies."

"This isn't like a three-choice thing where I have to pick after some suspenseful deliberation?"

"No, I . . . don't believe so?"

"Allies it is! Our Party is looking a bit thinner now, with two spaces to fill."

"I thought that may be the case." Humphrey nodded. "There is a bandit encampment not too far away. I have reports that it is being led by a Unique Monster."

"Reports from whom?" Sally frowned before Theo's arrival from the side caught her eye.

"The Village Notice Board. We have access to some of the things Players had here."

Theo entered the forge and winced as the wave of heated air enveloped him. "Oof, how can you both stand it in here?" He passed a small basket over to the zombie.

"Real classes get resistances, pup." Sally peered inside the wicker container, a variety of cooked meats meeting her gaze as the cover lifted.

"I'm the first Level Nine Novice though." He shrugged, almost immediately regretting saying it.

"Correct." The Death Knight nodded. "I do not believe there would be anyone else as . . . dedicated to such . . ." He frowned and rubbed the back of his neck. "*Folly?*"

Jaxk had been silent during the continuing conversation, seemingly patient enough to wait for the group to leave so that he could continue his new role.

"Leave Theo alone, Mr. Edgy Dark Lord." Sally waved her hand. "Shall we agree to set off against the bandits this morning, then? Sounds like a classic adventure that we'll have no issue with."

" . . . *Yes.*"

"Sounds alright to me." Theo shrugged.

"Oh, before we do—are the corpses still around? My skull collection hungers."

Humphrey nodded and pointed out to the back of the village. "About three dozen feet out that way. They shouldn't have despawned yet."

"Despawned," Sally repeated, letting the word roll out of her mouth. "Alright, Theo, go get supplies. And I'll meet you both in the square." She moved to leave but paused to hand the basket back to the Novice. "Sorry, not fresh enough."

She strolled her way out of the village. It was another pleasant day, which she was moderately content about. Part of her did miss the gloom of the Cemetery. There was something about the sunlight that brought the feeling of hope, of safety, which she was surprised to realize was something that felt good right now. Her unlife had been fraught with uncertainty and danger so far, so a break was a warm welcome.

The pile of corpses had been unceremoniously stacked in a pile a reasonable distance away from the village, behind a small group of trees. As she approached, her STAR *bloiped*.

Theo: Let me know if you run into any problems
Sally: I've been gone two minutes!
Theo: Sorry—trouble just seems to follow you

She tutted and closed the window, also ignoring the Daily Gift notification. It would take ages to sift through and loot all these bodies when they were so stacked without opening up some of them repeatedly by accident. They'd better have something decent on them.

As she crouched down to begin sifting through, a figure among them moved, backing away from her.

*"K-keep away!"*

Sally tensed and peered through the stacked bodies. A pale and familiar figure sat, panicked, trying to escape her gaze.

Her mouth hung open as she silently mouthed a curse.

## CHAPTER THIRTY-SEVEN

# Reborn

C*huck?"*

The figure paused their attempt at escape, confusion mixing with their panic. They licked their lips in an attempt to whet reality, to make it make some sense. "S-sally?" his tentative reply came.

"Oh, buddy, why are you hiding under all this death?" She frowned as sadness crossed her face.

"Well, why do you *look* like death? Where are we?"

She sat on the grass and gave the floor a pat. "Come on out, and we will talk. I won't hurt you, despite my appearance."

"Okay . . ." He did not sound convinced but worked his way out of the pile and nervously came to sit nearby—but not too close. He looked like a normal human, though his dark hair was matted slightly from the various corpse juices, and his hooded top was similarly dirtied.

"How long have you been in there?" Concern painted Sally's face as she looked him over.

"Since dawn."

Sally wrinkled up her nose. "Gross, no wonder you're so spooked."

"Plus, *you* look like a zombie," he added, his eyes still darting all over her to try and make sense of her current look.

"Yeah, I am a zombie." She watched his nerves turn into a frown. "Or only partly one, at least. See, there are Players, and there are Monsters—"

"Oh, I've always been a player," he interjected.

"*There you are!* See, you're late to the party here because everyone except you and I started in this world almost four weeks ago." She smiled at his wavering acceptance.

"So it's like a real-life video game, huh?" Chuck wiped the sweat from his forehead. "Apparently I'm just called Chuck here now too?"

"It was close enough." She shrugged. "How good is your memory?"

He closed his eyes and sighed, trying to bring forth what he could last remember. "I . . . work in a diner? I remember you there and then the kitchen. Someone was nagging me—"

"Doris."

"*Doris*—yes. Then I felt sleepy. There was a period of . . . I don't know— nothingness?" He shook his head and opened his eyes. "It's hard to explain, but then I just woke up here under a pile of dead bodies."

"My tragic backstory is similar—except I woke up partly as a Monster."

"That does explain the bad complexion."

"Ass." She flicked a clod of dried dirt at him. "So now you're a Level One Novice. Want to join up with my Party and destroy the System?"

Chuck rolled his tongue around in his mouth. "I feel like I am missing several days of context for all this."

"I'll fill you in on the boring stuff when we travel. We have another Player in the Party, so you're not the only normie."

"Ugh." He rolled his eyes. "I'll join I suppose, just don't call me that."

Chuck has joined the Party

Almost immediately, both of their STARs lit up with chat notifications.

Theo: Huh, how?
Humphrey: Interesting
Theo: But also—what?
Chuck: new reality, who dis

"No memeing in chat." Sally scowled at the young man half-heartedly.

"So, you have a cute guy and some kind of *Gundam* in your Party?" Chuck raised an eyebrow. "*Theo* seems familiar though?"

"Maybe you saw him as he left the diner. You came in after him. You think he is cute?"

"Not my type, but good on you." He tilted his head. "Unless that sort of thing is illegal here, right?"

Sally rolled her eyes. This was definitely the Chuck she used to know. "I don't have that kind of attraction anymore. I do really, really want to eat him though. In a zombie way."

"Should *I* be worried?" He narrowed his eyes to see if she was eyeing up his brain already.

"Strangely, no." She shrugged and stood up, brushing off her skirt. "It's like . . . you're family or something." There would be no point telling him about his recent undeath—it could only confuse him more.

"Lucky me." He smiled despite the sarcastic tone and rose from the floor himself.

She gave him a light punch on the shoulder. "Yes, lucky you. I'm kind of a big deal around here."

Sally gave the bodies a quick loot, while Chuck averted his gaze. "Theo is probably the most experienced Novice in this world, so you've got a great mentor before you choose a class."

Skull (6)

46 Gold

Cheese (1)

Common Basic Spear (2)

"Rest of this stuff is pretty broken or terrible quality, plus I can't reach some of the corpses because of the loot box clipping." She turned around and opened up her Inventory. "Here are some items for you."

She transferred over a spear, eighty gold, and the cheese.

"A spear, fantastic. I feel just like a medieval peasant now." He withdrew it and gave the nearest tree a few test pokes. "This is a fantasy world I take it?"

"So far." She nodded. "Like a type of RPG."

"Sad. I'm more of a shooter guy, myself." He awkwardly managed to work out how to stow the weapon into his Inventory.

"Jeez, alright—here." She transferred him over her crossbow. "There are Ranger and Mage classes at the least, for when you get to Level Five. I'm not a Beginners Guide though, you know?" Sally scrunched up her face at the echoed sentiment.

"Yeah, yeah. I'm sure I'll pick things up quickly enough. Do we need to go meet your boy-toy and the robot?"

"Yes. He is not a robot though; he is a Death Knight, and—"

"Same difference."

*Chuck was a lot less annoying when he was a zombie*, Sally thought to herself as her eyes narrowed. Not that she wished death upon him. Not when she couldn't even stomach eating him after.

She gestured toward the village and then headed back. Chuck was attentive enough to silently take in some of the information dumps she was able to vocalize on the short trip over. Classes, Players, Monsters, Parties, and skills. The overview was brief but enough to give the poor lad some grounding in the new world.

"Welcome to Sanctuary." She gestured widely with her arms as they entered the town. Goblins turned to eye Chuck with suspicion, but they carried on as normal.

"Cliché, and the locals are not what I was expecting."

"Remember, there are no System-created humans. Also, do not leave the Party, as the goblins may kill you." She turned to the new Novice, who was looking a little overwhelmed. "Sorry, Novices usually have their hand held at the start—not that I'd know, of course."

Chuck nodded but said little. It was somewhat unlike him, but perhaps understandable given the circumstances.

As they reached the village square, the imposing figure of Humphrey along-side the delicious stack of Theo stood out among the shorter goblins. Both of them looked at the approaching pair with a heavy amount of curiosity and con-fusion. Chuck extended his hand for shaking.

"Humphrey." The Death Knight nodded as he clasped the smaller hand in his plated fist.

"Not a very edgy name for a Death Knight." Chuck beamed and then shook Theo's in turn. "And you looked taller in your chat picture, Theo."

"A pleasure to . . . meet you, Chuck." The Novice narrowed his eyes as Sally tried to communicate something to him, silently mouthing *don't mention the dead stuff?* "That's the first time I've been negged in this world."

"Sorry." Chuck shrugged. "I spent all morning covered in dead bodies. I'm only half this salty, usually."

"It's slightly better than having someone threaten to eat you all the time." Theo smiled, avoiding the gaze of the zombie. "Let me sort you out with some Novice gear."

"Hey! I've had plenty of chances but haven't done it yet!" Sally scowled and looked out around the village as the two men dallied with their equipment. All this around her was now under threat. Whether they were System-created or not, this little community stood for their hope and as the first important step in their journey to ending this charade of a world.

Humphrey stood beside her. "We should leave. Defending this village will not be easy, but the most important thing is that you survive. If it falls, it can be retaken, but they need you. *We* need you."

She looked up at the metal Monster, the warm flames of his helmet making the air wavy behind him. "You're remarkably soft and considerate for someone designed for impassively monitoring the world."

"They will come for me." He ignored her comments. "And I want you to be safe even without me. Without these inept Players."

"What's got into you?" Her eyes searched the stoic face of the Death Knight. "Do you know something that you aren't letting on?"

"*Yes.*"

She frowned and looked back out at the village. Her five Leaders were now running the place. They should be able to hold out against random Players that may come investigating. If it took Poppybrook two days to reach here, then it must be quite far away. Even walking from the Cemetery to Yarch—now Sanctuary—the distance had surprised her. She would have to give the map a proper look once they got walking.

"How soon?" She looked back up at Humphrey with a raised eyebrow.

"Hmm." His eye sockets narrowed, and he raised a finger to the air just above them. "About now."

Out of the air, a skull bathed in eldritch green energy appeared and lowered to meet them.

"Hello, rogue unit HM-3.3," the Observer hissed in a dry tone.

## CHAPTER THIRTY-EIGHT

# Punishment

Hello, Observer P-2T." Humphrey crossed his arms.

"We had reports that you went dark. You find yourself in interesting company."

"Ha, Patootie is a funny name." Sally grinned. "What did you come here for? To tell Humphrey off?"

"Humphrey? How amusing. *Ho-ho*." The green skull nodded in the air. "I am just here to *observe*—"

"Heard it before." She stuck her tongue out and pulled a face. "Are you going to eventually join me too?"

"Sally, please." Humphrey shook his head. "Green has a deeper knowledge of the System; they would be able to see—"

"I can see how you are all *wrong*. Far too much Strength, Constitution, and sass for a zombie. [Player: Theo] has circumvented his class selection, [Player: Chuck] is a whole bundle of issues. Observer HM-3.3, you have broken protocol and become a Monster—not to mention the destruction of the Novice village of Yarch." Patootie hovered in the air.

"So what do you intend to do about it?" Humphrey narrowed his eye sockets, and the flame behind his helmet flickered brighter.

"For now . . . nothing."

"Then why assault us with the unnecessary tension?" Sally growled.

"My directive is to ensure the System is believable and cohesive. Your Party and their actions are cause for concern, but I am yet to determine if you threaten the—"

"Oh, so you're just giving us a vibe check?" Chuck piped up from the back, the pair of Novices having been quietly listening in on the conversation.

"Despite being borne of error and malpractice"—the green Observer glared at the Death Knight—"you are still working within the terms of the System. I anticipate that the regiment from Poppybrook shall overtake Yarch in due course and any anomalies shall be taken care of."

"Ah, so you're not reporting us to the big boss, because you think we'll be dead soon?" Sally shook her head at the indignation.

"Very smart for a zombie," the green glow said, "very *astute*. The Peacekeeper Regiment is the cure to the disease that you represent—*they* are the System working as intended."

"That's a bit harsh," Theo murmured, rubbing the back of his neck.

Humphrey grinned, a twinkle of red fire lighting in his eye sockets. "What if we repel the Peacekeepers?"

"I don't deal in hypotheticals. *I will* be keeping watch over you all." With that, the Observer vanished from view.

"Creepy." Chuck grimaced. "What was that?"

"Monitoring bots. Humphrey used to be one," Theo said.

The Death Knight sighed. "It's fair to assume we will be under constant observation now. It is unlikely they will show themselves, nor will we be able to detect them."

"They felt it needed to come to taunt you though. Sounded personal." Sally nudged the plated undead. "Our plan doesn't change, right?"

"*Yes*. The plan does not change. Let us head out to the bandits."

The group turned to leave as Chuck flipped off the empty space where the skull had been with both hands before he caught them up.

"Like I'm going to follow the advice of the guy carrying a wooden sword."

Sally sighed. "Would you two stop bickering? You are worse than Humphrey and me."

Humphrey frowned and shrugged at the insinuation as she continued.

"Theo is actually rather effective, even if he has chosen a really stupid build."

The Level Nine Novice opened his mouth but then thought better of arguing. Likewise, Chuck rolled his eyes and looked off into the surrounding woods.

*Traveling with people who can talk is a lot more hassle than when it was just Humps and me,* Sally thought. She liked both of the men individually, but the drudgery of walking just caused them to find ways of annoying each other. Only Humphrey didn't seem to be too perturbed, which was surprising given the now real threat of the System watching him.

She shook these thoughts away and turned to the Death Knight. "What do we know about the bandits?"

"Should be a small outpost, maybe several dozen bandits at most. Not too powerful, but we should exercise caution; the Unique bandit will be a complication."

Sally nodded despite *several* leaving a lot of smudged detail. "Before the bandit camp . . ."

"You want to get the newb leveled up first?"

"Perfect, glad you're on my wavelength, Humps." She beamed at the crimson-plated figure. Sure, it may be because he was her bodyguard, but there was a link between them—a trust and understanding that she didn't feel with anyone else.

"There's a short detour we can take." He turned his head to Theo. "There's an orc encampment slightly to the west—not as far as you encountered, but in that direction."

The Novice nodded. "Seemed a bit weird at the time, like a hunting party. That was the first time I'd seen them that side of the woods though."

"Interesting." The helmet flames briefly flickered wildly.

Sally knew what that meant—more bugs or glitches to contend with. Hopefully just something like the cyclops, and not anything to distract them from their task.

"Am I going to be able to get to Level Five and change class?" Chuck nudged up between the zombie and Humphrey.

"Killing some orcs? Probably not, although—" The Death Knight stopped dead in his tracks.

Chuck tripped over the now stationary plated feet and landed face down on the road. As Sally and Theo exchanged a look, they helped the young Novice up.

"Hmm." Humphrey knelt and observed the road before looking into the woods on the right.

Sally joined him and narrowed her eyes. The grass just off the road had been flattened, and patches of trampled mud showed through. A handful of bushes between the trees had been shredded and equally thrashed to pieces as if something, or many things, had blazed through the area.

"What does it look like?" She crossed her arms.

"Looks like . . . boars?" Theo offered with a shrug. "There's the occasional group spaced around parts of the woods."

"Theo is correct." The Death Knight stood back up. "Though they are not normally so destructive. They graze or run from Players but return to their area. This looks like a stampede that tore through, across the road into . . ." He turned and pointed to the left side of the woods, where they could now see some similar damage.

"Must have been a lot of lil piggies to churn up that mud." Chuck idly gestured to the turned earth. "How many boars are usually in a pack?"

Humphrey shrugged. "Between five and ten, at a guess. This looks like two dozen or so, at my estimation."

Sally rubbed her forehead. Just once it would be nice to go half a day without some part of the System doing something untoward. "You seeing this greenie?"

She looked up into the clear sky. "Much more pressing matters to attend to than our group of weirdos."

If the Observer was there, it gave no sign of acknowledgment.

"I'm not sure if 'weirdos'—" Theo began.

"Hush, puppy." Sally wagged her finger. "There's been too many words and not enough sustenance. You'll want to be on the good side of these gnashers." She pointed to her sharp, pointed teeth for emphasis.

"Wait," Chuck interjected. "So if Players are humans, and you only eat them—you're murdering actual people?"

An awkward silence fell among the group as they stood still on the road. Theo especially looked down at his feet as the zombie tried to come up with a concise excuse.

"Short answer . . . yes?" She shrugged sheepishly.

"In fairness," Theo added, "Players are hunting Sally down, so it's mostly self-defense."

"Mostly." She agreed with a nod. "It's not like Theo, who didn't even eat the ones he killed. Oh—maybe we should have swapped Leaders for that?"

"You're not helping your case." Chuck swept his messy hair from his forehead, scowling up at the bright sunny day. "It's not that I judge the morality of it—this must be some kind of weird dream or virtual reality thing, right? We might just go back to our normal lives when we die."

They all cautiously eyed up Humphrey, who returned a blank expression. "I know nothing of your previous lives or how you came to be here. I apologize."

"It's okay, Humps." Sally nudged him. "We'll just assume we aren't committing wholesale slaughter on innocents until proven otherwise."

"I plan on repressing and avoiding any thought of it." Theo rubbed the sweat from his hands across his Novice armor. "And hopefully just die before becoming accountable."

"That's the spirit." Sally nodded, shooting him finger-guns. "Now let's go kill some orcs so Chuck can be more useful than you."

Chuck rolled his eyes.

They set back off up the road in the hopes of not coming across the rampaging boar horde. Sally ran up her STAR menus, checking for any notifications. Naturally, the daily reward sat unclaimed—as was now tradition. With no better way to build a little suspense, she decided now was as good a time as any to retrieve it.

| Day 8 Reward |
| --- |

Her right eye twitched; it was definitely not day eight.

## CHAPTER THIRTY-NINE

# Seeing Green

Sausage (1)

**W**hat? She shuddered with absolute anger . . . *Disgust*. Literally, *what?*

"Are you okay, Sally?" Humphrey frowned at her. "You've gone an odd color."

"I feel like this is some big joke sometimes," she hissed like a deflating balloon. "Like, maybe the Architect is just watching over me and having a good laugh."

"They did not seem to have much humor from my interactions."

Sally narrowed her eyes at the Death Knight. "Have you met them or just spoken to them?"

"Just . . . spoken." He gestured for them to leave the road into the woods.

The trees here were darker—a deeper, almost redder brown, as well as being sturdier-looking. The foliage began to look more like pine trees than wide verdant leaves. As the zombie kept her narrowed gaze on Humphrey, she stumbled over a rough stone sticking from the floor. Looking down, this area was also less grass-dense and sparse rocks dotted around bare patches of dried earth.

"This is the woods east of Hillan," Theo said, trying to be helpful.

"*I have a map.*" Sally shrugged. "I just don't want to look at it."

"Willful ignorance isn't an attractive trait, you know," Chuck murmured loud enough for them all to hear.

"Neither is being Level One—try not to get killed by orcs." She stuck her tongue out and smiled, almost biting her tongue in the process. These sharp teeth were pretty wild now that she thought about it.

Thankfully, their back-talking was quickly curbed as they entered this section of the woods. The change of scenery brought with it an air of tension, a thick foreboding texture to the very air. Quietly, they traveled until the Death Knight held up a plated fist before he pointed to the southwest.

Through the tree line, some darker wooden structures could be seen, and the faint whisper of smoke rose into the sky. It was reasonably likely that this was the orc encampment. As a group, they crouched down and began to sneak closer.

"*Nice gloves*," Sally whisper-hissed at Theo as they crept between trees.

"Thanks," his hushed reply came. "I had Oleb enchant them."

"Whaat? That's a thing?" She screwed her face up in envy. Perhaps she shouldn't have slept in so late.

"Attack Speed Increase." He winked before he caught the scowl of the Death Knight trying to keep them quiet.

Even if she eventually decided not to eat him, Theo might be useful to keep around just because he seemed to have more of a clue of what he was doing in this world. There was something about him that concerned her, but she couldn't place what. Perhaps it was just that he had been here nearly a month before she had even awoken. That was plenty of time to learn the ins and outs.

Humphrey paused, and they sidled up to him, peering around a dead tree that had wrapped around a dirt-smeared boulder. The orc camp lay ahead of them. It was both smaller than Sally had expected but also more than anticipated.

A group of five houses sat on the left side of a clearing as they looked down at it: roughly made circular structures of dark wood, with a thatched roof that rose to a point like a cone. In the middle of the camp, the campfire itself was surrounded by several half-log benches and small stools. Metal frames sat beside the fire, most likely for drying meat. The right side of the camp had a raised platform, as it looked as though the camp had been built against a plateau. The ground at the higher level had two buildings but was otherwise lacking interesting details.

There were three orcs on the raised ridge and six milling about the camp area. *No doubt there will be more in the houses,* Sally thought.

"Okay." Humphrey turned back to the group, his helmet flames licking against the boulder they hid behind. "There's an Elite here—I can feel it."

"I bet they have a nice dagger for me." Sally rolled her eyes before they huddled together for their plan.

Heavy, plated footsteps were the first thing to alert the orcs. Barreling down the shallow decline toward the camp, the Death Knight burst into a red glow as

*[Adrenaline]* activated. The brief confusion painted across the brows of the orcs gave way to anger, even if this wasn't a Player—they were under attack.

"*Attackers!*" one of them at the front bellowed out in a gruff, guttural voice as they withdrew an axe from their belt.

Around the top of the camp, the lighter armored figure of Theo ran across to meet the three orcs readying bows at the top of the platform. Chuck trailed a distance behind him, crossbow drawn, trying to keep as far away from the danger as possible.

Four more orcs had emerged from the group of huts by the time Humphrey slid into melee, raising his sword to meet the gathered throng of greenskins. Sally popped out from behind him, having trailed him closely on approach.

*[Will of the Dark Lord] [Summon Zombies]*

The pair posed dramatically as they activated their new skills at the same time. A pulse of black light flashed through the orcs as the greatsword struck the ground and fell energy pulsed from Sally's hands to the ground beneath her.

Five orcs grasped at their heads or lolled around stunned. Three were unaffected, and two were slightly out of range as they clambered from their housing.

Four zombies erupted from the dry earth, scratching and groaning. Two of which immediately latched onto stunned orcs and began biting into them.

Three steps closer Sally rammed her dagger into the throat of one of the stunned opponents, dark crimson blood spraying to the floor.

Two bloodied orcs fell down from the platform, a whir of pink energy overhead as Theo battled with additional orcs from the structures up top.

One crossbow bolt flew across the clearing, striking one of the reinforcements in the chest. Their roar of pain echoed around the clearing.

*Zero chance this could go wrong.* Sally beamed—red eyes blazing with excitement.

The door of the biggest hut burst open.

A cloud of dust and debris obscured the figure that emerged from within. With the melee truly engaged, it drew Sally's focus away from the new opponent.

Theo dived and swung upwards, the wooden sword almost moving against his will as his set activation drew him to make continual attacks. The orcs were large—a head taller than him and twice as wide. These were just like the ones he had to fight the other day; full of muscle and tribal barbarism. He had taken an axe to the arm, which stung, but had felled three of the seven now atop the platform. More than they had expected, but not more than he could handle.

A crossbow bolt struck his attacker in the shoulder, interrupting their attack, which gave his *[Novice Strike]* two further chances to do damage. The extra attack speed from his gloves was fantastic, but he could feel the lethargy from the repeated fast movements—he could do with some Constitution. At least he had heard the Novice behind him level up once, maybe even twice so far.

Sally and Humphrey fought back-to-back. As he struck an orc with the pommel of his weapon, she darted forth to the briefly flatfooted Monster—a quick stab to the leg, followed up the arm, and then another stab into the eye socket. A second orc with a greataxe came her way, so she quickly withdrew the torch from her Inventory and blinded it. The Death Knight swung his large blade over her head and decapitated the opponent.

The zombies weren't a great match for the orcs—two had been sent back to the ground already—but they had taken down three orcs with a fourth in progress. Sometimes the extra distraction would be worth the use of the skill, and she had no emotional attachment to these shamblers.

The figure of the Elite loomed into view among a throng of even more orcs emerging from the buildings. Slightly larger than the others, with a large headdress and pauldrons of thin reed, skulls, and other small adornments. Pale yellow eyes glared from their darker green skin, and large fangs rose up on either side of their wide jaw. A jagged branch of dead wood formed a magic staff, and some manner of animal skull sat at the top.

Tendrils of bright green energy began swirling around the top of the magic staff as the shaman began chanting a spell. A single beam shot out, weaving through the air and striking one of the standing zombies—exploding the corpse in two; residual green energy crackled around the impact.

"Watch out—magic user," Humphrey growled as he lopped a hand off his assailant.

Sally rolled beneath an overhead axe swing and sliced the calf muscle of a bloodied orc. "*Duh!*"

Theo threw up and dropped his sword to the floor. This extra attack speed was nauseating at best, and now his arm ached. The orcs had been dealt with. He allowed himself a moment to recover as his bleary eyes looked out over the platform to see the shaman emerge into the fray. *He should go help.*

"You alright? Perhaps we should call *you* Chuck?" Chuck came up beside him, crossbow still loaded. "You know, like the food you just chucked—"

"I get it." Theo wiped his mouth and stood up straight. "But you should be staying back, still."

"Rats to that. Now that it's clear I can better shoot down at—" He turned his head to the noise from the smaller shacks on the ridge.

An orc emerged, taller and much thicker, with more muscle than all the rest, wielding twin scimitars that gleamed with magical energy.

The real Elite of the camp.

## CHAPTER FORTY

# Seeing Red

**S**ally dropped to the floor as one winding bolt of fell energy surged off into a tree someway off behind the melee. A second one struck Humphrey in the shoulder, letting off a blaze of green that crackled as it petered out, the smell of burnt ozone filling the air overpowering the scent of gore and sweat. If only she still had her crossbow.

As if the System could read her thoughts, the crossbow clattered to the floor just behind her. Shortly followed by the hard thud of Chuck's bloodied body.

She cursed and rolled over to his prone form, grabbing the ranged weapon along the way. Her eyes darted over the prone Novice. *Definitely broken bones and plenty of sources of bleeding.*

"*Ow,*" Chuck groaned toward the hard ground. "*. . . Elite.*"

Sally popped a Healing Potion from his belt and helped him imbibe it. "Humps, guard Chuck," she growled, her eyes scanning the top of the platform. She couldn't see Theo or the Elite.

With a *twang*, she shot the bolt out at the shaman, striking the orc in the hand holding the staff, pinning it to the wooden focus and interrupting their next spell. As she quickly loaded another bolt and stowed the crossbow in her Inventory, she turned back to her plated bodyguard. "Throw me!" She ran at the Death Knight.

Humphrey dropped his greatsword briefly to crouch ready, then boosted her into the air as she ran onto his braced forearms. She leapt into the air, her fingers just reaching the rough lip of the platform.

*Thank the Architect for my high Strength.* She pulled herself up, pausing halfway as she saw Theo. A brief shiver of cold ran through her core, followed by a burst of red-hot rage. Her fingers clenched into the wooden floor as she lifted the rest of her body up, eyes blazing at the Elite orc.

Theo's wooden sword glowed pink as his *[Novice Strike]* tried to strike out at his opponent. His arm was held back at an odd, unnatural angle so the blow couldn't land. Gashes of crimson ran up the side of his torso and across his face. He was in a test of Strength against the massive orc and was slowly losing. The orc had its fair share of damage too, and the arm not currently twisting away from the Novice's attack held a scimitar sluggishly.

"Leave him alone!" She withdrew her dagger and balled up a fist in her free hand, *[Hex: Slow]* barely casting correctly as she shook with rage.

The Elite looked over at her, his bright yellow eyes furrowing in confusion at seeing a Monster—or at least something that looked like a Monster—and being hit by the curse. With a grunt, he headbutted Theo and dropped him to the floor. The pink glow of the wooden sword faded as the Novice sunk to the floor, unconscious.

"Nobody bleeds my boy but me," she hissed through clenched teeth. She watched as the large figure picked up their second scimitar and rolled their shoulders out. The orc was much larger and better armed, with more reach. If this was the time to unlock some hidden potential, then it'd better happen soon.

"What are you?" the deep voice of the Elite boomed out.

Sally grinned and checked the UI. *Krudd the Bloodthirsty.* He wasn't Unique and was only a Level Three Elite. If she took down the cyclops, then this chump should be easy enough. The fact that both men had been taken down by this one guy would have to be a stern conversation for later on—Chuck had a bit of an excuse, but with Theo being Level Nine, he shouldn't be this paper-thin. She was ignoring the group of dead orcs already littering the floor that the pair had managed to dispatch.

"Answer me!" Krudd bellowed again, hesitating.

"I am *Sally the Unliving*, eater of the System, slayer of Monster and Player alike, and you are in my way!"

The orc huffed and hunched down, ready to sprint. "Too many words." He launched forward, closing the gap between them in a couple of brief seconds. The first scimitar tore through the air, the power of his large arms blurring the glowing blade as it careened toward her.

Sally took a deep breath to cool her temper and sidestepped the first attack. As fast and strong as it may be, it was heavily telegraphed. The second blade was slower—dark blood ran down this arm in streams, and she was able to block it with the edge of her rare dagger. Trying to block was not a great idea, just due to the surface area of each weapon, but the act knocked on the confidence of Krudd.

His glare faltered as the amount of strength this slim zombie seemed to possess was much higher than expected. As his blades twisted through the air, she seemed to be one step ahead, just outside his reach or able to deflect his assault. He didn't feel helpless, though—in fact it just enraged him further. With a burst of amber flames, he activated *[Endless Fury]*.

Humphrey slid his blade through the last of the orc defenders, foul intestines dropping to the floor as he stood in front of the injured Novice. No orc had made it past—even the shaman had been unable to send magic that way, even if the Death Knight had to take a couple of those eldritch blows himself.

The shaman, now the only orc left in the lower campground, licked their yellowed fangs nervously. Most System-created, especially low-level Monsters, were not built for self-preservation. They would not run, or give chase over great distance, or even beg or plead for mercy. Thus, all they could do was send further bolts of green magic out at the slowly approaching plated figure.

Humphrey grinned, crimson flames like a furnace from the back of his helmet. Dark energy swirled around his greatsword as he readied a final *[Grave Strike]*.

Sally caught the sharp edge of a scimitar across her forehead as she leapt backward. Blood ran down her face, threatening to blind her as she cursed at the orc. Whatever his skill did, he had renewed speed and focus and had become a whirling dervish of continuous attacks. Splinters of wood had shot up from the platform along with blood and shredded leather as Krudd struck everything in his path.

Foolishly, she hadn't bought her own Healing Potions or saw fit to get a portion of the supplies that Theo had gotten from Sanctuary. There would be time after the fight, she had thought. It would be a quick in-and-out, twenty-minute battle against some weak orcs. A fresh cut against her thigh reassured her that she was correct on being completely wrong.

Could she hold out until Humphrey finished down at the bottom and was able to circle around? *Doubtful.* Plus, Theo was bleeding out, and she didn't have the space to properly check the Party UI and see how everyone was faring. Why the System couldn't be accessed mentally was something she would add to her long list of questions for the Architect.

She ducked and dived toward the Elite, sliding along the wooden platform. A scimitar struck next to her head, cutting off a chunk of hair as the blade stuck into the wood. With a quick strike, she stabbed the offending hand, heavily slicing through two fingers. In the brief respite, she clambered up and sliced across his stomach as she moved away from him. The streak of crimson was her reward, but the orc was too tough-skinned to be so easily disemboweled by a small weapon.

Krudd growled and let go of the scimitar embedded into the wood, his skill was draining him of stamina, and the small injuries were adding up. He raised his blade up for the attack—expecting the duel to continue, but the zombie ran away, leaving him briefly perplexed.

Sally jumped over a dead orc and bashed away at her STAR, the menus spinning erratically as her shaky hand tried to find her Inventory. With a brief yelp of jubilation, she withdrew the crossbow and turned toward the Elite.

The orc roared as his weapon flashed through the air, knocking the projectile out of the air with a clang. As he lowered the scimitar with a grin, a sharp, warm feeling clouded his vision in one eye. It was . . . *uncomfortable*.

She watched as Krudd raised a hand up to feel for the bolt protruding from his eye socket before the Elite slumped to the floor and collapsed. "Ass," she spat, "now I'll have to find where my dagger went." She stowed the crossbow and ran over to Theo.

Thankfully, he also stored a Healing Potion on his belt. Why he didn't think of using it himself was another cause for her to shake her head. She lifted him onto her lap so she could feed the potion to him. He looked pretty bad—not only was his sword arm limp and clearly broken, but the gash on his face was pretty deep, and his breathing was haggard from his side injury.

For a brief moment, this was as human as she had felt since awakening here. She felt sorry for him; there was a pit inside her that wanted to care for him and was alarmed to see him in such a state. Despite the lives she had taken and the differences in their existence here, he was just as fragile and Unique as she or Humphrey were.

She slowly licked a line of blood from his face.

# Beside the Flame

*W*hat are you doing?"

Sally slowly turned to the side, tongue still extended from her salivating mouth. Chuck and Humphrey stood at the end of the platform. The Death Knight didn't seem to be passing any judgment, but the Novice had a confused scowl across his bruised face to match the question posed.

"Goog to see 'ou're up, Chufk," she said, trying to play it cool as her tongue slowly slid back into her mouth.

"Yeah." He shook the situation out of his head. "Would have been nice to know that was a possibility."

Humphrey jostled the limping Novice. "That Sally wanted to taste Theo or that the Elite would spawn up here?"

"The Elite, obviously." Chuck frowned at the floor.

"It was a bit rougher than we expected." Sally nodded. "But you got what, three levels out of that?"

"I almost got *dead!*" He threw his arms up in the air, which caused him to wince in pain. "But . . . yes, I'm very close to Level Four now."

Sally smiled at the Death Knight. They had done a pretty good job—they certainly fought well together. Whether that was because of their boss-bodyguard bond, or they were just naturally pretty neat, it didn't matter too much. It was a shame the zombies had gotten mulched so quickly; that skill was perhaps more useful if she got a whole horde from it with all three activations. She hoped it scaled better as she leveled up.

Theo spluttered, and his eyes opened slowly. His wounds had already healed up to some degree, and his arm had set itself back to an unbroken state. He sat forward from her lap and rubbed his temples, letting out a slow groan.

"You alright, meatbag? *I didn't eat you,*" she spoke softly and mostly truthfully.

"I'm starting to wonder if the system has anything that fixes PTSD." He grimaced and shrugged at her. "I was just broken, bleeding, with my arm twisted off. Some of that is healed, but the memory of the pain lingers."

Sally adjusted her dress as she sat beside him. "That's pretty deep, hun. I've been trying to maintain a Sunday-morning-cartoon sorta vibe. It helps that my brains got kinda scrambled on the way in." She placed a hand softly on his leg. "I'm sorry."

"It's . . . not your fault." He looked away from her as an exasperated tear ran down his cheek. "I blame the Architect. I'm not a violent person . . . To be forced into this . . . the pain, the death—it's not right."

"Maybe. I didn't need to drag you along into all this danger though."

"True—you didn't," Chuck interjected.

Sally rolled her eyes. "But there might be a way for us all to escape this. Well, not Humphrey, I suppose?"

The Death Knight said nothing but stood with arms folded.

Theo sighed and stood to his feet, dusting himself down, before offering a hand down to Sally. "If that is possible, then we must endure this, correct?"

She took his hand and stood too. "*Yarp.*"

"Enough of the sap." Chuck waved his arms despite the discomfort. "Let's just loot these bodies and head on our way."

Humphrey tilted his head to the side. Parts of his crimson armor looked cracked and tarnished. "I will try and remember if there is anything we can level you up on as we travel to the bandits."

"I have a *[Campfire].*" Theo nudged Sally as he saw her check the Party UI. "It's slow healing, but we can rest together and get healed up."

"Righto. Let's loot and reconvene outside of this encampment. Wouldn't want a respawn atop us—it's bound to happen eventually, right?"

"Guaranteed." He smiled before hobbling off to the nearest body.

It took them a short while to make their way around each of the corpses before they moved farther into the woods, away from the orc spawning area. After dividing up the spoils, Sally received her share of the bounty, along with recovering her *[Rare Dagger of Luck].*

---

173 Gold
Red Cape
Bracers of Defense
Medium Medicine Kit (2)
Iron Bars (4)

Theo had enough Strength to use the *[Orc Scimitars]*, but still chose not to due to his odd meme-build interaction. Chuck did not have the right stats for it but seemed content enough with the crossbow anyway, which Sally relinquished back to the Novice. There were a couple of basic Chance Boxes that they let Chuck open. *Two maces and a shortsword.*

She put the bracers on. They had a little weight to them, but she already felt comfortable in wearing them. Until she found something better to stab people with, the extra defense to block blows with was worth everything. The *[Iron Bars]* could be given to Jaxk back at the village, and hopefully, he could make something nice out of them. She made a mental note to check out crafting and the requirements when they were in less imminent danger.

Humphrey was given the *[Red Cape]*. Despite him not having a proper Inventory or way to equip items, he made do with the old-fashioned way. The cape was large, and even though it was slightly worn and rough around the edges, it suited his look perfectly. He posed dramatically, and it shimmered in the breeze. "*Ha-ha!*" Crimson flame blazed from his helmet.

The two men brought out some food to eat as the *[Campfire]* was set up—the warming flame comforting and relaxing. Sally was a little jealous she was not interested in partaking of the meal—the memory of the way Theo's blood made her tongue tingle was too fresh in her memory to find purpose in anything else. Why couldn't she have been a vampire instead? At least then she could turn him or at least turn him into a thrall.

She glanced over at Chuck. Perhaps a mindless follower wasn't the best idea. The thought of how he had come to be—how his soul had lingered in some other space before joining to his body . . . Some of that was scary to think about. The other people in the diner . . . Were they in a similar position? Her thoughts busied her mind enough that she didn't notice Chuck staring at her at first.

He looked . . . tired and stressed. Perhaps the ordeal was working him over harder than it had with Theo. Chuck had almost died, too, if he had landed slightly different from the drop off the platform—or even if he hadn't been pushed and got trapped in melee. Something told her he didn't still have the ability to come back from zero Hit Points at some level loss . . . Though . . .

"Have you thought about what class you'll pick?" Theo was the one to end the awkward silence.

"Probably Rogue." Chuck shrugged, still looking over at Sally. "Evasion chance, ranged damage with the crossbow—try not to die."

"Ranged support would be useful." The zombie nodded. Part of her wondered if she should have gone for Ranged or Spellcasting Affinity with how the Party was now stacked—but the extra HP and defense had certainly saved her so far. "Do you know what the Unique bandit boss is like, Humps?"

"I do not. Generally, bandits are a mix of ranged and melee. Spellcasting is rare. They aren't very skilled, but it depends on how the Unique has been glitched—if that's what they are."

She nodded. It was a reasonable assumption that the Death Knight would know if the Unique was System-created or not. Having named one-life Monsters seemed like a short-lived endeavor. Any Party worth their salt would have hunted them out at this stage in the . . . game? That word felt awkward but sat in her mind like a slowly melting ice cube.

Chuck's hand shook as he tapped on his leg, something clearly playing on his mind. "So the plan is to recruit this . . . other Monster, then travel back to Sanctuary and beat off the approaching city guards?"

Sally stifled a snicker as she nodded.

"We won't be walking back, though." Humphrey held up a hand. In this hand was a rolled-up scroll. "*[Scroll of Town Teleport]*. I had to twist Oleb's arm for this. Not literally, *ha-ha*."

"Neat!" Sally's eyes gleamed. "So we can probably do the bandit thing, get Chuck leveled, do some adventuring, and just pop back in time to help defend the village?"

"In a manner of speaking, *yes*."

Theo rubbed his chin. His facial wound had closed up, and a fresh scar ran down the right side of his head. "I haven't been around this side of the woods. It would be great to find out if there is anything else that could be useful for my build."

Humphrey tilted his head and put the scroll back away on his belt. "Let me consider what I know and furnish you with any pertinent details."

"I await your response eagerly." The Novice nodded slowly in return. However, anything that made him attack faster might break his arm or kill him quicker than any opponent.

Chuck just looked ill. His eyes had a sunken look to them, glazed over as he stared into the lapping flames of the *[Campfire]*.

Sally ran her tongue across her sharp teeth. The woods around here were oddly quiet—there was no ambient noise of animals or insects, only the brief rustle of pine needles as the gentle breeze meandered its way through the area. Maybe it would be a good idea to get Chuck back to the village for some proper rest soon; there was obviously some coming-to-terms-with-the-situation that he needed to get on board with.

"Hey, Chuck, what do you want to do after you get your class?" A verbal branch of peace she offered across the flames.

He looked up, the fire dancing in his darkened eyes.

"I want to kill more Monsters."

## CHAPTER FORTY-TWO

# Morals / Morsels

The mood of the group was somewhat somber once they had finished recovering. Humphrey led the way through the woods, with Chuck falling slightly behind the other two.

Sally pulled an awkward expression at Theo, who responded in kind. It was nice that despite their differences, they were on the same wavelength. The scar from his earlier wound was just a slim line of pink now, hardly noticeable except in certain lighting. She looked away and swallowed the gathering saliva. It was even more conflicting now. Not only had she become more attached to his existence and well-being, but after tasting his blood she also wanted to eat him all the more too.

Chuck had taken a similar route but in the opposite direction. His attitude was concerning, and there was part of her brain that told her to be wary. Both Humps and Theo she trusted with her life—unlife—but the shorter Novice had already begun showing contempt for Monsters. Not that she particularly cared for them either, but she and the Death Knight were Monsters—just like Bella and the rest of the goblins.

As far as she was concerned, there was no difference between the Unique Monsters and the Players who had a soul. Not until they found out how people were brought here and if they could be sent back. On reflection, this decision made her actions more villainous. Or at least as terrible as whatever the Players did . . .

Sally shook her head. There was no time for moral quandaries.

Humphrey held up his hand. "Movement ahead."

Sally sidled up beside him and looked into the distance. "Bandits?" She could now hear footsteps ahead but didn't have visuals yet.

The Death Knight shrugged. "I suggest we approach ready; better we get the jump than they."

She cursed under her breath and drew her dagger. Nodding at the two Novices, they similarly prepared. Although their physical Health Points had recovered, they would be too mentally drained to get into a new fight so soon before the bandits. Hopefully, this would be some basic Monsters and not a high-level Party.

Soft voices carried out from behind a wall of dried shrubbery and trees leaning away from a mottled gray boulder. With a sharp intake of unnecessary breath, she gave the signal that they should jump out at the approaching group. Internally, she was glad that Chuck was less clumsy and more silent—leaving the Death Knight to be the clunkiest among them.

"*Wait, can you hear something?*"

Sally sighed; their attempts at subtlety still needed work. Instead, she led the Party into a charge, barreling around the obstacles and sliding into a wide pathway through the trees. Ahead of them by twenty feet were four very startled-looking women.

She quickly ran her eye over them—two Level Four Novices, a Level One Cleric, and a Level One Fighter.

The Fighter was the first to speak up, taking a tentative step forward as their Party leader. "Who or . . . what are you guys?" Beneath short black hair, her green eyes shifted uneasily between each of the *Outsiders*. The axe held in a tight fist shook visibly.

Sally licked her lips. "We are a Party, same as you . . ."

"Don't look it!" one of the Novices with a blonde ponytail piped up, trying to hide behind a wooden shield.

"You look like Monsters . . ." the Fighter continued. "Well, half of you do."

The eyes of the new group looked up at the bounty on Theo—the clear signal that he was a Player Killer. It did little to improve their trust in the odd Party before them.

"We aren't particularly bad . . ." Theo shrugged sheepishly. "We are more against the System than we are against Players."

"We aren't going to kill them, are we?" Chuck murmured out of the side of his mouth.

"I am sooo hungry," Sally hissed. "They might want to kill us too."

The Cleric moved forward to join her Fighter. "We don't want any trouble—we were just heading away from Yarch." She pushed brown hair from her tanned face. "It's been taken over by goblins."

Sally grinned and opened her mouth to speak before the Fighter interrupted.

"Our friend and fifth, Chloe, was attacked before we realized . . ." A sigh shuddered from the woman. "She died."

The smile on the face of the zombie turned into a frown. She hoped the goblins were okay. "Group vote?" She raised an eyebrow to the team.

"*For.*" The Death Knight crossed his arms.

"Indifferent." Theo bit his lip and tried not to make eye contact with the nervous Party.

"Against!" Chuck threw his arms up, startling the four women. "I can't believe you are discussing this; especially you, Theo." He shook his head in frustration. "But *also*, especially you, Sally."

Sally opened her mouth to counter him, but again the Fighter interrupted.

"Do you need rescuing? You seem normal. We can fight them if need be." Her expression hardened, but her weapon didn't shake any less.

"No!" Chuck held his face. "*No fighting.*" With a deep sigh, his face rose to face the zombie, his eyes looking even more tired than before. "I'm sorry, Sally, I can't do this."

Chuck has left the Party

"B-but, Chuck?" Sally stammered as she watched the Novice walk across to the other group.

"You girls have a free spot, yeah?"

The Fighter nodded and added him to their Party while still trying to keep her eyes on the three remaining. She whispered something to Chuck, and he shook his head.

"Probably asking if he wanted to attack us now," Humphrey said with a small shrug.

"We are going to leave now. We will not attack you if you do not attack us." The voice of the Fighter wavered but seemed earnest enough.

Sally clenched her jaw. The pit in her stomach wasn't just from the escaping meal. Her mind felt cloudy, and her mouth refused to move to form words. Instead, she just nodded.

With brief nods of their own, the group of women plus Chuck exited from the clearing, still keeping wary eyes on the *Outsiders* until they were out of sight.

The zombie boss slumped to the floor and exhaled. "*Fffffffuuuuuuuuuuuu—*" *Bloip*

Chuck: Keep in touch
Chuck: I don't hate you . . . I just can't walk your path
Chuck: Can't become a monster too . . .

Sally smiled and wiped her eyes. If only the little jerk knew he had been a zombie.

Sally: Just don't die
Sally: ass
Chuck: The group name is White Foxes
Chuck: don't ask
Chuck: Let me know if you find a way out of the System

"Everything okay?" Theo knelt beside her and put his hand on her shoulder.

"You know how they say, 'if you love something, set it free'?" She looked up at him, her red eyes softened.

"Yeah—"

"Well, do you love that hand?" Sally ran her tongue across her teeth as her eyes bore into the tasty, warm handburger upon her.

Theo slowly removed himself from the situation and stood back up straight. "We need to find you some food. Any way we can ethically source it?"

Humphrey rubbed the side of his helmet, the scratching sound of metal upon metal making the Novice wince. "That seems unlikely. If we only killed *bad people*, then that would be closer to ethical."

"Depends how we define 'bad.'" Theo shrugged. "Am I not bad?"

Sally stood back up and brushed her skirt off, mostly by habit. It was still dusty and covered in dried blood and worse. *Typical zombie aesthetic*, she supposed. "Morality is relative, right? Especially if we are talking about who I can kill and eat. The best we can do is run into Players who will fight us outright for the honor of being in my belly."

"Like that Cleric." Humphrey nodded sagely to the agreeing nods of the zombie.

"Wait, which Cleric was this—haven't you seen a few?" Theo raised an eyebrow.

Sally shrugged animatedly. "It was the one LARPing like there was an achievement for being aggressively in-character. I wonder why he didn't get a bounty for clocking that Ranger?"

"I suppose he only did some damage; he didn't outright kill the Ranger himself."

They stood in silence for a few moments, the lack of action and subsequent questions leaving them awkwardly unfocused.

"I wonder where they're going, then." Sally raised her eyebrows innocently.

"There's another Novice village about half a day's travel from here." Theo looked out in the direction the *White Foxes* had been traveling.

"Belberry," Humphrey added. "Slightly more popular than Yarch, but probably just as deserted these days."

"Probably not full of goblins, either." Sally narrowed her eyes. They would have to find five more potential Leaders if they wanted to steal another village from the System. She caught Theo's eyes; the Novice was able to see what she was plotting in her head.

"Let's save what we have first; best not stretch ourselves too thin."

She rolled her eyes in response, despite him being correct. "Any chance of snacks on the way to the bandits, Humps?"

"Possibly. It would be a popular place to gain experience. There is a chance some Parties may be camping in the area."

"I suppose we should go find out, huh? At least we don't have the liability of getting Chuck leveled up and keeping him from dying." Sally got her bearings and started to head back in their original direction.

"Think he will turn back into a zombie if he dies?" Theo caught her up, and Humphrey lagged behind.

"Don't put that out into the world, Mister." She wagged a finger at him.

The Death Knight turned his head to watch the smallest shadow of movement flicker between distant trees behind them.

His eye sockets narrowed before he turned back to the Party with a grin.

## CHAPTER FORTY-THREE

# Fewer Still

Sally slumped against a large rock as they stopped for a breather. The temperature had been consistently mild all day, but the amount of walking in their armor was slowly draining their stamina. Theo withdrew a water flask and wiped the sweat from his brow.

Humphrey was the only one of the three who didn't seem to be too bothered. "Theo, have you used a *[Skill Book]* yet? I assume not."

The Novice gasped as he gulped down some of the fresh water and nodded. "Never found one and I was not in the villages often to purchase."

"What's a *[Skill Book]*?" Sally frowned. "And why is this the first I'm hearing of it?"

Humphrey shrugged. "There's a lot of things you don't know—I can't stand around talking about everything. It is more efficient to just bring it up when it is most important."

Sally said nothing but narrowed her eyes at the Death Knight.

"It's basically an item that lets you unlock a new skill. My understanding was that it works on First Classes and above—since, you know, Novices only get the one skill." Theo rubbed the back of his neck, reminded of his inadequacies.

"Do you have one Humphrey? Is that why you're bringing it up?" She stood back up and ogled the plated bodyguard—maybe he got one from the village?

"No, *ha-ha*. I would have given it over already or used it myself. They are worth their weight in—"

"We'd all need one," Theo diplomatically interjected, having seen the twitch in Sally's eye start-up. "If we can all use one, anyway."

"Hence my question. I do wonder if an over-leveled Novice could use it to gain a new skill. Or could a Monster?"

"Or half-Monster half-Player," Sally added, not wanting to be left out of the decision. "It would be a big boost in power to any of us."

They all nodded in silence, perhaps secretly plotting to be the first to attempt to use something that they didn't have or know how to find. Sally slyly glanced between the other two. Humphrey had pretty decent skills already that suited him, and he had a clear progression for what may come next. Theo only had one skill, so a second one would be swell if he could even get anything, considering Novices don't have any to achieve after *[Novice Strike]*.

She, however, had the whole breadth of the System to draw potential skills from. What if she could suddenly *[Summon Dragon]*, *[Remove Soul]*, or *[Eat Theo]*? The skill could also be as useless as *[Novice Strike]*, she supposed. With great randomness came risk. Maybe she could eat loads of these books and become overpowered? There was probably some limit to them—she would wait till they had at least one before getting disappointed by the reality.

"Did you know Henkk had a whole thing like *The Matrix* going on?" Sally shuffled her feet on the loose stone as she glanced at Theo.

"How so?"

"It was like . . . a video game." Those words burst forth into her brain with a warm but uncomfortable energy. "*Video game*," she repeated to herself.

"Huh? Hmm." The Novice looked into the air and sucked at his teeth, although he was having the same word-gasm. "Like . . . he could see past the code? It wasn't just a teleport power, then."

Humphrey was silent, his arms folded as he regarded the pair discussing. They really should get moving again if they wanted to reach the bandits before dusk . . . but observing was a habit hard lost. He glanced out toward the woods behind him to watch for movement.

"There was a little room he'd made, sort of outside the System—though I'm not sure how true that was. It was like if you clip through the terrain in a game and there's just emptiness." She placed her chin in her palms as she sat on a warm rock.

The Novice contemplated this for a while, staring now at the ground with a furrowed brow as if he expected to see through the illusion. "It definitely makes some manner of sense. That we are in a game, I mean." He looked up at the zombie, but his frown remained. "The stats, items, skills; everything kind of reminds me of something like . . ."

"*Hobgoblincide?*"

Theo snapped his fingers. "Yes! Like a tabletop role-playing game . . . just kind of real. And painful."

The Death Knight tilted his head and finally spoke. "Players are usually not aware of the past life. Certainly not details of . . . whatever it is you're talking about."

"An RPG is like the System except you play it by proxy with your imagination." Sally rolled her eyes. "Instead of the opposite, here. They usually have progression and classes, and Monsters to slay and loot."

Humphrey returned a blank stare. For a moment, the only sound was the lapping of the red flames from his helmet. "Well," he finally announced, "that makes my existence seem less . . . *I don't know*. I suppose I was always a meaningless pawn of something greater."

Sally shook her head. "Naw. Humps, you are part of the *Outsiders* now—remember? The Party that will be the *[Death of the Party]*. Wait, why did that box up?"

"Hmm." Theo tapped at his STAR. "It seems that links to an archived text document—like a lore file or something. It's locked though; I can't access it."

"Tease." Sally clucked her tongue, eyeing the Novice over for double measure.

"We'd best head out." Humphrey rolled his shoulders out and flexed his plated legs. "Let's get the bandit Unique on our side before dinner, huh?"

She threw up her hands in resignation.


By the time the outskirts of the bandit encampment were visible, the sun was indeed waning toward the horizon. Why had the System decided that everything had to be so bloody damn far apart? It was one of the things that irked her most about this world. It made finding people to eat difficult—especially if they just let some of them go. She glanced over to Theo.

"You know much about the layout, Humphrey?" the Novice said, narrowing his eyes at the wooden log walls ahead of them.

The Death Knight rubbed his metal chin. "You know, it is harder to recall certain details since severing my connection." He tilted his head at Theo and grinned. "There are three sections of the camp—an outside within the walls, a secondary camp built around the entrance to a cavern, with the third being structures inside the mountain."

"Each tougher to blast through, I assume?"

"*Yes, ha-ha.*"

Sally bit her lip and forced her gaze away from the Novice and toward the walls ahead of them. As much as her confidence wanted her to blaze ahead, the prospect of trying to take down such an entrenched encampment with just the three of them was a slight concern in the back of her mind.

"What level are they?" she asked, idly tapping a finger against her sheathed dagger. She was pretty sure he had said the camp had been smaller before they set off.

"Mostly two. The first area has a Level Three leader—the second has a Level Four."

"The third area?"

Humphrey grinned at her and shrugged. "That will be the Unique Monster, I presume."

Sally slowly exhaled through her nose. "Well, let's get started before it gets dark. Game plan?"

"I think our orc plan worked out pretty well, *ha-ha*."

"Right? So you take aggro, I'll bring out some zombie friends while you stun, then Theo can take on those outside the stun range while we mop up?" She beamed at them both as they nodded their agreement.

Humphrey lumbered out in front as Theo opened up his STAR menus.

"Here." He withdrew something from his Inventory and passed it to her. "I forgot I had this because it requires First Class to wear—but you might be able to wear it?"

He placed a small metal ring in her dead hand. A plain band in a dirty silver color with etchings in light green across it.

"A ring, Theo? I feel that is just too easy to make a joke about. So I'm not going to." She bit her tongue to stop something coming out and slipped the ring on.

"Looks like it works, then." He smiled sheepishly. "It has Resistance against Slashing damage. So unless all the bandits have hammers, it should help."

"The orcs dealt Slashing damage too . . ."

"Like I said, I only just remembered!" He edged away from her as they walked toward the outpost.

"Well, better late than never. I do appreciate it." She moved some hair from her face. "You just earned a few more days of remaining uneaten."

"Hey, I'm a hardened outlaw now; those sorts of threats don't—"

"If you two could please stop." Humphrey stopped to look over his shoulder. His cape fluttered dramatically as the flames from his helmet rose higher. "Some manner of surprise would be beneficial to our assault."

Sally waited for the Death Knight to turn back around before sticking her tongue out at him. Theo smiled but turned his attention to the fight ahead.

"Hmm, in saying that . . ." Humphrey tilted his head as he pointed a plated hand forward. "The gate is already open."

The log walls, which stood a good twenty feet high at pointed tips, broke at one section where a large gate would presumably be closed. Two watchtowers over each side of the opening were vacant, and the entrance was indeed wide open as the Death Knight had noted.

They sidled up to the wall and moved slowly toward the gate opening, drawing their weapons. Sally could hear no sound coming from within. She wasn't too sure what noises she expected, but a group of people would make some kind of noise.

She pushed to the front of the three of them as they reached the thick post that the gate would hitch to when closed. Slowly she peered around the edge to observe the camp.

Her eyes narrowed over empty wooden shacks, topped chairs and crates, a dying campfire, and two scores of bloodied bodies strewn across the area.

## CHAPTER FORTY-FOUR

# Bad Bad Banditry

They're already dead," she hissed to the pair behind her.

"Are you sure?" Humphrey bore down over her despite her glare in response.

"You think there are Players inside already? Or they've killed the bandits and left?" Theo waited patiently, despite also wanting to look.

Her eyes narrowed again as she tried to pick out more details. "The door to the second area of the camp is closed. There's a walkway over it, but it's sheltered—too much shadow to see if anyone is on it. This first section has no movement—lots of corpses." *And probably looted*, she thought.

"Well, let's investigate further, but stay on guard." Humphrey nudged them both before taking point.

There were two, maybe three areas where it looked like the bandits had been gathered in melee before being slaughtered. The bodies lay there, mouths agape and eyes wide in shock. Broken bones, blood, and some kind of burns. As much as it may be some kind of video game, the attention to detail was pretty realistic—as far as Sally could imagine anyway. She vaguely recalled being somewhat squeamish in real life, but here it didn't bother her one bit.

Slowly, they stalked around the outside of the almost circular camp, trying to keep out of sight of the walkway. Not the most straightforward of tasks, but between the roughly made shacks and a bit of crouch-walking they were able to block most lines of sight.

Theo grunted and pointed a finger out toward the center. "There's a second campfire, a smaller one—like our *[Campfire]*."

Indeed, next to the larger built-up campfire that had a black metal pot beside it, there was a smaller one that was spent and cold. The fight against the bandits had perhaps not gone as swimmingly as it seemed, and the supposed Party had rested before . . . heading out. Or farther in?

They squeezed behind a couple of shacks, nearing the back end of this first area. The smell of damp wood overpowered the gore and slight remains of smoke. Suddenly, Humphrey stopped, and they both paused behind him.

Humphrey: Two figures on the walkway
Humphrey: Bandits
Sally: Nodders
Sally: Let me take lead

She pushed past the Death Knight and strode confidently into the clearing in front of the closed door. "Hey! Open up!"

Two crossbows peeked out over the shadowed wall into the light.

"Who are you?" a gruff female voice called down.

Humphrey and Theo sheepishly slid out of the hiding place to join her.

"We are the *Outsiders*, and we want to speak with your boss." Sally put her hands on her hips and glared at the shadowy figures. She heard a second voice speak to the female bandit.

"Weird, they aren't adventurers, right?"

"One of them is; can tell by the smell of him."

"No, you can't. That's bullsh—"

"Ahem," Sally interrupted, "it's rude to whisper! When we are so eagerly waiting for your response." She cast a side eye at Theo and murmured from the side of her mouth, "I'm totally going to do it too, though."

The bandit turned back to them with a growl. "Doesn't matter—you seem like assholes. I won't shoot you, but you can't come in neither."

Sally pouted. "Anybody have crossbow resistance?"

"I implore you to reconsider!" Theo raised his voice, clearly not too enthused at taking a bolt for the zombie.

"No." The crossbow turned slightly more toward the Novice.

Sally raised her hands; she didn't want holes in her foodstuff. "Well, could you at least pass on a gift to your boss?"

The pair of bandits grumbled to each other before one spoke up. "Alright, no funny business though."

She turned around to mime taking something out of a bag, stifling a laugh. *No funny business* indeed. Withdrawing an item from her Inventory, she spun around and launched her torch at the battlements. After a brief sputter of surprise, the bandits fired off their shots.

Humphrey stepped in front of one, deflecting it with his greatsword. The second struck the earth beside Theo, narrowly missing his thigh. Sally charged forward and swung her fist against the locked wooden gate, while the bandits above her tried to prevent their walkway from catching alight.

To her surprise, her punch shattered through the gate, breaking whatever locking mechanism was on the other side. She shook her fist and kicked the doors wide open, the rest of her Party standing alongside her.

The wooden door shuddered as it swung over the broken parts of the lock, opening to reveal the second camp. Wooden buildings of better construction loomed in the distance, as this area almost resembled a small village. There was a well, an archery range, a large hall, a ramshackle tavern, and several houses of modest size. Most impressive, however, was the number of bandits standing around—now gawking at the trio.

"I am Sally the Unliving," she bellowed out. "You have breathed your last!"

"Choke point, near the tavern," Humphrey growled out.

"*Shit*, that was a terrible battle cry, huh?" She glanced at Theo.

The Novice didn't reply; he had a determined expression across his face as his eyes darted between the many bandits now drawing weapons and heading toward them as they ran to an alleyway.

"This seems more like a death trap?" Sally slid as they stopped in the passageway. Both wooden buildings on either side of them ran straight up to the mountain wall. A pretty apt *dead* end.

"It is." Humphrey grinned as *[Adrenaline]* flashed crimson over his plated body. "But not for us."

The alley was a good ten feet wide. With the size of the Death Knight and his blade, it would make it difficult for any bandit to make it back to her or the Novice. Humphrey stood a few feet inside the alley so only one or two bandits could make an attack at the same time. A simple plan. Ranged weapons would be the main problem.

"Hey, gimme a boost." She nudged Theo as the first bandit made it into melee with Humphrey. Blood flicked up the wall as the greatsword severed off an arm.

With a little effort, she climbed atop the roof of the shorter building and wobbled as the uneven material almost didn't support her. *They really needed to get better contractors.* She withdrew the *[Zap Wand]* from her Inventory and watched as Humphrey sliced a third bandit from leg to neck with a quick flash of his blade.

Around fifteen bandits had gathered at their choke point, almost politely waiting their turn, with a variety of weapons drawn. They obviously weren't that smart if this was their idea of an attack plan. A handful of bandits stood near the back with crossbows and shortbows at the ready but unable to make a shot with their companions blocking the way.

The flames from the torch had been extinguished and had caused little damage—the only evidence of the attempt being the slight burning smell in the air and a slight haze of smoke over by the platform. The two bandits had climbed down to join their fellows in combat. Perhaps the higher ground would have been the smart option for them though.

If only she had a Resistance to Piercing damage ring instead, she mused, as a couple of these ranged bandits noticed her on the roof. What she was actually hoping to find was the higher-level boss of this second camp area. Her eyes narrowed—but she almost needn't have bothered. In the middle of the clearing, an absolute unit of a man stood, a large axe in one hand and a small crossbow in the other. *Hank Redfang*, she read from the UI.

She watched as Hank scratched his messy beard with the butt-end of the crossbow. He seemed rather unperturbed at his fellow bandits running (somewhat) literally head-first into the blazing sword of the Death Knight. However, he also seemed less inclined to get involved in that melee and risk the same fate himself.

Humphrey continued to carve bloody swathes from the bandits, his reach and experience sufficient enough to keep them at bay from getting into the alleyway. Theo looked mostly useless and glum, only occasionally withdrawing some kind of basic weapon to lob over the Death Knight into the crowd—to some minor effect.

She turned back to the leader and winced as an arrow flew overhead, clattering against the rough mountain rock behind her. Several of the bandits were now drawing their bows or aiming bolts in her direction. Hank was probably out of range of the wand for now—she would have to draw him closer and quickly.

"Hey, ugly! Why don't you—" She ducked to the side as a crossbow bolt almost took her ear off. The roof below her shifted and buckled slightly at her movement.

"I said, hey! Ugly—" Two further attacks whizzed past her, barely missing. She bared her sharp teeth as her temper started to rise. The bandit leader slowly looked up in her direction.

*There we go.* "Hey u—" She jumped to the side as a bolt clattered off the wall behind her.

With a short but dramatic *creak*, the roof collapsed, sending the zombie down into the tavern below, shattering through a table as remnants of the ceiling clattered down around her.

She let out a long hiss of pain as the sound of heavy boots stomped toward the door.

## CHAPTER FORTY-FIVE

# Crime Doesn't Pay

Sally clambered to her feet and winced as a sharp numbing pain shot up her left leg. A brief glance showed a shard of splintered wood impaled straight through it.

*[Summon Zombies]*

The dirtied and poorly made floorboards of the tavern burst upwards as three zombies emerged from the ground. The door flung open, and the first bandit was silhouetted against the gap.

*[Zap Wand]*

A crack of blue lightning shot out and burst a chunk out of the unlucky bandit's shoulder. As they stumbled backward from the shock, the first zombie moved in front of the door and gave Sally a brief moment to compose herself. She spent most of these handfuls of stressed seconds cursing internally. With her reduced mobility, melee would be difficult. There was a second doorway down the other end of the dimly lit room—so a choke point wouldn't be her saving grace.

She hobbled from her pile of broken furniture and roofing and used *[Command Dead]* to send the other two zombies toward the far door. At the least, they would be able to slow down any assault long enough for Humphrey or Theo to catch on and come assist. She had hoped the first one through the door would be the boss. As she went to bring up the STAR to call for aid, the zombie in front of her had their head caved in and dropped to the floor as a pair of bandits surged in.

The first bandit, with more red curly beard than face, swung an axe toward her. It struck her left forearm and scraped off—her new bracers barely deflected the blow. She stabbed into the outstretched arm, but it slid along the wrapped linens worn by the bandit, only causing a shallow line of crimson. As the bandit grasped onto her raised left arm, she lunged and bit into . . . a mouthful of greasy beard.

They spun as her unstable footing caused her to stumble, the bandit letting her go as she tripped backward, landing unintentionally deftly atop a tavern chair that had avoided any damage so far. As he lunged, a third bandit came through the doorway.

*[Zap Wand]*

The quick flash of blue energy struck the axe-wielding bandit in the thigh, blowing a crater of singed flesh and causing the man to drop to one knee in his approach. Sally stood and jammed the inert wand into his eye socket and hissed in anger at the two bandits waiting to engage.

The far door crashed open as five more bandits poured in, two of them taken down by the zombies before they too were dispatched. She bared her fangs and readied her dagger, her left hand twitching as she sought the opportunity to retrieve the dropped axe. The three bandits joined the two, and the doorways darkened further to signal more approaching.

Just as she was about to make her move, a heavy *thunk* struck the wall behind her. Risking the slight glance over her shoulder, she saw the end of a blade, blazing crimson, stuck almost a foot into the ramshackle wooden wall.

All eyes were drawn to this odd sight as the sword tip carved around in a wide circle. It left a trail of bright red embers as it passed through the dark wood, the smell of burning filling the tavern. Just before it reached a full circle, it suddenly shattered forth. The figure of Theo rolled into the tavern, popping up to his feet beside the zombie, his sword ablaze in pink.

"Need assistance, m'lady?"

"Gross, don't even." She shook her head. "You can go back outside if you're going to be cringe."

Theo rolled his eyes. "Where's your sense of humor gone?"

"Somewhere between screwing up my leg and chewing on a gross beard."

The Novice took a brief glance down at the dead bandit, one eye still open in shock, and then saw her injured leg. "Use your *[Med Kit]*, then, while I deal with these uncouth yobs."

"Ugh, don't you start character LARPing too." She sat back down on the chair and opened up her Inventory with a scowl.

The Novice leapt forward at the bandits, his *[Novice Strike]* leaving a trail of energy as his first attack flickered into the slow-acting opponents.

Sally watched him as the little progress bar on the *[Med Kit]* rose, pulling the shard of wood from her leg with a grunt. Theo seemed a lot more confident when it came to fighting Monsters—though, in fairness, she hadn't really seen him fight much in person, aside from against the Yarch guards.

*He hadn't seemed so athletic in the diner*, she thought, her memories perhaps not exactly picture perfect. Here he was, shredding through these opponents like a natural. She almost swore he had his eyes closed half the time as he weaved and darted around the throng of bandits. The trail of light from his wooden blade left an afterimage in her vision, and despite the smells and noise of the melee, it was beautiful to watch.

The wooden sword did damage beyond what its simple form belied, even though Level Nine didn't give the tasty meatbag any bonus aside from his Strength going up. Watching the bursts of blood from his strikes was mesmerizing.

Her Health bar ran back up to around 85 percent as the kit completed, a warm burst of comfort flowing through her body—and, most importantly, her leg was now usable, if still stiff. She stood, grabbing the discarded axe up off the floor and ran, barreling into a figure coming into the doorway.

They tumbled out down a couple of rickety wooden steps onto the hard floor of the campground. Light temporarily blinded her as she got used to the sunlight once more, but in finding herself on the top of the two-person pile, she hacked downward with both weapons.

Humphrey slid across the dusty floor beside her, leveling an approaching bandit with a hefty upward slash. The Death Knight was spattered with blood, his whole armor a brighter crimson than usual—and he didn't seem to have taken much damage in the process.

Theo stumbled from the second door of the tavern, also covered in mostly-not-his blood. He was sweating heavily and looked queasy but otherwise unaffected. He furrowed his brow as his eyes focused, moving to stand alongside them while keeping eyes ahead.

Sally stood as she too looked in front of them. Most of the bandits had been culled. The only few that remained were the boss, three melee, and four ranged bandits. The Death Knight had been way out on his estimation of how many enemies there were here. She licked her lips, eyes darting between the larger bandit leader and the ones holding ranged weapons. Why hadn't they attacked yet?

"Not as eager to join your fellows?" Humphrey taunted, flicking the blood from his greatsword across the floor.

Hank spat on the floor and grunted. "Don't 'ave to be 'Unique' to 'ave some brains."

The Death Knight tilted his head.

"Huh." Sally frowned. "You're pretty self-aware."

"And you're not." The bandit grinned, a foul twinkle in his eye.

A snap came from above, where the mountain cavern began to overhang the encampment, and something weighty fell down toward the group.

With a flash of crimson and pink energy, both Theo and Humphrey cut through the air above them, slashing the heavy rope net in half and it fell apart around them, ineffective.

"Now what?" Sally grinned and cracked her knuckles.

Hank scowled and dug through his tunic, retrieving a small piece of crinkled paper. He silently mouthed some words as he read through it before turning his gaze back to the trio—stuffing the paper back into a pocket abruptly.

"That was just a distraction," he growled, "for this!"

The Party tensed briefly . . . and then relaxed as nothing came to pass. The bandit leader looked frustrated, and his eyes darted among his lackeys. Sally sucked her teeth.

"Well, you boys have fun with this, I'm going to . . ." She narrowed her eyes around the camp—they lit up as she hopped over to a nearby corpse.

She grabbed a loose crossbow to put in her Inventory. "*F to the yes*," she murmured to herself as she wound it back to load a new bolt. She glanced back up to see all the ranged bandits trained on her. She still fancied her chances.

"Perhaps we can parley?" Theo suggested, if for nothing more than to keep the large bandit busy.

"We ain't pirates, ya bastard." Hank shook his head, much to the smarmy grins of the remaining group behind him.

"*Yeah, Theo.*" Sally strolled back over to the Novice. She was perhaps enjoying the growing confusion on his face a little too much.

"I'm pretty sure that it isn't a pirate-specific term," he said, wrinkling up his nose.

"Do you see any ships here?" she continued, much to the amusement of the bandits. "How about you, Humps. Any boats?"

"Not in the traditional sense." The Death Knight shrugged.

Theo raised an eyebrow. "What does that even mean?"

"It means . . ." Sally tilted her head at him with eyes wide. "*That it's time to kill the bandits.*" She flicked the crossbow toward Hank and her finger tensed against the trigger.

"*Hey!*" A voice called out from the deeper cave encampment, putting a pause on their anticipated brawl.

"Hows about you assholes stop killing my goons, and we talk?"

## CHAPTER FORTY-SIX

# Lost in Translation

Weapons lowered as they all regarded the source of the voice—too darkly lit to be seen from where they stood, however. The gateway to the third and final part of the camp was even darker than the second due to it being deeper into the hollowed-out cavern of the mountain.

With an awkward glance around, Hank eventually shrugged. "Go ahead, then. Boss'll see ya."

"Was a pleasure." Theo nodded. "Good luck next time you set sail."

Sally shoved him along as the bandit narrowed his eyes, trying to decide whether to attack anyway.

"Time and place," she murmured. "Read the room, bud."

She was able to resist the urge to loot the few bandits that were dead this side of the camp—it was briefly odd that they were this far away from the tavern where most of the fighting had been, but it was not the most pressing thing on her mind right now.

"You think this is the Unique, then, yeah?" She leaned back to address the Death Knight heading up behind them.

"*Yes.*"

Sometimes she wondered why she even spoke to anyone. There was something to be said about having minions that just (mostly) did what you told them without the need for snark. How did the saying go? You didn't pick your family, but you could eat your friends? Maybe she couldn't eat her friends. Certainly, neither Humphrey nor Chuck had been appealing, but Theo was a toughie. She knew at least that eating the System-created was not for her. They would just have to hope to come across enough Players that the Novice wouldn't have to be eaten.

*Not yet, anyway.*

They approached the gate—a more fortified wooden one—which opened as they got to it. A bandit gave them a nod as they entered into a passageway lit by wall torches. This part of the encampment was fully within the cavern, and the dark ceiling rose high above a small town of properly constructed wooden buildings. Periodic lanterns hung from posts as they traveled farther in.

"Boss is in 'HQ,'" a hunched-over bandit with an eye patch grunted, stubby finger leveled at the biggest building in the town.

Sally nodded her thanks. It was pretty odd that the apparent boss yelled at them and then scarpered back to their base of operations. If it smelled like a trap then her nose must be blocked. If anything, it just tasted like the eccentricity of a Unique Monster.

The apparent headquarters was rather dull—perfectly matching the bare decor of the rest of the buildings. The double doors in front looked more like the swinging saloon kind, which made Sally wonder if it was just a repurposed tavern. Bandits must like to drink. With a silent gesture to the others, she led the way and pushed into the building.

Two lanterns illuminated a wide desk covered in paperwork. The smell of tobacco was only barely overwhelmed by the almost palpable aroma of alcohol. A staircase on the right-hand side led upward, and, likewise, on the opposite left side a staircase headed downward. Behind the desk a long painting adorned the wall, the murky shapes of the design barely congruous in this lighting.

On the other side of the desk, sitting with hands steepled together, was the alleged Unique boss. A woman in a dark gray pin-stripe suit, a trilby in a similar design atop her head barely containing long, purple hair. A scowl sat across her pale face as a humorless smirk regarded the odd Party.

"Hows about yous guys take a seat, huh?" She unclenched her hands to gesture at (conveniently) three chairs on their side of the long desk.

Sally nodded and approached. "Sure, my name's—"

"Not the refrigeration unit though." The woman scowled as she lit a cigarette. "Just you and the boy."

Sally turned back to the Death Knight with a raised eyebrow, but he just shrugged. "I will wait outside the door."

"Hot smokes, he can talk." A cloud of smoke blew from the woman's thin mouth as she watched Humphrey exit the building. "Name's Jackie, by the way. Jack is fine too. *Jacques* and we have issues—and you don't wanna see how I solve issues."

"Sally." The zombie nodded. "And this is Theo."

"Alright, toots, so the question is—why's a bunch of oddballs like yous killing all my goons?" Jackie leaned forward against her desk and took a long drag.

"Oh, well—we are actually here to see you." Sally tilted her head, not sure what to make of the woman yet.

"An' why's that?"

"Short answer." Theo scratched his chin. "We are taking down the System, or at least making it more Monster-friendly. Have you heard about Yarch yet?"

"The Player town? Nah, word doesn't really reach back here. My goons have a rememberin' problem."

Sally wiggled her eyebrows as she leaned back on her chair, crossing her legs. "It's a goblin town now."

"No shit?" Jackie tapped her ash onto an obsidian-black tray. "And you two tall glasses of fresh air did it?"

"With some help." Sally nodded. "There are quite a few Unique Monsters out there, and we want to give them a chance at living their one life as good as any Player can."

"You do know *this asshole* is a Player, yeah?" The woman leveled a long finger at the Novice.

"He's a what?!" Sally leapt to her feet, knocking the chair back, before relaxing. "Well, yeah, of course I know."

Theo shrugged apologetically.

Jackie blinked slowly as a trail of smoke wiggled gently from her cigarette. "Ah, I gets it. You're the manic risk taker. Yer pal here is the nerdy straight man. So what's the tin can outside?"

Sally opened her mouth to argue but closed it, eyes narrowing.

"Humphrey was an Observer; he is very competent and informative." Theo diplomatically nodded. "He is also Sally's minion."

"Ah, it sounds so reductive when you say it like that," the zombie grumbled. "He became my bodyguard to help unglitch my leveling process."

Jackie nodded and pushed her hat back to scratch at her head. "So what's this gotta do with me? I have a home here already."

Sally looked around the mostly bare room. "If I may ask, Jackie, in what way are you glitched? Why are you Unique?"

The woman again stared blankly at her before she put her cigarette out. "I'll assume yous aren't being a wise guy." She held her arms wide for the reveal, a half-smirk on her face. "A typo."

The pair looked at each other in brief confusion before the Novice groaned and rolled his eyes.

"*See*, ya guy here is a smart one. When they made me, uh, instead of being a Monster—well, I'm a *mobster*."

"Ohhhhhh." Sally nodded slowly. "That explains the weird theme, huh."

"My boys and gals here don't seem to notice it . . . but every time I look in that damned mirror." She shook her head and looked at the mess of paper on the desk. "*Assholes*. I'm not usually this open with whatever group of mooks show up on my doorstep. Mostly because they're Players and need to get whacked."

"How many have you, uh, whacked?" Theo asked, idly rubbing his armor.

Jackie shrugged and put her feet up on the table, hands clasped behind her head. "Only as many as what deserved it. I have a whole stash of trinkets and baubles from the idiots. It's not the best loot, but when yer goons can't even go on raids, ya take what you can, aye?"

Sally slowly nodded again, mostly tuning out everything after the mobster had mentioned she had cool loot to look through.

"Well, perhaps . . ." Theo began, "we can make you an offer you can't refuse?"

Jackie scowled and shook her head. "Don't *patronize* me, buttercup; this is a condition."

"Oh, I'm sorry—I just—"

"Ah hah, just jerkin' yer chain." Jackie grinned and closed her eyes. "Not just keeping this one around for his good looks, I hope?"

"No!" Sally pouted. It was mostly so that she could eat him one day. Maybe not mostly anymore—just partly.

"Lay it out for me, then, toots; what's in it for me?"

"You get to kill Players and join a Party of like-minded individuals." Sally's eyes wandered as she tried to pitch this. "If you don't want to stay with us, we are planning on taking over more villages—you could become a proper leader of a functional bandit town."

"Mm-hmm, go on."

"We feel the System is unfair and we want to wrestle control from it or at least get some answers from the Architect . . ."

"Anything else?"

Sally felt herself start to sweat—or at least the feeling. "Erm, you can also do some neat things like—"

"I'm just shittin' ya, gal. You had me at hello." Jackie stood and stuffed her hands into her pants pockets. "Bandits 'round here are thicker than the plate on your tin can outside and aren't much for conversatin'."

"You'll join us, then?" Theo raised his eyebrows, a few seconds of processing time behind the dialogue.

"Having my own town with a buncha other Uniques sounds like a more sane, and more lucrative, way o' livin'."

---

Jackie has joined the Party

"Yessss," Sally hissed, watching the picture pop up into the UI. "Now, show us your loot?"

"I guess that'll be okay." The mobster rolled her eyes. "Everything is in the basement."

The zombie boss hopped down the steps before Theo had even stood up. "So, uh, if I may ask—what kind of skills or weapons do you use?"

Jackie smiled humorlessly. "Ranged damage, ranged damage skills, and adjacent abilities."

"Understood." The Novice awkwardly nodded as they started down the stairs.

Sally stood wide-eyed with amazement at the boxes and crates stacked in the small room. A dim lantern hung from the ceiling, casting shadows into the corners behind the storage units. The nearest ones were filled with all sorts of weaponry—the next was gold and gemstones.

"I don't have an 'Inventory' like 'Players'—and you assholes do, so feel free to store it for me." Jackie rolled her eyes as she leaned against the wall.

---

674 Gold
Ruby (4)
Sapphire (2)
Amethyst (2)

---

Theo squinted his eyes as he looked through items, trying to see anything that could be useful for his build.

Sally hopped about, glancing at everything too quickly, before stopping by a half-covered crate.

"Ooh, what's this?" She brought out a swirling orb of pale pink and orange.

Immediately it felt warm in her hand—and then, suddenly, the color within shunted to a muted gray. Vertigo and an overwhelming sense of nausea flooded her body as she dropped to the floor.

Prickles of pain tapered up her body, covering her skin, as her blazing crimson eyes tried to focus on the text boxes rising above her STAR.

Panic and wonder filled her as drool spattered down to her dress.

## CHAPTER FORTY-SEVEN

# To Consume

Are you okay?" Theo crouched down beside her, his warm hand resting on her shoulder.

She shuddered as her eyes focused.

Zombie Path Unlocked
New Skill: Eat Brains
Stats Increased
Brains Consumed: 0
Bonus: N/A

The words spun around in her head, her vision shifting as the hunger roiled around in her stomach. And then, there it was.

Heartbeat. The dull thud of someone nearby. Slightly elevated—maybe nervous or concerned. Briefly, it blinded her, consumed her, a beating drum encouraging her to act. To silence it.

Her shaking vision twisted round to the figure beside her. The warmth radiated from him, his features blurred and his voice distant and muffled. It wasn't just his throat now. His head brimmed with potential.

Sally leapt up from the floor, knocking Theo back and landing atop him. Her red eyes blazed fire as she bared her fangs.

As she went to bite him, a wave of lethargy washed over her body. Several strong blinks didn't seem to shrug the feeling, and as she slowly lowered sleepily onto the Novice, her tired eyes met with Jackie. Embers from a disintegrating scroll fell from the hand of the mobster.

*　*　*

The Cleric rubbed his left forearm over his robes. A burning pain shot down the bone every time the coach jostled as it was pulled down the stone road. His jaw was stiff from clenching it.

"You alright, Bossss?" The hissed voice came from the seat opposite.

He looked up to regard the large reptilian warrior sitting across from him with tired eyes. The sickly green scales almost looked luminescent in the dim lighting of the coach interior. A wide jaw full of sharp teeth arranged in a humorless grin was no less disconcerting than when they had met.

"Marius is fine; he will just be happy once we are back in Yarch." A female voice came from beside the lizardman, the woman shrouded equally by shadow and the pitch-black cloak she wore. Snow-white hair ran out from beneath the hood.

"A necessary, but unfortunate, distraction." The Cleric looked out of the window. If the operation was successful, then it would prove paramount to his cause. For the fight ahead.

"You really think th' zombie girl issss there ssstill?"

Marius winced at the repeated extended *s*'s. *So cliché.* "I have my information. The bug needs to be squished, and she has a Party now."

A growl emanated from the other side of the lizardman. A small figure no more than two feet tall sat behind a newspaper. A series of clicks and chirps followed.

The Cleric frowned and watched the trees pass by them. "It's simple: we use the System to defeat the Party."


Blurred, gray shapes started to filter into the zombie's vision.

"Hey, you, you're finally awake."

The voice was familiar. *Theo's?* Color started to brighten the shapes as they sharpened every time she blinked. Yes—the Novice was crouching nearby where she was sitting.

"Sorry, hun. *[Sleep Spell]*. Good thing you didn't resist it, huh?" Jackie leaned down into her vision.

"Blurf," Sally replied. Her tongue still felt sluggish. The wall behind her was cold, even through her armor. Dusty floorboards felt rough beneath her fingers. "What happen?"

The shuffling of armor replaced the mobster as the Death Knight squatted down next to the Novice. "You interacted with some kind of magical item that unlocked the zombie skills that you didn't have before."

"Ya look with yer eyes, not ya hands," the mobster chastised from out of view.

"Then you tried to eat me, for real," Theo added helpfully.

Sally shook her head, trying to shift the fog clouding her thoughts. Clumsily, she got to her feet. The group eyed her warily. With a sigh, she relaxed into a normal posture and frowned at them. Seeing their faces, the weight in her skull felt lighter, and she grabbed hold of her faculties.

"I now have the desire and ability to eat brains," she stated plainly.

"*Yes*." Humphrey nodded and folded his arms. "It would have been nice to know what you used to do that. It is now an inert ball of glass—no System-related information."

Her eyes glazed over as she looked at Theo. "Sorry about almost eating your brains." It would have been nice if he had been her first though. There was an itch—what sort of bonus would she get from eating brains?

"Wouldn't have been much of a meal." He shrugged sheepishly. "I am Partied up with you guys, after all."

"This *is* kinda weird, huh?" The mobster wrinkled up her nose with a sour expression across her face. "Your lad here found ya some items from my store. Let me go get my things before we head out."

The Novice stepped over with his STAR up as the mobster ascended the stairs to the main floor.

"Jacks is pretty nice." Sally smiled weakly at Theo. "We need more morally questionable jerks in our Party."

"I can't tell if you mean that genuinely or not."

Rare Sword (Empty Socket: 1)
Belt of Constitution
Healing Potion
Medium Medicine Kit (2)

"A sword?" Sally cooed and brought it out of her Inventory. She gasped. "Is this a *katana*?"

"No." Theo shook his head firmly. "We aren't doing that. It's just a nicely made blade. It's not enchanted, but it has an empty socket—if we find any gems."

"There's *gems*?"

"*Yes*." Humphrey nodded. "You probably won't find any in this area. Whoever died with this sword would be kicking themselves. If they weren't dead."

The zombie slowly slid the blade into the scabbard now on her left hip. Looks like her dagger days were over. She gave herself a few bonus points for not swinging it around the rather cramped basement. With a nod toward the stairs, she gestured for the group to leave. "You get anything nice, Theo?"

"Boots with Movement Speed and Belt with Evasion Chance. There were a few other things, but I can't use them as a Novice."

"Perhaps the greatest boon is the inclusion of a new member to our group." The statement from the Death Knight was flat, but Sally chose to gloss over it.

"Only one space left now. I'm sure we can fill it super soon." They reached the top of the stairs back into the main room of the headquarters to see the mobster slam down a large wooden case onto the desk, paperwork fluttering off onto the floor.

Two catches popped open on the front and Jackie lifted the heavy lid. Inside, a contraption of wood and steel was revealed. "This's my pride and joy. I call her Betty." With slight strain, she lifted the large object out.

It was a crossbow, although larger and more complex than Sally had ever seen. Beneath the polished wooden frame, a cylinder of metal framework sat. The dark steel atop the weapon was engraved with a golden pattern of symmetrical swirls.

"A repeating crossbow?" Theo asked. His mouth hung open.

"*[Hellfire Trigger]*, *[Rapid Reload]*, *[Pin Down]*, and *[Explosive Shot]*." The mobster grinned as she wielded this behemoth of a crossbow, perhaps the first genuine smile the group had seen.

"You're Level Five though, right? What's the other skill?" Sally squinted at the UI pop-up, her vision perhaps not 100 percent yet.

Jackie deflated a little, the smile draining from her face as she glanced over to the Novice. "*[Extort].*"

"Well, that could be useful." Theo rubbed his neck, trying to be diplomatic. "Like if we come across some ornery traders, or—"

"Don't forget I saved your life, wiseass. You owe me." Jackie frowned and stowed her crossbow.

"Way to get indebted to everyone." Sally nudged the Novice in the side, only slightly relishing how his soft body moved beneath that useless armor. "Shall we get moving, then, team?"

"I'd say goodbye to the fellas, but they'd forget soon enough." Jackie shrugged, looking away idly.

Sally nodded and headed toward the door. She felt sad for the mobster. Having to watch your brainless friends go off and die to the Players but come back and remember nothing about their previous lives. Them not having a purpose except to follow the path the System had set out for them.

As they walked from the headquarters and out along the pathway to the middle camp, thoughts ruminated in her muddled mind. Before she had awoken, if she had been like Chuck, a zombie that was killed and reborn until her . . . soul had somehow made it into almost the correct place . . . Is that where a lot of her resentment for the System came from? Seeing herself and her friends killed over and over by Players?

"What are we doing next, Sally?" Theo roused her from the thoughts as they entered the second bandit camp.

"Is there anything that we can find to help us out, Humps?"

The Death Knight rubbed his chin in thought as they passed the remaining bandits.

"At least you didn't die, Hank." Jackie nodded before looking around the rest of the camp. "Shit job of defending though. You're in charge while I run some errands."

"*Yes, Boss.*"

Humphrey eventually shrugged. "Depends on whether you want to level up, find more loot, or fill the last place in our Party."

"Why is it always three choices?" the zombie grumbled back.

Theo drummed his fingers on the hilt of his wooden sword. "Generally a fifth member will be a better power increase than whatever we may be able to find nearby, probably more than leveling too."

Sally stopped before the opening of the door they had smashed open. "Any leads on further Unique Monsters? Sympathetic Players?"

They all produced a gathering of shrugs and heads shaking in the negative.

She sighed and stepped through the opening into the more open and airy first part of the camp. "It's not like our problems are going to be solved by—*oh!* Look, a cat."

About a dozen feet in front of them, sitting expectantly, was a small ginger cat. His eyes widened as the odd group moved toward him.

Just as Sally went to pet him, he shirked away and opened his little mouth.

"Greetings," the cat announced. "I am the Architect."

## CHAPTER FORTY-EIGHT

# Feline Fine

Humphrey crouched down next to the zombie. "No. He is not."

The cat opened and closed his mouth. "Okay—I'm not. I'm actually a Player that is stuck in a—"

"No, you're not." Sally furrowed her brow. "Can I pet you or not?"

"I mean, *alright.*" The cat closed his amber eyes as the zombie gently petted his scruffy head.

"What's yer name, and why are ya hanging around my turf?" Jackie loomed behind Sally with hands on her hips.

"I-I'm the Architect-t, and I come with a w-warning," he managed to get out as Sally continued to pet him.

"Aw, well let's just call you *Archie,* you lil liar. Want to join a Party and destroy the System?" She sat down and patted her lap in invitation.

"N-no, I bring you a *warning.*" Archie resisted moving onto her lap.

Theo crossed his arms and sighed. "So what is the warning?"

" . . . I forgot."

"I'm *highly* likely to eat you." Sally leaned forward and scrunched up her nose. "You don't look like good eating, but I've recently got the hankering to try brains, so you'd best start explaining why you're a talking cat and interrupting my, uh . . . vibe."

"R-right. Well, I've been trailing you for a while, as there is an odd smell to you. I don't know why I'm able to talk though—is that not common?" Their silence was enough of an answer. "Most importantly, there is a group of people coming to attack you soon."

Jackie rolled her eyes and lit a cigarette. "I feel like ya shoulda led with that."

"You mean a Party of Players? You have to use the right terminology; branding is important." Sally looked up at the gate as if expecting the danger to arrive dramatically at that moment.

Archie shrugged, an odd movement for a cat. "I don't know what those are."

"I feel like you are lying to me." She dusted her skirt off as she stood once more. "Just based on our interactions so far, you don't seem very honest. How soon are they coming?"

"N-no, why would I put myself in danger like this?" The cat twitched nervously. "I'm not a very good judge of time . . . Tomorrow afternoon?"

Sally huffed. "There is one way you could prove your loyalty." She turned to Humphrey and wiggled her eyebrows.

The Death Knight glanced past her to look at the Novice who shook his head slowly. "*Ha-ha*, at your level you only get two—"

"Perfect!" She beamed, turning back to address the small cat. "Archie, would you swear to become my bodyguard and keep me safe and serve under me until one of us dies or something? That's how it went, right, Humps?"

The Death Knight clenched and stretched out his jaw. "Pretty verbatim, my liege."

"*Ass*. Well, you'll get to be Level Four and come adventure with us. We *are* kinda bad guys though." She shrugged and held out a hand to be shaken, bringing up her UI to see what she knew about the small feline already.

---

"Archie" Domestic Cat - Critter

---

*Nothing too untoward there.* Critter Level was something new, but it was a fair assumption to think of it as a Level Zero—something not intended to benefit from the crunchy part of the System, as they weren't going to advance or see proper combat. She had no idea what kind of skills he may gain, *which was half the fun.*

"B-but, I'm the Architect?"

"Compulsive lying is the one trait we don't have in our Party though. Right, unless . . . " She turned to the Death Knight. "You're not hiding some secrets, Humphrey?"

" . . . "

"Humps??"

"*Ha-ha*, no, I do not hide anything from you. I may be vague on occasion, but I'm as boring and straightforward as Theo."

The Novice spluttered and took a step back. "What? I'm not boring—I'm just not eccentric. I've killed, you know. I've paid my lumps."

"I'm not sure that is the expression." Sally frowned. "But okay—try not to make us look silly in front of the newbie, guys."

"I'm used to dealing with useless men." Jackie blew a cloud of smoke. "As long as you're leading, princess, I'm good."

"Alright, I'll join," Archie growled cutely. "*If* it means you all talk less."

Sally spun back to the cat and bent over, hand outstretched once more. "I promise."

Theo rolled his eyes at her other hand behind her back, her fingers crossed.

Archie has joined the Party
New Bodyguard: Level Four Domestic Cat
Subtype Error: Hash 064804

"Neat, errors. What skills did you unlock?"

The cat looked confused and paced around in a circle looking at the floor. "No idea."

"Huh, almost regret my decision already. What's that called?"

"Buyer's remorse?" Theo shrugged.

Sally stretched out her back as she looked at the sky. It was nearing dusk now. Walking most of the day sure burnt the sunlight hours. "Yeah, I'm really remorse-ing you right now, Archie—what can you tell me?"

"I . . . I know things?" The cat stopped his circling and looked up at the zombie.

*It would have been a lot cooler if he had grown in size when he leveled up or had some sign of what abilities he had gained,* she thought. Sally narrowed her eyes. "Go on."

". . . Like, how people got here. What this place is . . ."

All eyes bore down into the small ginger cat. Curiosity but mistrust on their faces.

Theo nodded to the middle of the camp. "Let's set up the old-school campfire and settle down for a bit. Then we can have words and rest."

They moved over to the inert camp and waited for Theo to relight it. Jackie and Humphrey went to close the gates, barring them with a thick plank of wood, before they all reconvened, sitting in a semi-circle around the cat, who became silhouetted against the fire.

"Remember, no lies, or you go in the fire as my next meal," Sally bluffed. She knew that she couldn't eat him now that he was a bodyguard—plus he wouldn't be much of a meal. *Not like Theo . . .*

"So what do you want to know?" Archie's ears twitched nervously.

Theo and Sally exchanged glances. "How we got here."

"Magic."

The Death Knight had to hold her back from leaping at the fuzzy creature.

"You'll have to be more specific than that." Theo agreed with her outburst.

"As a cat, my understanding of it is very limited." He leaned back away from the zombie. "Imagine, if you will, a bowl of food, full of giblets and chunks of meaty goodness. Then someone brings their own homemade bowl and places it nearby, but this bowl is empty. So this new person, the bowl's Architect, if you will, takes a handful of chunky meat bits from the first bowl for their own. But they only like certain bits—like, uh—chicken—"

"So, that's why all the Players are in a similar age range," Theo interrupted, scowling at the floor in thought.

"Chicken," Archie confirmed, licking his lips in reflex. "Where was I?"

"I think you've said enough, terrible metaphor aside." The dry voice of the P-2T rang out overhead as they shimmered into view.

"Shove off, spoilsport," Sally hissed before murmuring to Humphrey, "*Can we kill it?*"

"The shit is that?" Jackie leapt up and brought Betty to bear, the cylinder of bolts clacking as it rotated in place.

Humphrey shrugged, perhaps keen on finding out himself.

"I would advise against hostility. I am just here to level a warning," the dry voice intoned. Nevertheless, the Observer floated slightly farther away from the aggressive mobster.

"Always with the warnings and observing." The zombie shook her head. "Is it against the law for us to have a conversation now?"

"It is not permitted for Players to know where—"

"I do not permit *you!*" Sally growled, slowly drawing her not-katana from its scabbard and pointing it at the green skull. "I challenge you to a duel."

"*No.*"

"But I *challenged* you."

"Obstinance is not a precursor to ability. I am an Observer built in the infallible image of the Architect who—"

"I'm the Architect," Archie interjected.

Theo scratched his chin. "I don't think the Architect would look like a floating skull."

"*Ha-ha*, not so infallible are we, my once brother."

A pink-red light quickly flickered over the Observer as it tried to combat the deluge of words from the Party below. The eldritch green energy quickly returned, enveloping the skull once more. "No. This will not work on me. Consider *this* a mercy."

The skull blinked out of view once more. Sally cursed under her breath and stowed the sword. She looked down at Archie. "Care to tell us more, then?"

"Meow," came the response.

"You're kidding me, right?"

"Meow."

Humphrey rubbed the side of his head. "I can almost hear the *ho-ho* in the breeze."

Sally kicked a loose stone off into the distance as she spun around, exhaling. They were *so* close to getting more information. Raptured from the real world to this fake one, all people of a certain age, apparently by magic? Magic probably wasn't the right word for it, just some convenience pasted over the gaps in understanding. But what other details did he have in that cute little skull?

She saw that Theo looked conflicted. After she picked Archie up, with no complaint from the furred creature, she went and nudged the Novice. "Look, it's harder to eat you if I'm holding the cat. Penny for your thoughts?"

"I'm gonna go keep watch from the tower," Jackie butted in before walking off. She threw the stub of her cigarette into the campfire and adjusted her hat.

The Novice rubbed the accumulated sweat and grime from his forehead and gave her a glum smile. "If we came from the real world, there is a chance we can go back, right?"

She nodded as Archie began to purr within her grasp.

"But does that mean we have also doomed the people we have killed to . . . What? Never have that chance?"

"Death could be what releases them back to their old lives?" She shrugged and tried to remember a good anime comparison to make, but that area of her brain was still mud.

"I don't know." He sat down, leaning against a pair of overturned barrels. The low flame of the campfire flickered in his anguished eyes.

"We'll camp here for the night," Humphrey said from nearby. "Think of some plans for tomorrow."

Sally shot him some awkward cat-laden finger guns as she sat down beside the Novice. "What do you remember about the old world?"

He gave her a slight smile and after a few moments gathering his thoughts, he began to tell her what little information he could. About the friend group that he had abandoned, the different RPG games he used to play, and even the failed attempt at learning guitar. Sally, too, told him about the things she could remember. It was dark by the time they finished talking, tired from the events of the day. They were perhaps unsurprised that the most vivid memories they shared were of the diner and the short time before they had been brought here.

As Sally looked out at the fire dancing in the slight breeze, she smiled, and her eyelids hung heavily.

It had been a decent day.

## CHAPTER FORTY-NINE

# Theo-logy

Sally awoke with a start and sat forward. She had fallen asleep against Theo, and it was well into nighttime now. As she wiped the drool from her mouth, she stood and moved away from the Novice and low flame of the campfire. Theo may have trusted her enough, but she wasn't sure she could hold back if the urge to eat him came suddenly.

It was nice and cool away from the body heat of the Novice, and it helped awaken her. Humphrey sat on the other side of the fire facing the bandit campground gate. The fire from his helmet was barely visible, and he was statuesque, sword out and placed downward in his hand like some kind of crimson-plated sentry.

Jackie was also asleep on a chair over by one of the gate watchtowers, slouched at an awkward angle with her repeating crossbow leaned against the side of the chair, easy to reach in an emergency. A small pile of cigarettes littered the ground around smart dress shoes slightly scuffed from the dusty dirt of the encampment.

Archie was curled up near the fire atop a barrel. She briefly wondered if the odd cat could talk through Party chat like Chuck used to be able to. What had the green Observer exactly taken away from her feline bodyguard? Something to prod the cat about in the morning—but if he couldn't see his skills, then she didn't have much confidence.

The zombie yawned and stretched her arms. It was rare to have a bit of quiet time to herself. A handful of days under her belt and it had been full tilt. Maybe she was just a bit too scared to face the voices bouncing around in her head. She exhaled. Slowly, and as quietly as possible, she crept up the ladder to the other watchtower. The smooth wood of the ladder felt comforting under her hands before she clambered through the open hatch.

It was even cooler up here—the slight breeze that had become signature in this area came through the walls unabated. Dark shadows of the trees surrounding the camp became an almost impenetrable wall of pitch black a few dozen feet past the first few layers of muted greenery. She sat down against the back wall, looking up above the woodland ahead of the camp at the tiny specks of stars covering the night sky. Were they even real?

Folding her arms, she jostled the STAR by accident. Hmm.

Sally: hey, Chuck, hope you didn't get dead yet
Sally: but if you did — hit me up!
Sally: we found a new friend, and a talking cat
Sally: haven't done any evil yet
Sally: further evil*

She paused and closed the chat. Morality had been buzzing around the back of her head since Chuck became human. Theo may have been swayed by her methods and intentions to defeat the System easily enough, but it had stung when Chuck had decided he couldn't be . . . evil.

Killing Players was certainly evil to some degree, sure. When she was attacking the village to give a home to the goblins, it didn't feel so black and white. She rested her head on her folded arms, knees up to her chest as she squished herself into sitting in the corner of the watchtower. Anti-hero was the title she thought she could inherit. But she knew the real words that had become mired in the thick mud of her existence.

*Selfish. Hypocritical. Impulsive.*

There was no punchline there. No amount of manic quirkiness that she could use to slide across reality as if on ice. Was she still even the same Sally as in the diner? Did she even want to be? She had no anxiety, no mind goblins holding her back—she was powerful now. Her gut wanted out of the System as soon as she gained her soul, but maybe she wanted to stay here.

She shuddered at the thought. But . . . what about instead of breaking the System . . . they just bent it. Her brow furrowed as the words flowed through her head like the breeze. Priority One was seeing if there was a way to get the Players back to the real world. If that was not possible . . . what would the goal be? Equality for Unique Monsters so they were the same as Players? Change the System so it wasn't built on bloodshed?

*Hypocritical again*, she mused. Half of her still wanted to kill and consume everything. Grow stronger. Eat the System. It was like a curse—something driving her whether she wanted to or not. That was probably why she awoke with such resentment toward the System and Players.

A creak of the ladder drew her attention, and the ready-to-eat brain bowl of Theo popped up into the hatch. He turned to face her, his eyes squinting in the dark to pick her out in the shadow of the corner.

"Everything okay?" he whispered, hauling himself fully into the watchtower and sitting against the side opposite her.

"Just . . . Chuck got me a little shaken up." She brushed her hair from her face. "Like, I know I'm a train off the rails already—but am I at least careening in the right direction?"

There was a silence where she thought the Novice wasn't going to reply before he shifted and exhaled. "A derailed train is going against the grain no matter where it's headed. What really drives you?"

"*The System is unfair*—and there's no reason for it to be. Monsters deserve the same chance at living as Players do, and Players shouldn't be demigods in comparison just because they are human. If we are stuck in this world—"

"Othea."

"Then—*Othea*? That's what it's called?" She frowned at the shadowed shape across from her.

"That's what the map says. We are on an island called Grace of Light. Looks like a croissant."

"*Huh.* Guess I should start paying more attention." Sally shook her head. "But anyway, if we have to stay here then I think it'll be fair to make things equal. Maybe just because I'm straddling both lanes."

"I can understand it." Theo shuffled to get more comfortable against the wooden logs of the wall. "It's like . . . *Hobgoblincide*, right? To a degree—doesn't matter whether you are human, elf, orc, a living skeleton, you are just as valid a character that can live and play the game."

"Unless you are a hobgoblin, of course," she added. "The only creature that is naturally evil and beyond redemption."

"So who are the 'hobgoblins' here? The System-created on both sides are without agency. Players and Unique Monsters have the choice of how to act and how to live."

Sally clucked her tongue and looked up at the peaked roof of the watchtower blocking what would be an otherwise lovely view of the night sky. "That's the thing, then. There are no 'hobgoblins' as such. Or is that us? We've done our share of punching down."

"Players punch down at any Monster they can."

She grinned, her sharp teeth catching the barest of moonlight, leaving her an intimidating visage in the dark. "So it's decided, then? We raise up Uniques and punch down at Players. Eventually, there should be some kind of equilibrium. Maybe end up with both sides just fighting the System-created?"

Theo scratched at his chin, the mild stubble rough. "That's . . . a *moderately* valid goal."

The zombie stood and looked out to the woods. "We will always be seen as evil though; we are Monsters, after all. Well, you aren't."

"Maybe just a lower-case one?"

She grinned and nudged his side. Theo had done his share of the hard work, especially in the assault at Yarch. He seemed to be taking things well enough, even after she almost ate his brain. Either he had an iron will or he was disassociating. She would need to keep an eye on him. Not just for wondering how to cook him up.

Her eyes narrowed out to the woods—and then she ducked, grabbing the Novice and dragging him to a crouch too. Thankfully, he had the wherewithal to keep his surprise to hushed murmurs rather than a panic that she was about to eat him. She raised her eyes just over the wall.

A group of shadowed figures moved between the trees, getting close to the encampment. Theo followed suit and gulped as he squinted at the silhouettes. Sally licked her teeth and tried to pick out their details.

All Level Five. Paladin. Monk. Bard. Wizard. Rogue.

Her ability to see this information partially negated their attempt at subtlety—though had she not been awake and looking in this direction she would have never known. The group of five paused and huddled together.

"Probably talking through chat," Theo whispered. "Should we . . . ?"

Sally slowly shook her head. She knew Humphrey was now awake, Archie too, and would be getting Jackie up. It had something to do with the bodyguard condition. She didn't know exactly, but there was some kind of connection there. Like a shared mood or warning system. Her mind was wandering to avoid the current situation. A full group of Level Fives . . .

Humphrey still had the *[Town Scroll]*. At her word, they could be safe in Sanctuary. She was salivating though. Her tongue itched.

*Quiet bloip.*

She lowered down to cover her STAR as she opened the message.

Humphrey: Hillan special?

As the reference clicked into place, a sinister grin of sharp teeth widened across her face. Anticipation danced in her red eyes, and she turned to the Novice.

"How good are your knees, Theo?" she whispered, almost purring with malicious intent.

## CHAPTER FIFTY

# Punching Down

The Paladin stopped and raised their hand, slowly turning to the group behind. With the gesture of a metal-clad finger, they brought up their STAR Party chat windows.

Clive: Silence now.
Clive: Usual battle plan. Confirm roles.
Vanessa: I will cast [Night Vision] on us all. It is Concentration, so I will assist with low-level spells until we know how things stand.
Lars: [Exploding Fist] the doors open. Then just punch stuff.
Claire: [Stealth] to [Assassinate] any open target or flank the enemy.
Roger: Buff with [Song of Valor] to start with, [Ode of Recovery] if things turn hairy.
Clive: Confirmed. I will lead the charge once Lars has destroyed the gate.
Clive: Move as quickly as possible while we have the element of surprise.

The Party—*Voice of Gaia*—nodded their acknowledgments as they closed their chats. Clive stretched out his shoulders and lowered the visor on his helm as he turned his gaze back to the bandit encampment. The low murmur of the Wizard casting *[Night Vision]* got his nerves up. It was always the preparation right before the battle that got him antsy.

They just had to kill this boss Monster and whatever Elites were in the area of the camp, and then they could get closer to both their Second Class advancements as well as entry to the second area—the Wastelands. Sure, they were behind the curve, but they were alive.

A flare lit his eyes as the spell was complete, and the bandit camp came into view. As bright as day but at a slightly off hue—almost without any saturation. The low light of a campfire was less apparent now, but the shadowed areas had melted away by the vision spell.

The watchtowers looked clear. Not surprising, really. Clive gave the nod to Lars and let the Monk take the lead. This first area of the camp was often farmed for experience—heck, the *Voice of Gaia* had cleared it twice about a week ago. The inner two camps were less frequented, as you could easily draw aggro from way too many bandits. Too risky.

As they reached the gate, the Rogue went invisible in preparation. Roger held his fingers against the strings of his lute in tense anticipation. The Wizard began a familiar rhythmic breathing to prepare herself for the fight ahead. Clive gave Lars a nod.

*[Exploding Fist]*

The wooden gate shattered inward, splitting into fragments that scattered into the camp. As the group stepped into the threshold, the Paladin paused.

Before them, a small ginger cat sat all on its own.

Clive opened his mouth to give an order—but the shadow of movement from above distracted him.


Sally leapt from the watchtower accompanied by Theo. Sword drawn, she cast *[Summon Zombies]* on the way down. With a flash of crimson, she cut a line down the surprised Bard. A full five zombies ruptured from the earth as the Novice landed next to the Monk—his attack was blocked, but the weight of his descent knocked back the young man with a shaved head.

The Paladin raised his sword into the air, and it burst into holy fire—even the look of it hurt Sally's eyes. As he turned toward her to get her attention, Humphrey charged out from the side of one of the small huts. His greatsword burst into dark energy as he ran toward the throng.

A table flipped over, and Jackie hopped atop two chairs, the cylinder of her weapon rotating with an orange glow as she used *[Hellfire Trigger]*.

It was at this moment full chaos bloomed.

In slow motion, as she cast *[Hex: Slow]* on the man she struck, Sally watched as the Paladin turned back to face the Death Knight. The injured Bard stumbled backward to try and withdraw a knife, but his feet got caught up on one of the emerging zombies, sending them falling to the floor.

The Monk had recovered and began an assault on Theo; the Novice's sword blazed with pink energy as he prepared his *[Novice Strike]*, waiting to see if he needed to block before starting his wild attack. The Rogue was nowhere to be seen.

A change in temperature drew her attention to the back of the pack as the Wizard released a *[Firebolt]*. The glowing orb zipped across and struck Sally in the left shoulder—pain flaring up as her dead flesh burnt beneath the flame. She growled and pounced forward to attack the panicked woman before a shape emerged from the shadow beside her.

Learning from experience, she twisted away by instinct. The Rogue appeared with a long blade that only just missed piercing her side and instead gashed her back and shredded her shirt. Sally spun with her sword out, but the cloaked woman evaded, moving backward into the shadows again.

*[Uncontrolled Growth]*

A large figure barreled past her—a blur of orange fur that pounced at the Wizard, knocking the spellcaster to the floor. Sally blinked as Archie had now grown to the size of a lion, disrupting the second fire spell with his attack. The growled mews as his large jaws snapped at the prone woman were off-putting. Patches of red soaked through silver robes as the Wizard dropped her *[Night Vision]* buff to cast *[Shield]* on herself.

The clatter of a bolt hitting the wall sounded near where the Rogue had vanished to—followed by a second to the left, a third to the right—and then the fourth bolt fired from Betty stopped in the air as the cloaked woman became visible again, struck by the projectile. She cursed and leapt over a pair of barrels, withdrawing a red potion from her belt.

*[Exploding Shot]*

A burst of fire erupted from the hiding place as the barrels splintered to pieces, the Rogue rolling away injured, her black clothing smoldering and alight in places.

One of her zombies had been felled by the Bard—stabbed in the eye socket— as two more currently clawed and bit at the fallen man. Sally licked her lips and approached, ready to stab her sword into her trapped prey.

*[Unstoppable Flurry]*

A force knocked into her, waylaying her from the potential killing blow. Punches—striking her one after another. She turned to face the Monk while her arms raised to protect her head. The punches were strong but not massively powerful—not for someone with her Strength and Constitution. But they were unrelenting. They chipped away at her health and resolve as each fist powered into her while leaving her few chances to counter.

With blazing red eyes, she looked at her assailant. Theo was behind the Monk, his *[Novice Strike]* repeatedly flicking into the back of the Monk. Spurts of blood accompanied the flash of strikes, but the Monk remained persistent— either unwilling or unable to end his constant barrage of strikes.

The Paladin pushed back Humphrey from their clash and cast *[Salvation]*. Radiant energy flowed through the *Voice of Gaia*, healing them and providing them with some temporary resistance.

Archie howled as he took some form of magic damage, cowering away from the Wizard trying to stand.

The Bard was able to fend off the two zombies, his lute finding its way back to his hands.

Fury painted the face of the Monk. Sally started to feel weak, her arms numb and thoroughly tenderized.

"Should do this t'Theo next, make 'im easier to eat," she growled out.

"*You can talk?*" Surprise and confusion filled the Monk's face, relenting his assault enough to catch the *[Hex: Slow]*.

*[Will of the Dark Lord]*

Humphrey had pushed through as he clashed with the Paladin, taking some damage in the process but putting himself in range of everyone except the Rogue.

All of the *Voice of Gaia* Party members passed the Willpower check against the Stun.

*Except one.*

The fists of the Monk went lax as his expression slunk. Theo continued battering him from behind, his wooden sword starting to cut chunks from the exposed back of the man.

A strum of music emanated from behind her as the Bard began casting something to support the Stunned Party member. The Wizard was contending with Archie, who—Sally had to resist doing a double take as it looked like the cat had doubled in size again. The clash of metal past Theo signaled that the two heavily armored members were still at odds. If there was one thing the Death Knight excelled at, it was keeping tanks occupied.

A bolt from Jackie struck the lute, interrupting the intended magical song. The follow-up shot came slower than previously, with *[Hellfire Trigger]* now worn off, and the Bard was able to dodge out of the way.

"Ow, you *fuck stick*, yous gonna get it now!" Jackie seethed, a dagger sticking out from her thigh, thrown by the Rogue to stop her from harrying the Bard.

Sally slashed twice with her sword—her amateur swings were still effective against an unresponsive foe. Blood dripped to the floor, causing her to salivate. She ached, both arms were sore, and her left shoulder still felt like it was burning. Perhaps this would be an opportune time to pop a Healing Potion to top up—the Monk might be close to death, but the rest of his Party had lots of tricks left to pull.

Instead, she was enamored by a text pop-up.

A new skill that had certain conditions to be used. Conditions that were currently fulfilled.

Her eyes widened as she dropped the sword to the floor, hands outstretched. They held the warm, bloodied face of the Monk. As the stun wore off, pain and confusion sank back into his features as his pale brown eyes met the blazing red ones of the zombie.

*[Eat Brains]*

## CHAPTER FIFTY-ONE

# Queen of the Dead

The environment melted away. Sound, smells, and even the feeling of her injuries, everything became mute to Sally. It was like splitting a pistachio nut in half. Except instead of a little nut there was a lumpy and slimy prize within. Like an oyster? But made of cocaine.

As the husk of the Monk slunk to the floor, a warm bliss filled the zombie. She wiped her mouth on her gore-covered arm and her hands on her dress. All eyes were on her.

> Brains Eaten: 1
> Bonus: +5% Melee Damage
> Unlocked Passive: Carrier - Players killed by you turn into Zombies

Fresh tears ran down her face, cleaning thin lines between the grime and crimson caked around the wide grin of sharp teeth. *Proper Zombie skills. A proper meal.*

She bent over slowly and retrieved her sword. Warmth continued to flow through her whole body. Elation. Confidence. The glances of the human Party told her all she needed to know—their morale was broken. Fear and disgust overwhelmed them. Even Theo looked panicked. *Perhaps warranted,* she thought as she winked at him.

"I'll give you all one chance to leave." Her words came out slightly slurred. It reminded her of when she had gorged on the Novices.

The sword of the Paladin shook as eyes looked to him for answers.

Was it in fear—or rage? Sally beamed at the plated man. It was hard to tell between the slits in the faceplate of his helmet. Was there ever a time that Players had given Monsters this option? They must be confused.

*Could they even trust her?* The power her apparent offer gave her almost made her laugh out loud. Either they accepted the mercy, and became high-roaded by the evil that they so sought to destroy, or they fought back against the injustice of their fallen friend and potentially also died. There was also the choice of betraying them and getting an easier fight if they relented. Get some easy brain food.

"Why?" The Paladin's voice shook through his clenched teeth almost as much as his held sword.

"Because I have the choice to." She smiled, wiping her sword off on her dress. She should really get cleaned up sometime soon.

The corpse of the Monk groaned and staggered up to its feet, turning around to walk over to Sally with glowing yellow eyes as she continued.

"We all have the right to live or die. The choice to kill or live. What do you choose?"

A strange mew that grew higher in pitch followed the extremely large cat unceremoniously shrinking back to his normal size. The Wizard looked rather relieved by this fact—and somewhat more confident. The Bard still looked sick, almost trembling in place.

Sally turned back to the Paladin and narrowed her eyes. The Rogue was nowhere to be seen. She shot a gaze over to Jackie, who just shrugged. There was an art to reading a situation. Sally could read the broad strokes of the scale tipping to an imminent attack. Somewhat desperate on the side of the *Voices of Gaia*—they were a full member down, and the *Outsiders* were only marginally hurt.

"What would you have us do should we decide to leave?" The muffled voice from inside the metal helmet did not have the same level of confidence that the rest of the Paladin's Party seemed to be gathering.

That stood to reason—if he was their leader, then trying to keep his Party alive would be more important than dying in a futile fight.

She shrugged. "Hope that we don't cross paths again. Or if we do, you'll either immediately yield or have powered up enough that your victory could be more decisive."

"You're . . . not like—"

"Normal Monsters? Yeah, I get that a lot." She crossed her arms. "But I'm not in the habit of giving my unlife story to everyone I meet. Unless you have any more brains to trade."

"Well . . . *no?*" The Paladin gingerly lowered his sword as he shook his head.

"What if we can direct you to people to eat?" The trembling voice of the Bard came from behind.

Sally turned to observe the man. A floppy hat of green and yellow had somehow managed to stay atop his head, matching the slightly extravagant outfit he wore. A small brown goatee was matted with blood and spittle, and he leaned slightly to the side where she had slashed him with her sword.

"*Roger!*" the Wizard hissed at the Bard. "You can't do—"

Sally held up a hand to silence the spellcaster. "Hmm, Roger? I always forget Players have names." Slowly she began walking toward the nervous man, hands clasped behind her back. "It's rather dehumanizing of me to refer to you all as your class only—but that's how you guys see Monsters though, right?"

She stopped a few feet from the Bard and smiled. Approaching him had raised the tension again, but it also showed who was in control. They hadn't attacked. She ran her tongue across her teeth. That might mean they could be trusted to leave. "Best tell the Rogue to stand down, huh?"

"*Claire,*" the Paladin ordered through clenched teeth.

The Rogue appeared, now a dozen or so feet closer to the mobster than when last visible. The cloaked woman sighed and crossed her arms.

"Yous lucky the boss is in charge," Jackie spat, lowering her weapon to light a cigarette. "I'd fill ya like a pincushion for stabbin' my leg."

Sally grinned and looked around. Humphrey looked relaxed with his greatsword resting over his shoulder—still keeping a close proximity to the Paladin but with a pleased smirk across his metallic skull face. Theo had collapsed to a sitting position on the floor and was applying some healing. Exhausted from his own efforts as usual. On the other side of the gate, behind the Bard, Archie was keeping his eyes fiercely affixed on the Wizard, despite his normal small stature.

"So . . ." she continued, eyes idly focusing back on the musician, "where are these brains at?"

"There's a planned r-raid at the Kobold Mines tomorrow—two Parties going in at the same time to f-fully clear it."

"Level Three area," Humphrey added from the back.

Sally tilted her head. "Why are you giving them up to me? That seems *callous?*"

"They're griefers," the Wizard said with a hint of hesitation. "They don't PvP directly, but they use their numbers to make leveling difficult—or trap other Parties . . ."

"*The Flying Swords.*" The Paladin shook his head. "A Party of three that those assholes got killed."

Theo stood up, stumbling on his feet briefly. "What are the two groups called?"

"*OnetoFive* and *SixtoTen.*" The Bard shrugged. "It's not against the rules to raid together, but they do it to the detriment of everyone else."

Sally nodded thoughtfully and turned, walking slowly back toward the low campfire before sitting atop a crate. The buzz from her first meal was starting to wear off, and she was tired of the bravado. Would getting the jump on ten Players be a danger or an easy meal? Numbers often had the advantage when the levels were so close—they would have a lot more skills at their disposal.

She scuffed her trainers through the dry dirt, trying to get her head clear. It would be a nice way to get some of their own power up and utilize her new ability. Killing the Monk wouldn't be enough experience, and her bloodlust was cooling off. One of her summoned zombies looked up at her from the floor. It was the last one remaining but had its legs hewn off at some point.

"Hey." She glanced up at the Paladin. "What was the Monk's name?"

". . . Lars."

---

"Lars" - Level Three Zombie

---

She tilted her head at the information and then looked back down at the half-corpse. How was she supposed to move the zombies around? If they used the teleport scroll, then they might end up left behind. The thought of leaving them to fend for themselves made her feel sad.

"I feel *sad*," she stated, "and I'm telling rather than showing because it might be hard for you to see with all your friend's gore caked across my face."

An awkward silence followed.

"Time for yous to scram." Jackie blew a puff of smoke. "Boss lady is getting tired, and I'm sure you don't want the very generous offer to be revoked?"

Slowly at first, then with some haste, the four members of *Voice of Gaia* began to gather at the gate before heading out into the darkened woods—the Bard only briefly looked back at the zombified Monk.

"Whatcha think, metal-head?" Jackie raised an eyebrow at the Death Knight as she flicked away the end of the cigarette. "They'll come at us for revenge down the line?"

"*Ha-ha*. I trust that they have been sufficiently scared off." He stowed his blade as he continued to watch the shadowed figures vanish into the distant tree line.

Archie came up to the campfire and licked at patches of his fur where he had been injured—otherwise showing no acknowledgement of his dramatic size increase.

Theo came and stood by Sally, hesitantly putting his hand on her shoulder. "You alright?"

Her message was sent from her STAR to Chuck.

---

Sally: okay, did a *little evil*

---

She sighed and looked up at the Novice, her red eyes dull and tired. "I gave them the choice, like we spoke about *right* before."

"Morality stuff is difficult, huh?"

"Yeah." Sally looked up into the sky at the two pale moons. One distant, almost hiding behind the brighter one. "I wanted to eat them, though. *So bad.*"

"The brain-eating was . . . uh." Theo brought his hand back to rub the back of his neck. "Horrifying, I guess?"

She smiled and wrinkled up her nose, swinging her feet back and forth idly.

"Aw, pup." Bright light filled her eyes once more. "We are only getting started."

## CHAPTER FIFTY-TWO

# Foul Intent

The rest of the night was uncomfortable, but after retreating to the middle encampment, the Party eventually got some rest to round off the day. The half-zombie had vanished—apparently, only some kind of temporary summon—but Lars remained and kept watch alongside Humphrey.

Sally rolled out of the bedroll onto the hard earth. The fight from the previous night seemed like it was a dream. Mostly a good dream, on account of the fact that she ate a brain. Despite being a zombie for nearly a week, it hadn't felt like something she wanted to do until that skill was unlocked. Maybe that was her Player side overriding the natural zombie stuff.

Her STAR blinked with notifications.

> Chuck: it was only a matter of time, huh?
> Chuck: pretty late though, you okay?
> Chuck: we saved some goats or something
> Chuck: seems weak, but I leveled and I'm now a Druid
> Chuck: no judgements, zombie girl

She smiled and closed the chat. There would be no point in clueing him in on the whole eat-a-brain thing. *Druid* was interesting though. He had also leveled up without having to kill things—a thought both almost as uncomfortable as the ground she lay on and not as comforting as the meal the Monk had been.

It reminded her about the quests that she had pretty much ignored after getting Bella back to her mother. Things had just snowballed from there, and they had Monster'd around with no proper direction. Perhaps she would check it out—after making sure everyone was alright.

As she clambered to her feet, she saw the Death Knight sitting, arms folded, in a wooden chair that looked about ready to give up under the weight. With a yawn, she gave him a nod. "All is well, Humps?"

"Nothing to report." The flame of his helmet flickered a little higher. "You know, we could have tracked them down after they escaped?"

She narrowed her eyes in response. "True. I think we need to work on our soft skills though. Having more allies—or at least people that will keep out of our way—will further our goal more than killing and eating all."

"Very measured of you." Humphrey crossed his arms and looked around the encampment at the death and destruction they had leveled the previous day. "*Meditate* on that, did you?"

"Don't you sass me." She wiggled a finger at him. "The brain actually gave me some melee damage boost. Let me guess: the bonus depends on what kind of brain I eat—the level and class?"

The Death Knight grinned. "Soon you will be done with my mentorship, and I can die a nice dramatic death to further your growth arc."

"As your boss, I forbid it." She sighed and looked around the middle camp—most of the remaining bandits were keeping to themselves or doing repairs on the tavern. It was slightly surprising that the building didn't regenerate like how the Monsters respawned. "Where's the rest of the gang?"

"First camp." He stood and rolled out his shoulders. "Theo was trying to find a way for the cat to speak again. Jackie went to watch in amusement."

"What do you think of our new pal?"

"Effective in combat and fills the missing role of ranged damage that we lack." Humphrey looked around to make sure nobody was listening in. "*Abrasive personality*—and I'm not sure I commend the smoking."

"You are *literally* constantly on fire." She gestured her head toward the fixed gateway. "But, you are correct. We could really do with a healer of some sort. If I could rely on the System to give me a clear class, then it would have been easier to stack the Party to be more fleshed out."

"Four melee unless the cat has something interesting going on."

Sally shrugged and pushed through into the start of the camp once more. The bright daylight, unhindered by the cavern or any wooden structure, was painful to her eyes. She shielded them with her hand and looked out to see the rest of her Party.

Theo had seemingly given up on trying to communicate with Archie, the ginger cat now asleep on his stomach as he lay back on some crates. Jackie was similarly reclined in a chair nearby, her hat dipped down over her eyes. On hearing the pair approach, the mobster lifted it to squint at the zombie.

"Hey, Jacks." Sally nodded. "Any chance your bandit friends can join us?"

"I tried before, but the buggers won't leave the camp past"—she loosely gestured with a wave of her hand—"about thirty feet? Then they turn tail back here."

That made some sense. Monsters had some kind of tether to their spawning place—perhaps not all Monsters did, but certainly those who were trying to defend a specific place. A regiment of bandits against the regiment sent from Poppybrook would have made for a nice standoff, though.

"Shame. We have to be back at Sanctuary tomorrow, Humps?"

The Death Knight nodded and looked out toward the sky as if there lay a more detailed answer out in the clear blue.

"Remind me what's going on?" Jackie sat forward to light a cigarette. "I kinda tuned out most of the pretty words you were yabberin' yesterday. We're doing some adventurin' and killin'?"

"Short answer, yes," Theo murmured from beneath his forearm. He tilted his head to the side to regard the two women talking, not wanting to disturb the cat. "Only death follows the path we take."

Humphrey grinned at the morose Novice.

Sally rolled her eyes, despite the delightful juxtaposition of her reflective mood and his sour one. *That's what you get for not eating brains.* Or something more normal adjacent. "Hush, but yeah, kinda. We ousted a village from the humans and elves there, and Poppybrook is sending a regiment of . . . people to come un-oust it."

Jackie let the slim stream of smoke from her cigarette idly wave in the air. "Alright—and you said you would get me a village next, yeah?"

"Sure, we'd need to find four more Uniques to be Leaders." She shrugged and turned to the Death Knight. "How many villages are there in this first area?"

"Six."

"How many do we need to take to march on Poppybrook?"

Humphrey paused, a flicker of hesitation crossing his skull before the answer was released. "Three."

"Easy, then, right?" She beamed and counted on her fingers. "First up, we need to secure Sanctuary—that's the big crux of our movement. Then with that under our belt, two more villages should be the priority before another climax in taking Poppybrook."

"This isn't a movie trilogy." Theo groaned into his arm. "If we have to get to max level and go through all the areas to find the Architect then that's like . . ."

"Could be ten movies. Or we could just find a way out of the System or some way to circumvent leveling and travel options before then. I'm sure if we put our brains to it"—she licked her lips by reflex—"we can wrap this up in a neat and tidy way."

The Novice just groaned in response.

Humphrey and Jackie gave each other a shrug as Sally brought up her STAR menus. *Time to actually use the map!* The island they were on was indeed croissant shaped—or like a crescent moon. They were on the left side—a large chunk of that tip being verdant green with the mass of woodlands that comprised most of the area.

She zoomed in and wrinkled her nose. "Humphrey, come point out the mines for me."

The Death Knight moved behind her and pointed with a plated digit. "There, *ha-ha*."

As Sally selected the waypoint, the transparent arrow appeared over her head again. There was a button to share it with Theo—but it kept rejecting the transfer every time she pressed it.

"Oh, I don't do *quests*." The Novice finally sat up, disrupting Archie. The cat stretched and yawned as Theo continued, "Just went out into the wild as soon as possible to start hitting things"

"Punching down at Monsters?"

"Yeah, that."

Sally scowled at him, more so because she had completed more quests than he had—he was a terrible excuse for a Player. No class, no proper equipment, no skills, no quests, and no decency to offer up his brain to her.

"Well, get packed up. We are heading out—and you can leave the bad attitude here, Mister." Her sneakers tapped against the dry dirt as she continued her scowl. She gave a *[Command Dead]* to Lars, who had been stowed away in one of the small shacks near the second camp gate as an alarm. He stumbled out with a low moan.

A zombie army of one was a small start—if she could keep him alive and eat more brains, then it would soon grow. If she was supposedly a carrier now, any bite should do it. She brought up the ability description while she waited for the Party to gather.

> [Carrier - Passive] Players killed by you turn into Zombies under your control

As always, the System was as vague as expected. The Death Knight caught her confused glare at the text window.

"It makes it sound like a guaranteed thing." He shrugged. "But there are degrees of success. Every scratch or bite has a chance to pass on the *[Zombie Curse]*—against a Constitution Save. Eating their brains is a 100 percent chance. When they die—no matter in what manner—if they have the curse, then they turn."

"They should get you to write these things." She sighed, closing the window. "You'd do a better job."

"*Ha-ha*. That is a light-blue Observer job. My cousin is in that field."

"Like an actual field or—"

"*No*. Why was that your take from the conversation?"

"I just thought that . . ." Sally turned to see the rest of the *Outsiders* waiting for them to finish their meandering chat.

She glanced at her wrist; the Daily Item Reward notification was lonely and ignored. Briefly, her finger hovered over it . . . before she decided against it.

"Let's move out," she growled, pointing in the direction of the Kobold Mines.

## CHAPTER FIFTY-THREE

# Travel Encounters

Dried earth crumbled beneath the footsteps of the Party as they made their way through the woods.

Sally was in a good mood. Despite Jackie complaining of the heat, Humphrey giving the mobster constant evils over her smoking, Theo groaning almost as much as Lars as he looked ill, and Archie mewing to be picked up every so often.

They were going to beat people up and steal their lunch. And by lunch, she meant brains. And by steal, she meant eat. The Death Knight had reassured her that they were likely to turn up as the raid was already underway. Due to the nature of the excursion, the ten-strong group would want to get in early and spend most of the day in there. Apparently the mines had enough Monsters to sustain that.

She had wondered if there would be any Unique Monsters among the kobolds and whether they were the dog-type or the dragon-type. It seemed rude to ask, so she kept that as a little surprise for herself. They might be unlike anything from the pop culture of her previous world—even though a lot of the System seemed to have been vaguely made with them as a reference.

"Say, Humps? Do you know how the regiment is comprised?" She raised an eyebrow at the plated figure.

"*Yes.*" His skeletal features somehow relaxed. "Well, not exactly. This is rather unprecedented. However, my educated guess is that it will be twenty Level Ten guards led by a Level Ten Elite."

Sally and Theo exchanged glances.

"Shit me, that's a lot," Jackie exclaimed, dropping the lit cigarette from her mouth. "What level am I—like, twenty-something, right?"

"Close." Sally grimaced. "Five."

The mobster pulled a sour face and reached for her seemingly unending cigarette packet.

"It's not as terrible as it sounds!" Sally hopped ahead of them and raised her arms as she turned. "We can probably get some experience today and level up! With some smart planning, we will be able to do some damage despite the power difference."

If her speech had roused their spirits and washed away any doubt, none of them showed it. Only Archie seemed to be somewhat enthused. Lars probably wouldn't complain either, if you excluded the moans.

"One death trap at a time." Theo shrugged. "If we can kill ten Level Three Players, then twenty Level Ten NPCs should be . . . a walk in the park." Whatever energy he had for the statement had drained by the conclusion.

Sally snapped her fingers with a wink and turned to lead the way again, the smile fading from her face. They were up against the odds—but it wouldn't be just them. The goblins in Sanctuary, including the Leaders. Hopefully some more zombies too—not only from the mines but all three *[Summon Zombie]* charges. That was exciting. She could almost match their number if she was lucky—and although they wouldn't stand up to much of an assault, the corpses were always great distractions.

Slowly exhaling through her nose, she brought up her chat with Chuck.

Sally: yeah, we are still alive
Sally: off to do some evil
Sally: proud of you, snot
Chuck: doing an escort quest
Chuck: zero chance of combat
Sally: how's that feel?
Chuck: rain check
Sally: that a Druid spell?

She waited a few seconds for the reply, briefly stumbling over a tree root as she focused on the UI.

Chuck: we'll talk later . . . about something
Chuck: stay alive
Chuck: or dead, yknow wtev
Sally: remember to lift with ur knees

The chat closed, and she wondered what he could have to say later. Was he just giving her a cliffhanger? Was he *allowed* to do that?

"Everything okay?" Theo had caught up to her.

"Just Chuck; he's on that pacifist grind."

"Is it working out for him?"

She shrugged. "He isn't dead and probably isn't leveling up his trauma stat."

"Huh." Theo looked out into the woods.

Despite it being his choice to follow along, she did feel bad for the Novice. She was at least able to suppress some of the horror due to being part Monster. There must be a breaking point for him—she doubted all the Strength he stacked helped his mental fortitude.

After a short while they reached a small stream running across their path. There didn't seem to be a walkway or small bridge to cross it as far as Sally could see, neither up nor downstream. The embankment sank at a sharp angle on each side, and she estimated a good eight or so feet from one flat side to the other.

"We can just jump it, yeah?" Jackie peered over the edge, her face scrunched up as she regarded the running water.

"Not all of us are so spry." Humphrey nodded toward Lars trying not to give away that he also meant himself.

"It doesn't look that deep." Sally knelt beside the muddied slope. The water was remarkably clear, perhaps two feet deep at the most, and they should have no trouble Strength-wise at wading against the flow.

"I'm not a fan of water." Theo rubbed the back of his neck, giving his own scan up and down to see if he could see a bridge.

Sally rolled her eyes. "We aren't being bested by a bit of wet. Humphrey, I am delegating the problem to you—I am going full send."

"I am not aware what that means—"

They watched as the boss zombie took a dozen or so steps back and sprinted toward the edge. She leapt into the air, sailing over the river. Her foot slipped on the edge of the opposite embankment turning her landing into an impromptu roll. She quickly spun up onto her feet, raised her hands in the air, and turned back to the watching group.

Theo mimed holding up a scorecard. "Eight."

"RIGGED!" She stomped her foot and crossed her arms. "Now hurry up and get across."

Jackie held out Betty to the Novice. "Here, put this in your big pocket." She paused as he went to take it. "Don't make any mistakes. We are at a handy junction where I can drown ya."

He nodded awkwardly and stowed the weapon away in his Inventory.

The mobster took a few steps back and performed the same sprint-jump as Sally had. Jackie's longer legs made an easy go of it, and she landed with a slide beside the zombie.

"Hey, what score'd I get?" She brimmed with confidence, brushing a chunk of purple hair from her face.

"Uh—a nine?" Theo shrugged.

She crossed her arms and looked proud of herself as Sally pouted.

"Hurry up, Humps, so I can lecture Theo about my insecurities."

The Death Knight scratched his metal chin and looked at the remaining group: the Novice, the cat, and the walking corpse. With a brief shrug, he withdrew his greatsword from his back, a pulse of unholy energy flickering along the long blade. He turned, after briefly drinking in the slight worry in Theo's eyes, and moved to the nearest tree.

With a quick flash of crimson, the large sword carved straight through the trunk—a straight line of bright red glow across the width of the dark log. As the glow faded, the tree shifted across this slice, and with the cracking of breaking branches, it fell to crash across the small gorge.

"I got my skirt all dusty for no reason," Sally murmured to herself.

Jackie just looked down at the zombie's outfit. The dried blood, brain matter, mud, and who knows what else made the dust seem like the least of the issues.

The pair watched as one by one the rest of the Party made it across the log to their side of the water. Theo took even longer than Lars to slowly shuffle along the fallen tree.

"Never imagined you to be hydrophobic." She tilted her head as the sweaty man hopped down from the thickening branches. "Y'know, after all the gore and murder didn't ruin you."

"We all have our Achilles' heel." He tried to get his breath back. "I'm not usually that bothered by it; it's strange."

"Well, at least I know what to do if I ever need to chase you down." She gave him a pat on the back and allowed Archie to hop onto her shoulder.

Jackie came and stood beside the Novice as the boss walked away. "*Betty*." She held out her hands as Theo removed it and returned the repeating crossbow to the mobster.

They continued along their path for another hour or so. The weather remained as mild as it seemed to always be. Sally squinted at the almost clear sky. It was probably saving all the rain and stormy weather for when the stakes were the highest. She knew the System understood how to set a good scene.

After a while, the Death Knight stopped and turned toward the right. "As much as I don't want to tip the scales with my meta knowledge." He craned his head back to Sally who had now paused. "We should take a brief detour this way."

Seeing no reason to doubt him, the *Outsiders* changed course briefly.

A few hundred feet later, as they worked their way through denser trees, there was an opening—a circular clearing with some kind of stone structure in the middle.

Twenty feet tall, made of a gray marble that was similar to the fountain they had previously seen, it was a rounded cone shape, with two sets of carved wings jutting from near the peak. As they rounded to the front of the shrine, a rounded indent was visible on the lower bulge of the main body. Carvings of a language that Sally didn't know spread out in spiral patterns around the small alcove and across the floor in a wide circle.

"Shrine of Regret." Humphrey grinned. "And it looks like it isn't on cooldown."

Sally raised her eyebrows to the Novice, but he shrugged and shook his head.

Seeing their confusion, the Death Knight reveled in the reveal. Crimson flame flickered higher from his helmet, and he narrowed his empty eye sockets.

"It lets you unlearn one of your skills and replace it, *ha-ha*."

"Dibs!" Sally immediately shouted and ran toward the shrine, hand outstretched to try and activate it.

"*Stop there!*" a gruff voice shouted out from behind them.

## CHAPTER FIFTY-FOUR

# Arrogance

Sally almost slid on the carved stone base of the shrine as she stopped and swiveled around.

A figure stood on the other side of the clearing. Dark leather armor contrasted with the occasional silver armor plates that caught the light, one on the knee, one on each shoulder, and one on the left arm bracer. Small pouches lined across their chest as well as along their belt. As he stepped farther into the light, his black beard and tanned but scarred face aged the man beyond his years.

"I have come here for that shrine, madam." His gravelly voice was harsh but calm, almost apathetic.

"But I'm closest," she whined in return, narrowing her eyes. She gulped. Level Fifteen Swordmaster. That must be a Third Class Fighter.

"I have traveled from the middle of the Wastelands just to use this and change my keystone ability." He slowly walked toward her. "Every shrine I have seen along the way was on cooldown or camped by a Party."

She shot a glance over to the *Outsiders*. They all looked tense. Could a Level Fifteen solo their whole group? Somehow she managed to prevent herself from blurting out the question to the Death Knight. Instead, she tried to keep the man engaged.

"You don't have a Party?" For all she knew, they could be nearby in hiding—or on their way.

"No." He stopped around fifteen feet away from her and regarded her Party with cold eyes. "You seem to have a very *interesting* one."

"We're a bunch of misfits, those glitched or shunned by the System." She attempted a pleasant smile, which was difficult with how sharp her teeth were.

The man scratched at his beard as his gaze slid between each member, then back to Sally. He seemed totally relaxed as if they were no threat. "System's been real weird for the past couple of weeks."

"We are looking to fix it, in a manner of speaking."

"Interesting." He looked past her at the shrine. "If I could just reset my skill, I'll be on my way."

"The name's Sally." She seethed through a clenched jaw. "And I'd really like to change a skill as I don't have a proper class."

His eyes flickered back to her. They were pale blue and pierced through her. He licked his lips before he spoke, which she read as a small sign his patience was being tested.

"Miss, I don't care to bloody my sword on those who aren't a challenge. I'd hate to end your little crusade so early." There was a slight inflection to his words now.

She glanced over at the *Outsiders*. Humphrey remained impassive. Jackie looked like she was itching to let loose with her tensely held crossbow. Theo was trying to give a signal; his face said, "Panic, run away," but the actions of his hands looked more like he was encouraging a fight. The cat was just asleep. She clucked her tongue at how cohesive everyone was.

Intrusive thoughts told her that a Level Fifteen brain would be very tasty—and maybe worth the risk. She quickly did the math. The numbers did not look good. They did not have enough crowd control to tie him down—he would probably likely pass Humphrey's Stun check and would blaze through her zombies even if she summoned all of them.

Her eye twitched as she stepped to the side.

As the man walked toward the shrine, he stopped beside her. "Name's Dent. You have a STAR, right? If you make it to the Wastelands, come meet me, and I'll repay you."

She held her wrist out to match with his, a brief glow appearing as his contact information was added.

"What, nothing you can give a gal now for her trouble?" She wrinkled her nose up as he continued up to the shrine.

"Nothing for your level or class." He shook his head as he placed his STAR into the alcove. "I can only use swords, so I don't keep much else."

A yellow sheen flashed over the shrine, circling around the outside of the alcove and increasing in intensity before it flickered out—and the shrine was now inert. Instead of the off-white of the marble-like material, it was now a dull gray.

"I'm surprised you didn't want to kill us because of what we are, even if it wouldn't be worth your time."

He turned back to her, his eyes looking at System messages that she couldn't see as he chose a new skill to replace another. "Some Players are more monster than some of the Monsters are. After my Party . . ." He trailed off as his eyes focused back on her. "Let's just say only the numbers matter to me now. Being the best Swordmaster in the System. Anything else is inconsequential."

Sally nodded but wasn't sure what to say.

"As it is, then, goodbye and good luck, Miss." He held out a scroll, which burnt up in his hand. A quick blue light flooded over his body and then dissipated as he teleported away.

After a few moments of silence, she kicked a loose stone away. "Dent is a silly name." She turned to the Party. "Cat got your tongues? Just because I'm the main character doesn't mean I have to do all the talking."

Archie meowed.

"I thought I was the main character." Theo frowned as he murmured to himself.

"Yous seem to have a level enough head for it, and yous is the boss, Boss." Jackie shrugged and lit a cigarette, looking disappointed that there would be no fighting.

The Death Knight stood impassively, his gaze still on the shrine. Slowly, he turned back to face her, the light breeze gently caressing his helmet flames. "No comment."

Sally closed her eyes and exhaled. She wasn't even really that annoyed at the group. As comically oddball and reliant on her as they were, that was part of their charm. What she was most frustrated by was being insignificant compared to the sole Swordmaster.

Knowing that they could have done almost nothing if he had attacked them burned her up. And that was just Level Fifteen! While the fights in this starting area had been rough at times, she had always felt that they had the upper hand—whether through plot armor or just convenient luck. But they were still small fry in the world.

Why was the world just an island? She let the question distract her mind from the simmering anger. Opening her eyes, she looked up briefly at the location marker pointing them to the mines still.

"I guess this is a long cooldown? We should just head out." She curled her fingers around the hilt of her sword and then relaxed them, trying to trick herself into thinking something had been accomplished here.

Humphrey nodded. "Yes. Several days to a week usually. It is not a set time, and usually not worth waiting around for."

With one last forlorn glance at the tall gray-marble structure, Sally slouched in resignation and resigned herself to leaving the area. It probably would have just glitched for her anyway, she told herself. The last thing she needed was to lose all her skills or to be given something useless like *[Novice Strike]*.

The *Outsiders* fell into step behind her, Archie now settling on the wide shoulder plate armor of the Death Knight.

"As far as random encounters go, that one was pretty dull." She raised her eyebrows higher in an exaggerated effort toward Humphrey as if he was the sole reason it ended as a flop.

"Perhaps a wake-up call," he replied bluntly.

Theo groaned and rubbed his face. "Of course. The higher our notoriety gets, the more likely we are to attract the attention of someone who could easily wipe us from the System."

"Imagine a Level Twenty Party that hears about our uprising, and they want to be the heroes to stop it." Humphrey turned his empty-socket gaze toward her. "*Ha-ha.*"

Sally exhaled. *Mood killer.* "So what do you suggest? Is there a way to go 'off-grid' or hide ourselves better? By nature, we are going to make noise if we are killing and toppling civilization."

"*Yes.*" The Death Knight grinned at her frustration. "Let me consider some options." He looked into the air and frowned.

"Meow," Archie stated from beside his head.

She waited for either of them to elaborate before giving up on that as well. Her earlier mood had been completely run over by the series of miserable events. Still, she tried to shirk them off, looking into the distant woods with determination. There was a big fight to be had and potentially brains to be eaten.

Another half an hour of bland scenery passed with little fanfare. Other than Humphrey occasionally looking into the air, the Party seemed to be content enough to walk in silence and contemplate the trial ahead.

Eventually, they reached thinning trees, and with a quick check of her map, Sally gestured for everyone to slow and quiet. As they stepped with as much stealth as they were capable of, they reached the edge of a clearing.

Ahead of them, as they crouched behind the sparse amount of trunks, was an unmistakable mine entrance built into the side of a rocky hill. A square of wooden beams bordered the entrance and continued inward into dim light, bracing the sides of the tunnel. From within, a rusted minecart track spat forth like a snake's tongue before it ended at the side, a couple of overturned carts having spilled their contents.

Alongside the dirty footsteps in the gray dust, discarded mining tools, and roughshod wooden furniture the exterior of the mine was also splattered with crimson. Half a dozen kobold bodies lay dead in various states of injury. They were the dog-like kind. Sally hid her pleased grin.

*The Players must be inside.*

Gingerly they began to make their way across the clearing to the entrance. Weapons were drawn. The corpses looked to have various stabbing and slashing wounds, along with some burns—one was even partially frozen. Sally licked her lips as she reached the open maw of the mines.

A faint echo of battle came from within.

"They are not far inside." Humphrey narrowed his lack of eyes to the dim wall torches farther in. "They must not have started that long ago."

With a nod and wry smile, Sally met the eyes of each of the *Outsiders*.

Sword in one hand, Dagger of Luck in the other, she exhaled and led the group down into the unknown below.

## CHAPTER FIFTY-FIVE

# Into the Bowels

Sally had to stop herself from humming a tune. Despite the imminent danger, the overwhelming joy at the anticipated full-course meal awaiting her left no room for any doubts. Her dead fingers gently caressed the cold walls of the mine tunnel as it slowly twisted and descended.

Every so often a lantern hung from the wooden bracings. *Every fourth one,* she counted. Though sometimes every three, annoyingly. Slightly less frequent were corpses of the furred kobolds.

As she entered a small room, a handful of the short Monsters were splayed across the toppled furniture. One of them, dark brown fur with mottled beige around his paws and snout, lay atop the table—his blood soaking through the maps and plans spread beneath him.

Theo knelt by one of the bodies and ran his eyes up the wall. "At least one slashing weapon," he whispered as he ran a finger over a slightly lighter line in the rock wall. He frowned as he stood and observed the rest of the room. "Maybe multiple?"

Humphrey grunted but had nothing to add.

Sally nodded and gestured to the continuation of the tunnel. The sounds of battle were still reasonably distant—but definitely closer. She assumed their quarry was moving into the mines farther as they ground the poor pups up. If there was any loot to be had, then that would be something for the way out.

Two further rooms in a similar state were passed. The occasional partially frozen dead kobold was an interesting keynote among the crimson gashes of the others. A few dozen feet farther down the mine shaft, it turned to the left sharply. The sounds of the Players were very close now.

The zombie boss paused, flush against the wall before the opening, and looked back to the group. She had picked Jackie to be her second in the surprise attack—much to the pouting of the Death Knight. He was just too noisy in his plated boots and had to keep up the rear with Lars. Jackie could at least provide covering fire and some near-instant damage while she and Theo had time to run into melee.

She closed her eyes as footsteps from the next room came briefly closer.

"Goddamn, they weren't kidding when they said the spawns were crazy here."

"Almost as dense as you, Benny."

"Up yours!"

"This is only the first depth too. I think there's supposed to be three?"

"Hold still so I can heal you."

At least three different voices, maybe four. It was hard for her to tell with the pounding of her heart. Slowly, she wiped the drool from her mouth and gave a nod to the mobster.

As soon as she heard the start of the healing spell, she pounced into the opening and cast *[Hex: Slow]* on the nearest figure, who happened to have their back turned to her. Five Players stood in various states of brief shock in the medium-sized room. Sally leapt over dead kobolds as Jackie moved into the opening with Betty.

*[Hellfire Trigger]* blazed as four bolts were fired in short succession. The first didn't pierce the armor of the slowed Paladin, but the second, third, and fourth landed squarely in their back—the last struck just as Sally reached them.

*[Eat Brains]*

The unaware victim had their skull cracked like a watermelon, blood and gore spraying into the room as Sally devoured a chunk of their gray matter.

Theo ran into the room just as soon as the bolt volley stopped but slowed to a stop with a confused look on his face. "Who . . . who are you guys?"

+2% Physical Defense

Sally dropped the body to the floor and looked at the remaining Players. The look of abject horror and disgust was becoming familiar now. Her brow furrowed at them; her vision was wavy as warmth and power flowed through her body.

They were only *Level Two*, and there were definitely only five of them. Well, four now. They were also all Fighters, except for the Paladin she had just consumed.

One of them near the back exit of the chamber, a man with short blond hair, threw up—his sword dropping to the floor in the process. The other three didn't look confident in doing anything more useful than that, their eyes not able to get any wider as the rest of the Party entered the room.

"These are not the Players you are looking for." Humphrey intoned, waving his hand across to signify their levels. "They are called *the Warriors*."

"I respect a theme," Sally slurred as she wiped her mouth. "Why are you down here, though?"

The closest Player, a female Fighter with red hair tied into a bun, nervously spoke up. "W-we keep getting griefed by a large group, so d-decided to level h-here." She was on the verge of tears as her eyes kept darting between their dead member and the one who perpetrated the violent murder.

"Bit on the nose," Theo murmured, trying to avoid eye contact with everyone in the room.

"What do you—? *Ah, sh—*" The realization hit Sally, and she paused as Jackie raised a hand. Over the panicked breathing—there it was. The sound of footsteps. "Too on the nose," she groaned, awaiting the inevitable.

The zombie Paladin rose to their feet, yellow baleful eyes briefly regarding their former teammates before they turned to face the boss and await orders.

"*Warriors, come out and play-ay!*" A mocking voice echoed down the tunnels, followed by the sound of potion bottles clinking together.

"That's just ridiculous." Sally sighed, to the nods of the Novice. "Listen, we'll help you kill all these jerk-offs. I'm sorry for killing . . ."

"Ben," the vomit-Fighter offered.

"*Ben*, thank you." She renamed them on her UI. "We were here for the two griefing Parties—just a case of wrong place, wrong time."

"If it's any consolation, there's a small chance they are back in the real world." Theo rubbed the back of his neck with a shrug.

"What real world?" a leather-capped Fighter asked, brows furrowing beneath their messy black hair.

"No time for that." Sally shrugged. She wanted to get back into battle before this energy wore out. They were at a disadvantage here though; if they fought them at the mouth of the tunnel, the bad guys would have the choke point. When what they deserved was being choked out.

"Alright," she hissed at the remaining *Warriors*, "you're going to help us now." Her eyes blazed red as a sharp-toothed grin spread across her face.

The first of the gang of ten walked through into the chamber. A wiry Rogue with more teeth than morals led the pack. Shriveled ears hung from a chain around his neck. His beady eyes scoured the room as his companions filtered in behind his step.

"Well, well . . . what do we have here?" He snarled at the huddle of Fighters crowded around a prone figure at the braced exit of the room.

"It's our friend; they tried taking on too many kobolds . . . You have to help." The eyes of the red-haired Fighter were puffy, and tears had marred her face.

"Oh, *I have to*, do I?" the Rogue scoffed as he pushed back his greasy hair to the murmured chuckles of the group filtering into the room behind him.

"H-he has a special sword; we need it to carry on in here."

"They want to carry on." A burly woman stepped in beside the Rogue. "Good thing we were here to help *push* them forward."

"Idiot," he snarled back. "First—let's see that special sword, eh" With a wicked grin, he strode toward the huddled group. The two newcomers converged on the *Warriors*, equally interested in why the sword was special and to maybe get some gloating in over the injured person.

The Rogue loomed over the small group; his eyes narrowed as they parted, revealing the body of a man lying sprawled awkwardly with a sword across his chest. A man with a bounty? Something wasn't right . . .

He pushed one of the Fighters away as he knelt, shooting a scowl at them before he turned his attention to the sword across the man's chest. It seemed to be made . . . of wood. As he slowly reached his hand out to touch it—it burst into pink flame.


Sally grinned as she peered around the corner. Seeing the pink glow of the *[Novice Strike]*, she gave Humphrey the signal. *Classic duo time.*

The Death Knight thundered around the corner and leapt over the prone Novice, sending the remaining *Warriors* scattering to the side. Sally had never seen him move with such dexterity or purpose as the plated figure crashed down heavily the other side of Theo and barreled into the throng of surprised Players, with her in tow right behind.

Theo rolled to his feet and began attacking the Rogue, who was still hastily trying to draw his weapons while trying to get a bearing on the situation.

Jackie stood in the corridor and spun up Betty, waiting for the signal to engage *[Hellfire Trigger]* now that it had cooled down. Archie stood back and watched as Lars and Ben slowly walked their way into the ensuing battle.

Sally threw *[Hex: Slow]* on the Rogue as she passed. The sooner Theo could join them, the better. As soon as Humphrey made it into the middle of the fray, he burst into crimson flame with *[Adrenaline]*, bathing the stone chamber in a red glow.

*[Will of the Dark Lord] [Summon Zombies]*

She glanced around to see who of the large gang failed their saves when something caught her eye.

They were all Level Five.

## CHAPTER FIFTY-SIX

# Rumbled

Her mind spun as the battle went into slow motion. The *Voice of Gaia* Party didn't actually say what level the two griefing Parties were. Humphrey had said it was a Level Three area, so she had made the false connection. You know what they say about assumptions though—they get you killed, *you ass.*

Three fresh, temporary zombies burst from the hard rocky floor as she made a quick slash-then-stab with her two blades into a Ranger who was currently stunned. Despite the unprotected damage, it was still not enough to kill the equal-level Player—so she gave them a headbutt for good measure.

Her panic about higher-level opponents was quickly washed away by the excitement of Level Five brains. Instead of turning to her next opponent, she again stabbed at the falling Ranger, jumping on top of them and plunging her dagger through leather armor into their chest.

A flurry of bolts flew overhead, striking at the few members of the gang who were about to try and stop her.

[Eat Brains]

+5% Ranged Damage

She sat up from her victim, blood soaking into her already filthy white shirt. *This was exhilarating.* Turning to the Novice, she watched as Theo battered the Rogue—despite his attempts to block Theo's whirling blade, it was just too unrelenting. Sally stood warm and calm, barely even registering the clash of weapons and shouts of pain and anger mixed with the groans of the undead.

She could sense the Rogue was on low health.

As she blissfully walked toward him, the Rogue suddenly went invisible, one hand fumbling for a red potion as he quickly faded from view. The *[Novice Strike]* wore off as the wooden sword clattered against the stone wall. She watched Theo growl and search the flickering shadows for signs of the Rogue.

*But Sally could smell the blood.*

She ran full pelt toward a plain wall, colliding with a soft and dense Rogue-shaped figure. With a crack against the stone and a further burst of the potion bottle breaking on the floor, the injured opponent shifted back into view. His beady eyes were wide with panic, and he opened his mouth to speak.

*[Eat Brains]*

+2.5% Melee Critical Chance

A hand shot down toward her, and she opened her gore-caked maw as if to bite it before realizing it was the hand of Theo. She instead took it with hers and stood with his assistance. He looked different. There was a cold indifference mixed with an anger—*no, not anger.* Some kind of primal determination to stay alive.

"Get back into the fight," he growled.

Her head lolled back around to the swirling battle. The mass of their opponents had become their detriment at the start. As Humphrey had pushed them back and engaged, they had tripped over each other or been pushed out of their effective ranges. Even now, the shocked head of some manner of spellcaster lay detached from their body in the middle of the melee—the first casualty of their bad positioning.

The Death Knight had killed two. She had killed two. Jackie had killed one—and between the mobster and the zombies another handful of Players were injured. The tide had stabilized now, as the support characters were able to buff and heal the remaining Fighters, and the Death Knight had come to be very outnumbered.

"*Retreat!*" a voice called from the back—a Bard with a bolt in their upper arm.

As she leapt toward the fray, three of the remaining members vanished in a shimmer of blue light. *Teleport scroll.*

Two of the gang remained—a Fighter and a Cleric. She watched as the Cleric readied a healing spell in one hand, aimed toward the armored Fighter squaring off against Humphrey, and with his other hand, grabbed at a teleport scroll.

Sally growled and threw her dagger as she ran the short distance with her sword raised. A bolt struck the outstretched hand, halting the spell. Her dagger struck the forearm of the grabby-hand, the teleport scroll instead falling to the dusty and crimson-stained floor.

Unholy light flickered along the Death Knight's blade as he feigned a swing to instead slam the hilt into the face of the Fighter, breaking their nose. He followed up with a swift kick of his plated boot into their unguarded stomach, knocking the wind from them. As they dropped to their knees, Humphrey grabbed them by the hair, his own crimson helmet flames dancing wildly.

Sally barreled past the Cleric, only briefly slashing out with her sword, dismembering the outstretched hand. She slid around to the held Fighter and used *[Eat Brains]* again.

+5% Health Points

She stood and laughed. Her clothing was drenched and stuck to her cold skin. As her jubilations echoed around the now quiet chamber, her blood-red eyes turned back toward the Cleric, burning with evil intent.

Theo handed Humphrey a Healing Potion, which he downed into his skeletal maw with a thankful nod.

"I'm . . . not s-sure I can talk." Sally turned her head to the pair abruptly, shuddering all over. "Feels like h-had quest and done c-cocaine about it."

"I can interrogate, then." Theo shrugged, nervously patting the shaking zombie boss on the shoulder. "Unless, Jackie . . . ?"

"What? Just because I'm a mobster you think—"

"*Okay, okay*, I'll do it." The Novice rubbed the bridge of his nose.

"Yous wanna look out for this cat though. He ain't normal."

All eyes, including the panicked Cleric and *Warriors* trying to sink into the background, turned toward the small ginger cat as he waltzed quietly out of the exit tunnel.

"H-how so?" Sally twitched. *It was hot down here, right? Was it just her?*

"I did feel . . . something." The Death Knight put away his greatsword, slightly scraping it across the ceiling. "Level Fives would normally put up more resistance than that, even with their disadvantages."

Theo scratched his chin. Whatever grim determination had powered him through the fight had faded, and he looked tired now. "Felt like fighting Level Threes, right?"

No response was given, but they continued to watch the cat preen himself, oblivious to their conversation.

"Well, uh . . . take a seat." The Novice nodded toward the Cleric, who collapsed against the wall, pale and clutching at his stump. "My name is Theo, and I'll be your good cop." He turned back to the Party behind him before regarding the injured man with a shrug. "You have your pick of bad cops."

"W-who are you people?" The spittle of the panicked man ran down his chin as he shook with fear and rage.

"We're assholes like you guys were." Theo sat down on the floor. "Emphasis on the were." He paused for dramatic effect as the bodies that Sally had killed rose to their feet as zombies. "In fact, with your resume, we'd love for you to *join us*."

The Cleric gulped. His green eyes darted between the gathering of odd figures in the room. A small spark of determination pushed away the brief fear. "You're all idiots." He smirked, between wincing from the pain he was in. "Can I at least heal my hand?"

"No." Theo shook his head. "Not after you just insulted us."

A growl emanated from the pained figure. "Shoulda just killed me, then; they'll come here for you."

"Who w-will?" Sally stuttered as she came to loom behind the Novice. Being this close to his head . . . Her attention was drawn to his hair, the rounded shape of his head—imagine what a tasty brain he must have! *Level Nine too!* But . . . the bonus from killing a Novice must be pretty weak . . .

"*Zero*." The smirk remained as sweat ran down from the Cleric's dusty blond hair. "The leaders of—"

"Oh, that makes sense." Theo turned to give the zombie a scowl as her drool pattered on his head. "You guys are just goons for a higher-level Party, right? They must bully you, huh? Do you run their errands in the low-level area for them? Or you're just too weak to—"

"*Shut up, shut up!*" The Cleric seethed. "Just have your pet zombie eat my brains already. They'll kill me if they teleport here, or worse . . . "

"I'm n-not his pet!" Sally pouted, turning away from them both.

"It's more of the other way around." Theo sighed. "But I perhaps am interested in increasing my bounty—maybe I'll—"

"You don't get it. Sure we grief and have caused Player deaths. But we don't PvP. *Zero* does." The man closed his eyes. "They are Level Ten, and they gatekeep the progression through the Swamp to the Wasteland."

Humphrey grunted. "Level Ten First Classes, or Second?"

"First."

"Not too bad then." The flame flickered at the back of the Death Knight's helmet. "Though our ace card may have already been spent." He looked down at the cat, who was now halfway to having a nap.

"What's your call, Sally?" Theo stood up and stretched as Jackie stormed over.

"Yous didn't even do any interrogating, useless *ass-having-ass*." She squatted down by the Cleric and shoved Betty against his temple. "Who ya working for?"

"I-I just said—it's *Zero*—" The man winced away from the cold metal of the weapon.

"Oh, yeah. Well, I guess we didn't need much information anyway. We just came here to murder ya after we got a tipoff."

"W-who told you we were here?"

"Huh?" Jackie cupped an ear as her finger tightened on the trigger. "I think *we* are doin' the talkin' here, punk."

"*She's good,*" Sally whispered into Theo's ear—he was startled, not realizing she was that close, but he nodded in agreement.

The Cleric squinted his eyes down toward his STAR; his arm was hanging limp with the dagger still embedded in it, which made it a hard angle to read.

"It's too late." He grinned widely. "They are on the way."

The Party tensed as a wave of static filled the chamber. Sally looked at the *Warriors*, who had still been too scared to move, and then at Humphrey, who had started reaching for his sword.

With a pop and flash of blue light, five new figures now stood in the chamber, the digital "Ten" of their level searing into the widening eyes of Sally.

## CHAPTER FIFTY-SEVEN

# Unchewable

Sally paled. As intimidating as Swordsmaster Dent had been, this group was on a whole different level. In part this was due to the red Player Killer notifications next to their classes, showing high bounties—but it was also how they stood, the manner in which they held themselves. They were *killers* through and through.

A Fighter at the forefront turned his head to the side, observing the *Outsiders* and gathered zombies. His pale face had two deep scars across it, cutting blank spaces from his right cheek over his eye and into his short dark hair. His studded armor had been dyed white but was dirtied and unwashed.

"Well, this is certainly interesting." His words came out slowly as if he was savoring each word.

Behind him, a Knight in full plate mail dyed a bright yellow stood with their hands on their hips. Two Wizards—one in pale gray robes and another in light blue—scowled at the undead Party, poised in anticipation. The last of the group was a female Rogue in a dark leather trench coat and black goggles.

Sally's hands shook, a mixture of the brain-high wearing off and the pressure from the powerful foes now in this small chamber with them.

The white-armored Fighter turned his gaze slowly away from the *Outsiders* down to the injured Cleric against the wall.

"Disappointing." He sighed. "We had information that there were a couple of Parties about to head through the Swamps today—and you brought us here for this?"

"I-I'm sorry, Walter—they had something—"

"No excuses. The whole ten of you were here, and yet this Party of . . . odd low levels were able to almost wipe you?" Venom dripped from his words, yet his eyes remained calm.

The Cleric said nothing in return and just lowered his head, cowering away.

"You will be dealt with later," the Fighter continued as he turned his dead-eyed stare back to Sally. "Naturally, we respect that you seem to be killing Players too—your bounties are decent for . . . *Players* your level."

Humphrey narrowed his sockets. "How is it you were able to get yours so high without the System intervening?"

"It tries." A humorless grin spread across his slim face. He raised a hand and snapped his fingers.

The Rogue opened up her trench coat, revealing two belts and a bandoleer of scrolls and small magical stones that Sally hadn't seen before.

Walter widened his slim smile. "Teleport scrolls and stones. Jess there has all points in Dexterity, Evasion Chance, and Movement Speed. No faster hands in this area. Anything untoward comes up—we can jump between places in almost an instant."

The Death Knight said nothing but slowly nodded.

Sally huffed and crossed her arms—partly to hide them shaking. "So what's the good of killing people in the Swamps and never getting your Second Class?"

"It's for a purpose." His dark eyes focused on the zombie. "If we were Second Class, then there would be fewer rewards for killing the First Classes. We get some nice items from the idiots trying to level and progress. Potions, magical items, Skill Books—"

"You have Skill Books?" Theo blurted out.

"Sure do. Level Nine Novice? You might be the biggest newb yet!" This time the smile met his eyes, and his Party chuckled among themselves. "I bet you'd like one, huh?"

The Novice paused, briefly licking his lips as his eyes darted between Sally and Walter. "What would I have to do?"

"Easy. You're the only one close in level." He withdrew a sledgehammer from his back. It was a simple and brutish weapon, the end of it a dull, flakey red. Not rust—dried blood. "Why not duel one of us for a chance?"

Sally scowled at Theo. This was no time for heroics—a Skill Book wasn't worth him dying and denying her a tasty brain. These Player-killers were outfitted and experienced in getting rid of fools like the Novice. Yellow Knight was clearly the decoy, most likely full Defense and CON to weather the attacks. The two Wizards would be Crowd Control and Status Effects. Walter would be the one picking off the easy targets as the Rogue gave them an easy exit.

If it was that clear to her, she assumed Theo would know too. He was smart;

his brain was not just a pretty face. She doubted they would play fair in any kind of duel. And yet it came as no surprise that the Novice nodded in agreement.

"Okay, but I get to pick who?"

His answer was met with laughs. Walter shrugged. "Sure, why not? If you think you have a chance."

Theo leveled his outstretched finger at the Rogue.

"Interesting choice. Jess does need to pad her kill count, I suppose."

Theo brought up his STAR.

"Hey, no funny business?" The Rogue stepped forward, drawing a thin rapier from beneath her trench coat.

"Just sending a last love letter, in case I die." He replied flatly, closing the menu and not meeting the gaze of Sally.

The zombie narrowed her eyes and opened her STAR—but there were no notifications, except for the Daily Reward. As she looked up, she was surprised to see him in front of her.

He leaned in close and whispered to her. "Master, forgive me, but I'll have to go all out . . . just this once . . ."

"Asshole. I hate you," she hissed back as he turned away.

Pink flame enveloped his wooden sword as he stepped forward. Both Parties stepped back to give more room to the pair.

With a brief nod, they began.


The lizardman wiped the blood from his curved blade on the long grass, painting a dark crimson streak through the verdant green.

With a short growl, the Cleric spat on the corpse of an orc. "Useless Monster."

Avoiding his glares, the lizardman and the pale, cloaked woman looked away. They had no interest in invoking his ire as he shook with anger.

"This is why Uniques are infernal and must be cleansed. They have one life to live, and they waste it. *Waste it.*" He kicked at the limp body to further his point.

A series of clicks and chirps came from behind him.

The Cleric spun around and glared at the short figure, his fist shaking as his face reddened. "Don't you start again. It's only because you are useful that you haven't met the same fate. We need our fifth Party member before tomorrow, and this heretic just wanted to be a *trader?*"

A single chirp sounded out from the small insectoid, who then also avoided the gaze of the looming Cleric.

Marius sighed and looked toward the sky with eyes closed. He let the rage lower, but his left fist remained clenched. Pain had been flaring down his arm, pulsing along with his heartbeat. He had taken to wearing a glove to hide the discoloration of his skin. *Perhaps the four of them would be enough.* They were running low on time.

"Maybe I can be of service?" A low, scratchy voice came from the trees behind them.

They turned to watch the source of the voice appear in mid-air, a black-red flame flickering around a floating skull.

*[Novice Strike]* missed for the third time.

Sally clasped at her face, a nervous energy making her want to join the fray. The Rogue was clearly playing with the Novice, as she hadn't made a single attack yet. Instead, she had dodged away, the flicker of pink energy arcing through the air and then disappearing as the attack failed.

"Pretty quick for a Novice," Walter admitted. "Looks like it is mostly gear-dependent though. Stats make a bigger difference."

Sharp teeth were harder to grind together, Sally found, especially when they slotted together like some kind of cartoon character. "*What are we doing? Shouldn't we . . . ?*" she hissed toward the Death Knight.

Humphrey slowly shook his head, his hands clasped and folded across his chest. Instead, he turned around away from the fight to murmur something to the panicked *Warriors* huddled in the corner.

She looked between Jackie and Archie for some help. The cat was just sitting, watching intently, seemingly more interested in the flailing colors of the sword strike. A puff of smoke came from the mobster, but she seemed pretty serene given their danger.

Sally turned back to the fight just in time to see the Rogue make her first attack. The rapier was almost a blur in the air as it darted out and struck the Novice in the shoulder of his off arm.

Theo grunted in pain and redoubled his efforts. Again and again, the flare of his skill lit the small chamber before it was extinguished, unable to land a blow.

"You're trying to hit me with a wooden sword?" Jess scoffed. "You must be a brainless zombie too."

A second rapier attack snaked out and struck Theo's off arm again—a few inches below the first puncturing attack. She was still toying with him.

"Play fair, Jessica." Walter rolled his eyes with a smirk on his face.

She blew out some air in exasperation. "Alright. Go on, then, Novice. You can strike me once—just not the face."

Theo wasted no time—his attack blazed through the air and struck the arm of the trench coat in a similar place to where he had been stabbed.

Her smirk quickly changed into confusion at the amount of pain from the impact. "Ow, that actually—"

The wooden sword flickered around in a bright arc to strike her again before she had finished the sentence. A third one was already on the way as she gathered her senses—only just having enough time to parry it. Theo spun immediately out, the Rogue dodging it, but he continued the rotation like a whirlwind, catching her on the backswing.

Sally allowed herself a smile as she watched the concerned expressions grow on the Player-killing Party. The Rogue was probably in no danger still, and they would intervene if she were—of that she had no doubt—but for now, their discomfort was her pleasure.

Clangs of wood against metal resonated through the small space as light from the attacks blazed through the air. With the increased blocks and parries it seemed as though the Rogue had gotten used to the attack speed of the Novice.

"*Stuff this,*" the woman hissed.

*[Heartseeker Strike]*

Her rapier was enveloped in shadow as it shot forward, piercing straight through Theo's torso and out his back.

The pink light of his attack faded away.

## CHAPTER FIFTY-EIGHT

# Flame Grilled

The Death Knight held the zombie back, shaking his head despite the pleas of her eyes. "He made his choice."

Sally shook with rage and turned back to the impaled Novice. That was her meal. *And her friend.* She tried to relax. Humphrey was perhaps right; this was Theo's choice—and it would make the situation worse to get herself killed too. The thought of running in and eating his brain was only a very brief consideration.

"Missed your heart—though I don't think the skill name is literal." The smile across the Rogue's face was wide and menacing.

Blood ran from Theo's mouth as his brow furrowed in pain. "Think that really h-hurts?" he stammered as his sword arm wavered. "I eat strikes like that for b-breakfast."

"Then let me give you your *late lunch!*" The rapier withdrew backward, causing the Novice to twitch in pain.

*[Heartseeker Strike]*

A second strike pierced him in the stomach, and he bent over, growling out in pain. Sally seethed, a lump of nausea settling into her own gut.

The wooden sword clattered to the floor as Theo dropped to his knees.

"Not a bad show." Walter slowly clapped from behind. "I can see how you have a bounty—you would be easily underestimated. Shame this is how it ends."

Jess leaned down, her trench coat hanging open as she put pressure on her embedded blade. "Any last words, Novice?"

Theo looked up at her with blurry eyes. He looked pale and sickly—about to pass out if he also wasn't about to die. He had certainly done some damage to the Rogue, but eventually, he had just been outclassed.

A slight smile twitched across his face as sweat ran down his temples. "I . . . t-think you d-ropped a scroll?"

She looked down at the scroll held in his off hand. "Huh, I—"

*[Scroll: Fireball]*

A blinding blast of amber followed by a wave of superheated air washed over Sally and the Party—briefly—before a cooling blue light and the sense of immense vertigo enveloped her whole body.

She fell to the floor. Cold cobbled stone lay beneath her. As her two brain cells stopped clattering around in her skull, she focused on the surroundings.

*Sanctuary.*

A metal-plated hand came down to help her up, which she took.

"You two planned this?" She seethed as she shook the blur from her vision.

"*Yes. Ha-ha.*"

Sally turned around. Jackie and Archie were there, looking just as disrupted as she felt. Lars, Ben, and the asshole zombies were also here. The *Warriors* were here—something just as surprising to her as it was to them. A village full of goblins was only slightly less traumatic than an underground mine of Player-killers and undead.

"They are *allies* now. It is like a loose guild structure; we can't formally—" the Death Knight cut off as Sally ran over to the prone body of Theo.

He looked rough. Not only from the blood loss and puncture wounds, but he had taken some fire damage too—though not as much as she had expected. His eyes were closed, and her own slowly looked over to the *[Eat Brains]* ability showing the conditionals were active. With shaking hands, she pressed her STAR and withdrew a Healing Potion from her Inventory.

"Hi, Sally!" The voice of the small goblin Healer, Bella, rang out of the gathered crowd of goblins. She hadn't even noticed them.

"H-hey, Bella—can you heal Theo?"

"Sure. That'll be twenty gold, please." She gave a brief curtsy. "Sorry, he is just really beat up."

After pocketing the potion once more, Sally handed over the money and watched the small goblin do her work. A pulse of energy was released from her hands and washed over the Novice. His wounds healed, and color slowly returned to his face. As the glow of the magical healing faded, his eyes fluttered open.

"Come see me soon; I've got some goblins to heal!" Bella beamed at the zombie and then scurried off back through the crowd.

"Didn't get a Skill Book." The Novice groaned weakly.

"I'm . . . not even going to bully you about it." Sally sighed and lay down on the street beside him. "I didn't think I could get emotionally exhausted like this, but you managed to do it."

"Usually I just tire people out with my extensively bad lore takes."

She smiled and closed her eyes. "We would have gotten along well in the real world."

The Novice shuffled onto his side and propped his head up on his hand. "Don't we get along well in *this* world?"

"Of course, but I'm a flesh-eating Monster, and you're a self-destructive meme." She opened her red eyes. "No offense."

"None taken." With a grunt, he righted himself to his feet and offered a hand down to her, which she took.

"So what was even the point in that, huh?" A brief scowl came back as she wondered why he had decided to put his life in such danger.

"Fireball damages things, whereas Fireblast——"

"Yes, yes, I've had this lecture before." She waved her hand toward the Death Knight.

Theo watched as Humphrey awkwardly waved back. "Okay, so it wasn't guaranteed that I would kill the Rogue even with the Fireball—but it should hopefully have destroyed a bunch of her scrolls. Serves her right for having them on display instead of in her Inventory."

"So they can't move about as well. Either getting them caught out with the System or being unable to patrol the Swamps as effectively." She punched him on the arm, which he reeled away from. "I'm sure there will be no repercussions for that."

"Bought us some time at least." He shrugged. "Best case is we have to fight them at the Swamps when we are ready?"

"Worst case is they're on their way to crush us." Sally put her hands on her hips and raised her eyebrows.

"Gotta die someday?" Theo rubbed the back of his neck.

"If you two are done yabberin'," Jackie yelled out from the other side of the crowd of goblins, "it looks like we leveled up."

They both looked down at their STARS, which now glowed a tarnished gold color. They had killed a good number of Level Five Players, even if the Level Ten Rogue didn't die.

"Neat, enjoy your *nothing*!" She skipped away to join the Death Knight. She punched him on the shoulder, a dull clang ringing out. "That portal scroll was something, huh?"

"Yes. If you are going to be amassing a lot of followers, I knew I couldn't go for the *basic* option." He turned his head downward to meet her gaze. "Only the best for you."

Sally pushed her filthy blonde hair from her face and stuck her tongue out at Humphrey. "Alright, Ainz, what skill did you get?"

"I can't choose until you have leveled up." He crossed his arms and looked out at the village.

It was pretty much how they left it the previous day. It was a slight guess that the structures and layout of the village would be set—any modifications to the defenses they'd want to do before the regiment arrived tomorrow would have to be done after the nightly reset.

"Ayyy." Jackie grinned. "I got *[Critical Aura]*. I'm off to schmooze around."

"Alright, but no *[Extort]*ing people." Sally wagged a finger to the eye-rolling of the mobster.

She jabbed at her own STAR. Archie probably wouldn't know what he got— nor would he be able to tell her anyway.

"H-hey."

Her eyes rose from the UI messages to see the red-haired Fighter from the *Warriors* standing nervously before her, the other members behind her.

"We wanted to thank you, kinda? You killed our friend, but not us, and you saved us from the PvPers, and these goblins currently aren't murdering us, so . . ."

"Sure." Sally waved them off, away from her impending skill choice. "If you want to leave the ally-ship or whatever it's called, just do it outside the village."

"That's—we are considering *staying*."

The zombie looked up properly from the UI messages. *This was unexpected.* "Are you sure? We are kind of evil, blah-blah."

"Seems to be safer on your side than against it," one of the other *Warriors* interjected from behind. "We will help raise the gold so you can make a proper guild if you allow us to join."

Sally said nothing for a few moments, allowing the conversation to settle inside her skull. "Okay. Go now, though—go see the innkeeper; she will take good care of you."

She watched them leave and then focused on her Level Six skill choice.

---

**Pick One**
**[Triple Bite]** Melee Attack - Attack three times
**[Necroblast]** Ranged Spell 10s Cooldown
**[Foul Aura]** Passive Aura 20 ft - Enemies have reduced save chance for CON checks

---

"Necroblast!" she yelled out loud, much to the displeasure of the Death Knight.

"What are you doing?"

"If I pick really quickly, then it doesn't become a cliffhanger—livin' da vida loca and all that."

The Death Knight shrugged. "I have no idea what you are talking about. I am now Level Five and have a keystone, *[Dead King's Court]*, and also the passive skill *[Undead Regeneration]*."

"What's the first one do?"

"Mostly stat enhancements."

"Mostly?"

"*Yes.*"

Sally narrowed her eyes. "Let's go see what Mr. Novice has gotten. At least that should be a straightforward enough answer."

The crowd of goblins had all but cleared now; only a few of the nosiest had stuck around to observe the idle zombies and the odd Party who had made it to the town. It was therefore not a huge undertaking to find Theo sitting on a bench, not far from where she had left him.

His eyes were glazed over as he read through something on the UI.

"Another love letter?" Sally rolled her eyes.

"That was just a message to Humphrey to tell him to prepare—"

"Humps, you *cad*." She jostled into the Death Knight, to no effect. Instead, the large plated figure walked around and stood behind the Novice to see his UI.

"I forgot you could do that," Theo murmured. "What do you think?"

Humphrey's empty sockets briefly scanned over the window the man had been deliberating over, then looked up at the waiting zombie before back to Theo.

"You not only have the class selection of all Player classes, but most Monster classes too."

Sally's mouth hung open.

"This is an overwhelming number of options." He mimed scrolling through a list. "How do I see more information on a class? Do I just click—"

"No."

Theo paused, his finger outstretched before the Death Knight had even responded.

"Oh," he stated, before the color drained from his face and his eyes rolled back in his head.

Then he flopped off the bench onto the floor.

*Dead.*

## CHAPTER FIFTY-NINE

# Fangs for Nothing

Theo shuffled uneasily. His eyes felt heavy and sore as he opened them, trying to blink away the blur. He was *somewhere* dimly lit. Dead? Was he in the real world? There was something about the room that said *hospital* in his head. Whatever blankets were on his aching body were heavy.

And then—a bright light blinded his vision. A shadowed figure loomed over him—was this a nurse, a doctor? He fought against his complaining body to try and right himself.

"Rise and shine, Mr. Theo, rise . . . and shine."

The voice was young and had a distinct scratchiness to it. It itched inside his laggy mind. The familiarity. It was . . .

As the light rescinded, the familiar green face of Bella, goblin Healer, was now in his face.

"All fixed! Pay up, Mister."

With a deep breath, he managed to lift himself up on his elbows. Sitting across the room on a very small chair was the very visage of death. A large, armored Knight of deep crimson with a flaming skull helmet. He watched as Humphrey passed some gold to the small goblin, who promptly turned and waved to him as she left the room.

Theo laid back down and closed his eyes. "Why does it feel like I ate a three-foot-long burrito made of tube socks and iron filings?"

"You have absorbed all your equipment. It is most . . . concerning." There was a hint of interest hidden away in the tone of the Death Knight.

"I changed into part-Monster and reset, huh?"

"Astute. It seems you are as reckless and impulsive as Sally."

He furrowed his brow. Even his face ached. "Where is she?"

"Currently organizing plans for tomorrow with the mobster. She was very angry with you. It has been several hours." The sound of the Death Knight shifting on the tiny painted chair vibrated around the room.

Theo lifted up his arm with great effort and checked his STAR. "She sent me thirty-seven messages."

"In a row, *yes.*"

"I'll save those for later." He gingerly closed the chat menu, not wanting to see what mean things she had to say about him. He felt his eyes close again, heavy against his wishes.

"Are you not going to ask?" Humphrey tapped his plated boot on the floor.

"What?" Theo's mind was still fuzzy. "Like, what they're talking about—if they mention me or have their own contained conversation about—"

"I don't know what you are prattling on about." Even with his eyes closed Theo could see the flare-up on the helmet flame. "I mean your class."

He vaguely remembered selecting something. Tentatively, with some feeling in his gut about what the answer would be, he brought up his Character Information.

Theo - Undead Humanoid - Level One Vampire Lord
Health: 100% Mana: 100% Stamina: 20%

"*Oh,*" he said.

---

Sally took a deep breath. Her voice was getting hoarse from shouting at goblins. It was perhaps unkind to yell at the little goobers, but her zombies were useless at planning and doing what she asked. It was perhaps even more unfair to be so mad at Theo. She had tried not to think about it.

Was she mad because she thought he had died briefly? The only thing that prevented that meltdown was the lack of a System message confirming it. Was she mad that he had cursed himself to be half-Monster half-Player like herself? It was nice to have a kindred spirit, sure, but she wouldn't wish this kind of existence on anyone. Was she mad that he had stolen his tasty brains away and now she had no culinary interest in him? *Yes.*

Probably for the best, as their long-term working relationship was eventually going to turn into bloodshed otherwise. She was mostly just jealous that he got to be a cool vampire.

She turned, and immediately all the jibes and vampire jokes she had stored up melted away on seeing him. The Death Knight followed behind Theo like a disappointed parent.

He approached sheepishly as she crossed her arms in a put-on show of displeasure. "I know, I'm an asshole—sorry." He rubbed the back of his neck.

She wrinkled up her nose at him. He was definitely more vampire-looking now. His skin had a pale, almost blue sheen to it. His eyes were sharper, despite how tired he looked, and his hair was a shade or two closer to black than brown now. He was still wearing his Novice gear, however.

"You are . . . but I'm mostly glad you're okay." She relented with a sigh. "I'm partly annoyed that you are Level One and we have big trouble tomorrow."

"I can get a few levels in the night. Humphrey said I absorbed all my items from before—and I'm a Vampire *Lord*—so I'm not super weak."

She rolled her eyes in response. "Sure you are, *Blade*. Here—in fact, have my sword for now. Tell me about your skills."

"I have a whole bunch of passives," he began, trying to speed over the details as he watched her eyes narrow further. "Resistances, low light vision. I have *[Vampire Bite]* but none of the other cool stuff."

"Ah, you would have lost them because of your low level, like Humphrey did."

The Death Knight chose to ignore her and looked off into the village square, now bathed in dusk.

"Apparently a proper Vampire Lord is like Level Twenty-Five or something." Theo gave a sheepish grin, which Sally did not fail to notice now included a pair of fangs.

"Alright." She stomped her foot. "Hold down the fort, Humps. I'm taking fresh meat here out to kill and eat some Monsters."

"Head southeast." Humphrey nodded. "If you are after humanoids, there may still be cultists at this time of night."

"Perfect. Jackie is currently bending the ears off Henkk at the garrison. Go make sure she isn't trying to fleece him." With a salute and awkward wave, she nudged the vampire into following her.


Sally tripped over a tree root in the waning daylight. "So one of the *Warriors* had a Sword of Frost? I guess that is one mystery solved."

"Yeah." Theo nodded. "And I didn't die from the Fireball, as I had a necklace that reduces self-damage from spells."

"Hmm." Sally stopped to frown at the vampire. "You had a lot of little convenient secrets, huh?"

"A few." He stopped too and grinned, which again revealed his fangs. "Not anymore, of course. I lost all my Inventory."

"But you absorbed what you had on? Your weird meme build?"

He nodded once again, and then they continued walking. "I still retained *[Novice Strike]*, but I just need something to deal really low damage, as my wooden sword did."

"Can't you just punch people? Your Strength stat must still be off the charts for your level." She knew hers was also higher than intended for a zombie.

"Huh, true." Theo removed the rare sword and gave it back to Sally. "It sure is weird not being able to see my stats, though."

"*Right?*"

She was slightly envious of his better vision in the low light. Stumbling in the woods near nighttime was perhaps not an ideal way to spend the end of the day, but getting the jump on the cultists would smooth the quick leveling adventure process.

Bringing up her STAR menu, she was a little disappointed to see there had been no messages from Chuck.

---

Sally: there are some terrible people in this world
Sally: might have made some enemies
Sally: also Theo died

---

She waited a few seconds, narrowly avoiding walking straight into a tree—and also ignoring the concerned scowl of the vampire—as she stared at the UI.

---

Chuck: What? How??
Chuck: are you okay?
Sally: yeh, he is a vampire now
Chuck: like a cool one, or . . . ?
Sally: not yet. I'm his mentor tho
Chuck: good luck—oh
Chuck: I will send you a mail about the thing
Chuck: night
Sally: night chuckz

---

"There's some kind of mail feature?" she asked out loud, not surprised that she didn't know but already knew what the answer would be.

"I know that was rhetorical. But yes." He waved his hand in the air in frustration. "Unfortunately, I can't offer you tech support, as I can't see your menus."

"Humphrey and Bella could. Maybe if I just open and close it really fast lots of times?" The zombie repeatedly jabbed the STAR, causing the menus to open and close in her vision.

"I'm not sure that—"

"Oh, there we go!" Notifications popped up as a familiar twinge in her head came—this time with only a brief amount of pressure before it cleared.

---

14 New Mail Messages

---

"Why do we have these if there's a chat?"

Theo shrugged—or at least the gray shapes near his head moved up and down. She scrolled through; some of them looked like boring System messages or hate mail from that diner Cleric. The most recent one was from Chuck, which she read through.

---

Hey Sally,

Chat is pretty terrible for long-form text, and I know you'll end up walking into a tree if we are texting back and forth. Some things never change. Anyway, I had a quest to deliver logs to some goblins near Sanctuary. Like an actual helping-the-monster-village quest. The rest of the Foxes hadn't heard anything like it. We did it, and we received some kind of . . . goodwill currency with Sanctuary, and they are friendly to us now. Took a bit to convince the girls since they lost their friend there, but things are changing. You are making a change in the world. Players and Monsters could live more equally. We are doing some errands to help with the village defense—see you tomorrow.

Chuck

---

"You alright, Sally? Your eyes are leaking."

She nodded and wiped her face. "Yeah, just a little bit of rain."

The vampire put his hand on her shoulder to stop her. He moved his face down closer to hers, a slight glimmer of red reflecting in the back of his dark eyes.

He opened his mouth to whisper to her. "Quiet now. There are a couple of cultists patrolling just through there. Let's go eat."

Sally shuddered as he moved away, and a wide grin crossed her face.

## CHAPTER SIXTY

# Initiated

Two cloaked figures approached the lantern-lit doorway partially obscured in the backroom of the ruins. Amber light flickered across the gray stone, casting long shadows from the two advancing. A guard in similar orange robes regarded them warily, his pointed hood with white stripe falling back as he looked up.

"Password," he grunted, hand idly at the hilt of a sword.

One of the hooded figures turned to the other as if to gesture to them to provide the information. A shrug was returned before they cleared their throat.

"Uh, praise the cone?" the female voice stated.

The guard's face screwed up, and the sword was drawn. "Just who are you—"

The female figure leapt toward him, her own sword flaring through the air as it came out from the robe and pierced into the chest of the man. Red soaked through the orange robes as he slunk to the floor.

"*Praise the cone?* Really?" Theo lowered his hood to raise his eyebrows.

Sally stowed her weapon and shrugged as she pulled her own hood down. "This is like traffic cone iconography, right? Orange triangles with white stripes?"

"I think it's meant to be . . . teeth? A tooth?" The vampire tilted his head to look at the carved shape on the door.

The zombie checked the Loot window of the cultist guard. A set of *[Keys]* and a *[Half-Eaten Apple]*. She took the keys. "This is fun, though." She turned back to Theo with a smile.

"Yeah, I've always wanted to do something like this."

"Well, just don't get staked or whatever. I'm sure they won't have holy water here since they are an evil cult." She wiggled her eyebrows before raising her hood back over her face.

"Well, you just don't get your brains blown out."

The cloaked figure crossed her arms.

"Sorry." Theo rubbed his neck before putting his own hood up. "That sounded better in my head."

Sally unlocked the door, and they entered into a downward staircase. They descended for about a dozen feet before finding the torch-lit bottom—some manner of cellar had been converted into an underground cultist sanctuary.

In the cellar proper a small table with two chairs sat. Across from them, a farther door led into whatever weird church had been constructed. Pinned to the frame of this door was a piece of paper. Sally moved up closer to it and lifted the hood slightly to get a proper view. It was a map with brief instructions.

> Advocates of the Fang must report to the shrine to be cleansed before heading to the main hall where the ritual will be attempted TONIGHT

Theo read it too and nodded back to her. She smiled beneath the shadow of the hood. Subtlety was not one of her strong suits, but the prospect of surprising all the cultists made her giddy—even if they were just System-created.

She pushed through the door into a chamber beyond. A downward ramp continued for two dozen feet before opening up into a wide room. Rows of benches covered the floor of this room, populated by little cones of robed cultists sitting and observing the front. At the front, a large statue painted orange with a white stripe across it took up the majority of a raised stage. In front of it, a small lectern or altar sat unattended.

To their left, a doorway led to the noted shrine—and with eyes on the main room, they entered here to play the part. Rows of candles ran along the walls of this small chamber, and a table sat at the far end. Around twenty cones of various sizes sat atop the table.

"Careful," Sally whispered, "hazard."

Theo nudged her with his elbow. Thankfully there were no other cultists in here, so they didn't have to pretend they knew what they were doing. After a brief minute of looking around the shrine, they left to go and find seats in the ritual chamber.

There were maybe three dozen other figures sitting either in silence or briefly murmuring to each other. Sally chose somewhere as far away from others as she could. She scrunched her nose up and stared at the large statue at the front—she wondered what kind of ritual they were going to be doing.

"You new here?" a voice said from behind them.

They both slowly turned as a robed figure with a long gray beard extending from his shadowed hood sat beside them on the bench.

"Praise the Fang?" Theo responded.

"Yes, yes . . . Praise the Fang indeed." The mysterious man turned to face the statue at the front. "You're just not the sort who usually . . . worship here."

The three sat in silence for a brief moment. Each not wanting to break the silence and possibly reveal more than they needed to. Eventually, this new man relented.

"Name's Baldrick. They've attempted the ritual at least a dozen times since I . . . can remember. They never seem to listen."

Sally kicked Theo's foot in a manner to communicate that this guy may be a Unique Monster.

"Uh." The vampire shuffled awkwardly. "You've never thought of leaving?"

Baldrick kept on staring at the statue. "No. Well, yes. But I am an evil cultist—what options do I have? There was another here . . . who was . . . different."

"But?" Sally interjected, leaning over Theo to listen intently.

"Adventurers killed them. After that, I dug a pit in the library, which I sleep in every night—hidden away. I don't *usually* come out for the ritual anymore." His wrinkled hands clasped at the fabric of his robe.

"We are currently, uh, recruiting—if you are a learned man, we have a space for a librarian in a proper town where you won't have to hide in a hole."

Sally nodded. "Unless you still wanted to, of course."

"Really?" The man seemed taken aback but quickly came to a conclusion. "Only on one condition."

"Sure!" Sally beamed.

"Prove your worth by surviving after I blow your cover."

Theo shuffled away, a task ineffective due to the zombie still leaning across his lap. "*What?*" he whispered.

"I did say I was an evil cultist." Baldrick cackled and grabbed at their hoods. "Initiates of the Fang, intruders!"

Sally and Theo leapt to their feet as their hoods fell back. All eyes in the chamber fell toward them. A mix of Level Ones and Twos—she grinned as she drew her sword.

"Ready to level, vamps?" She chucked her robes and withdrew her dagger and sword.

"Always." He returned a wide grin, his fingertips illuminated in a pinkish-red glow.

As one, the cultists withdrew all manner of simple melee weapons: swords, maces, daggers, and even some improvised farming tools. With a roar of defiance, anger that these two were invading and besmirching the holy place of their foul god, they surged forth.

*[Summon Zombies]*

Four corpses broke through the stone floor—a welcome distraction and hindrance. Sally stepped forth and side-stepped an awkward swing of an axe, jamming her dagger into where the assailant's throat was. She ducked and spun around, sweeping the legs of her victim and allowing the recently emerged zombie to grab them.

There wasn't any real need to use *[Hex: Slow]*. As a Level Six, she could walk through half of the room even without Theo's help. She watched a figure run across the top of the stage. A spellcaster at Level Three—this must be the boss of the area! Just as the slightly more-ornately robed figure arrived at the altar, she raised her sword and pointed to him.

*[Necroblast]*

A quick bolt of green energy zapped through the air and blasted a hole in the man's neck. She watched in morbid fascination as he spluttered and struggled to breathe as his blood sprayed out from the wound across the altar and floor beyond.

"Hey, Theo," she began, ducking a widely swung sword, "did you see that?" But Theo was otherwise distracted.

She watched the newly borne vampire slash through foes. Just using his fists and fingertips, his *[Novice Strike]* had turned into a barrage of martial ferocity that reminded her of the Monk. *Ah, her first brain.* Not only did a pinkish hue blaze in a trail behind his hands, but a glow in his eyes shone dark crimson and illuminated his face.

He dodged the stabbing action of a pitchfork and rolled along the length of it, a flurry of blows striking their torso twice, then their left arm, left shoulder, and finally, he twisted the bloodied cultist around, pushing their head to the side to bite into the neck of his victim.

Sally shuddered as she dropped her knife to grab the wrist of her assailant, twisting it back until it snapped and forcing the cultist to the floor. A quick stab of the sword and then *[Eat Brains]*.

It did not taste great. She felt energized and fulfilled, but there wasn't the power behind it, the wild elation. Most importantly, there were no stat bonuses. She looked up to see Theo drop the drained corpse, fresh blood covering his lower face and his chest.

"These guys don't taste great, but *wow!*" He beamed, eyes alight.

"We need to get you a Player to drain." She smirked back at him, her own face caked with cultist gore. She blocked a wooden club with her bracers and headbutted the cultist. "You level up yet?"

"Yeah!" he shouted back, breaking ribs with a strong punch before grabbing the dazed cultist and twisting their head around fatally. "I'll give it a prod once we are done."

Sally looked around. There were still plenty of panicked but aggressive cultists for them to have some fun with. As she leaned down to pick up her knife a burst of heat rocked the chamber.

Wide-eyed, she looked over to the altar. It was now glowing with an amber light—and, more importantly, so too was the larger statue behind it. Even the cultists paused their assault to observe the odd phenomenon as the cultist Leader slowly slunk from the bowl now filled with his blood.

"You've only gone and summoned him!" The voice of Baldrick rang out from the back of the room, a mix of jubilation and mortal fear in his tone.

Sally readied *[Hex: Slow]* as the statue shimmered, a further wave of heated energy pulsing through the room.

From within the statue, a large paw of flame and darkened fur stepped through.

## CHAPTER SIXTY-ONE

# Worse Than His Bite

Holy balls," Sally whispered to herself, mouth open in awe as she watched the creature tear itself through the magical portal.

A second paw and then a long wolf head burst through into the ritual chamber. Waves of heat followed, the creature itself aflame as if it crawled from hell. Three bright white eyes beamed out across the room as the rest of the body slunk onto the raised stage. As the burning tail passed through the portal, whatever magic that had summoned it vanished.

The zombie looked over at Theo, who looked up from his STAR. She jerked a thumb over to the giant fire wolf, who leapt down off the stage to pounce upon one of the cultists—tearing into their body and scorching the robes from their torso. The vampire nodded and ran over to her, knocking a distracted cultist over.

"Level Five Elite." She grinned. "I'm not a fan of fire, but we could take it, I reckon."

"Sure. I did my Level Two stuff—I think I'm almost Three."

"I can't even see my experience bar, can you?"

"No—but I have a feeling?"

She wrinkled up her nose. The Fang had killed or maimed five of the remaining cultists, and her zombies had taken down another. This was not great for helping Theo level up.

"Hey!" Sally yelled out. "Cats are better than dogs!" As the flame-covered wolf turned its three eyes to her, she leaned over to Theo. "I actually like them both the same; I'm just doing a bit."

"Yeah, I got it." He stood in an approximate martial stance as his fingertips glowed pink-red.

The Fang leapt forward as Sally hit it with *[Hex: Slow]*, giving them both time to roll to either side.

*[Sanguine Weapon]*

*[Necroblast]*

Her magic shot blew a chunk of furred flesh from the flank of the beast as it turned to face the vampire. With a further roll, she spun with her sword, taking a slice through the back leg. The blood that sprayed from the wound hissed and burned her skin where it landed.

"Don't bite this one!" she called to Theo as he came into view.

His *[Novice Strikes]* were landing repeated blows on the Fang—but there was something else. A third hand, floating in the air and made of pink energy was attacking at the same time. A blur of pink energy followed the quick arcs of all three strikes. Pain wracked his face as the impacts of his punches burnt at his skin.

Struggling against the relentless assault, the large wolf recoiled and opened its large maw. Suddenly, a jet of fire spewed forth like a dragon's breath, enveloping Theo fully.

"Theo!" Sally yelled and leapt at the beast, stabbing repeatedly into the Fang's side and ignoring the spattering of painful blood.

The beast swung around with its tail of fire, and she ducked under it, some of her hair singeing from the proximity. Large teeth gnashed out at her as it turned its attention to her. Theo wasn't where he had been just a moment before; only a scorched and blackened patch covered the area of the room where the flame had touched.

She blocked the next snapping jaw attack, and the force knocked the sword from her hand. The knife switched to her main hand as she waited for the next bite. As soon as the attack was started, *[Necroblast]* left her free hand and struck the overgrown pup in the nose. As the beast whined in pain, Sally jammed the dagger up into the bottom of the mouth—unable to reach the throat but doing enough damage to make the Fang choke in pain and surprise.

As she rolled away backward, she retrieved the crossbow from her Inventory with practiced precision and quickly aimed the bolt into the middle eye of the beast. As it struck, the Fang lifted a paw to rub at the protruding bolt as it yelped in pain.

Then a darkened figure dropped down from nowhere, landing atop the beast's neck.

*[Vampire Bite]*

Sally watched as Theo, burnt and blistered, his armor scorched black and half missing, dropped to sink his fangs into the wounded creature. Her mouth was agape in horror, expecting the vampire to suddenly combust from within from the boiling blood.

Instead, his wounds started to heal. As Fang lowered, weakened, to the floor, Theo's face became as new. He withdrew with a gasp, his eyes ablaze with red energy, and turned to focus on her.

"Here, left some for you." He beamed, hands shaking.

Conditionals were met, but should she? Drool pattered to the floor as she did it.

*[Eat Brains]*

---

Trait Unlocked: Increased Fire Resistance

---

"You get the trait?" She gasped, stumbling back from the open skull of the beast. It had tasted almost as plain as the System-created, but . . . spicy? Even saying that sounded ridiculous.

"Sure did!" He hopped down from the felled animal, his face once again covered with blood.

The ritual chamber was now a ruin. Blood covered the light gray stone, corpses lay beaten and hewn to bits among the benches, and the large body of the fire creature lay inert.

Sally struggled to get her breath back as she looked up into the glowing eyes of the vampire. He too was panting, a wild excitement having taken the eaters of the living.

"I guess this is the point where we'd kiss in a cliché romance novel?" She beamed, stretching her back out.

"Seems really unhygienic with all this blood around." He frowned at the state of them both.

"Right? There's nothing romantic about death. I crave nothing but eating brains."

"And I nothing more than to drink blood."

Sally grinned and held out a fist. "Platonic care gang?"

He returned both the bump and the grin. "Of course. Even Monsters need found family, right?"

"This is all very sweet," Baldrick interrupted, removing his hood to reveal a bald head and piercing blue eyes, "but can we get out of here now?"

Sally looked around at the carnage wrought. Any cultists remaining must be hiding in one of the side rooms. "What say you, Vampire Lord? Need any more experience?"

"I'm good—I'm Level Four now." He gave his stomach a pat as if that had any bearing on how it worked.

* * *

Baldrick had the foresight to grab the lantern from the outside door before they headed back to Sanctuary. It was near pitch black outside now, so Sally was thankful for that.

"Imagine if we came across a couple of Novices," Theo thought out loud. "Just putting that out into the world."

"Keep it in your . . . mouth." Sally nudged him as she opened up her STAR. "There will be plenty of opportunity tomorrow I bet. If the news of the regiment has gotten around, then some Parties will want on in the action."

Humphrey: Status report?

Humphrey: Status report?

Humphrey: I can see Theo's HP bar—it's really low

Humphrey: Oh it's better now

Humphrey: Sally

Sally: alright dad, on our way home

Sally: bringing an evil old man with us

Humphrey: Okay

Humphrey: We will talk when you're back

"Hey, Baldrick." She motioned toward the cultist as she closed the chat. "You keep saying you are evil—what do you do?"

"Mostly, extract goblin juice for the ritual."

Theo gave her some raised eyebrows. At least there wasn't a text box around it, right? As much as they could do with a librarian, perhaps the goblins in Sanctuary would not be too pleased about his presence.

"Goblins probably don't regard you too highly, then?" Theo asked as politely as he was able.

"Oh no, the things I did to their children. You just have to wait for them to reappear, though, after the process—it was like growing a crop. A *squealing* crop."

"About time you got back, young lady." Humphrey tapped his foot on the cobbled stone of the square. "And you should know better, Theo. Where is the old man?"

The pair wiped their mouths in reflex.

"What old man?" Theo shrugged. "I got to Level Four though; quite the feat for one evening."

"You had the best trainer, to be fair." The zombie punched him on the shoulder, but this time he didn't get displaced by the jovial strike.

"What did you unlock?" Humphrey narrowed his sockets further, ready to judge his choices.

"At Level Two I chose *[Sanguine Weapon]*. At Three, *[Blood Shift]*. Four was tough, but I eventually went with *[Crimson Aura]*."

"You picked your Level Three while you were being burnt alive?" Sally frowned and crossed her arms.

"Uh—yeah, the health increase is what kept me standing. *[Blood Shift]* has three charges based on recent kills of a certain strength. That's how I got atop the beast."

The Death Knight gestured for them to head toward the tavern part of the inn. "There was a beast?"

Sally grinned and looped one arm with Theo's and her other with Humphrey's large plated one. "We accidentally completed some kind of summoning ritual; it was a large fire wolf called—"

"The Fang, *yes.* You didn't tame it?" The question caused the zombie to pause, stopping the other two with a brief jolt.

"That was an option?" She pouted at the vampire. "We kinda ate it and received Fire Resistance."

"Interesting. I had never considered that an—"

Humphrey stopped mid-sentence and dropped to one knee, a plated hand grasping at his head. A whining hiss escaped his skeletal mouth before he righted himself with the help of the two undead Players.

"Humps? Are you okay?"

The Death Knight turned his head to the sky in silence as a faint shade of green flickered into view.

"HM-3.3?" The dry voice crackled as the skull lowered to their level. The Observer was lethargic, and the normally blazing eldritch energy was flickering and dull.

"*What has happened?*" Humphrey growled.

"It's the Architect . . . They have been . . . murdered."

## CHAPTER SIXTY-TWO

# Behind Green Eyes

*What?"* Red flame jettisoned from the back of the Death Knight's helmet.

"How is that possible? Aren't they a god?" Sally darted a look to the vampire, who shrugged in return.

The voice of the mobster shouted out from behind. "Got your message, tin-can, what's the—oh, hey, Boss. Fangs."

Humphrey turned and plucked Archie from the floor, grabbing the ginger cat by the scruff of his neck. With arm outstretched, he held him aloft toward the fading skull.

"*Merge.*"

"I . . . cannot. Too . . . weak . . . Against p-protocol . . ."

"Merge or *perish.*"

Sally had never heard the Death Knight sound so serious or on edge. Things could not be good if the Architect was no more—what did this mean for them? Would the world as they knew it start to collapse?

She watched as the green Observer relented and hovered slowly toward the presented animal. With a green flash, they merged.

Humphrey turned Archie to face him. The once amber eyes of the cat were now bright emerald green, but he looked otherwise unchanged. The Death Knight narrowed his eye sockets. "How successful was the transfer?"

Archie blinked a few times before he opened his small mouth. "I'm still Archie, I think. But now I have . . . memories . . . and understandings that I did not before."

The cat was placed on the floor. "P-2T did not have the necessary strength to fully control you, but his will persists within you."

"Do you know what happened?" Sally crouched down beside him to stroke the fluffy head.

"Poison, in simple terms." Archie nudged into her hand. "Something had been weakening them for a period. I am sure even Humphrey had suspicions."

The Death Knight nodded and crossed his arms. The flames behind his head had lowered but still simmered with an above-normal ferocity. "Glitches are a result of that; that was my presumption."

"It was minor at first," the cat continued, "but the connection was just severed. In the odd memories I now have, I can tell you that thirty-eight Observers have perished, and thirteen have bonded with Monsters, excluding the two of us. That leaves eighteen unaccounted for."

Theo scratched his chin. "Is there any way for them to survive without merging?"

The cat shook his head. "Though most of the world is no longer directly connected to the Architect, the Observers were more closely bound to their power."

"Unless the eighteen merge, they too are lost. For many, the choice to be erased is the correct one." Humphrey looked out to the darkened horizon. "We will need to keep an eye out for the merged. Their prior knowledge of the System's inner workings may prove problematic in our adventures."

Sally scrunched up her face and resigned herself to sitting down fully, allowing Archie to climb into her lap. The warmth and slight purring just reminded her that they needed some good sleep pretty soonish. Tomorrow was a whole other barrel of trouble.

"What does that mean for this world?" Theo looked like he was trying to process twenty things at once. He also needed a good wash and replacement armor.

"It means"—the Death Knight grinned—"there needs to be a new Architect."

"Dibs!" Sally shouted, disturbing the cat.

Theo rubbed the back of his neck and shot Humphrey a glance. "I'm not sure that is the best use of your talents—plus that is probably on the other side of the croissant."

Jackie blew a cloud of smoke into the gathering. "So, uh, do I still get my castle?"

"If we aren't dead tomorrow." Sally beamed, looking up at the mobster with bright red eyes. "I'm assuming this doesn't change our little scuffle tomorrow?"

"No." Humphrey shook his head.

Archie looked up toward the zombie boss. "Are you sure this is wise?" His green eyes shimmered.

"It'll be rough, Arch, but twenty guards should—"

"Twenty? Who'd you get that information from?" Archie scowled toward the Death Knight, already knowing the answer.

Humphrey opened his mouth to respond but then closed his skeletal maw and turned to look off into the distance.

"Sixty," the cat continued. "Three Elites and a Champion."

Silence fell over the group. Arranged awkwardly in the twilight of the village square, the torchlight that illuminated their impromptu meeting didn't seem to be enough to warm them. Sally bit down on her tongue as she tried to concoct some plan. A glance over to Theo showed that he was trying to do the same, a confused frown across his pale face as his unfocused eyes darted back and forth.

"Do you think we can get another *[Town Scroll]*?" She looked up at Humphrey.

"Depends on how much gold you have, but yes."

"Oh." Jackie awkwardly stuck her hands into her pockets, Betty slung across her back. "I kinda came into a lotta cash recently. For the guild, right? Should have enough for a scroll too."

Sally narrowed her eyes at the mobster. No doubt she had used *[Extort]* on as many goblins as she could to acquire those funds. Still, better those resources found some use in keeping Sanctuary in their control. Jackie avoided her glare but jerked her thumb back to the inn.

"It's in a box in my room; don't have big enough pockets, ya see."

"Only Players can join a guild, but if you have allies, then it'll confer some benefits." Archie purred from her lap.

"So many different boxes to put people in now." Sally shook her head. "Speaking of, how have my zombies been doing?"

"They have remained in a pen." Humphrey leveled a finger over to behind the forge. "The goblins threw them meat, like some kind of zoo. It felt conflicting."

Theo snapped his fingers. "If you know what a zoo is: are there some in this world?"

"*Yes, ha-ha.* Of course. What kind of question is that? You are just too low level to go there." Humphrey grinned and gestured toward the cat.

"What my big brother is trying to say"—Archie yawned—"is that the fourth zone has what you might call more 'modern' architecture and amenities. However, I suggest we focus on our toes before we start climbing trees. They will arrive at midday."

"*Big brother?*" the Death Knight murmured to himself.

"Alright, alright." Sally fumed as she rubbed her temples. "Enough yapping. Theo, we'll have our platonic date at the zoo eventually, if we live that long. Humphrey, I need to take all the spare gold and get a list of things, plus anything you think would be helpful—Jackie help him."

The zombie stood up, lifting the cat with her. She snuggled Archie with a smile. "Arch, you go help Theo plan things. I'm going to create the guild and see what allies we have."

With nods and murmured agreements, the Party split up to move around the dark village. For the first time in a while, Sally stood alone. It was briefly overwhelming—the emptiness of the square, how quiet it was, the looming strife tomorrow. She shuddered and headed toward the library.

The door opened quietly. Inside, lanterns lit the corners with dim amber light. Humphrey should be in later to wake Oleb and pry some items from the new librarian if he wasn't already with the goblin Leaders—but for now, she would take the peace for herself. She sat on the nearest chair and put her feet up on the table. Her clothes really were filthy. The normally bright red skirt was now various shades of dark brown from mud and dried blood. Not to mention her white shirt, which was anything but.

It was about time she updated her signature look. Maybe Archie could help unstick some of her bugs with the little power of the Observer he had in him. She leaned the chair onto the back legs and brought up her STAR menu to open chat.

> Sally: hey bud, your mail was 10/10
> Sally: lil thing tho
> Sally: Sanctuary has 63 dudes on the way tomorrow
> Sally: arriving at noon

She paused and wrinkled up her nose. Archie had been pretty off time-wise when it came to the *Voice of Gaia* assault at the bandit camp. Was he at least speaking with the Observer knowledge now?

> Sally: maybe
> Sally: making a guild if you want in
> Sally: we're looking at some ultraviolence tho
> Chuck: don't you guys ever sleep??
> Chuck: you got the gold already, how?
> Chuck: no, don't answer that
> Chuck: but we're in. We also have a quest to assist Sanctuary so?
> Sally: see you at dawn?
> Chuck: at dawn

Sally smiled and closed the chat. With the *White Foxes* and *Warriors*, that gave them a Player count of . . . eleven? Quite a few low levels—but any help was help.

She considered messaging Dent, but he was unlikely to assist. He barely cared for their existence. It was unlikely he would be able to get here in time too. After Yarch fell, all the teleport options became invalid.

Her brain ached from wracking it as she tried to think of any further allies she could call on. *Skullsplitters*? Definitely not. *Voice of Gaia*? Very unlikely. Whatever that annoying Cleric was called? He would more likely be fighting on the side of the System, no doubt.

Perhaps eating people was not the right way to make friends. Not that she was short any, in fairness. She had turned a nice duo of her and Humps into a guild in formation—not to mention those who were unable to join.

No matter—that just left her to focus on planning her next daring gambit to give some advantage for tomorrow.

A knock from the door drew her attention away, and as she turned the chair, she almost tipped over backward.

"Whoa—hello?" She managed to control her descent by hastily grabbing onto a bookshelf.

"Oh, hello?" A nervous voice came from the doorway as a short, furred figure came into the light. "Is this the right place for fighting against the System?"

An excited grin spread across her face at seeing the Unique kobold—he must have heard about her from the mines!

"It sure is!" The chair clunked forward as she stood to greet the still-nervous figure. He was about two feet tall and snowy white—his shaky disposition almost gave the impression he was extra chilly. Yellow eyes widened as she approached to shake his paw. "Always glad to have more on board; I'm sure we could find you a Party to—"

"Oh no." His head shook, tiny ears flopping back and forth. "I already have a full Party."

Behind him, further figures stepped into the room.

## CHAPTER SIXTY-THREE

# War Room

Sally's eyebrows raised higher as she turned to the doorway to greet the rest of the kobold's Party.

The first was a stout female goblin, who nodded toward the zombie as she stood awkwardly. "Hi, I'm Cass. I can predict the weather, I-I think?"

Sally nodded politely. To her knowledge, the weather in the area was mostly stuck in the permanently-pleasant-with-a-light-breeze mode. But perhaps before she came to unlife, it had been more varied—it *had* only been a week or so.

Second to enter was an exceptionally slim and frail-looking orc—almost deathly so. His skin was a dull gray-yellow, and as the light of the library came to illuminate him, she saw that his face was dominated by empty, sunken eye sockets. He bumped gently into the goblin, who held his hand.

"They call me Scratcher," he intoned, his voice crackling with age as he leveled his blank gaze toward the zombie.

"Did you . . . scratch your eyes out?" Sally tilted her head. That seemed like a reasonable guess.

The orc smiled and shook his head. "Oh, no. My eyes can move independently of my body and work just the same."

Sally wrinkled her nose. "Where are they now?" Given the appearance of the orc, she half expected him to be the perverted old guy trope.

"I've been watching the regiment approach for the last day."

She was somewhat taken aback. Perhaps she shouldn't judge a book by its cover, even if she was in the library. "So you know how far they are out, what they're doing?"

Scratcher nodded. "They are currently sleeping. They have set up a camp about—"

"*HELLO!* I'm a fuckin' horse!" The orc was interrupted by a large horse's skull ramming its way into the open door. The skull was both attached to a normal horse body and also flamed wildly with a golden orange hue.

"Hello, horsie." Sally waved diplomatically. "Did you used to be an Observer?"

"*Neigh!* Actually, yes." The flames flickered wildly for a second. "I've just always wanted to say that."

Another figure pushed past the overly excited horse-observer, one that she recognized.

"Oh! You have a Theo too?" She beamed at the vampire.

He frowned and came to stand beside her. "No—it's just me. I found these guys outside hoping to gain entrance. Humphrey didn't seem keen on meeting them for some reason."

"How strange." She shrugged.

A small voice croaked up from the floor. "I'm Adam!"

Sally crouched down to see a snail slowly crawling along the floor. There was something to be said about this odd Party. It was like she had just stepped into a weird twilight zone or alternate reality. But, then, maybe other people thought that about her Party when they met them.

"What can you do, Adam?"

"I'm a wizard," the high-pitched voice replied.

She stared blankly back before standing. Things had just gotten a lot stranger, and, briefly, her mind reeled from the whiplash of the last few days. Theo becoming a vampire was one thing, but a second Party of oddballs was just too much seasoning to the broth. Mostly she just thought they shouldn't get too attached right before the big battle.

"Oh—what was your name and ability again?" She wrinkled up her nose at the kobold.

"They call me Foreman. I, uh, was one of the driving forces behind the mine expansion." His furred paw grabbed out at one of the nearby books. With a deep sigh, he opened it, grabbed a single page, and tore it from the book.

As they all watched, he took the held page and pointed to an open space beneath the walkway that led up to Oleb's rooms. A wooden beam sprung into view as the paper turned to cinders in Foreman's grasp. An oaken support almost a foot thick now helped prop up the second floor—though it didn't match the rest of the furnishing.

"Ah, just the same as in the mines." Theo nodded. "What are the limitations?"

Foreman twitched his ears as he snapped the tome shut. "How many books have you got?"

Blankly, the vampire gestured slowly around the room with a hand outstretched.

Sally cleared her throat. "So, I'm Sally, and I'm a zombie with some of the facets of a Player. This is Theo." She nudged the pale man. "He is the same except also my emotional support vampire."

The new Party nodded and murmured their greetings, with the added "*Nice!*" of the horse at the back.

"I'm going to message the others, Theo. I think we should meet at the . . ." Sally trailed off as her eyes narrowed from the STAR to the new Party. "I . . . can't see what level you guys are . . ."

The vampire furrowed his brow and leaned backward to look between the zombie and the group. "I can't either, nor yours."

A weight gnawed at Sally's stomach. The Architect had died, and now parts of the System weren't working. Things had also gone weird when they had assaulted Sanctuary—a coincidence or another symptom of things going wrong?

"Heh, would be ironic, wouldn't it?" Theo shook his head with an exasperated sigh. In seeing her confused look, he continued. "We wanted Monsters to be equal to Players. What if the STAR stops working and we no longer have Inventory and the like?"

Sally felt around the inside of her mouth with her tongue. That *would* be ironic—but also pretty terrible. That's where she kept her skull collection. Well, all but one of them. Her mind idly wandered. Would Jackie have been more antagonistic if they had stopped to remove the heads of all the bandits they had murdered?

With a brief pause, she opened up her Party chat.

---

Sally: everyone to the Garrison — planning time
Sally: AND HUMPS the bandits were human??
Sally: you said only Players were human
Humphrey: No, they were Bandits.
Sally: human bandits
Sally: the cultists were human too . . .
Humphrey: No, they were cultists.
Humphrey: I fail to note the distinction.
Archie: Jackie is currently . . . preoccupied
Archie: On my way n_n

---

"Did he just . . ." Sally shook her head.

"Alright." The vampire clapped his hands to address the room. "We are going up to the garrison to plan with the goblin Leaders. I assume Oleb must be already up there. Otherwise, he'd eat you for tearing up a book."

Sally wrinkled up her nose. Oleb hadn't been especially book-centric before his term as Leader started, but perhaps after the System-assigned position had its grip on him, he had found a new passion in life.

The group started to saunter out of the library; Foreman scooped up the snail, and the goblin held the forearm of the orc to guide him.

Cass looked up at Theo, then past him into the upstairs of the library. "Eat literally, or . . . ?"


The garrison had a large hall with a round table at the center. Banners depicting goblinoid skulls hung from the stone walls, and bright torches illuminated the open space. Sitting around this table was the oddest collection of characters one might ever hope to see. And yet, they were the salvation of Sanctuary.

*Intended salvation*, Sally thought as she looked at those present. Jackie was still absent from their group, but the new Party of Monsters—apparently called *Us Against*—and the five goblin Leaders filled in most of the other spots. The *Warriors* sat in a huddle, their faces painted with the same confused and overwhelmed expression that Sally felt inside.

Henkk had a case of constant stress painted across his pale face. His fingers tapped at the table beside piles of paperwork as the orc relayed the message about the regiment's current situation.

"Troubling, indeed." His smooth voice wavered as though his confidence was cracking. "Though, perhaps not as bad as if they marched on us without pause."

Sally dug her fingernails into the padded arms of the chair. Her first ploy was to go and raid the regiment, knock over as many as they could, and *[Town Scroll]* back to Sanctuary for the morning. Apparently, travel would take too long—plus they would miss out on sleep.

"We tried to set up some pits and spikes along the road." The muscled Jaxk shrugged. "But we are tied to the town; after fifteen minutes we just teleport back to our housing."

"And the town's goblins are useless," Oleb added. "They literally won't pick up arms to heed the danger until the regiment actually arrives."

The zombie nodded but dug her fingertips in tighter, piercing the cloth. She wanted to kill and live, not wait and die. Her eyes turned to the *Warriors*, and her thoughts dallied over Chuck and the *White Foxes*. Even if they were allied, she didn't want them to die here. It made more sense for them to go on even if the village was retaken . . . This was her fight and burden to bear. Bare? She wished she had some bears.

She watched across the table as Bella brushed at the Observer-horse, whom the goblin had named Petal. Petal had been staring excitedly over at the Death Knight since the meeting had begun. Humphrey, however, had been sitting at an angle facing away from the horse. It was *amusing*, and she was itching to dig into the details there. Instead, she turned her gaze back to the white goblin.

"How far can your teleport-y thing work, Henkk?"

He sighed deeply. "I knew that question would come eventually. It's . . . well it's not a teleport as such . . . but at this range . . ." He furrowed his brow further and rubbed his chin. A small map of the area lay beneath his intense stare, the location of the guard camp roughly denoted with a cross.

"You can say it's too far." She gave him a glum smile. "We have to be realistic."

The goblin closed his eyes and leaned back in his chair, face angled toward the ceiling. He took one deep breath, in and out, before responding. "I could do it. But it would be one . . . two people at the maximum. It would be inaccurate too—the distance makes it harder to judge."

"Two people," Sally repeated in a hushed tone as her eyes scoured past all the occupants in the room.

Theo sat up a little straighter.

"Humphrey." She stood and put her hands on her hips. "Go and get Jackie and tell her to bring all the gold."

A sense of excitement built up inside her as the pieces of half a plan began to slot together.

## CHAPTER SIXTY-FOUR

# Exploit

A weighted feeling pressed down on Sally for what felt like hours. Whirling vertigo compressed her as she shot her way through the System under the strange power of the pale goblin.

Then, it ended. She felt cold grass beneath her hands. Slowly, she raised her head and saw that the sky was an odd off-white . . . No, this was a tent. A reasonably large one if the peaked roof was any measure. The sound of snoring hit her ears, and she gingerly turned as she got to her feet.

A single bed sat on one side. There was one male figure sleeping rather soundly. Sally narrowed her eyes and quietly adjusted the heavy backpack. Her belt of potion bottles had extra padding to ensure they didn't clink together. To be in a tent on his own, this must be one of the Elites.

Sure enough, the dimly lit marquee was furnished with various things that one might expect a generic soldier's living quarters to have: a stand for his armor, a table with maps and paperwork strewn across it, and even a worn rug that didn't cover much of the floor. *What luck to be teleported right in the middle of the camp*, she thought sourly.

Still, zombies can't be choosers. Softly her feet approached the sleeping guard. She withdrew her knife from its sheathe as she licked her lips. She could only assume she was among a large group of tents just off the road, dozens upon dozens of sleeping soldiers ready to attack her once the alarm was raised.

She hovered over the man. He was portly, aged, and had a whiskered moustache that waved as he breathed in and out deeply. Both hands gripping her *[Rare Dagger of Luck]*, she rammed it down into his neck. As his eyes shot open, she switched to his heart and chest. Two, three, four times, and then, eyes wide, she crunched down with *[Eat Brains]*.

Crimson soaked through his sheets and dripped onto the grass below as the zombie wiped her mouth. It wasn't good eating. Energizing perhaps, but more like one of those protein shakes that just taste like powder. She briefly paused to loot his *[Skull]* with a smile on her face before she started taking the potions off her belt. From each one in turn, the cork was popped and the liquid imbibed. They had a lot of their gold riding on this.

Colors flashed and waved through her vision as pulses of warmth and coolness alternated through her body. The effects wouldn't last the whole fight, but there might not be another opportunity to down them. Two Healing Potions stayed on her left hip as an emergency. *You never know.*

"Okay, here we go, then," she whispered as she withdrew the first lit torch from her Inventory.

Stepping out into the cool night air was both refreshing and frightening. A forest of white tents dimly lit by lanterns and candles surrounded her. Slowly, she put her dagger back away and scoured the darkness for any patrolling sentries. None that she could spot. With that being the case, she opened up the Inventory again to withdraw a second torch.

Arms reaching back, she lobbed the first onto the largest tent within reach—it was hard not to hit one even if her aim had been terrible. One after another, in a loose circle, she turned and threw a total of eight. As the flames began to grow, the first soldiers started to wake and raise the alarm.

The smell of burning fabric carried with the breeze. Shouts and the donning of armor followed suit, and Sally withdrew both sword and dagger. Silhouettes in the tent to the right showed guards getting ready to fight but were not on fire. She ran and slashed out at the fabric, rolling through the gap into the tent.

She had taken a *[Potion of Strength]*, *[Potion of Attack Speed]*, and *[Potion of Battle]*. Her sword was coated in *[Burning Oil]*, which added extra fire damage—despite not showing the effect.

Her weapon caught the first guard in the back, severing a bright crimson gash through his skin. She blocked the swing of a sword with her bracers and stabbed into a hand trying to grasp her. Five guards in here. She pushed into the grabby one and kicked at his shin, stabbing the other thigh, his flank, and then the side of his neck in quick succession. No time to eat brains.

She barely deflected a swing of an axe as the swordsman then made a cut into her shoulder. Sally hissed and dropped low, hitting one of them with *[Hex: Slow]* as the axe arced wildly over her head.

*[Necroblast]* blew a decaying chunk from the leg of the other guard, and then she spun to the side to avoid the sword again. With a flick of her weapon, she cut another slit through the tent and dove into a roll, back into the open.

"Ow," the backpack said.

Level Tens were hard work. As the figures clamored behind her, she hissed at the throng of guards pouring from the tents. One of the previous combatants tried to stick his head through the gash she had made, and she slashed out at his neck. Blood sprayed across the white of the tent as he collapsed, gurgling.

The sharp pain of a crossbow bolt struck as she turned back to see a group emerging around a tent with leveled ranged weapons. Her cover was definitely blown now. As she stepped toward some cover, she was struck. A bolt through her arm, one cutting into her hip, and a third narrowly missing her neck. Sally stumbled to her knees behind one of the tents and gasped as she pulled one of the bolts free.

Then a warm glow flowed through her, and she got back to her feet. Immediately, she had to block the assault of another group of guards. She cast *[Hex: Slow]* and then *[Necroblast]* on the first, finishing him off with a stab with the sword. A duck and a block with her bracer sent her rolling away, carving another entrance into a different tent. This one was partially on fire.

She ran and stabbed a burning guard to put him out of his misery, switching her *[Hex: Slow]* to a man trying to assist a wounded woman and plunging her sword into the back of his neck before he could respond. Her eyes blazed bright crimson as she turned to face more guards bursting into the doorway. As the first one swung a heavy mace, she jumped backward and kicked a bit of burning debris toward the group. The distraction allowed her to level a *[Necroblast]* at one and blow their neck out. Sally turned to make a new exit but found the debris blocked her route.

Gloved hands grabbed her and pulled her onto a sword, piercing her through her lower back below the pack. She swung her head backward and was rewarded with a crack of a broken nose as she pulled away from the blade. Warmth flowed through her again, and she turned to flurry repeated swings of her sword at the blooded guard. He blocked most of them but not enough.

She was struck in the side, knocking her to the floor with a crack of bones—then warmth again as she rolled away from a crushing blow that dug up clods of earth. *[Necroblast]* struck out into the group again, doing damage but not felling any opponent. The smell of smoke and heat had become thick in the air, and the flicker of light from dancing flames painted the backdrop of the tent like some hellscape.

Sally threw her dagger—it was last ditch and without proper aim, yet the Luck must have come to fruition as it embedded into the eye socket of an unprepared guard. Using the distraction as intended, the crossbow was already in her hand—the bolt quickly found the throat of a second assailant. The single remaining guard blocking the tent doorway stared at her with open mouth, unsure whether to attack or flee.

Sally was taking no chances. With *[Hex: Slow]* and a sprint, she dropped the crossbow to hold back the sword with both hands, diving into a wild two-handed stab that broke through the armored plate of the guard and pierced their chest. She allowed herself a quick *[Eat Brains]* as she retrieved the dagger.

As she tried to run from the tent, she immediately slammed into the armored body of another guard, knocking the woman to the floor. The zombie turned it into a spinning slash with the dagger, catching the neck of another guard. There were *so many* guards. Stuck between four tents with no doorways, she was assailed by more guards alerted to the fray.

She threw out *[Hex: Slow]* and *[Necroblast]* with reckless abandon, her sword and dagger silver arcs in the night air. The yelling, sounds of pain, crackling of wood aflame, and her own complaining body blurred into one as she whirled in melee. She would take cuts and gashes—and even almost lost her whole arm at one point to a critically damaging axe swing, but every time her health went low a pulse of warmth healed her.

The mass of guards trying to fight her didn't have the room to assault her at once, so she barely clung to fighting five or six at once. It was both mentally and physically exhausting, and healing only helped one of those. Bodies had piled up around her, and the grass was slick with spilled blood. She was caked from head to toe in gore, matting her hair and causing her clothes to stick to her skin.

And then another Elite joined the fray. She could tell because he immediately struck her with a large war hammer, knocking her into the air. Sally landed atop one of the tents, the wooden beams collapsed, and she was covered by the fabric. The melee piled on her, sprays of red marring the white of the fallen tent before the zombie emerged—rolling to her feet away from the fight and straight into a peppering of crossbow bolts.

As a warmth passed through her again, a voice peeped up from behind. "My feet are getting itchy, Sally."

With one last burst of energy, she burst forward at the Elite, throwing every spell and weapon she could at him—with a final leap into the air and both blades raised high, the war hammer swung around in a wide arc.

"Cabbages!"

## CHAPTER SIXTY-FIVE

# Coming Storm

Sally spat out a mouthful of cold grass.

She blinked and tried to absorb her surroundings as her muscles ached and burned from every slight movement. Something fidgeted from behind her and with the popping sound of a clasp, the small goblin girl rolled from the backpack.

"Ew, that made me dizzy." Bella stumbled to her feet and held her head.

The heavy footsteps of Humphrey's plated boots stomped closer to the zombie as she rolled over to look up at the stars.

"How was that?" The Death Knight grinned.

"Bad. Even Level Ten *guards* are a menace." With a pained groan, she sat up to see the sickly orc being led over to where she had reappeared. She narrowed her eyes to pick out it was Oleb giving the assistance.

"You did well; the carnage is still ongoing." The orc smiled. His empty eye sockets turned toward the sky. "At least fifteen dead, and many wounded by the fires. Some of their supplies were lost to the fires."

"They'll be tired too," Humphrey added, "since you interrupted their rest."

Sally nodded. "I killed one of the Elites too. I was hoping for more, though."

The Death Knight shrugged. "Considering the level difference, you did well enough. It's no surprise you leveled up."

She held up her wrist to see the glowing golden STAR awaiting her input. Perhaps her little adventure had done a bit more than just weaken the approaching forces. With a sigh, she scrunched up her nose. "Where's Theo at?"

"He thought he could get another level, I think. He said he wasn't tired."

Humphrey crossed his arms and shook his head. "Possibly he was just a little jealous not to be included in the fun."

Sally rubbed her temples. "Just warm up Henkk and let him have a go too, then." He had some catching up to do, and he would be too weak to take on the higher-level guards. She had barely managed herself, and she was pumped up on what potions she could get her hands on.

"Henkk is . . ." Oleb shrugged sheepishly. "Well, that took a lot out of him. He will need to rest if you want him to assist tomorrow."

She nodded and frowned. "They have to . . . remove the Leaders, right? Bella is invincible, no?"

Their eyes turned to the small Healer, who had been listening in with her hands clasped behind her back. It was hard to consider the possibility that everyone could get killed as the remaining guards tried to off the last goblin but wouldn't be able to. That sounded like a big glitch waiting to happen.

"Invincible, or just high regeneration." The Death Knight looked down at the goblin. "If the latter, then sufficient damage in a short period would . . ." He looked out to the surrounding forest as the flames of his helmet burned brighter.

It looked like they had returned to Sanctuary just outside of the garrison area. The breeze was nice and cool here and a far cry from the maelstrom of heat and violence she had just left behind. She took a moment to allow nature to just exist around her. Tomorrow would be further carnage; a light bit of contemplation would settle her mind.

"Meditating again?" Humphrey grinned and extended a hand down to her.

Sally rolled her eyes and took it, standing up on her aching legs. "Being able to regenerate like that was pretty neat, but I think it would drive me insane after a while."

The Death Knight raised an eye socket as they turned to head back into the village.

"I'm just saying, I like my fights to be brief and dramatic. When it turns into a slog it wears on the emotions, maybe more than on my stabbing arms." She sighed and looked to the floor.

"Sleep well and choose your new ability. Knowing the System, it'll be some deus ex machina skill that'll win us the day tomorrow."

"That'd be kind of anticlimactic, Humps." It was certainly a possibility— maybe if she had chosen the Puppy skill, then things would be different. Even with the number of bugs she had been amassing, it seemed unlikely there would be something powerful enough to lay waste to the force arriving tomorrow.

The dimly lit village square seemed so serene now, considering the battleground it would be tomorrow. Humphrey filled her in on some of the details of the preparations made, but she largely tuned it out. It had been a long day. If she could just ignore the possibility of imminent danger for the rest of the night, that'd be swell.

They passed Cass, who was sitting on a bench and staring into the clear night sky. "It's going to rain tomorrow," she warned with a nod, "maybe even storm."

She waved off the Death Knight and retired to her room in the inn. No sooner had her head hit the pillow than she fell asleep—arm stretched out as if she was about to press the STAR.

A shadowy figure loomed over her as she startled awake. Dark clothes rose to a pale face, shadowed despite the bright morning sunlight illuminating the bedroom. Her hand went for her dagger before she paused.

"Theo? *Ass*, what are you doing in here?"

The vampire was now wearing what was essentially a smart suit—velvety dark black with a dark crimson tie and white dress shirt. The cape that hung from his shoulders was almost too cliché to be believed. "I just came to wake you. You wouldn't want to miss the big day."

She rubbed her eyes, wondering how late she had slept in. "Aren't vampires supposed to get permission before intruding?"

Theo shrugged in response. "This is the Player side of me talking to you. I heard you leveled up; what did you end up picking?"

"Oh, I hadn't—I fell asleep after all that fighting." Sally frowned down at her wrist. Now was as good a time as any to do it. There was some amount of trepidation about making the choice—especially with Theo watching. "Did you get to Level Five?"

"Sure did!" He beamed, wrapping his cape around himself dramatically. "Vampire keystones are really cool, but I went with a ranged stun. I figure it would be a good support skill so you can do your eating thing."

"That's really thoughtful, Theo. Just don't wake me up like that again." She scowled at him but almost immediately softened her glare. "Did you not sleep?"

He shrugged. "I'm not sure vampires need it. I feel great. *Real great.*" The slow nod with wide eyes did little to convince the zombie that his statement was totally true. "Anyway, I'll leave you to it. Meet at the garrison?"

Sally nodded and watched him depart. No sooner had the door closed than she deflated back into the bed. As if reading her mood, the tip-tapping of raindrops started beating on the window. Slowly the bright day retreated, and the first rainfall she had known in this world had begun.

She slunk from the bed to move over to the window, pushing it open. The drops were cool against her skin. A breeze rolled through the room, bringing with it the scent of wet grass and vegetation. Homesickness rolled through her stomach at the scent. The familiarity was comforting, but the prickle of nerves sat in the back of her mind.

For a minute, she held her eyes closed and just listened to the noise. Eventually, she turned around and brought up the STAR.

---

**Pick One**
Skill Upgrade
**[Improved Necroblast]** Projectile has a chance to strike further targets.
**[Improved Eat Brains]** Gain percentage of target's stats for short duration.
**[Improved Summon Zombies]** Raised zombies are higher level.

---

All very interesting options, and at least they were her undead-themed ones. She let her stomach do the picking.

*[Improved Eat Brains]* was one of those clutch skills that probably wouldn't see a lot of use, but when it mattered, it could be a huge boost. It already gave a permanent boost depending on who she ate, so an extra temporary boost could be a force multiplier—especially if it worked on the System-created. Actually, she selected it on the basis that it *should* work on the System-created. A buffet was on its way.

Before leaving the room, she went to the bathroom sink and selected the *[Wash Clothes]* option. Somehow this seemed even more arbitrary after all they had been through. Whoever the Architect had been must have been undecided on where to draw the line on gamifying things. After a few seconds of a progress bar, her clothes were suddenly back to pristine. A similar bar could be utilized by the bath and the rest of her became clean too.

She added taking a real bath to her to-do list. Right after surviving the System apocalypse.

As she left the inn, she largely ignored the goblins having a good time in ignorance on the tavern side.

The distance between the inn and the garrison was similarly filled with villager goblins who seemed happy to see her and still oblivious to the danger they were about to be in. The constant rainfall didn't seem to dampen their spirits either. A wooden barricade had been built at the northern road entrance—the kobold had created an alcove for the guards to funnel into. Atop the garrison, a raised platform had been built, where Jackie sat among boxes of bows.

She gave the mobster a wave, which was returned. The information that Humphrey jammed into her tired mind the night before slowly started to emerge to the surface of her thoughts. The Leaders were going to stay in their buildings. They weren't particularly combat-focused, and their survival meant the town would stay in their control.

Most of the Unique Monsters weren't too fighting capable but had agreed to do what they could to hold the garrison. Sally hadn't wanted them to—she thought they should escape with the Players and ensure they survived the day.

The *Outsiders* and the village militia would handle most of the meat of the fighting. Outnumbered and lower leveled.

She rubbed her chin as she pushed into the garrison, thankful to be out of the rain for a bit. It was nice to hear, but being damp was no way to go to war.

The eyes of all present turned to meet her, including the empty sockets of the orc.

"They are on the move. In about an hour, they will arrive."

## CHAPTER SIXTY-SIX

# Rolling Thunder

Sally sat atop the barricade and swung her feet back and forth nervously. On the surface, it seemed like they were well prepared. Oleb had eaten a series of trenches along the road to at least one hundred feet out. Jaxk had filled a couple of them with coal, which had now been set alight—the hiss of the light rain striking the heated areas almost drowned out her panicked internal voice. Almost.

The sound of light footsteps drew her attention away as Theo nimbly hopped from beam to beam before landing beside her.

"You alright?" He opened up his cloak to reveal Archie, who he placed down on the barricade as he himself sat.

"Yeah—it just seems too . . . easy?" Her brow furrowed as she idly petted the ginger cat. "I mean, this is a pretty defensible position."

Archie began to purr and looked up at her with emerald eyes. "It's the Champion you should be worried about. They are extremely tough."

"Well, that's reassuring." She looked back out at the road. The waiting was not fun. At least if they were here, she would be able to do something. Even against impossible odds, she could rip and gnaw.

One of the pits was filled with all her zombies. It was a difficult choice to expend that skill so early, but with how low level the undead were they'd hardly be a hindrance against the regiment. At least this way any that stumbled or fell into that hole would not be able to climb back out.

Theo leaned back on his palms and closed his eyes to the sky. "Any other insights you're able to give us?"

"The guards have a breaking point; they will not fight till the last person standing."

Sally nodded. That's what she was hoping and why she went on the risky solo mission the night before. The lower their numbers got, the closer to that threshold they'd be today. Between the traps and the looming archery towers they had set up, she had allowed herself the small mote of hope that the day could be won without needing to get into a large brawl.

The vampire was less convinced. "This is definitely the only attempt they'll make to try and take the village back?"

"Yes, that's the way I—that's the way the *Architect* designed it."

Both of the undead Players turned their gaze to the animal. Sally prodded him atop the head.

"*Are* you the Architect?"

"Short answer, no." Archie recoiled away from the bop. "Long answer . . . the Observer that merged with me is trying to find out what is going on."

"Schrodinger's Architect," Theo murmured, rolling his eyes.

"Keep us updated." Sally sighed and brought up her STAR. There were a couple of messages awaiting her notice.

> Chuck: uhm
> Chuck: I'm no good at this sort of thing—so don't die thx
> Chuck: Foxes & Warriors outside village limits
> Chuck: ping us if need us

A morose weight sat upon her shoulders. If she hadn't spent the guild money on the night raid, then maybe they'd be more use—but she didn't want them to die or become enemies of the System on her behalf. Not at such a low level. Fighting with your friends was the most fun, but she wasn't keen on burying any of them.

> Sally: thanks chucky
> Sally: no promises, but you guys need to level
> Sally: if we survive this, I want to take the guild to the second area as one
> Chuck: understood
> Chuck: once we receive the signal, either way, we catch up

With a slight smile, she closed the private chat and switched to Party chat.

> Sally: everyone good?
> Jackie: just peachy, boss
> Humphrey: Just finishing something with Jaxk and I will be there.

"I'm great." Theo grinned unconvincingly.

Archie curled up on the zombie's lap. "Meow," he said.

The three of them sat in silence for a while, save for the purring of the contented cat. As the rain increased in severity as the clouds overhead darkened, visibility down the long road decreased.

"Theo," Sally eventually said softly. "What do you want to do after this?"

"Like get a drink, or?" He recoiled away from her glare and gave a sheepish grin. "Two more villages, right?"

"Yeah. Equal, three each. I'm not sure taking the capital was a great idea—it would constantly be under siege, I would have thought."

"I suppose so. Maybe we can just elect some council members to represent Monster rights . . . or is it a monarchy?" The vampire pulled a face.

They both briefly waited for Archie to interject, but he had fallen asleep.

"Beats me," Sally eventually relented. "My question was more, do you want to keep doing this?"

He didn't reply straight away. Instead, they both remained staring at the waves of precipitation breaking across the slick road. Eventually, he offered up his thoughts.

"I'm a vampire in a weird video game world. Is it real? The pain and the trauma sure feel it. But so are the friendships." He turned his tired eyes to meet those of the zombie.

"Theo . . . that's really sickening. Like, my mouth actually tastes gross now. Were you planning on pitching that to a greeting card company?" Her tongue stuck from her mouth.

Theo rolled his eyes. "Be real for once. You're having the time of your life, right? You'd rather be in the diner still?"

Her mouth opened and closed in response. Would she rather be in the diner? There was pretty much zero bloodshed she could remember in what scant memories her brain had arranged into a pile. Were they even real memories? She had been in this odd world long enough to where her original life was a distant blur.

"I'd rather . . . not live in fear."

The vampire wrapped his cape a little tighter around himself. "How often has that been? You seem pretty capable. The only times I've seen you freak out are when your friends are in trouble."

"That's not true!" She tried to quickly scour her mind for other times. Certainly, the times meeting the higher levels had been nerve-wracking—but perhaps she handled those situations fine. Exasperated, she gave up the mental exercise. "Fine, but with the Architect being dead, we might have to change up our goals."

"You're not allowed to be the Architect." Theo raised an eyebrow but smiled.

"Spoilsport." The zombie shook her head and returned the grin.

Heavy footsteps vibrated up through the wooden beams as the Death Knight gingerly came up to join them. "I have no confidence in this construction." He wobbled, eye sockets wide, before reaching the wider area they were seated at.

"Anything to report, Humps?"

"Bella's mother has been scouting this morning. There appear to be two Player Parties in the nearby area that aren't known allies. One of them may be the *Skullsplitters*."

"Ooh, I can finish them off if they want to get involved!" Sally punched a fist into an open palm.

"Otherwise, we are all prepared. The villagers will arm themselves once the alarm is raised. Level One goblins with bows probably won't do much damage— but it at least keeps them out of our way."

The Death Knight moved to sit down on the edge between the two half-Players. Sally leaned against the large plated former Observer and continued to watch the rain. Theo closed his eyes and softly hummed to himself. It was a rare moment of peace where the Party was not at odds against some foe, on the trail of adventure, or trying to rile each other up. The low rumble of thunder in the distance reflected their collective mood.

"Hey, Boss?" Jackie leaned over the edge of the garrison roof to look down at them. "Spooky orc up here says ten minutes approximately."

"Isn't it so poetic," Theo said with eyes still closed, "the culmination of our tribulations and beliefs joined here under the narrative weight of the inclement weather, a dramatic climax to test our unwavering willpower?"

Sally leaned forward to see past Humphrey, frowning at the vampire. "Humps, vampires need to sleep, right?"

"*Yes.*"

"I am doing *great!*" Theo opened his eyes widely and turned to her, his exaggerated grin exposing his fangs.

She rolled her eyes and sat back, deflating at the wait still dragging on. "I guess *you're* back to being the foil for my manic personality, Humphrey."

"I am very normal." The Death Knight nodded slowly.

"Pretty terrible at differentiating from human species and Monster designations, though."

"*Yes.*"

Sally softly rubbed Archie's ears as she pondered. They were an odd approximation of found family and even more strange when they were at peace like this and not barreling toward misadventure. "Humps, can Observers merge with Players?"

"No. Not even Player corpses. Only the System-created and probably dead Uniques."

She chewed on her tongue. At least that meant they wouldn't have to worry about fighting against some weird, empowered Players. A shiver ran through her. Fighting in the rain would be miserable. Dying in the rain was only marginally worse. Her mind idly drifted to daydreams of being injured and held by Theo as he cried out against the storm. Her blood was probably as unattractive to him as his brain was to her now. The daydream popped like a balloon.

Her legs swung back and forth again. She was impatient, but a small smile had crossed her face. Even if they fell now, just the thought of what they had accomplished excited her. Closing in on Level Ten, they had fought off Players, and bandits, cultists, and the giant dog thing. If they took Sanctuary at their low level before, the next two villages should be easy pickings. She was breaking down the System, and while she wasn't getting any more "normal," she was at least becoming a more valid entity within it.

"Boss? The reg' is here!"

The smile from her face faded as a large bell began to ring in the village square. Yelling and the scuffles of movement came from behind as the villagers organized into a militia. She picked Archie up and stood, soon followed by the Death Knight and Theo.

With eyes narrowed, through the misty fog of the constant rainfall, she saw a flash of lightning briefly illuminate scores of darkened figures marching in formation.

The fight for Sanctuary had begun.

## CHAPTER SIXTY-SEVEN

# Lightning Strike

You'd have thought there would be horses or wagons." Theo scrunched his nose up as the group glared out into the curtain of rain.

Sally shrugged and looked up to the firing platforms. "Fire at will, Jacks."

"Understood, Boss."

The clattering footsteps almost drowned out the yelled response of the mobster as village goblins ascended the ladders and steps to grab their bows and take a position on the defensive walls.

She pointed her finger out and squinted an eye. "Still too far out for my spells. I think I'll keep *[Hex: Slow]* on the Champion. If we can defeat them, then that will be a huge blow to their morale."

The Death Knight nodded. "Agreed. It will not be that easy, of course."

"Of course." She idly tapped at the handle of her dagger. The dark shapes had become more clear now that the regiment was closer—individual marching bodies could be made out through the rain. "Where'd the snail Wizard go?"

Humphrey shrugged and then pointed out to the middle of the woods away from the path. "He said he was going to climb a tree and cast something. Very slowly."

"Ominous." Sally wondered how many last-ditch saving graces they had in their deck now. Probably enough; statistically speaking, the defenders always had an advantage—especially with the time to make the preparations that they had.

The Death Knight turned to the vampire. "Here, got you both some last-minute gifts." He held out two bladed fist weapons to Theo.

"Punch-blades? Oh, thank you. I guess they—"

"Are low enough damage for your *[Novice Strike]* meme interaction, *yes*."
With a nod, he then turned to the zombie.

His plated hand held out a metal crown—a cold silver, almost blue in tone,
with a green emerald in the center of the spiked front.

"Humps! It's been too long since I've had an accessory." Sally eagerly took it
and propped it atop her damp blonde hair.

Title Unlocked: Queen of the Dead
Grave Crown: A focus for necromantic power

The blue text windows that popped up shifted and flickered as if unsure of
how to conduct themselves with the Architect gone. Sally gasped as it faded away.

"A new title!" Her eyes blazed bright red as she hopped from foot to foot.
"Does the crown actually do something?"

"*Yes*, probably." The Death Knight shrugged.

Theo, having donned his pair of bladed gloves, threw some test punches in
the air. The jagged black blades whizzed through the air as his fists shot back and
forth. "Attack speed too; you shouldn't have."

"Just don't die and let them go to waste. You're still lower level, so the more
you can hit, the better." Humphrey huffed, a big grin across his face. "There
wasn't much I could get for Archie—"

"That's okay, big brother." The cat mewed from by their feet.

"—and you should see Jackie's one soon."

Sally nudged his plated arm. "Get yourself something too?"

The Death Knight just turned and gave her a brief nod; perhaps a wink
would have accompanied it if he was capable of such an act.

"*Alright!*" Jackie yelled from above, drawing their attention away. "You little
green shits better know how to aim. Fire at will in five . . ."

Sally squinted back at the shapes. Definitely closer. A large figure of an
armored woman led from the front, towering over the rank-and-file guards
marching in formation behind. There was no risk in betting on that being the
Champion.

"*Fire!*"

The twangs of bowstrings rang out in an offset pattern, quickly followed by
the sound of cutting air as the dark arrows leapt through the rain toward the regiment. Most fell short by twenty feet or so, clattering on the road. Others went
completely awry and ended up in the woods to either side. Two arrows from the
first volley landed among the guard but were deflected by the silver metal armor
most of them wore.

"Not a bad start," Sally murmured to herself, feet itching to run and begin
the melee.

A deluge of curse words and panicked goblinoid screeches came from the firing platforms as Jackie chastised their first attempt. Bows were drawn once more for the second volley. The mobster herself leveled Betty into the air, slowly adjusting the angle as red energy flowed around the metal frame.

As the second volley of goblin arrows whipped into the air, they were joined by the flaming bolt of Jackie's *[Explosive Shot]*—then a second and third quickly followed. The flaming bolts arced through the darkening sky toward their target.

"*[Triple Shot]* and *[Increased Fire Damage]* scrolls." Humphrey grinned.

Explosions rang out across the first group of guards. Amber light flared and lit up the impact points, joined by the pained yells of those struck. As the glow faded, the Champion at the front remained unaffected—a translucent orb of light blue energy fully encircled her. A handful of guards were not so lucky to be defended as such, and four or five had fallen, their position in the regiment quickly replaced by those behind.

"We keeping count of the remaining guards?" Theo asked, eyes darting around the approaching group. "I kind of want to, for some reason."

Sally didn't respond. Instead, she ground her fangs together nervously. The Champion had magic abilities, she could tell. Not just from the glowing orb of protection, but the sheer presence the armored woman commanded—the brazen confidence as she strode forward . . .

"Forty-four." The vampire licked his lips, mentally double-checking his math.

The third volley went into the air.

"One more volley and they'll be at the pits," Humphrey growled, his eyes focused on the Champion.

Arrows clattered among the road and the regiment; on the whole, a much better result than the first two attempts.

"Forty-three."

Sally went through her Inventory and cleared all the consumables out. Stat boost? Activated. Weapon and Armor Enhancements—now spent and used. Hoarding was one thing, but there was no joy in being a really lootable corpse. One by one, she removed a *[Skull]* from the flickering UI screen and walked along the edge of the defensive wall, placing one of them down every couple of feet.

The next volley went out as a crack of lightning illuminated the background. They were close enough that they could see where each arrow was hitting among the rain-slick silvers and muted brown armors.

"Forty . . . uh, forty-three still." The rumble of thunder punctuated the vampire's count.

Low steam swept across the approach to the village as the increased rainfall had all but put out the coal fires. The Champion stopped just before the first trench that had been dug out.

The woman raised a staff into the air, and her voice boomed out across the area.

"Invaders of Yarch! We have come to remove you from the—"

An errant arrow from a nervous goblin sailed through the air and clattered to the floor by the Champion's feet.

"Promote that gobbo!" Sally yelled out through cupped hands.

"Yeah, these lectures and proclamations get old pretty quick." Theo yawned before quickly pretending he wasn't tired.

"Invaders of—"

Sally released her own crossbow bolt. The flare of the protective orb lit up as her attack struck but was absorbed.

The Champion growled and gnashed her teeth as a full volley of arrows came from the firing platforms, accompanied by repeated shots of *[Hellfire Trigger]*.

"Forty-one." Theo scratched his chin and tried not to poke his own eye with his bladed fist. "That was mostly Jackie's doing."

"To arms! Reclaim Yarch for the Throne! *Kill the Leaders!*" The Champion, now unable to get her monologue out, resigned herself to sending the guards to battle. With her staff leveled out toward the Party, she cast a spell.

*[Neutral Ground]*

The road returned to normal. All the traps and pits dug, trenches, and the zombie hideaway they had planned to slow down the assault were now rendered to nothing. A clear path of cobbled stone lay between the Champion and the defenses. A flash of lightning brought the angry charge of the scores of guards as they surged past the large woman.

"That's not particularly fair," Sally grumbled as a weight lurched in her stomach. "*My zombies!*"

"Ah, well." Humphrey turned to her, a grin still across his skeletal face. "It never is fair for the underdogs. Scratcher said that your attack last night destroyed all their ranged ammunition. So I consider that an even trade."

The Death Knight then leapt down from the battlements and landed on the road, standing to withdraw his greatsword. Sally and Theo joined him, landing each side of the plated undead.

"Watch this." He held out his sword toward the onrushing enemy. The flames from the back of his head, sizzling from the rain, petered out and disappeared. There was a brief second of nothing, and then his extended weapon burst into crimson flame.

"Neat party trick, big brother!" Archie called down from atop the defenses.

"Now you made it less cool." Humphrey pouted, deflating slightly. "At least the horse isn't here."

"Where *did* he go?" Theo asked, limbering up his shoulders.

"As far from here as I could send him," Humphrey growled.

*[Dead King's Court]*

A pulse of energy flowed through the trio of undead. A volley of arrows peppered the guards now no longer in formation as they charged.

"Forty," Theo whispered to himself.

"Stick together, heal if you need to, don't get overwhelmed. Stay alive." Humphrey assumed a stance with his sword, the blade at the ready.

"Yes, Dad." Sally rolled her eyes and drew her pair of weapons. It was now seconds before the two sides would clash and her muscles felt tense.

"I have reports that the two Player Parties are moving in closer," Archie called from above.

She bared her fangs at the first wave of guards. Lightning flashed, and thunder rolled across the village soon after. One last easy breath was taken.

When it rained, it poured.

## CHAPTER SIXTY-EIGHT

# Impending Doom

As the trio ran forward to meet the charging guards, goblin villagers began to pour down from the battlements armed with knives, shortswords, and spears—while they lacked the levels to do significant damage, their number would at least slow the battle down.

A barrel appeared over the middle of the road about fifteen feet in the air, then dropped to the ground and split, sending black tar across a large area. Henkk had been weakened but still lent a hand. Arrows continued to rain down on the large column of armored assailants, doing little damage but at least providing constant pressure to anyone attempting to retreat from the front lines.

"For Sanctuary!" Sally growled as she ducked and spun from the first guard, turning as they passed over her to stab her dagger into the back of their knee. As the guard fell, a blazing red sword cleaved their head from their shoulders.

Theo clashed with his first opponent. As he used *[Sanguine Weapon]*, a glowing blade appeared beside him and mimicked his flurry of strikes as he lashed into the guard with his glitched *[Novice Strike]*, several strikes finding their mark before the figure dropped. A second guard swung a large mace toward him, but the vampire vanished in a cloud of dark mist to appear behind them and continued his blurred attacks.

Sally cast *[Necroblast]* and burned away at the shield arm of her next opponent, stabbing out at that shoulder as their defenses dropped. A follow-up attack was not possible as already another guard had moved into melee with her. She jumped backward to avoid the slice of a sword, almost bumping against the Death Knight.

Humphrey blazed with energy as he activated *[Adrenaline]* and swung his flaming greatsword through the air, the blade hissing as it passed through the falling rain. He had the advantage of size and reach over the generic human guards and used it to slash at the injured opponents of the Party and slow the approach of the oncoming horde. A wide grin was illuminated by the crimson sword as his empty eyes tried to search out the Champion ahead.

From the battlements above, Archie stretched out his back. He knew that he should use some skills to help out his new friends. Neither he nor the Observer inside of him knew what abilities he actually had access to or how to activate them. His emerald eyes flashed as he watched over the battlefield, and then they narrowed as he tried to focus.

Pain flared up the zombie's flank as the sword found purchase in her left side. As her arm sagged, she sent *[Necroblast]* into the leg of her opponent, and then as they stumbled, she lunged at their neck with her sword. The scrape of metal plate deflected the attack, lopping off the ear of the guard instead of being a killing blow. Sally followed up by barging into a headbutt against the wounded guard, knocking them to the floor; the *[Eat Brains]* conditions were only barely met.

She was knocked to the floor as soon as the brains slid down her gullet. She rolled across the rain-slick floor as a war hammer cracked the cobblestone where she had been. Energy flowed through her as she became buffed by a portion of the Level Ten guard's stats. A gore-stained grin twisted across her face as her red eyes regarded the Elite from last night.

The vampire had become a sickening blur, with all three attacks launching one after the other, he began to dart between the loose group of guards, slightly damaging them here and there like a spiked pinball. Every kill gained him a use of his short-ranged teleport. With a pained, dizzied expression, he zipped his way back to the Party so as not to get too out of place and sunk his fangs into the neck of a wounded guard.

Humphrey moved with precision, the defensive abilities that he had picked up combining with the zombie boss's auras to make him a powerhouse in melee combat. His *[Dead King's Court]* passive made him slower, but he had been able to parry or absorb most of the attacks levied at him. Activating the skill to share half of the boons with the Party had made him slower still, but that was his position in the group. Gradually he tanked and supported the two whirling damage dealers as he slowly progressed toward his intended quarry.

An *[Explosive Shot]* flew overhead and struck past the road, almost in the tree line. The brief surge of amber light silhouetted a group of seven. Sally grit her teeth as she withdrew her dagger from the warm guts of a slain guard. This was the interloping Players. A pulse of nausea shuddered through her—briefly, she thought it was maybe panic, but no, it was something else. The guard beneath her looked up with glowing yellow eyes and shambled to their feet.

The ginger cat was pretty pleased with himself. He was sure the new Queen of the Dead would be happy with the new buff, even if it was only temporary. He was also secretly relieved that it had been something useful and he didn't blow her up instead. *Speaking of which* . . . He frowned up toward the sky as a large orb glistened against the dark clouds.

Jackie spat on the floor. "*Buncha assholes.*" She seethed as she reloaded Betty. She had told the goblins to switch targets to the woods where the Players had appeared from. It wouldn't be enough to kill them but might make them think twice about getting involved. From her vantage point, it seemed like things were going okay. At least more guards had died than Party members. The goblins who had joined the fray were something else entirely, but it had kept the trio of undead down there from getting overwhelmed. Oddly enough though—she leaned over the wall—some of the goblins seemed to be getting back up.

Sally felt powerful as she weaved beneath another strike, lashing out with her sword. *[Necroblast]* missed the target but struck a different guard behind, who then received a downward arc from the Death Knight's greatsword. The Elite swung for her but missed and struck a zombie goblin, splattering the small living corpse. That was almost as big a surprise to the Elite as it was to Sally. Her eyes quickly darted to the side; all the fallen in the battle were now clambering to their feet, hunger for living flesh in their eyes. *This crown sure is nice!*

Something in the air caught her gaze, and she flinched, expecting it to be a spell cast by the Champion. If it was, it was huge. It looked like a ball of fire . . . only closer to a meteorite.

"Adam says 'sorry, it's not usually that big,'" Archie called from the battlements.

It was hard to judge how much time they had before impact as she deflected a sword strike. If there was any consolation, it seemed to be at least aimed to where the Champion had been standing and wasn't coming down straight on their heads. Somehow dying to a friendly fire meteor strike would annoy her even more than any other presented danger.

"Do not worry." Humphrey beamed as he blocked a mace, twisting his sword to lop off the offending hand at the wrist. "We will have enough resistance to survive it."

Sally wasn't so convinced, but other than abandoning the road and defenses, there would be no way of avoiding it. The Elite blocked or absorbed her *[Necroblast]* before kicking away at another goblin zombie. The man was struck by a bolt as the mobster fired *[Pin down]* from the platform, keeping him in place. Sally ran around and got some distance from the large guard with the war hammer. As the surge of undead began getting into the fight alongside the still-living goblins, it bogged the melee down substantially.

She watched as his eyes darted around through the curtain of rain to try and seek her out. As soon as he became distracted by a nearby goblin, she released the bolt of her crossbow. The Elite raised his arm to protect his face, but a clambering zombie slowed his movement, weighing him down. A sickening gurgle spurted from his bloody lips as the bolt found its mark beneath his jaw.

*[Eat Brains]*. Sally was there beside him, hardly remembering making the short trip. She felt warm now. Must be all the strenuous activity? Possibly even all the buffs she was now stacking up. Everything seemed brighter now—as if her eyes were aglow with the . . . She looked up. The orb of fire was much larger now. Perhaps thirty . . . maybe forty feet across. It illuminated and warmed the area.

"You sure about this?" Theo winced away from the bright light. Both of his arms were soaked in blood, and his cloak and shirt had been slashed through in a few places.

"*Yes. Ha-ha.*" Humphrey barely paid any notice to what lay above, instead simply content to hack slowly through the guard toward the Champion.

"Jackie says the Players are on the road ahead now with the Champion," Archie called out. His voice was getting harder to hear over the battle, as the three had fought their way away from the village.

"The numbers are thinning." Theo licked the blood from his lips as he cut through a guard in three swift strikes. "I think twenty-eight remaining."

That was better than Sally had been expecting. She took one of her Healing Potions as there was a brief lull in combat. Even the guards seemed slightly distracted from the burning ball about to strike down upon them. She had taken more damage than she realized, and it would be a smart move to keep on top of it. She dodged out of the way of a reckless swing and smashed the empty potion bottle into the guard's face. *[Eat Brains]*.

And then pain as three arrows found their places in her leg, torso, and shoulder.

"Players," Humphrey growled as he lowered into a more defensive stance.

As she pulled the arrows from her wounds, her red eyes blazed and the crowd parted. The Champion and the Players stood together and were making their approach.

Sally licked her sharp teeth and slunk behind a zombie to avoid a further arrow from striking her.

It looked like *lunch* had arrived.

## CHAPTER SIXTY-NINE

# Nice Fireball

Blazing heat bore down on them as the trio of undead ran to clash with the Champion and Players. The amber orb of fire was now maybe eighty feet in diameter, and the impact was imminent.

Humphrey withdrew a scroll from his belt and with the sizzle of spent magical energy, it faded to ashes. A red circle of light illuminated beneath the Party.

Ahead, the Champion raised her staff, and a beam of light shot up toward the impending meteor. The descent slowed almost to a stop as the white line of magical power maintained a connection to it. Arrows and spells shot from the enemy group, blasting some of the goblins and raised zombies.

Sally couldn't see the levels or classes of the opponents, but at this point it didn't matter. She swerved around the remaining guards, avoiding their attacks and slashing out with her sword as they passed.

The Death Knight shoulder barged a guard to the floor, sending them sliding several feet away. With the majority of the space now clear, he leveled his greatsword toward the Champion.

*[Compelled Duel]*

*The sneaky bastard,* Sally thought. Her level up had of course leveled him, too, as her bodyguard. He hadn't seen it fitting to let her know that he had regained that ability.

Eyes ablaze with fury, the Champion fought against the ability. She slowly lowered her staff to stare down at Humphrey, her concentration of the spell broken.

"Looks like you failed your Willpower save." He beamed, swinging his sword around in an arc and taking a defensive stance.

Now unhindered, the fireball struck.

Briefly, everything was awash with amber light. A heat seared at Sally's skin. It hurt, but she didn't feel dead. More dead. As the light faded from her vision, the scene around her was awash with those without as powerful of a resistance as their group.

Charred remains of goblins, zombies, and guards alike littered the road behind and before them. While a few lucky ones remained, the attack had been devastating. Flames continued to lap at some of the corpses, and the grass and foliage on either side of the road smoldered.

"*Fuckin' shit!*" Jackie's voice carried out across the brief silence.

Someone grabbed Sally's elbow. She turned to the blazing red eyes of Theo.

"C'mon, let's end this," he hissed, before running toward the enemy.

She shook the disorientation from her head and started after him. The Death Knight was slowly advancing toward the Champion—if only he could have waited, then she could have put *[Hex: Slow]* on her. Instead, she leveled the spell at the human Cleric ahead of them—the familiar blonde hair of the *Skullsplitters's* healer was now slightly singed.

Concern filled her as Theo took an arrow to the chest, and then a second— the blue glow of a third held shot illuminated the face of the Ranger. Theo then vanished as this *[Ice Shot]* flew through the black mist and struck the road behind them both. The vampire appeared behind the surprised Player and began strik- ing out with his blades.

Sally threw out *[Necroblast]* toward the Cleric, but the dark-haired female Fighter from before stepped in the way and took the hit. There was anger in the faces of the Players, but also some amount of trepidation. Their desire for revenge had looked like a tastier dish before most of the "good guys" had been all but obliterated. Enough seemed to remain to keep the battle going, or perhaps the forced duel between Humphrey and the Champion prevented the order of retreat from being issued.

A Rogue appeared beside her as she launched herself at the Fighter. Pain burned across her left arm as a blade cut into her dead flesh. Her feet stumbled as a numbness slid through her, but she shook it just in time to slide out of the way of the Fighter's axe swing. Jumping backward, she circled around the two opponents until *[Necroblast]* snuck past them and slammed into the Cleric, interrupting her healing spell.

The Fighter spun in response, and a flare of orange appeared as her attack turned into a *[Whirlwind]*. Sally jerked backward as crimson flashed in front of her eyes as the axe bit a gash across her face. Warmth trickled down her cheeks as the woman stopped the attack and stared at her in confusion, eyes now tired and staring blankly across the battlefield.

A beam of red light ran between the dizzied Fighter and somewhere behind her—Theo. *[Stunning Gaze]* had caught the frenzied woman. Sally surged forward, a crossbow bolt from Jackie striking the Rogue in the back with *[Pin Down]* and preventing him from interfering. The rare sword jabbed up beneath the ribcage and into the chest of the stunned Fighter, landing a critical hit.

*[Eat Brains]*

---

+7% Health Points

---

Theo vanished from his position and appeared behind the Cleric, immediately using *[Vampire Bite]* on the back of her neck. Sally ran up to the dazed woman and watched the crimson leak from the wounds until her conditions were met.

*[Eat Brains]*

---

+7% Magical Defense

---

Their blazing red eyes met as the vampire discarded the consumed Cleric to the floor. His gore-caked grin was quickly ended as he was struck in the side of the head with a blunt weapon. Theo's body slumped to the ground as an armored Paladin pushed into the zombie and began to glow with a holy light.

Sally barely blocked the follow-up attack as a burst of radiant energy knocked her backward. She tried to get a glance at the vampire, but he hadn't moved from the floor. Behind her, the Rogue had now vanished. *[Hex: Slow]* switched to the Paladin, and she rolled to the side to avoid a crack of golden thunder. She felt lethargic in his presence, despite the stacking buffs from the eaten Players.

There must be some kind of aura. She tried to back away, but he moved closer more quickly than she thought possible. Out of the eight Players, four still remained. There was another crack as the Paladin's hammer struck her left arm, the dagger dropping to the floor from her grasp. The plated foe went for a follow-up swing but stumbled as something ginger darted and weaved between his legs.

Sally grabbed onto the Paladin with her good arm and threw her body weight backward to pull the Player off-balance. They landed side-by-side on the charred cobblestone road, and she scrabbled at his neck, trying to get through the fabric and layers of armor. An *[Explosive Shot]* rang out nearby as Jackie tried to guess where the Rogue had gone.

"Foolish," the Paladin hissed as he put his hand against her bloodied chest. A radiant glow started to flare around his plated fist. Even with her hand finally around his neck, she couldn't puncture his skin or choke him in such a short time. *[Necroblast]*. Gore shot out across the nearby stone as the eldritch ball blew out most of his neck. *[Eat Brains]*.

+7% Physical Defense

She stood again as pain wracked her body and turned to see where Theo had gotten to. The vampire was standing again, but half of his clothing had been burned away by acid and patches of his pale skin were raw and bloodied. He stepped away from the pool of steaming green liquid, creating bloodied footprints on the darkened ground. The offending spellcaster paled at the sight and tried to mumble another spell. Theo teleported behind him in a cloud of mist, sunk both of his blades into their back, and then bit into their neck. Even from here, Sally could see the vampire's burnt skin regenerating.

Instead of rushing over for the brains, she grabbed the second Healing Potion bottle and downed the contents, turning as she did; she kept an eye open for the Rogue. Unaccosted, she met the sight of the Death Knight and Champion duel.

Both combatants looked worn and exhausted. Humphrey had two holes pierced straight through him, and the flame on his sword looked dangerously close to going out. The Champion had split and dented plate armor and a cut up the side of her face.

Archie was sitting nearby, watching intently.

A heavy downward swing from the crimson greatsword was blocked by the staff but sent the woman down onto one knee.

Sally realized it had still been raining. The fireball had briefly blocked the drops from landing or finding purchase, and then the adrenaline had caused her to focus on other things. It was actually reasonably quiet now. The Players she had killed just now were raised as zombies to stand and join her, and Theo stumbled over to her, wiping his mouth.

"It is over," Archie proclaimed, causing the duelists to pause. "Your forces are spent and have been repelled. Sanctuary belongs to the Monsters now."

The Champion stood and brushed off her arm. Except for the rain beating down, silence filled the road as all living and not living waited to hear her response. Her breathing was haggard. After a long gaze into the emerald eyes of the cat, she lowered her head in resignation.

"The Crown yields. On this day you have—"

Humphrey stepped forward and without hesitation cleaved her head clean from her neck, the blazing arc sending it bouncing across the stone road. "*I won the duel.*" He beamed, resting the blade across his shoulders.

Any remaining guards turned tail and fled. They didn't make it far, as the Party and remaining Monsters cut them down.

Sally shuddered and sat down on the body of the Champion. "Losing the buffs is not a fun feeling."

Theo just stood, weaving side to side slightly as if listening to a tune in his head, his eyes focused up into the clouded sky.

"Not a terrible battle," Humphrey huffed, sitting on the floor.

"Sanctuary is indeed safe for Monsters to live in now." Archie nodded. "As for *your* fates, they are still to be decided."

"What are you talking about, kitty?" Sally frowned at the wet cat. Then she heard a noise—faint at first but slowly rising above the rain.

The Party turned to look down the road. Fast approaching was a horse-drawn coach. A flash of lightning revealed a figure standing atop the roof, arms stretched as wide as his black feathered wings. A crimson halo sat atop his head.

Sally narrowed her eyes at the Cleric and drew her sword.

## CHAPTER SEVENTY

# True Villainy

As the dark sky rumbled with thunder, the coach slid to a halt, turning sideways. Figures burst from within and joined the Cleric as he hovered in the air.

"Sally the Unliving," he called out, slight mania in his voice, "I have come to wipe you, and Monsters like you, from this fine land."

"It's actually *Queen of the Dead* now!" She wrinkled her nose up and turned to Theo. "Or was it *Undead?*"

The vampire said nothing, but his tired, wandering eyes had returned to sharp focus as he glared at the newcomers.

She did the same as the floating Player seethed at her response.

There was a large alligator-looking man, a woman in dark clothing, a small insect in a business suit, and an orc with a black flaming skull. Oh—this last one might be interesting. She raised an eyebrow at her two ex-Observers.

"Do you feel that too, little brother?" Humphrey muttered in a low voice. He shook his head after realizing what he had said.

"Yes, he has become corrupt."

Sally frowned. A bad Observer? She wasn't really one to judge—technically her Party were bad guys, and two had joined her. But there was something about the Cleric and his apparent necessity to bug her that seemed even more evil. Like, at least she mostly didn't harass people.

"Your title means nothing; I will scour every memory of you from this place! I have killed you five times already. I can do it again just as easily."

A pang of nausea ran through her. So . . . *she had* been a normal zombie once, at the start of the System. Killed and reborn until her soul forced its way back in. There had always been a chance that was the case, but now knowing it for sure, it made her irrationally angry.

"It's like us," Theo's voice wavered. "Unique Monsters following a Player."

"He was normal before." She shook her head. "Kind of a prick, but not some demonic angel thing. Humps?"

The Death Knight exchanged a quick look with the cat before responding. "Must be a glitch."

That didn't seem super believable. She turned her head to watch the mobster run over, her long legs hopping over all the corpses along the way.

"Hey, Boss." She grinned, her hat dripping as rain pooled around the rim.

"Why didn't you stay up on the platform?"

"Oh. Seemed like we were doing a little gang versus gang thing here." She pointed a long finger out to the other Party. "The rest of you schmucks are here already, and I didn't want to miss out on getting some lumps of my own."

Sally shrugged. Her head was already swimming with conflicting feelings, and the line across her face where she had been cut still ached. "Hey, Theo." She nudged him, ignoring whatever the Cleric had started to ramble on about. "How bad does my face look?"

He turned to her and bit his lower lip, exposing his fangs. "Honestly? That's pretty gnarly—but I bet it'll turn into a badass scar."

"Did you just say *gnarly?*" She feigned puking. It did make her feel better about it though. Although you weren't supposed to scar here, it was certainly possible for bad enough wounds. Maybe she would delay her next healing item usage . . .

Archie stretched out and yawned. "Are they going to talk forever or what?"

Sally cleared her throat. "Hey, Monsters? Why not join with us? We won't force you to fight, and you can just live as you are."

A burst of crimson flared from the false halo of the Cleric. His Uniques gave each other a quick glance, but the red hue was reflected in their eyes.

"Aw." She leaned against Theo. Her arm felt sleepy. The break had mended, but it was still fragile. "I think he has them under his control—they are fighting under duress."

"Except for the orc." Humphrey shook his head. "We will need to kill at least two of them."

"I guess I have dibs on the Cleric, then." Sally rolled her eyes.

"I'll take the gal with the nice hair," Jackie blurted out quicker than she anticipated.

"Orc," Archie and Humphrey both said in tandem.

"Ah, I don't want to fight the lizardman." Theo rubbed the back of his neck. "What am I going to bite there?"

"Well, would you rather bite the bug?" Sally prodded him.

"I'll take the bug, I guess," Archie growled, shooting his emerald eyes at the Death Knight.

"Rock Paper Scissors for not-the-croc, Humphrey?" Theo held out a bladed hand.

Humphrey shrugged. "I don't know what that means, but I would like to face my fallen brother."

"*Fiiine.*" The vampire deflated.

Not being able to see levels certainly made things less stressful. Sally rubbed her chin. You would have thought that it would be the opposite, but they had enough Luck and plot armor to win something that was on approximately even standing. Having everyone pick an opponent was a simple way to keep them focused and made things . . .

"Hey, guys, what if we don't split five-on-five? Could we all just focus on the Cleric and pop him quicker?" She raised her eyebrow and raised her tired arms in an exaggerated shrug.

"I'm not sure how fair that'd be," Theo mumbled.

She watched his exhausted expression with concern. "Do you need a *coffin* to sleep in?"

His mouth hung agape, and he turned back to her, his eyes wide. "Yes! That sounds so nice!"

"*Quit talking among yourselves!*" the Cleric yelled out. A bolt of radiant energy formed in his hand. "You. Will. Listen." He threw the bolt down toward the zombie.

Humphrey stepped in the way to block it—the fizz as it struck his armor didn't cease, and he dropped to one knee in front of her.

Sally gasped and circled around him; the bolt remained embedded in his collarbone area, melting away at his armor.

"Don't touch," the Death Knight growled, grabbing it himself and wrenching it from the wound. His plated fingers smoldered just from contact. "I advise not getting hit by those."

The Cleric spread his arms wide, and five of the bolts appeared in an arc above his head. "Time to salt the earth," he spat, willing his Party onward.

"Alright, *Outsiders*, let's, uh, keep up our trend of not dying. I want at least four of you to survive." She gave them a wink and flashed her sword forward, ignoring the nervous glances between the rest of them.

Jackie immediately let off an *[Explosive Shot]* at the female Monster, the silver-haired woman vanishing from the impact and shimmering into view a dozen feet to the side.

Archie hopped forward and turned completely blue, activating some unknown skill.

Humphrey exhaled and activated *[Dead King's Court]* again, empowering his undead allies as he strode toward the orc.

Theo very unenthusiastically jogged toward the large lizardman.

Sally sprinted forward as the radiant bolts shot down toward her. She zigzagged and dodged, sparks flying from the cobblestone road as the attacks missed her. Two of the recent zombies were struck and exploded with golden sparks. Once each shot was spent, she waved a fist into the air. "You going to come down here and fight?"

Wild light danced behind the dark eyes of the Cleric. He dropped to the floor, his black wings relaxing and blowing a wave of dust dramatically toward her. In his hand, a mace of red energy appeared. "I've been waiting for this moment for a long time."

"Funny." Sally slid to a stop to size him up. "I hadn't thought of you at all."

*[Hellfire Trigger]* shot bolts from Betty in quick succession, each one hitting the blur of the moving woman. Jackie cursed as her opponent darted and then appeared right before her, sinking a blade into her side. The hood raised to reveal a beautiful dark elf, a slight sadness in her large opal eyes.

Theo cast *[Sanguine Weapon]* as the lizardman drew twin scimitars. His first punch was blocked, and he had to roll away from the second. Something struck him from behind, lacerating his thigh—the tail of the large Monster also held a scimitar. "Three against three." He grimaced from the pain as he watched the long mouth of the lizardman curl into a smile in return.

Archie stopped and blew a gust of ice spray at the insect-person; a cone of supercooled air and snowflakes blasted the air and iced over the rain-slick road. The Monster was no longer there as the hue faded. Dropping from the sky, the bug rolled toward the cat and lashed out with twin whips. The cat hissed as one struck his flank, flaying a patch of fur from his skin.

"I am the Architect!" He growled as energy began to pulse around his tiny feet.

The Monster clicked and chirped in response, antennae raised in challenge.

*[Adrenaline]* pulsed through the Death Knight as he leveled his sword toward the orc with the flaming skull for a head. "It is a shame to meet under such circumstances, brother."

"Hah!" Black flame pulsed from the Monster. "We are nothing like *brothers.*" He pulled a sword made of black metal from his back.

"You forget your station. The Architect—"

"The Architect is dead! And yet you cling to his teat still." The empty sockets of the orc narrowed as a crooked grin crossed along his teeth.

Humphrey growled and stood still in a defensive stance. "So soon you would fall in with those who would destroy the System?"

"Look who is talking, 'brother.'" The orc flourished his blade and stood, still opposed to the Death Knight.

"There is a new normal coming to the System, and we are trying to allow it to flourish. We are the protectors, and we must find out how the Architect came to pass."

The orc laughed, cackling out against the sound of battle and rainfall. A flash of lightning cast hideous shadows among them.

"Well, let me make this easy for you before I kill you." He crouched, ready to spring forth. "I am one of those who killed the Architect."

The two once-Observers leapt toward each other, anger burning within both of them.

## CHAPTER SEVENTY-ONE

# Death of the Party

Crimson sparks blazed from Sally's sword as she blocked the swing of the eldritch-looking mace. The Cleric had definitely not been this strong previously, and her numb arm was a testament to that fact. In fairness, she had done her fair share of leveling—it was only the inability to see levels that caused her concern.

She darted forward to lunge at him. With a pulse of his dark wings, he leapt backward, the resulting gust causing her eyes to narrow.

"What happened to you?" She growled and readied the blade. There was no chance that whatever he had become was part of the normal Cleric class progression. Certainly, there wouldn't be anything this demonic looking.

His eyes were sunken and manic. "I ascended! The so-called Architect was letting the System fall to chaos, and I intend to put it back into order."

"Did you become . . . part Monster . . . *Marius?*"

He rushed toward her, their weapons clashing in another spray of red light.

"Do not use my name, you wretched abomination!" The fallen Cleric feigned a swing of the mace before blasting a radiant bolt at the zombie with his other hand.

A burning pain radiated up Sally's side as she narrowly avoided the bolt. As she rolled across the floor she withdrew a crossbow and raised it—before the crimson mace immediately came down upon it, shattering the ranged weapon and knocking the zombie back.

"*Asshole.* Do you know how many times I've replaced that, Marius?"

"Stop calling me that!" Fury sparked behind his eyes, his angry voice echoing across the road.

Sally grinned, despite the lethargy and pain. Part of him must know why she started calling him by his given name. Players—she just referred to them by their classes. But Monsters had real names to show her kinship. His hypocrisy was expected but brazen. Knowing that he was one of the things he sought to destroy must eat him up inside.

"You should join us." She ducked a wide arc of the mace. "We need a moderately evil healer."

"I'm. Not. EVIL."

Jackie swung Betty around like a mace, always slightly too slow to catch the hooded woman. Her suit was soaked in blood from several stab wounds, and her face was pale and clammy. "Stay still, you miserable freak," she growled, spinning up *[Pin Down]*.

"Sorry, dear, I've *never* been touched." A flash of a smile appeared beneath the darkness of the hood as the woman dodged to the side.

As Betty rang out, the bolt hissed through the air and pierced through the side of the loose hood, knocking it backward. The silver-white hair of the dark elf fell forward, and a crimson line slowly appeared across her cheek.

"Well." The mobster winked. "First time for everything, eh?"

Theo spat blood on the floor. His own, unfortunately. Whatever was left of the top half of his outfit was now shredded pieces on the floor, and his bare torso bore several gashes, which were slowly regenerating. It felt as though his arms would fall out of their sockets with how fast he had been punching—and yet the large lizardman was barely hurt.

"It'ss like sswatting a mosssssquito." The large maw of the beast twisted into a grin as he flourished the three scimitars.

"You have *incredible* damage reduction." The vampire panted as he shook feeling back into his fists. "My whole 'thing' is doing lots of small amounts of damage."

"To take advantage of how realistic normal combat is in thessse low levelsss?"

"*Exactly*. Until it gets . . . unrealistic." Theo winced, aware that he was currently a vampire trying to win a fistfight against a crocodile to save a goblin village.

"Unfortunately for you, gnat," the lizardman said and hunched down, ready to power forward, "my level is doubled when it comes to defense." Green light flickered across his trio of blades as he leapt at the vampire.

Archie sat down and tilted his head. "Just what are you, anyway?"

The insectoid stopped casting whatever spell it was preparing and wrinkled up its face. A series of clicks and chirps came from beneath the mandibles—accompanied by a shrug.

"Obviously you're a *bug*, but I don't remember a creature like you."

A brief pause before higher-pitched chirps.

"I see. That is unfortunate." The ginger cat looked around at the ongoing battles before returning his emerald gaze to the agitated insect. "And this is what you want to do with your brief life?"

The bug clicked slowly, and a sharp knife of ice began to form in its hand.

Humphrey stepped back as the clang of the sword colliding weakened him. Despite his defenses, the previous battle with the Champion had taken a lot out of him, and there was something else going on that he was unable to put his finger on. Mostly on account of having lost a couple of them.

"Ah! A *[Stamina Drain]* enchantment?" His eyes blazed red as he stared at the orc.

"Is that what you've been worrying about?" The black-flamed skull shook his head and flourished the blade. "It's no wonder you're so soft."

The Death Knight surged forward and slashed out at his opponent, drawing blood from the orc's thigh. The follow-up attack was parried, and Humphrey then dropped to one knee as exhaustion dulled his flames.

The Observer chuckled. "After killing you and any other upstart Uniques, I'm going to become the next Architect."

"Over . . . my dead body," Humphrey hissed, trying to struggle back to his feet.

"That's my intention!" The looming pitch-black flame around the skull of the murderer blazed with greater intensity as he stood over the struggling Death Knight.

Sally rolled across the wet cobblestone, agony flaring up her side. Broken ribs for sure. Her grip on the sword shook as she got back to her feet, stumbling as her body convulsed with pain.

Marius grinned wickedly. "See? You put too much stock in being helped by your *Party*—they are nothing but tools, and you are nothing without them."

"Not true," she growled back, readying her off hand to cast *[Necroblast]*.

"Watch and see!" With a flick of his mace, crimson fire blasted forth from behind his wings and ran along the floor. A ring of fifteen-foot-tall raging flame encircled them both—cutting them both off from their respective Parties. With the way the duos had been fighting in opposite directions with her in the middle, neither pairing would be able to see any of the others.

A blur of red obscured Sally's vision as the mace whirled past her face. She already had a sore scar across there—a heavy hit from the bludgeoning weapon might just send the top half of her head bouncing across the road.

For all his posturing, Marius had not used many skills. If he had become a part-Monster recently, then that stood to reason. He was powerful though, more than Theo—and that guy power leveled better than anyone. *[Necroblast]* blew a darkened scar across the shoulder of the evil bastard but didn't seem to do as much damage as she was used to.

One of his skills must be a defensive shell—possibly against the same damage type that she was using. She whirled in with the sword, flickering attacks one after the other. The fallen Cleric was evasive, dodging three attacks before blocking the last with a swipe of his wing. Black feathers were shorn away before he pushed her back with a gust of air.

He growled, and the crimson of the mace grew brighter. "My turn now." Marius used the wings as a boost to leap into the air, starting with a wild overhead swing before landing where the zombie had rolled away from—immediately starting up with a flurry of angry swings.

The attacks came just as furiously as her own, but she was tired and numb from the extended battle. She dodged, blocked, barely blocked—and then jumped to the side to avoid a radiant bolt. This put her right in the way of a heavy swing of the mace, unable to guard against it at that angle.

With a horrible snap, Sally yelped out in pain and the sword clattered to the floor. Her right arm was broken and hung limply at her side. Quickly, she scoured her brain to weigh up her options as she tried to shake the rain from her eyes. Perhaps she would just have to try and bite him—

His fist loomed out from in front of her blind eyes and grabbed a hold of her shirt. Marius lifted her into the air and regarded the zombie with his cold eyes.

"Even if you were the strongest of them, you are still a cockroach. You will be crushed beneath my boot, and your little movement will lose all steam." His face contorted with barely contained seething hatred for all that she was.

"The System will continue to err," she spat back, "and you will be seen as the worst of us."

"I am NOTHING like you." His fist was tightly clenched around the crimson mace, the whites of his knuckles a stark contrast to the roving colors of the weapon. "Tell me, what can you hear, abomination?"

She tried to struggle against his grip, but she was all but spent. No healing and neither of her arms were very responsive. Over the sound of the pattering rain and the pulsing flames of the encircling wall . . . there were no sounds of fighting. No clashes or yells, just the tired gasps of her own undead lungs against broken ribs.

"The last thing you see before I snuff you from this world will be the corpses of those heathens you mistook for being your friends."

With tired eyes, Sally watched as the flickering heat of the fire wall slowly faded.

As her eyes adjusted to the gloom and she laid eyes on what remained of her Party, her jaw clenched tightly shut.

A single tear ran down her cheek as she shook.

## CHAPTER SEVENTY-TWO

# Freedom

The first person Sally laid eyes on was Jackie. The mobster was bleeding heavily from a multitude of stab wounds, her hat discarded from her rain-slick purple hair. She lay still, being held up by the dark elf that had assailed her. And they were . . . kissing?

Marius's mouth hung open as they turned slowly to the next pairing.

The lizardman stood and began laughing, hands on his scaled hips. Theo was a blur, attacking at ludicrous speeds with his bare hands—the *[Sanguine Weapon]* a streak of pink wavering over his head. The vampire was also laughing, almost as much as the large beast.

They turned again to see Archie and the bug sitting and talking, the insect Monster looking glum with its face in spindly arms.

Rage was almost tangible from the fallen Cleric. His crimson halo pulsed with energy, almost as if it was aflame. At least the last pairing was certainly going more to his plan.

"I knew I could trust *one* of you." He seethed; his fist holding the zombie up was twitching as his gaze bore into his other Party members.

"Humps," Sally whispered quietly as a lump sunk to her stomach.

The Death Knight was lying back, only propped up by an elbow as the orc stood above him. Across from the pair, the flaming greatsword now lay inert a few feet from their scuffle. A wide smile had crossed the jaws of the black-flamed skull as he reveled in his imminent victory.

"Let this be a lesson to all that stand against us in this corrupt System." He raised his blade high to strike down on the dull helmet of the Death Knight. For a brief moment only the sound of rain could be heard; everyone turned to start to object to the execution, their vision clear now the fire wall had vanished.

Then, the orc looked up. "What the—"

Something large and aflame slammed into him. As he jolted backward a pillar of wood appeared behind him and knocked the wind from his lungs. The flaming object landed and stood to its feet.

Jaxk flexed his muscles and withdrew a hammer from his belt, squaring up to the orc.

Sally turned as Marius twirled them both to see the village.

All of the Unique Monsters had come out. She watched with watering eyes as Bella ran up to the Death Knight and started to apply healing.

"You better be good for the gold, Mister," she hissed under her breath.

Henkk walked forward ahead of the rest of the group to address the fallen Cleric.

Marius twitched and took a step backward. "Stay back, you weak filth! I have your precious zombie, and I will cover you with her brains if you try anything!" Panic and fury both painted his outbursts.

The white goblin smiled and raised his hands in an open gesture. "We have fifteen minutes to fuck you up; how long would you like us to take?" Even with his smooth voice, the threat was steeped in menace.

Regaining his gusto, the orc began to chuckle. "You are all low level; you are not a—"

From a split in reality, a spout of amber flame followed by the heavy body of a horse barreled through and knocked the speaker to the floor. "I'm a *HORSE*, woo!" Petal yelled as he pranced past the target. Wooden beams appeared over the black-flamed ex-Observer, pinning him to the ground.

"I swear!" Marius growled, backing farther away from the throng of Uniques. "*One* more step and she gets it."

"Marius," Sally whispered, "I'll give you one last chance to repent and join us."

"Never!" Spittle shot from his mouth as he shook with rage. "I will never accept your kind."

"Then I have a secret to tell you." A small smile began to cross her weary face.

"What? Speak it so it may be your last words."

Her red eyes raised to meet his, a playful flame dancing behind them.

"I started carrying two crossbows."

Pain flared across the face of the Cleric as the *thunk* of a bolt buried itself into his gut. He dropped the zombie and stumbled backward.

Sally dropped the crossbow, which slunk low in her useless grip—barely able to raise her left hand she shot *[Necroblast]* at his right side. As he moved in reflex to block it, she lunged out and sunk her sharp teeth into his mace arm. Warmth flowed through into her mouth. It strengthened her. As he tried to stumble away, she bit down harder until he dropped the mace.

The Cleric managed to push her off, clutching his wounded arm to his chest and hunched over at the pain of the lodged bolt. He raised his other hand in readiness to send out a radiant bolt when a shadow loomed up behind him.

A figure sunk his fangs into the man's neck. Marius raised his hand to dislodge Theo, but *[Vampire Bite]* quickly hit his Stamina and his arm flopped downward ineffectively. After a few seconds, the Cleric dropped to his knees, and the vampire relented, spitting a mouthful of blood to the floor.

Sally stood over him, her shadow covering his weary eyes as they looked up to her. Once more, the only sound around them was the falling rain from the gloomy sky.

"Eat my brains. *Go on*, Monster. That is what you want." His voice came out in short pants.

The conditionals had been met. She swayed on tired legs as she idly looked at the skill pop-up.

"Hi, Sally." Bella tugged at her shredded skirt. "Did you want healing?"

"I . . . don't think I have the gold for it." She frowned and opened up her Inventory.

Marius ground his teeth together, blood and cold sweat running down his body. Theo stood behind him with arms folded across his bare chest.

"For some reason, I only have three gold left." The zombie tried to shrug, but her arms just painfully wiggled.

"I could at least fix your arm for that?" The small goblin wrinkled her nose up at the break. "Oh! I also found your dagger! Isn't that lucky?"

"Hah. *It is.*" Sally smiled as the warmth from the healing pulsed up her arm. It was amazing what a difference that made—not the fixing of the shattered bone, but the warmth in her cold, dead flesh. The goblin placed the *[Rare Dagger of Luck]* into her hand.

Humphrey's sword burst into red energy as he cleaved into the wooden beams and the orc beneath them. Kicking the remnants of the broken timber to the side, he lifted the wounded ex-Observer from the ground and threw him back atop the debris. The Death Knight stabbed his weapon down into the thigh of the enemy, pinning him to the floor.

He knelt by the orc and placed a plated finger against the bloodied chest of his opponent. "Merge or perish."

"Hah, *sure.*" The orc's skull managed to spit up blood. "A red Observer? I'll just take you over in no time and carry on in that nice shiny body."

"No, I am a purple Observer, and you are weak."

Archie walked over and sat beside them. "You are a purple, big brother? I thought red, too."

The Death Knight turned to the cat with a scowl. "You knew my name; how did you not know what kind of Observer I was?"

"What makes you think I want to become part of you?" the orc hissed and struggled against the sword keeping him in place. "Our ideals are opposite."

"All Observers live to serve the System. You can continue your duty and make amends for the wrong path you have traveled." Humphrey nudged the sword.

Archie climbed atop the body and gazed into the empty sockets of the black-flamed skull. "I will forgive you too."

The orc took a moment of pause as he maintained the glare of the ginger cat. Eventually, as his willpower physically deflated, he looked back up at the Death Knight. "Alright, I accept. I am ready."

Humphrey held out a plated hand, which the orc took with a weak grip. Swirls of black smoke began pouring from the skull as it slowly evaporated and swirled up and around the Death Knight's arm. It sunk into his body, and finally, as the inert corpse of the orc slumped to the floor, the plated bodyguard stood back to his feet and sighed.

"That will take some getting used to." He looked back down at Archie. "I will try and process his thoughts to find out about the Architect's murder and who else is responsible."

"If I am mortally wounded, will you absorb me too?" The cat stretched out and wagged his tail.

"If you allow it."

"What about ME? I'm a HOOORSE." Petal yelled from just behind them, causing the Death Knight to physically cringe.

"*Hurry up!*" Marius bit at the air, trying to shift from the weight of the vampire now holding his wings down. "End this already." He hung his head low in resignation.

Sally tutted and shook her head. "Normally, I'd be all for eating some brains—especially with whatever class you are now. I'm *literally* drooling. But that would be unfair to you—to become my zombie thrall when I can see that this existence is so troubling for you. Look at me, Marius."

The fallen Cleric slowly raised his head, the anger in his eyes now replaced by anguish and sorrow.

"The biggest mercy I can give you is freedom from this System. I hope that this sets your soul free."

With a quick flick of her arm, Sally buried the dagger deep into his eye socket.

Marius's mouth opened and closed slowly before he slunk to the floor, dead. The crimson halo melted away, and the wings of black feathers became limp and started to fall apart.

Sally stood and watched the dead body in silence with the cheers and conversations going on behind her muted and dull.

The rainfall continued to fall, and she closed her tired eyes.

## CHAPTER SEVENTY-THREE

# New Normal

Sally sat down by the bar on one of the wooden stools. The place was pretty packed, even for it being mid-afternoon. It had been a tiring week, and she was just glad for the chance to rest her feet. Now that she was able to change her clothes, the red shirt and black jeans combo made a nice change.

"Here ya go, hun—this one's on the house." The barkeep pushed an ale tankard across the wooden surface of the bar with a nod and wink.

"Thanks, Jacks." Sally beamed at the mobster. "How's Fran doing?"

"She's a doll as always. Out back cookin' up some meat Players dropped around for a quest. Things go well at Yewbridge I take it?"

"A lot less bloodshed than here—but the gang all being Level Ten helps out a lot." Sally idly tapped at the counter and looked around the tavern.

Jackie followed her gaze around the room as she cleaned out some empty mugs. "Waiting for Fangs?"

Sally raised an eyebrow. "Yeah, but don't start. We actually have a messenger from Poppybrook coming to meet us."

"Sure, sure. If he stands you up, just let us know and Fran will dig out the stakes." The mobster winked again and went off to greet some other patrons.

Images of the battle for Sanctuary filtered through Sally's mind. Theo had held her. At least until she told him to put a shirt on. Terrible way to get some kind of blood-borne disease, that was. Part of her wished they were both living so there could be something more between them. But . . . things were good. They had killed for each other and bled for each other. In some ways that seemed more important than any traditional romance.

Her mind wandered over to the doorway as the vampire walked in on cue. Having finally been talked out of wearing the cliché clothing, he now wore a smart dark gray suit with a crimson tie. Glasses with red lenses sat atop his nose—apparently to help him see better in the daylight. In the time spent being a vampire, he had become a little thinner and paler—but it suited him.

"Hey, Theo, good hunting today?"

He beamed in return, his fangs showing, as he came and sat at the bar beside her. "Two of the cards I need, still one missing. It's a shame we are hard capped at Level Ten."

Sally rolled her eyes. "It does suck that our keystone quests have to be done in the Wastelands—but, you level up fast enough; we don't need you zooming ahead of us."

"Can't help if I'm just a better Player." He winked and looked back to the door. "The other two meeting us here?"

"No. We are meeting the delegate just outside the village. They said they'd be there in a bit."

Theo rubbed his fingertips on the bar. Sally could see he was eager to get moving to the second area. They were a Party member short after helping populate both this village and Yewbridge with Leaders. Humphrey had told the vampire about some of the items he could find before Level Twenty, and now it was all he would think about.

"What *are* you thinking about, Theo?"

"Oh?" He turned his attention back to her. "I was just counting the clean mugs stacked back there." A gesture of his head to the wall behind the bar set her eyes rolling.

"Let's get out of here. It's a little walk."

They both waved to the mobster as they walked out into the warm afternoon weather. Sally looped her arm around the vampire's as she brought up the STAR menu to select guild chat.

Sally: Alright, gang, everyone has hit Level Ten now.
Sally: We are heading to Area Two at 8:00 sharp tomorrow.
Chuck: White Foxes are ready.
Jerri: Warriors are ready.
Xuan: Five Swords are ready.
Bran: Strength of Many are ready.

She closed her chat back up. As a parting gift, Jackie had fleeced enough people for them to found a guild. Twenty-two Players in total. Between the vampire and her own hunger, a few Players had found their way into their mouths—but the ones smart enough to yield saw the crimson writing on the wall and had allied themselves. Plus the world was a lot more vibrant now with neutral and friendly Monsters toward the Players that were still in the area.

After some strong words and bared fangs of encouragement, Theo had guided them all to get to Level Ten in no time. A small army of Players was certainly not what she had expected to be taking with her into the second area—certainly not living ones. But now if they needed to take a town as a home base, they could do that. Possibly even the nonviolent way.

"Everyone is ready for tomorrow." She nudged the vampire and looked out into the town. It was a strange mix of different System-created, but it felt . . . normal to her. Another place where she could belong. She couldn't help but smile as they passed through the streets of shops and residential buildings, back out into the wilds.

They followed the road in silence for about half an hour. Sometimes the quiet was nice, without having to be making quips or stabbing someone. Not that those weren't some of her favorite things to do, but it was nice to be stress-free for a brief time. Eventually, they reached the intended meeting space.

Theo walked around and wrinkled his nose up. It was a clearing among some trees with a small circular rock floor, long overgrown by grass. Two stone benches sat on either side of the center.

"Low chance of ambush, it's close enough to the road that we'd see anything coming, and the bushes are too thick through the trees to approach quietly."

She nodded and sat on one of the benches. It would be a shame to mar such a peaceful slice of nature with violence. Plus, she really didn't want to have to march on the capital. Sally watched the vampire stand off to the side in part of the shaded area, rubbing his chin as he stared off into nothingness. Undoubtedly thinking about leveling or items.

"Hey, nerd, why not come sit with me? It's shaded." She patted the cold stone next to her.

He tilted his head to her but almost immediately relented. "Sorry, I'm just a bit anxious is all. Humphrey said that sending a delegate was unheard of—in that sinister voice he does." The vampire sat on the bench and immediately slouched.

"Sometimes Humps covers for things he doesn't know with vague but ominous statements." She copied his slouch, and they both looked up to the clear blue sky.

"I think he is just grumpy that he has to haul my coffin around."

"Are you kidding? He secretly loves the visuals of it. Plus, we don't want you going without sleep for days again, huh?" She elbowed him in the side.

"I'm still sorry about that."

"Sorry doesn't bring the orphans back, Theo."

"And why were they orphans in the first place, *Sally?*"

An almost polite cough roused them from their glowing red-eyed death stares. They turned to see the looming figure of the Death Knight, the ginger cat Archie upon his shoulder.

"Terrible defense, as usual. I could have been someone of ill intent." Humphrey grinned but folded his arms across his chest.

"Pah." Theo rolled his eyes but didn't want to encourage him.

Archie dropped down from the plated armor of the Knight and ran up to the zombie to hop onto her lap. He began to purr as she ruffled his fluffy cheeks.

"Any breakthrough yet?" Sally raised her eyebrows but expected the negative again.

"Almost!" Archie beamed up at her with his bright emerald eyes. "Big brother says there's an item in the second area that will help us unlock the potential of the meowmeries hidden away in our skulls."

The vampire leaned forward with a frown. "Did you just say *meow*-meries?"

"No." Archie shook his head.

Sally beamed at them all. They had fought off three of the village-taking regiments in a row, and each had become easier as they leveled and grew as a team. Certainly, without insane Players trying to interfere, they had quite an easy go of it. The three of them were Elites in their own regard and, combined with the two brain cells shared between them, outsmarting the System-created turned things in their favor.

Of course . . . all that could change at any time.

The sound of a horse approaching came from down the road, and they all craned their necks to see who it was. It was three horses in fact—a woman in simple regalia and two male armored guards behind her. Humphrey moved to stand behind their bench as the figures dismounted and walked toward the small clearing.

"The *Outsiders*." She gave a small bow. "I am Steward Iona. I bring a message from the capital."

Sally stood to give a curtsy, briefly saddened not to be wearing a skirt. "Well met, Steward Iona—please join us in sitting."

Theo shot the zombie a furrowed brow as she sat back down, as if surprised that she had the capacity for manners.

She *was* nervous. Not for any kind of threat of violence—but the village captures were part of the big plan of *Making Things Equal,* and this could be a big turning point in how things progressed.

Iona sat on the bench as the two guards stood behind. "The Council and our patron Party have been watching your efforts since the capture of what is now Sanctuary. At first, we were shocked and appalled."

Sally nodded enthusiastically in hopes the woman would get to the final conclusion more quickly.

"We were in the process of sending an order for a larger army to combat the increasing problem you were causing—however, the patron Party called for an emergency vote."

She wondered who this mysterious Party could be, and the urge to blurt out a question was only barely held back.

"As such, we have decided to accept the validity of Monsters having a fair share of township under the Crown. In addition to the three villages you have taken remaining under Monster control, we would like to invite five so-called Unique Monsters to sit on the Council as representatives. This is under the condition that you don't attempt to capture further villages or incite violence in Poppybrook."

The zombie's mouth hung wide open, and tears began to well in her eyes. "You're . . . treating Unique Monsters as regular citizens—as equals?"

"To a degree, yes. There will be no more contracts or quests that target Uniques, and they will no longer be attacked by the Crown guards—further than that is beyond our control."

Theo adjusted his glasses and cupped his hand to his mouth in thought. "Crown, Council, Adventurers Guild, and a patron Party," he murmured under his breath.

"Well that's great news." Sally leapt to her feet, unable to control herself any longer. "What's the catch?"

"No catch—just that this only applies to this area, naturally. Beyond the Swamps is outside of our jurisdiction."

"You hear that, gang?" The zombie turned and placed her foot on the bench. "*We won*, and the Wasteland is ours to conquer!"

Out in the Swamps, the sound of a knife sharpening against a whetstone pierced through the gloom.

The leader of *Zero* slicked back his greasy hair and idly glared over at the gathering of twenty Players.

"They're coming tomorrow," he snarled, a twisted grin forming at the side of his thin mouth.

With a raucous cheer, dozens of weapons were held up in the air, the sound echoing out into the mists.

# About the Author

Kleggt is the author of the Death of the Party series, originally released on Royal Road. Upon clawing his way out of the depths of Scheduling Hell as a Forever DM, he began writing web novels, channeling his love of world-building and oddball characters into his own LitRPG and progression fantasy stories.

# DISCOVER
# *STORIES UNBOUND*

## PodiumAudio.com